Praise for Lexi Blake and Masters and Mercenaries...

"I can always trust Lexi Blake's Dominants to leave me breathless...and in love. If you want sensual, exciting BDSM wrapped in an awesome love story, then look for a Lexi Blake book."
~Cherise Sinclair USA Today Bestselling author

"Lexi Blake's MASTERS AND MERCENARIES series is beautifully written and deliciously hot. She's got a real way with both action and sex. I also love the way Blake writes her gorgeous Dom heroes--they make me want to do bad, bad things. Her heroines are intelligent and gutsy ladies whose taste for submission definitely does not make them dish rags. Can't wait for the next book!"
~Angela Knight, New York Times Bestselling author

"A Dom is Forever is action packed, both in the bedroom and out. Expect agents, spies, guns, killing and lots of kink as Liam goes after the mysterious Mr. Black and finds his past and his future… The action and espionage keep this story moving along quickly while the sex and kink provides a totally different type of interest. Everything is very well balanced and flows together wonderfully."
~A Night Owl "Top Pick", Terri, Night Owl Erotica

"A Dom Is Forever is everything that is good in erotic romance. The story was fast-paced and suspenseful, the characters were flawed but made me root for them every step of the way, and the hotness factor was off the charts mostly due to a bad boy Dom with a penchant for dirty talk."
~Rho, The Romance Reviews

"A good read that kept me on my toes, guessing until the big reveal, and thinking survival skills should be a must for all men."
~Chris, Night Owl Reviews

"I can't get enough of the Masters and Mercenaries Series! Love and Let Die is Lexi Blake at her best! She writes erotic romantic suspense like no other, and I am always extremely excited when she has something new for us! Intense, heart pounding, and erotically fulfilling, I could not put this book down."

~ Shayna Renee, Shayna Renee's Spicy Reads

"Certain authors and series are on my auto-buy list. Lexi Blake and her Masters & Mercenaries series is at the top of that list... this book offered everything I love about a Masters & Mercenaries book – alpha men, hot sex and sweet loving… As long as Ms. Blake continues to offer such high quality books, I'll be right there, ready to read."

~ Robin, Sizzling Hot Books

"I have absolutely fallen in love with this series. Spies, espionage, and intrigue all packaged up in a hot dominant male package. All the men at McKay-Taggart are smoking hot and the women are amazingly strong sexy submissives."

~Kelley, Smut Book Junkie Book Reviews

The Dom Identity

Other Books by Lexi Blake

ROMANTIC SUSPENSE

Masters and Mercenaries
The Dom Who Loved Me
The Men With The Golden Cuffs
A Dom is Forever
On Her Master's Secret Service
Sanctum: A Masters and Mercenaries Novella
Love and Let Die
Unconditional: A Masters and Mercenaries Novella
Dungeon Royale
Dungeon Games: A Masters and Mercenaries Novella
A View to a Thrill
Cherished: A Masters and Mercenaries Novella
You Only Love Twice
Luscious: Masters and Mercenaries~Topped
Adored: A Masters and Mercenaries Novella
Master No
Just One Taste: Masters and Mercenaries~Topped 2
From Sanctum with Love
Devoted: A Masters and Mercenaries Novella
Dominance Never Dies
Submission is Not Enough
Master Bits and Mercenary Bites~The Secret Recipes of Topped
Perfectly Paired: Masters and Mercenaries~Topped 3
For His Eyes Only
Arranged: A Masters and Mercenaries Novella
Love Another Day
At Your Service: Masters and Mercenaries~Topped 4
Master Bits and Mercenary Bites~Girls Night
Nobody Does It Better
Close Cover
Protected: A Masters and Mercenaries Novella
Enchanted: A Masters and Mercenaries Novella
Charmed: A Masters and Mercenaries Novella
Taggart Family Values
Treasured: A Masters and Mercenaries Novella

Masters and Mercenaries: The Forgotten
Lost Hearts (Memento Mori)
Lost and Found
Lost in You
Long Lost
No Love Lost

Masters and Mercenaries: Reloaded
Submission Impossible
The Dom Identity
The Man from Sanctum, Coming March 8, 2022

Butterfly Bayou
Butterfly Bayou
Bayou Baby
Bayou Dreaming
Bayou Beauty

Lawless
Ruthless
Satisfaction
Revenge

Courting Justice
Order of Protection
Evidence of Desire

Masters Of Ménage (by Shayla Black and Lexi Blake)
Their Virgin Captive
Their Virgin's Secret
Their Virgin Concubine
Their Virgin Princess
Their Virgin Hostage
Their Virgin Secretary
Their Virgin Mistress

The Perfect Gentlemen (by Shayla Black and Lexi Blake)
Scandal Never Sleeps
Seduction in Session
Big Easy Temptation
Smoke and Sin
At the Pleasure of the President

URBAN FANTASY

Thieves
Steal the Light
Steal the Day
Steal the Moon
Steal the Sun
Steal the Night
Ripper
Addict
Sleeper
Outcast
Stealing Summer
The Rebel Queen

LEXI BLAKE WRITING AS SOPHIE OAK

Texas Sirens
Small Town Siren
Siren in the City
Siren Enslaved
Siren Beloved
Siren in Waiting
Siren in Bloom
Siren Unleashed
Siren Reborn

Nights in Bliss, Colorado
Three to Ride
Two to Love
One to Keep
Lost in Bliss
Found in Bliss
Pure Bliss
Chasing Bliss
Once Upon a Time in Bliss
Back in Bliss
Sirens in Bliss
Happily Ever After in Bliss
Far From Bliss, Coming 2021

A Faery Story
Bound
Beast
Beauty

Standalone
Away From Me
Snowed In

The Dom Identity

Masters and Mercenaries: Reloaded, Book 2

Lexi Blake

The Dom Identity
Masters and Mercenaries: Reloaded, Book 2
Lexi Blake

Published by DLZ Entertainment LLC

Edited by Chloe Vale
ISBN: 978-1-942297-49-9

McKay-Taggart logo design by Charity Hendry

Sign up for Lexi Blake's newsletter
and be entered to win a $25 gift certificate
to the bookseller of your choice.

Join us for news, fun, and exclusive content
including free Thieves short stories.

There's a new contest every month!

Go to www.LexiBlake.net to subscribe.

Acknowledgments

Last year I turned fifty and I planned a decadent party for myself. I was going to go to Vegas with a bunch of friends and party like I'd just turned twenty-one. Those plans were obviously upended when we all found ourselves in the middle of a global pandemic. So instead of pretending to be twenty-one and carefree, I felt every year I've lived and maybe more. My birthday was lovely because some people who care about me took the time to bring everyone together online. It ended up being something far more than a booze fest. It became a moment of reflection, reflection on my life and what I want the next twenty or thirty years to be. And what I decided is that I want there to be as much listening as there is talking in my life. Shortly after that birthday revelation, I read a thread on social media by a young romance author who writes in a similar subgenre as I do. She was complaining about the fact that she was reading a book by an author she loved but the author kept talking about how the heroine's breasts were real and putting down the idea of fake breasts. She said it infuriated her that an author who otherwise seems so tolerant would take such a stand and that she was going to write a heroine who had her breasts done for no other reason than she wanted to. Because it should be her choice. Because if we fight so hard to say we're all beautiful, why can't that be beautiful, too?

I think she was talking about me.
I know she spoke to me even if she wasn't.

I sat back and realized I did that. I had my characters make judgments like that because deep down I was making them myself.

So that is how Vanessa was born. She refused to let me put her in a box. She does not apologize for what some people would call a scandal. Some will call her difficult, but only because she's honest and will not allow herself to be stepped on for someone else's comfort. Or because society told her that was what a woman should do.

This book is for the Britneys of the world. And for the women who refuse to let the media and society put them in a box. It is for the next generation of romance writers who are defying expectations of what they are "supposed" to write.

Keep writing. I am listening.

Chapter One

Between the elegant buffet set in the conference room and the sense of hushed anticipation that hung over the office, it was obvious something big was happening this morning.

Michael Malone just wished it wasn't happening to him. He'd been somewhat excited about the idea of a new assignment when it had first been floated by him, but now he wondered if life wouldn't be easier if he avoided this particular job.

"He doesn't even eat carbs," a deep voice argued. "These babies will be wasted on him."

"He eats carbs," a feminine voice replied.

"No, he doesn't. Julian Lodge lives off the blood of his enemies, baby. That's it. That's how he stays all lean and predatory. Also, should we be having this meeting in the light of day?" Yep. That was his boss. Ian Taggart.

Michael had been working for McKay-Taggart Security for…had it really been the majority of his adult life? He'd started out—like most MT employees—in the military. The Navy had led to the SEALS and the SEALs to the CIA. The CIA had turned into a clusterfuck of a job, and so he'd landed here and stayed.

He liked his job, enjoyed his team. So why the fuck had he started to think about quitting?

"He's not a vampire." Despite the fact that he couldn't see Charlotte Taggart, he heard the smile in her voice. She always seemed genuinely amused by her husband's antics. Which was a good thing because there were a lot of them.

"Think about it." The man most people called Big Tag chuckled. "Have you ever seen him in the light of day?"

"Yes. Many times," Charlotte insisted.

"Never even once." Big Tag continued like his wife had replied in the way he wanted her to. But that was his boss. He plowed through life like a steamroller.

That wasn't fair. A steamroller flattened things, and the truth of the matter was Big Tag tended to make life better for the people he met. The Taggarts were responsible for most of the good marriages around him. He'd recently been to one of the weddings Charlotte and Ian had a direct hand in.

How the hell had Hutch gotten married before him?

And when had he started to feel like a wallflower at some Regency ball? It wasn't like he was on the shelf or something. He was a man in the prime of his life, and he wasn't unattractive. It wasn't like he hadn't had some good shots. So why hadn't they worked out? After a while a guy started to wonder.

He should never have agreed to watch movies with his mother after her surgery. She'd suffered a hard fall while riding around the ranch she and his dad lived on. Shoulder surgery had followed, and he'd taken his turn making sure she wasn't alone. She'd made him sit through rom coms and a weird amount of Regency romantic drama, and now he was a Jane Austen character worried about his marital prospects.

"Is the big guy here yet?"

Michael turned, and Kyle Hawthorne was standing there. Kyle was a reminder that everyone was moving forward, including Michael's ex-fiancée. She was marrying Kyle's brother.

"No, he's still fifteen minutes out." And now his morning was complete because there she was. Tessa Santiago, soon-to-be Hawthorne. Never to be Malone because he'd been the dumbass who couldn't love her the way she needed to be loved.

He was starting to wonder if he could love anyone. Maybe his twin had gotten all those genes. It was weird. All of his life he and JT had basically been in the same place, but the last several years had changed all of that. His identical twin had gotten married and now had two kids.

Michael was still drifting through life.

"I don't get it. It's like we're entertaining the president or something." Kyle glanced into the conference room. "Charlotte threatened unholy hell on anyone who ate the pastries before the client gets here. I saw Li taking Boomer out of the office because he doesn't think he can stay away from a buffet. Is he a freak of nature or something? How the hell does he eat the way he does and not weigh a thousand pounds?"

"Boomer works out hard, and he's got a freaky metabolism. And we didn't do all this for the actual president," Tessa pointed out. "All he got was some drive-through. But this is Julian Lodge. For Big Tag, he's way more important than any president."

"He's intimidating." Kyle frowned. "You know how Big Tag explodes at least twice a day? Julian is the guy who never explodes. He's kept all that rage and hate inside for years, and one day it's going to come out. You do not want to be standing in front of him then."

Tessa rolled her eyes. "He's a sweetheart. I think you're projecting because you kind of defined yourself there, buddy."

Kyle sighed. "That's probably fair. But I still say Julian Lodge is scarier than Big Tag."

"How do you know Julian?" Michael was surprised Tessa was talking like she'd made a study of the man. Tessa had only been with McKay-Taggart for two years, and in all that time Julian had never once come to the office. She wouldn't have worked with him. Tessa was in the bodyguard unit. Lodge had his own full-time bodyguards.

Julian Lodge ran Lodge Corp, a multibillion-dollar company that he'd inherited from his parents. More importantly to Big Tag, he ran an investment group called the Masters Fund. It was also worth several billion dollars and was the very reason Big Tag was loaded. That was where a lot of people got it wrong. They thought Tag's money came from the company, and some of it did, but the big bucks came from shrewd investments and making the money he had work for him.

Julian Lodge had taught Tag that. He'd been the first investor in

McKay-Taggart and now was treated like royalty.

But he wasn't sure how Tessa knew that since she hadn't come to the yearly football games Big Tag and Julian threw that sometimes included one of them putting an actual athlete on the payroll in order to win. Those "family" picnics were vicious at times, with Big Tag and Julian going at each other like two T-Rexes fighting for territory.

"Oh, I had to meet with him when I started going to The Club." Tessa's tone had gone soft.

"It's so gross. She calls my brother *Professor*, and they run some hard-core scenes about her not turning in her homework." Kyle made a vomiting sound. "I joined The Club to get away from my family."

She was going to The Club with David Hawthorne. Well, of course she was. David was her Dom, her top in a way Michael had never been. Their sex life had been one of the many ways he'd failed her. There had been a spark in the beginning, but no magic need had come to life beyond a mutually pleasurable experience.

There was supposed to be more. He was almost certain of it. He saw it all around him. Never once had he called Tessa up to his office and fucked her over his desk. He wouldn't have disturbed her workday. It seemed rude, and yet he knew damn well not to walk into Big Tag's office without making sure it was safe. Because even after five kids and years of marriage, those two went at it hard sometimes.

He'd topped Tessa when they'd been engaged, but it had been play. And toward the end of their relationship, they'd stopped going to Sanctum altogether.

"Why The Club?" He hoped she wasn't avoiding him. Tessa needed Sanctum. She'd needed more than he could give her.

"Kyle and David both go to The Club instead of Sanctum," Tessa said. "It's weird for them at Sanctum."

"Because of my mom and stepdad," Kyle explained. "It's horrifying. I'm still traumatized from when I came home from college for the weekend and walked in on my mom tied to a chair. I thought it was a home invasion and maybe the attackers had forced her to put on that corset and butt floss. I'm still in therapy over it, so no, with the exception of my training class, I don't go to Sanctum."

"Kyle and David both have rights at The Club," Tessa continued. "It's a courtesy Julian's offering to anyone attached to McKay-Taggart who doesn't want to see their mom's boobs. I don't know.

I've seen Grace and Sean scene, and they're hot."

Kyle gagged. "Dude, they are about to be your inlaws."

Tessa shrugged. "They're the coolest inlaws in the world because I get to eat at Top all I want. All I have to do is head into the kitchen and beg for food, and suddenly I have a burger in my hand. Getting to eat in the kitchen is the best part."

Tessa had never been comfortable in his wealthy world. His family moved in the same circles as Julian Lodge. He'd actually met Lodge long before Ian Taggart had. He'd met him as a child, and the man was definitely intimidating.

"Well, they should keep their clothes on around tender young eyes. Like mine." Kyle sighed. "I'm going to grab my tablet. I'll be back before Lodge gets here."

Tessa turned her dark eyes Michael's way, an apologetic look on her face. "I'm sorry about the inlaw comment. I wasn't saying anything about your mom and dad. You know I think they're lovely."

He shook his head. "I didn't take it that way." Not entirely. There had been a momentary hurt, but she simply hadn't enjoyed the protocols and rules old money followed. She hadn't liked the fact that everyone watched her in that world, waited for her to fuck up. The truth of the matter was he didn't enjoy it either. "They still ask about you. Did you invite them?"

Her eyes went wide. "To my wedding? The one that isn't to their son? No. I thought it might be weird."

"You invited me." He'd gotten that invitation and had to sit for a moment. Not because he wasn't happy for her. He genuinely was, but it was another way the world seemed to be moving on. One more way he was left behind.

"I didn't want you to think you weren't welcome." She leaned against the wall. "I decided to invite everyone at the office, and it would have been wrong to leave you out. Besides, I hope you would invite me to yours. I would want to be there for you."

He wished she could have been the one. She was a genuinely nice person, and they'd gotten along well. They worked on paper. But paper hadn't been enough. "I'm glad to be there for you, too. Send my parents an invite and put something phenomenally expensive on your registry. They like to show off."

She breathed a sigh of obvious relief. "Good. I will." She glanced back to the conference room. "Are you okay with this? With me as your backup?"

"I didn't realize you were," he admitted. "I thought I was going in with Kyle. Like I said, I didn't know you played at The Club. Big Tag had mentioned you would have something to do with it, but he didn't say we would be working closely."

"I'm strictly there if you need me," she agreed. "I can watch the target in places you can't. Kyle's your physical backup while you're at The Club, and MaeBe's on call for all your hacking needs. She's got a big work-up on the target."

The target. Vanessa Hale. There was a "big" work-up on her for the simple fact that there was so very much information concerning her. Vanessa was one of Hollywood's favorite gossip targets. The blonde had pin-up girl looks and a thirst for money and fame that had led her to marry a man three times her age and get involved in one of the nastiest inheritance fights Michael had ever seen.

He could remember his mother shaking her head as she read one of the tabloid stories about the woman. His parents were both from old money, and they'd made plenty of new money with Malone Oil and Energy. Vanessa Hale was one of his mother's worst nightmares—the gold digger getting her hooks into a member of the family. So far his mother had been happy with the next generation's choice of spouses. She loved his twin's wife, Nina, and she'd adored Tessa. But then Tessa had never been interested in his money.

"I look forward to it, though I've done my own research," he admitted. He was sure MaeBe Vaughn had done a deep dive into the woman, so he was ready to find out what she'd learned. And to find out why Julian considered her such a threat.

"Are you okay doing this?"

"The undercover? It's not my first rodeo." He'd been undercover many times. It was more boring than the movies made it look. It mostly consisted of blending into the background and not getting caught. Though this time it would be a little different.

"Michael, you're probably going to have sex with her."

Yes, that was why it would be different. Although he wasn't going in planning to fuck her. "I'm going to be her training Dom. That doesn't mean I have to sleep with the woman."

A brow rose over Tessa's eyes. "You're going to top one of the sexiest women in the world and not sleep with her?"

"First of all, she's not my type." The woman was sexy, but he found her past distasteful. He was certain he could have sex with her and enjoy it on a base level, but he wasn't sure how he would feel about it afterward.

Yep, too many romantic movies.

"She's every man's type, but you need to remember that there's always a person under the makeup and push-up bras," Tessa pointed out.

"I doubt she needs a push-up bra. I'm pretty sure those aren't real."

"They're real. They might not be natural, but they're real breasts, and there's a real woman underneath all the scandal."

"You sound like you disapprove."

"I just..."

"Spit it out, Tessa."

Her arms crossed over her chest. "Honestly, you're not who I would put on this op. I understand why Tag picked you, and I worry it's going to bug you to be used as bait. And it bugs me that every single one of you is treating her like she's some craven gold digger."

Had Tessa not done her homework? "She married an eighty-year-old billionaire when she was twenty-seven, so yeah, I don't think she married him for love."

"Because no one could possibly love an old man?"

He stared at her for a moment.

Her hands came up in obvious frustration. "All I'm asking is that you go into this with even the tiniest bit of an open mind. You're already judging her because she got her breasts done, and that shouldn't be anyone's business but hers. She was barely nineteen when she started her career, and I've heard Hollywood is rough on a girl."

He sighed because he was being a dick. "I'm sorry. You're right. What a woman does with her body is her business. I'm playing into stereotypes, but you've got to admit the press around this woman is bad. Julian's got to have his reasons for wanting to investigate her."

Tessa pulled her cell phone out, glancing down at the screen. "I think he's seeing exactly what the rest of the world sees."

He trusted her, but she was a bodyguard. She'd never done the kind of intelligence work he'd done. "Have you met her?"

Tessa shook her head. "Not exactly. David is helping Lodge's daughter with her Spanish. He's got a group together, and they meet at Lodge's penthouse. Vanessa was there with Lodge's wife, and she seemed…sad, a little lost. I don't know, but she's not the same person you see on TV."

"I'll keep that in mind," he promised. "And don't worry about me. I'm not walking into this with my shields down. Trust me. They're completely up. It won't be the first time I've dealt with a woman who's interested in my family money."

She frowned and slid her phone back into her pocket. "And that's precisely why I'm worried you're wrong for this op. You made the first mistake in thinking I'm worried about *your* safety. I'm worried for hers. She's been through a lot, including losing her sister a few months ago."

He didn't like the way the words made him feel, but she was ignoring some realities. "We're not here to do the best thing for her. We're here to do what our client needs."

"And he's here." Tessa started for the door. "Please tell Tag I'm bringing him up now."

"Make sure the sunlight doesn't hit him," Tag called out from the doorway.

"I will be sure to tell him you care," Tessa replied without looking back.

"That'll put the old guy in a good mood," Tag said.

"He's not that much older than you." Michael walked into the conference room, and sure enough, the place had been set up for royalty.

"So he says, but have we seen a birth certificate?" Tag was in a suit for today's meeting. It made Michael wonder what miracles Charlotte had worked to get that tie around his neck. Tag was a little more laid back when it came to work. He only suited up when the client was important or he was playing out some mobster fantasy with his wife. "Vampires don't age. Like Lodge."

"Ian." Charlotte sent her husband a death stare he was pretty sure she'd patented and sold to the US government as a weapon.

Ian shot his wife a grin. "We're rivals, baby. Trust me. He's going to say some nasty shit when he walks in here. You just haven't seen him in a while. Hey, in office gossip, I have news."

Charlotte poured herself a cup of coffee from the carafe beside a lovely assortment of Danishes. "What?"

Ian leaned in. "Tessa thinks Michael can't handle this assignment."

"I'm right here." Michael hoped his own death stare was at least half as awful as Charlotte's.

"Why?" Charlotte completely ignored him.

"I think she thinks he's going in having already made certain assumptions about the target's background because of his class," Tag said.

"Hey, I'm not some snob." How long had Tag been listening? "And if Lodge is a vampire, then you are a gossipy old lady."

"A vampire? Heavens no. A demon perhaps, but then I'm known for making deals. Ian, it's good to see you."

Fuck. Michael turned and sure enough, there was Julian Lodge standing right there and looking every bit like a mafia don about to put out a hit on someone. Probably him since he'd called the man a vampire.

"Charlotte, what a pleasure to see you again," Julian said, holding out a hand. "You get more lovely every day. I still don't understand how a woman of your obvious intelligence ended up with Ian."

"I got her pregnant and trapped her." Ian didn't seem at all affected by the ribbing. "Every time she thinks she can get away, I put another baby up in her."

Charlotte laughed. "I think we're done with having kids. Five is more than enough. How are yours, Julian? Please come in. Can I offer you anything?"

"Some coffee would be lovely." Julian glanced back at Tessa. "Thank you for the escort, Tessa. You do your Master proud."

Julian also took the whole D/s thing way more seriously than anyone he knew. He was fairly certain Tessa and her professor kept the Dom/sub thing strictly to the bedroom.

Tessa simply nodded. "Thanks, Master Julian. I'm happy to help with this job, but you should know I'm going to be forthright and honest about how I feel about this assignment, and I hope it doesn't offend you."

"Not at all. You'll find I employ many people who submit in the dungeon and tell me what a moron I can be out of it. I married two of them," Julian admitted with a smile. "My Finn never misses a chance to tell me I'm wrong about some point of law, and my Danielle now challenges my every business decision. I consider that a point of pride. Charlotte, my children are doing well. Chloe is on the newspaper staff at her school. I'm surviving the boys, but only barely. I'm glad Danielle drew the line at three. I think Finn would have kept going until he could field his own baseball team."

"Don't I know it." Ian gestured for Julian to have a seat. "Why don't we get started now that Kyle and MaeBe are here."

Kyle strode in with his tablet in hand. He held the door opened and allowed MaeBe Vaughn to enter. MaeBe was the resident goth tech goddess. She'd recently changed her hair color to a bright pink in honor of spring. She was in her mid-twenties and looked so youthful and bouncy she made him feel old.

"Hello, Mr. Lodge. I'm Mae Beatrice Vaughn, and I will be running tech today." She held her hand out and Lodge politely shook it. "Everyone calls me MaeBe."

"Then I shall as well," Lodge said with genuine warmth in his tone. "Kyle, it's good to see you." He turned Ian's way. "When did they all get so young?"

Ian sat down, a lemon muffin in front of him. "I have to get them young. My old guys are all boring and married and whiney. I tried to get Theo on this one, but he was all *My wife will kick my ass if I top another woman*. But the good news is Michael there hasn't given in to the old ball and chain yet."

Charlotte's eyes were back to lasers. "I'm telling Erin you called her that."

"I wasn't talking about Erin. Theo's got old balls, and Erin wrapped a chain around them," Ian quipped. "They have pictures and everything."

"They absolutely do not," Charlotte began.

But Julian was already laughing.

The door opened again, and a large, muscular man walked through. Wolf Meyer. He'd handled Julian's personal security for more than a decade.

He nodded as he took a seat beside Julian. "The car is secure. Everything looks good."

That got Big Tag's brows rising. "You had Wolf do a walk-through of my building? You know I've been doing this for a long time."

"And so has Wolf," Julian replied. "I believe you'll find this was at his insistence, not mine."

Wolf Meyer sat back. "I check out everyone, Tag. Especially dirty cheaters. You paid that ref. I did not fumble that ball."

Ian's eyes flared, and Michael knew if he didn't take control of the situation, they would relitigate the last flag football game. It had turned into all the guys punching each other.

"MaeBe, why don't you start? If I'm meeting Ms. Hale this evening, I would like to know a little something about her," Michael said. This was his op, and he was going to run it without a throwdown between Julian's mentees.

"Yes, if you two want to fight it out, I can call down and Alex will be more than happy to set up a vat of Jell-O," Charlotte offered. "But after the meeting."

"Jell-O?" Wolf asked.

"The women like a good Jell-O wrestling session," Tessa replied. "Or you can lube up and go at it."

Wolf frowned. "I feel vaguely offended."

"You'll feel vaguely…" Tag began.

"So the subject of our investigation is one Vanessa Hale Benedict." MaeBe completely cut tag off and started her presentation. "Benedict is her married name. She goes by it."

"Hale was her stage name, if I'm correct." Julian seemed ready to get down to business.

"You are, sir." MaeBe hit a key on her laptop, and the image of a young woman with dark hair and stunning eyes came on the screen. She wore a green dress, and her hair was long and draped over one shoulder. She looked utterly unlike the woman he'd seen on magazine covers, with the exception of that fuck-me mouth of hers. Her lips formed a perfect pink bow that any man of the right persuasion would want to try out.

But not on this woman. This woman looked…innocent. Excited. Ready to take on the world.

God, was Tessa right and he was going into this whole op judging her because of the way she looked now? Because of stories he'd heard?

"She was born Vanessa Jones, but that was considered too boring for Hollywood. She was born here in Dallas. She won a teen modeling contest, and that was how she ended up going to Hollywood. She dropped out of high school to do her first movie," MaeBe continued, and the slide changed. Now it was a movie poster that showed a younger, but more recognizable Vanessa Hale. She was blonde and busty. "The classic *Terror in Walton Woods*. She played the flirt who gets chopped up by the crazy former summer camp owner. They liked her so much that she came back as a ghost in the second movie, and as her own evil twin who turned out to be the killer in the third."

"They're fun in a totally awful way," Kyle commented and then frowned. "MaeBe made me watch them."

"They're supposed to be tongue in cheek," MaeBe argued. "But that's beside the point. From there Vanessa Hale actually became something of an 'It Girl' in Hollywood for a couple of years. She did several romantic comedies, and even a drama she got positive reviews for. But then she got a reputation for being difficult."

"So she was hard to work with?" Ian asked. "Because I got a whole building of difficult here, and they're still working for me."

"I remember seeing something about her losing a part because she had crazy demands," Charlotte began.

MaeBe's slide show clicked through many of the numerous tabloids to feature Ms. Hale. In each photo she looked sexier and oddly more craven. The photographers caught her frowning and yelling. The headlines questioned everything from whether or not she slept with her married costars, to if she was eating enough, to if she was pregnant or simply letting herself go.

What they all had in common was criticism.

"That's one rumor, but I couldn't verify it," MaeBe replied. "She had an assistant she was close to. Ashton Banks. After she was hired, she moved in, and they lived together for a long time until it came out that Ashton was the one selling the stories to the tabloids. That was kind of where it all spiraled. She got fired from a movie for what they called unrealistic demands. She wanted to be paid what the male lead got. He had way less experience than she did, but he was the producer's nephew, so she was replaced."

"So you would say she had fallen on hard times when she met George Benedict?" Julian was carefully studying each picture.

MaeBe turned his way. "He was the producer on the last couple of films she made. He was a billionaire from Houston. He made his money in retail stores and real estate. One of his daughters was a director, and he produced her films. Vanessa starred in the last one, a kind of experimental piece. It did well on some of the festival circuits, but it never found an audience."

"I believe I remember hearing something about the daughter dying," Julian mused.

"She did. She was working on a film with Vanessa in France. Lara Benedict was found dead of a drug overdose in the house she'd rented while working there." MaeBe clicked, and the news headline came up. "Vanessa found her. By this point Vanessa was actually living with the Benedicts. She married George about six weeks after the funeral."

"That seems fast." Michael glanced through the folder Charlotte had placed in front of every seat. It was basic information, and he knew most of it.

"Grief can make you do odd things," Ian murmured.

"It can also make you vulnerable," Michael countered. He couldn't reconcile that sweet-faced young woman with the bleach blonde who wore five-inch heels to pick up her dry cleaning.

"While she was married to George, she seemed to try to stay out of the spotlight as much as she could." MaeBe turned on the lights. "But naturally there were stories. According to the press, she used George cruelly for cash and separated him from his remaining child, George Jr., who was not pleased with the marriage and tried to have his father declared non compos mentis. George died while they were in the middle of that battle, and then the real one began."

"She recently had to move out of the mansion, didn't she?" Charlotte asked.

"The judge awarded almost everything to Junior in the last go-round," MaeBe agreed. "She should have been able to stay in it through the appeals process, but George Jr. played hardball, and when she went to visit her sister here in Dallas, he moved in and changed the locks. She can fight it, but I don't like her odds."

"Did George Sr. have a will?" Lodge asked.

"Yep, and he left a huge amount to Vanessa." Michael knew this part. He'd studied up on her finances. It always came down to money, and George Benedict had a ton of it. Money that probably should have gone to his son and not the twenty-something he'd married on a lark.

"They've been fighting over it for the last two years," MaeBe continued. "The last judgment was against her. The judge ruled that there was enough evidence to believe that George Sr. was under undue influence at the time he wrote the will."

That told him everything he needed to know. Vanessa wasn't the same girl in that picture. She'd lost herself somewhere along the way and tried to take the easy route to money. She'd tried to steal it from a frail old man and gotten caught. "How did she come to be in your employ, Julian? She doesn't seem like the type of person you normally hire."

"My wife hired her," Lodge replied. "Technically, Vanessa works for Danielle's company."

"How does Dani know her?" Charlotte asked.

"Vanessa had a sister. Nicki. She worked for Danielle for ten years. She was one of the first employees Dani hired, and they were close. Nicki was in a car accident four months ago. They met at her funeral," Julian explained.

"She seems to go to a lot of funerals." He didn't like the way death seemed to be all around her. "So your wife decided it was a good idea to hire her friend's down-on-her-luck sister. Did she understand Vanessa's background?"

"My wife is one of the kindest people I know," Julian said. "She can look at all the information MaeBe laid out and see something totally different from me. She's grown close to this woman, and I worry about that. I've tried to make her see Vanessa could be dangerous, but she isn't interested in my opinion. I've got people watching her in the office. That was how I found her trying to look through reports she had no business with."

"So you think she's trying to steal from you?" Michael could see that possibility. "Why not use in-house investigators and surveil her online? I'm sure you have plenty of cameras around the office."

"I've tried that. We haven't caught anything, but I can tell you that someone managed to move more than fifty thousand dollars to an account I can't identify." Julian sat forward, his voice going soft.

It was suspicious. “So you want me to find a way to get into her house, to find out any secrets she might have.”

“She’s interested in D/s. She asked specifically about The Club. I think she’s looking for a new wealthy lover,” Julian replied.

“I suppose that would be me.” There it was. There was that nasty feeling in the pit of his stomach Tessa had warned him about, the one that made him wonder who the hell he was.

“All I’m asking you to do is to top her, Mr. Malone,” Julian explained. “If you happen to find her attractive and the two of you allow sexual relations in your contract, then that would simply be what happens when a Dom and sub connect. Otherwise, you can decide how far you choose to go.”

It wasn’t like she would be some innocent thing. She would be playing him, too.

“Michael, you don’t have to take this assignment,” Charlotte said. “We can find another way.”

Despite the feeling in his gut, he was also interested in playing the game with an expert. It wasn’t like he was in a relationship, and her heart wouldn’t come close to getting involved. “I’ll do it.”

So tonight, the games would begin.

* * * *

Vanessa Jones was sick of games.

She hung up the phone and took a deep breath.

“You okay?”

She looked up from the big desk her sister had once used. Danielle Lodge-Taylor stood in the doorway of her office, looking flawless in her designer suit and heels, blonde hair in an elegant bun at the back of her neck. The woman had been her sister’s boss for years, and now she was proving to be Vanessa’s savior.

Would Dani regret that when she discovered the real reason Vanessa had taken her up on her offer to slip into Nicki’s old job?

She gave Dani a weary smile. “I’m great. I’ve got those contracts ready for you, and I spoke with the caterer for the reception. She said it’s not going to be a problem to add an additional salad.”

Dani stepped inside, relief on her face. “Excellent. I didn’t realize the salad I chose wasn’t vegan, and given the crowd we’ll have for that one, it would be a huge mistake. That was a good catch."

Vanessa knew that crowd well. It was one of the reasons she felt slightly better about taking Dani up on her offer of employment. Dani was currently working on a big project that included attracting a celebrity spokesperson. Her line of resort spas focused on wellness, and getting the right celebrity endorsement was important. Vanessa knew how to handle a celebrity. After all, she'd been one once. "Alicia Kingman's been a vegan for a couple of years now, but she's not going to be upset that there are nonvegan options. I worked with the caterer, so her favorites will all be available. She won't actually eat the dessert, but it looks good to have it there."

Dani sank down to the seat in front of Vanessa's desk. "You are a godsend. I have no idea how I would have managed this without you."

Would Dani think she was a godsend a few weeks from now? Or would she be one more person who looked on Vanessa with contempt? It would be awful because she'd come to genuinely care for Dani and her family.

"You would have done fine," Vanessa replied in all honesty. "You're the single most capable woman I've ever met. You would have done a ton of research and landed her all on your own."

"I'm going to teach you one of the secrets I've learned over the years." Dani crossed one leg over the other. "Do not take credit away from yourself. There will be too many other people who do that. Don't do it to yourself."

She had to blink a couple of times to clear the tears that threatened to form. "That's very true."

No one gave her credit for anything but causing pain she hadn't meant to cause.

"So tell me why you look like you lost your last friend," Dani prompted.

Vanessa took a moment to compose herself. There were about twenty reasons to be sad and depressed. She picked the one most relevant to Dani. "The homeowner's association has asked me to vacate my sister's house as soon as possible. I recently got word that they are going to bring legal action against me if I don't move within the next month."

"What?" Dani's eyes had gone wide. "Why?"

"Why do you think?" It wasn't like it was the first time they'd had this conversation.

"Reporters? I thought changing your hair and how you dress fixed things."

She'd gone back to brunette when she'd moved to Dallas. Honestly, the only reason she'd stayed a blonde was that George had loved the long blonde extensions she'd worn, and she would have done anything to make him happy in those last days. Between that, gaining a little weight, and changing how she dressed, she looked different enough that she'd managed to avoid the press. She'd moved into the house her sister had left her, and for a while things had calmed down. The lawsuit over her late husband's estate was in limbo while waiting for an appeal, and no one seemed to care now.

Then a national magazine had published a tell-all story from her used-to-be best friend about how vanity and greed had ruined Vanessa's promising career. It was all bullshit, but it had made her ache because Ashton had been as close as a sister to her. Closer than her own sister since they'd lived in completely different worlds for the last decade and a half.

"It was only a matter of time before they found me again," Vanessa admitted. "There have already been a few incidents. One news van broke the gate trying to get in, and some of the photographers are jumping fences. They're going to send me a bill for the gate."

"That's not your fault," Dani insisted.

Fault in this case didn't matter. "The easiest way for them to solve the problem is to get rid of me. And honestly, I can't afford another lawsuit. Everything I have is tied up in legal fees over George's estate."

"Maybe if you told the press what you intend to do with the money, they would let up," Dani offered.

For all her money and power, Danielle Lodge-Taylor was still naïve about some things. Of course that's probably what happened when one found oneself married to not one, but two overly protective men. She knew some people would find Dani's personal life objectionable, but Vanessa was fascinated by how the trio worked. Julian, Dani, and their partner, Finn, had been married almost twenty years and had three lovable kiddos. Julian's fierce reputation and ties to every powerful person in Dallas had kept them off the press's radar. But that could change.

"They would never believe me. It would be just one more of my manipulations," Vanessa replied.

"You are not manipulative."

That was where Dani was wrong, and guilt wrenched through Vanessa. She had to give this woman an out. "I need you to think about what could happen…what will happen when the press eventually connects me to your business. They'll look into you."

Dani shrugged off that worry. "Let them. I don't care."

"What about Chloe? What about the boys? They'll get dragged into it."

"Chloe loves her family, and so do the boys. Do you think we haven't had to have this conversation about a million times?" Dani's voice had gone soft. "When you don't conform to what the world considers normal, you'll have trouble. And when you do conform there's different trouble. I don't care what the world thinks of us. I have the enormous privilege of my husbands' money and power, and that makes it infinitely easier to not care. But Chloe goes to a private school, and she's absolutely been teased about it. I sat her down once and asked her which dad she wanted to get rid of so we could be normal. She cried for a long time, and I cried with her, and the next day she explained to her friends and teachers that if they had a problem with her family, they could fuck themselves. And then we all got called into the office because she was thirteen."

"I hope you didn't punish her because they should go fuck themselves." She hated the thought of that little girl having to defend herself.

Everyone has to go through it. Why should you be different? Suck it up or lose your place.

The words of her ex-agent ran through her head. The woman had previously been an actress and thought anyone who didn't have to go through what she had didn't deserve a career. Unfortunately, what she'd been through was harassment and borderline assault. A pretty nineteen-year-old was fair game in Hollywood.

Don't get bitter, sweetheart. I'm an old man, and I've learned bitterness does nothing but make the world a colder place. You've been through bad things, so work to make sure the ones who come after you don't have to go through the same.

She felt a tear hit her cheek. She often heard George's words shortly after one of those negative voices hit her brain. Like he was still here, still telling her she was worthy. Telling her just because she'd been foolish for a while didn't mean she couldn't make a difference. Mistakes were how a person learned, and the person who never made mistakes would be hollow indeed because they would never learn empathy.

Using George's logic, she should be the most empathetic person in the world.

"We all have our challenges to face, and her unique family is one of my daughter's," Dani admitted. "Luckily she's got a lot of support on every level. I worry you think you don't."

She was alone in the world, and she couldn't admit to Dani what she was really doing. She actually thought Dani would help her, but Dani would also talk to her husband—the ruthless one—and she couldn't risk that. "Everyone's gone. I have a couple of cousins, but they don't want to have anything to do with me now that I don't have access to tons of money."

Her extended family had been perfectly happy to take her help but not to reciprocate. They didn't answer her calls or invite her to visit.

"You have me. I was close to your sister. I know you reached out to her in the last year of her life. I also know that the house you're living in was purchased by you," Dani pointed out.

She and Nicki had never stopped talking. They might have gone months without calling, but they always got in touch in the end. Her sister hadn't approved of her lifestyle, had thought she made poor choices, but Nicki had still loved her.

Which was why she had to do what she had to do.

"I did that years ago when my career was viable," Vanessa admitted. "And I put the house in Nicki's name, so until her will is through probate, they've got the right to ask me to leave. I think they're hoping if I leave I'll forget to pay the association fees and they can put a lien on the place. I won't. I'll have everything forwarded to wherever I end up next."

"Why not stay at The Club?" Dani asked.

She needed to be inside that secret domain of the wealthy and powerful and kinky. It was the whole reason she'd taken the job in the first place. The Club was part dungeon and part luxury hotel and apartments. Several of the high-level members of The Club lived in the building that also housed the offices she was currently working in. Dani's company had a big suite of offices attached to Lodge Corp. There was a secretive way down to the dungeon level. Anyone walking into the building would see nothing more than a private multi-use, elegant high-rise.

She needed to get into the dungeon.

"I don't want to cause you any more trouble than I need to. I can't tell you how much I appreciate this job not only for the fact that it allows me to eat and put gas in my car, but because it makes me feel close to Nicki. She adored you. But if I move here, they will follow me. I'm surprised they haven't shown up here yet, though I've been taking precautions. I've been parking in a lot down the street and going into that building before I sneak out the back and come here." It was the stupidest thing, but she had to do it. She actually went into a bathroom on the lower level and changed clothes and put on a wig that she ditched when she made it to the building that Lodge owned.

"That's ridiculous. I'll send someone to pick you up," Dani insisted.

She shook her head. "It's fine. I'll lay low for a couple of weeks at a motel, and they'll lose interest again. Ashton probably got enough off the interview to last her for six months or so. If she's quiet, I might get lucky."

"Laying low here would be perfect," Dani pointed out. "You don't even have to go out for groceries. You can have them delivered or eat with us."

"Dani, Julian doesn't like me." She needed to put things plainly. "It's best I stay off his radar."

Dani's head tilted slightly, and an amused expression crossed her face. "He hasn't spent time with you, and he can be a suspicious bastard. I know that. It's part of his charm, but I understand that he can be intimidating. You know going to The Club isn't going to change that perception. If you think Julian is overwhelming in a suit, you should see him in leathers."

"I can't tell you how much I appreciate him being okay with me going into training." She wasn't sure about this part. The idea of bondage and submission and all the other kinky things… She wasn't sure, but this lifestyle had called to her sister.

There's a new Dom, and I see the way he looks at me. I think he's following me.

I think he wants to kill me.

Sometimes she wished she'd never found her sister's notebook, never read the last few months of entries. Then she could have simply mourned her and tried to move on.

She could have believed the police reports about the accident.

She would never have known that her sister had been murdered.

"Of course." Dani stood up and straightened out her skirt. "Julian is a sweetheart once you get to know him. I wish you would let me put you up here, but I'm willing to be patient. What I'm not willing to do is throw that reception without you. We need to find the perfect dress."

She wanted to argue. God, the last thing she wanted was to be in a room with Hollywood hotshots. The reception was still weeks away. Maybe she would find her sister's killer and potentially cause an even bigger scandal than she had before and get her ass fired. Julian Lodge might find out she was trying to prove one of his powerful club members killed her sister, and he would bury her. Problem solved.

It was the way her world seemed to go.

She gave Dani what she hoped was a conciliatory smile. "All right. I'll consider it a work expense."

"No, you won't. It's a uniform. I'm paying." Dani started for the door. "Let's have lunch tomorrow. I want to hear all about the training Dom Julian found for you. He's being all secretive about it. I'm kind of excited."

Vanessa nodded. "Absolutely. I'm excited, too."

"I can tell." Dani gave her a wave and was gone.

And they called her a bad actress.

Vanessa sat back with a sigh. She had a couple of hours before she had to meet the man who would walk her through the world her sister had occupied.

The world that had cost Nicki everything—including her life.

It was a world she would take down if it was the last thing she did.

Chapter Two

Michael stepped inside the dungeon and had to appreciate the differences between The Club and Sanctum. It reflected the differences between the owners, and probably the people who frequented each.

Sanctum had an industrial feel and a loud, vibrant energy. The Club was old-school beautiful, with elegant lines and an edge of danger that matched Julian Lodge. Though it wasn't technically open right now, he could imagine a hushed, reverent crowd in this place.

"Have you ever been here before?" Julian stepped out of the elevator that had brought them from the lobby to the dungeon. It was a private elevator, and there had been a security guard who had tipped his head as Julian had approached. If it had been anyone but Julian, the guard would likely have reacted differently.

Security was tight here, but it potentially hadn't kept out a thief. Julian had indulged his wife and perhaps let someone into his home he shouldn't have.

"I've been in the building, of course. I haven't been in the dungeon. It's nice."

"I'm sure Ian would say something like it looks like a French brothel. Well, he would use a coarser word. He says French because it's the most elite descriptor he can think of and therefore some kind of insult, but the man literally met his wife in Paris, so don't let him fool you." Julian started down the hallway where they were met with another security guard at her post. "Ellie, how are you, dear?"

The pretty redhead gave Julian a bright smile. "Excellent, Master Julian. Your appointment is already here. I showed her to the conference room. There's tea and some snacks. Mr. Malone, is there anything I can offer you during your meeting?"

"Tea is fine." He needed a Scotch to get through this, but that wouldn't do when he was supposed to be a stern, in-control Dominant. Or a charming one. He would have to assess what was needed to get the best hold on the target. Mostly what he thought would attract her was his family name and money. But first he had a question. "Jones? She's going by her maiden name again? I would think she would hold on to Benedict as long as she possibly could."

He'd dressed for this first meeting in one of the slick suits he kept around for more formal occasions. He didn't need a suit in the office.

But he was going undercover, and that meant dressing the part. Including the Tiffany and Co. cufflinks he rarely wore and the Rolex his parents had bought him last Christmas.

"I think you'll find Ms. Hale has gone through a bit of a metamorphosis since she left Houston," Julian allowed as they continued down the hall. "I believe she's trying to reinvent herself."

He decided to ask the question no one had asked yet. "Julian, if you don't want her here, why hire her in the first place?"

Julian stopped and turned his way. His dark hair was slicked back, and there was a hint of gray at his temples. He was dressed in all black, from his three-piece suit to the loafers Michael recognized as Gucci and ridiculously expensive. In the low light, his dark eyes seemed obsidian. It was easy to see why some people referred to this man as the devil himself. "I didn't hire her at all. Danielle did, and she did not ask for my input. I'm afraid over the years my wife figured out how intelligent and independent she could be, and she does not compromise when it comes to her own business any more than I would."

"But you funded her business," Michael pointed out.

"No, I invested in her, and it paid insane dividends. Investing in Danielle has paid off in ways that have nothing to do with money and everything to do with peace and joy and light in my world." There was passion in the man's voice, and Michael realized that even the devil could love someone. Or in Julian's case, two someones.

"She also makes a lot of money," a lighter voice said. "She started out with one spa in a tiny town in East Texas. It catered to kinksters. She's moving into the big time now, and that's what our husband is worried about."

Finn Taylor was waiting in front of what was likely the conference room the guard had mentioned. He was shorter than Julian, light to the man's dark. From what Michael understood, Finn had once been a small-town kid. He looked very much like the high-powered attorney he was today. He also had that smile on his face that Michael didn't understand, the one his brother got when his sister-in-law walked in the room. The one his dad still had around his mom.

Julian moved in, crowding Finn and reaching around to cup the back of his neck. "You know why I worry."

Finn's face turned up, his smile slightly impish. "You're worried our wife will find out you're plotting behind her back, and then you'll be in for it."

Julian lowered his head to touch Finn's and breathed the man in like he was pure oxygen. "Perhaps. But I also know there's money missing from Danielle's accounts, and that started when Ms. Hale showed up. She's got a bad reputation."

"So do you," Finn whispered. "And she wants to be referred to as Vanessa Jones. It's her legal name. Master, I know you're worried, but don't be less a man than you are because of fear."

"Ms. Jones, then." Julian kissed Finn's forehead and then sighed and straightened up. "Is she ready?"

Finn shrugged. "I guess. I don't know. She's very nervous. I'll be honest. I don't know that she really wants to do this."

Julian opened the door, and Michael was surprised when it didn't open to the conference area but rather a small space with a window into the other. An observation room. Interesting.

"I would actually say the woman would be fairly submissive during sex." Julian stepped inside and stood in front of what Michael suspected was a two-way mirror. "She's rather hard to read, but she does tend to respond to what I would call benevolent dominance."

"She responds to you?" Michael followed them.

"Oh, she doesn't like to be around me at all," Julian replied. "She tends to avoid me, but she likes to work with female tops. I doubt she would recognize them as such, but it's what they are. Both Danielle and I employ several Dommes in our business, and I've found if I want to get Vanessa to talk, I send one of them."

"She's quite nice, though a little standoffish around me," Finn murmured.

That was when Michael got his first real look at the target.

"Another thing that worries me since you are incredibly lovable," Julian was saying.

Finn said something else, but it was lost because Michael couldn't take his eyes off the woman in the room.

She bore little resemblance to the woman on the cover of tabloid magazines. Gone was the bleach-blonde hair and the overdone makeup. She wore none of the flashy clothes she'd donned before. She had on a plain green blouse and a black cardigan. The clothes were cheap. He could see that even from here. Dark hair was pulled back in a low ponytail, and he noticed she wore no jewelry whatsoever. Not even earrings.

She was stunning. She'd gained weight, and it looked good on her. Some women could be very thin and it looked natural. For some women it *was* natural. Vanessa wasn't naturally thin. She'd likely had to starve herself to get that small.

How hard had it been to go into that world at such a young age? To give up something so normal and natural as properly feeding her body. Who had told her she needed to be someone else in order to make it in her industry?

Or she'd been ruthless even with herself. She'd had a goal and done whatever it took to achieve it.

He was getting drawn in by a sweet face and forgetting that this woman was an actress at heart, and she knew how to manipulate a man.

"Michael? Are you listening?"

He turned at Julian's question. "I'm sorry. She looks different."

"Like I said, I believe she's adapting to her circumstances," Julian replied.

"Or she's trying to find herself again." Finn seemed to need to fill the optimist role in the play they found themselves in. "Look, Mr.

Malone, I agree with my Master that we should look into Ms. Jones. She is close to Danielle, and she's gotten close to our daughter, Chloe. Some odd things have been happening around her. But I don't agree that she's some kind of monster. She's reserved and a bit distant. Given what she's gone through, I can understand that."

"What she's gone through is all of her own money and a good portion of her husband's," Julian said flatly.

"Then where is it?" Finn argued, proving their relationship wasn't so simple as Master and sub. Finn was willing to challenge his Master, though in this case Michael thought he was behaving more like a spouse. "I was closer to Nicki than you were, and she loved her sister."

"She did not approve of Vanessa's marriage. I remember that," Julian countered.

Finn didn't seem ready to back down. "Yes, but not for the reasons you think. She thought George Benedict took advantage of her sister."

Michael listened in, the argument between spouses telling him a lot about the dynamics in play. "Was she close to her sister?"

"They talked on the phone quite a bit in the last years of Nicki's life," Finn said. "After their mother passed, Vanessa and Nicki reconnected."

"Did the mother not approve of Vanessa's lifestyle?" He'd read a bit about her family but liked to learn some things organically.

"Their mother was extremely religious. She approved of very little, including Nicki working for Danielle. She was an angry, bitter woman. Nicki changed to a less restrictive church, and her mother cut her off," Finn explained. "So neither of them had much to do with their mother later in life, and the father walked out very early on."

So she had no strong male role models and had grown up in an environment where sex was more than taboo.

"What type of men does she like?"

Julian's brow rose. "Well, from what I can tell, eighty-year-old billionaires. Though there is a rumor that she was having several affairs with young members of her husband's household."

"You're going to get in so much trouble," Finn said with a sigh. He turned to Michael. "Here's what I know. I do believe she's straight and not bi. I believe she does not have a good relationship with her body. I'm not sure why she's insistent on training in D/s because I think she's terrified of all of it."

"Which is precisely why I'm suspicious of her," Julian added. "She wants access to The Club for some reason, and it's not that she wants to fit in. I've already heard that argument from Danielle. We have many employees who do not play."

So figuring out why she wanted to train would be his first order of business. "How would you suggest I approach her?"

Finn sighed. "I'm going to end up in the doghouse, too, aren't I?" He seemed to not need a reply as he moved on. "I would pretend to not know who she is. I would focus on making her feel safe. I don't think an over-the-top hard approach is going to work with her. I think you should ease her into the relationship, though if you have a chance to bring her any kind of sexual pleasure, that might be a way in. I've overheard her talking to Dani about how long it's been for her."

"If you disregard the rumors," Julian added.

"Charm, then?" He could manage a bit of that. He would do what he always did when he needed a little charm. Pretend to be his brother. Not that he himself couldn't get a woman in bed. He could, but JT was the one who was charming. Women flocked around him, happy to be in his company. Michael started to talk about his job and scared many of them off.

He needed to come across as pleasant, friendly, the kind of guy a woman could tell all her secrets to.

"I think kindness will work better with her in the beginning, and then you'll need to figure out how to handle her in the dungeon," Finn continued. "You're attracted to her."

It wasn't a question. "Physically, yes. This version of her is quite lovely. She's got a certain fragile air about her that calls to my dominant side. Unfortunately, I need more than that, as I've proven in the past."

"You've had long-term partners?" Julian asked.

"I've had girlfriends I played with," he allowed because he wasn't about to go into his personal history with Julian Lodge. "I've never had a permanent submissive, and I don't think I will."

"If Tessa is any indicator, you prefer a play partner to a sub." Julian didn't look his way but kept those dark eyes on the target, who was fidgeting now, looking back down at the contract Finn had no doubt recently gone over with her.

So they'd checked him out, too. "I'm not looking to pair up with anyone. This is a job, Mr. Lodge."

"Yes, but you could learn something about yourself, too. If I'm correct, I think one of Vanessa's talents is adapting to her circumstances," Julian said. "She survives. It's what she does. In some ways, I can understand and appreciate that. But I cannot allow Danielle and Chloe to be hurt by her. So figure it out for me, Mr. Malone. Tell me if I need to handle her or if she's an innocent victim in all of this."

"I doubt she's innocent." Michael needed to harden himself because she looked awfully innocent to him. She looked soft, and his protective side wanted to come out.

"There are many ways a person can be innocent, and I need to remember that," Julian said with a sigh. His arm went around Finn's shoulders. "You should, too. We'll be here watching. Good luck."

He didn't need luck. All he needed was his name and the call of the Malone billions.

Michael stepped out and got ready to perform.

* * * *

Vanessa pulled her thin cardigan around her and wondered if Julian Lodge was trying to freeze her out. Or perhaps the dungeon was kept cold for other reasons.

Not that it looked much like she'd thought it would. She'd envisioned some torture chamber, but what she'd seen so far resembled a decadent dream. It reminded her of a movie where the sex was tastefully done and likely ended in happily, if kinkily, ever after.

She could see Dani here. And Finn. She hadn't been able to picture it before, but the place had a timeless elegance, a beauty to it that would call to those two. She could see them playing in here. That was what she'd called it. Play.

Nicki had loved it here. Her sister had talked about how she'd found herself in this place, how she'd learned to love her body in this dungeon.

What would it be like to look in the mirror and not check off all the things she needed to change? She'd purposefully put on some weight to change her shape, and she knew it was healthy weight, but there was a part of her that panicked when she saw those curves.

She blinked back tears again. It was that kind of day, and she still had so much to get through. In a couple of days she would have to find a hotel she could afford and hole up there for a while, which meant packing what little she had and trying to sneak away without a picture being taken.

She liked the fact that no one had managed to take a picture of how she looked now. If they took her picture and plastered it everywhere, it would feel like she'd lost something.

The door came open, and Vanessa took a quick breath to banish the unwanted tears. The man walking in wouldn't be impressed. She stood, ready to face the man who would be in charge of her for the next six weeks. Technically this was supposed to be a meeting to figure out if she could accept Master Michael as a training Dom, but it wasn't like she was going to turn him away.

Of course, he could turn her away, and then it would take longer before she could get started. She had to remember that no matter who walked through that door, she needed to make sure he wanted to mentor her. It didn't matter how scary he was, how unattracted to him she was, how much she didn't want to spend time with him. She had to make him want to spend time with her. She'd gone through this a million times in her head. She expected Julian to send a hardass sadist to scare her away.

She turned and realized the situation was far worse.

He was gorgeous. Six foot three or four, and in an elegant suit that had almost certainly been made for him. She pegged him around thirty-five, perhaps forty, with stunning green eyes and a jawline any leading man would kill for. He was a supersexy comic book hero. Or a James Bond.

She was being stupid. She'd literally met *People's* Sexiest Man Alive. Four of them. And not once had she gone all drooling gaga on one of them the way she kind of wanted to right now.

She gave him what she hoped was her brightest smile and held out her hand, praying she remembered everything Dani had taught her. "Hello, Sir. I'm Vanessa Jones."

He gave her a smile that nearly knocked her over, and then that big hand of his was enveloping hers, sending a shock of warmth through her system. "Hello, Vanessa. I'm Michael Malone."

She nodded and tried not to get caught in those eyes. "Master Michael."

He hadn't let go of her hand, and she didn't want him to. She wanted to stand here touching the pretty man.

She wanted to be the Vanessa Jones she could have been if she'd never left Dallas in the first place.

"Let's go with Michael or Sir for now." His voice was deep and rich. He stared down at her like he was studying her. "You know we're being watched, right?"

She glanced to the mirror. "Finn told me it's a two-way. He said they use it to observe and make sure the chemistry is right."

He leaned in, and his voice went low. "They use it because they're perverts who like to watch."

He moved back, the grin on his face an intimacy between them.

Oh, Julian had done so much worse than she'd thought. She'd thought he would send in someone who she worried would harm her physically, but this one could do some serious damage.

Or it had been a long time since she'd been even vaguely interested in sex and having sex with an actual man, and she was making more of it than she should.

"Either way, they made sure I knew." She forced herself to pull away from him and get to the business at hand. "I've read through the…contract." It was so weird to think about signing a contract that would possibly lead to sex. "But I do have some questions."

She'd actually read through it the night before and forced herself to view this as an acting gig. What would she want to know before she started? She certainly didn't want to tell him that the contract didn't matter because she would do anything to get into that club. She needed to look thoughtful, fully interested in the lifestyle.

Michael nodded and then held out her seat for her. "Of course. That's what we're here for. The first thing you need to understand is that you are in control. If I do anything that makes you uncomfortable, you need to tell me, and that doesn't merely include physical things."

"I thought pain was kind of the point."

Michael moved around the table, sitting down across from her, and she was relieved he hadn't taken the seat beside her. "Then you don't understand D/s at all, and we should definitely have a conversation before you sign that."

Mistake number one. "I meant I thought it was about finding pleasure in pain."

"Only if pain brings you pleasure. It's about finding confidence, taking our bodies seriously, and discovering a place and people we can explore with," he said, that deep voice soothing her. "I'm going to be very forthright with you, Vanessa. We need to make sure we're a good fit because this won't work if we're not. Why are you here?"

Because I think someone in this club killed my sister.

It was right there on the tip of her tongue to tell him the truth. From what she'd read in the short bio she'd been given of Michael, he worked for an investigative firm. He might be able to help her.

Of course, if she did she would also be confiding in Julian Lodge and his husband, Finn. Julian was known for being good at hiding bodies. She couldn't trust that he didn't know damn well who'd done it and was protecting him.

She went with the easiest answer. "I want to explore my sexuality."

He stared at her for a moment. "I don't think so."

She bit her bottom lip and wished she'd kept the bigger implants. Of course they'd been far too big for her body and painful in the end, which was why she'd moved to smaller ones, but those double Ds worked on most men. They distracted men, and then no one thought she could possibly lie since it was obvious she didn't have a brain in her head. "Why wouldn't I want to explore? Do you think a woman like me has probably explored enough?"

She was out of practice because the question came out with an edge of irritation to it she hadn't meant. Well, she hadn't meant to share it with him. She'd certainly felt it.

"I don't think anyone's explored enough. I meant I doubt you're truly here because you want to have sex. You're beautiful. You could find a partner. You hesitated before you said the word contract because you find it unsavory. And despite the fact that you looked at me like you could eat me up, you're more comfortable with me sitting on the other side of the room. So why don't you tell me why you're really here."

She wanted to tell him to fuck off and walk away because she didn't like the way he was making her feel.

Though she had to allow that the words hadn't been said unkindly. He'd stated what he'd seen as fact after he'd told her he intended to be forthright with her. Finn and Dani had warned her this was a lifestyle that was all about truth, but she'd thought they were saying that like any lifestyle guru would.

"I want to understand my sister."

He was quiet for a moment. "Nicki Jones?"

"Did you know her?" She'd been told they were bringing in someone for her, someone who hadn't spent a lot of time in The Club but was up for membership now and needed to prove himself to Julian Lodge.

He shook his head. "No, but I have some friends who play here, and they talked about Nicki. I'm not a member of this club yet, but I work for a company that has ties to Lodge Corp. We intermingle quite a bit."

So she couldn't trust him. She'd known that, but it was good to be reminded that this was a small world, and she didn't have a place in it. Every person in this club would be wealthy or attached to someone wealthy. They were the elite of the elite, and they would protect their own.

Now that she thought about it, she wondered about Michael himself. Everything about him screamed money and power, but he worked for a security firm?

Or he had one good suit and he wanted to look his best. If she'd managed to keep any of her old clothes, wouldn't she have worn them today? Clothes could be armor.

A bit of truth wouldn't hurt, and now she understood what she was about to say was the truth. "Nicki talked about this place and how much it helped her. I want to understand. I want to feel close to my sister."

A sympathetic look crossed his face. "All right. I can ask Julian to make some appointments for you. He knows who her friends were. You could talk to them."

Her stomach knotted. That wouldn't help because the man she was looking for had been new to The Club. Nicki hadn't been friends with him. "I don't need that. I need to be where she was, to know what she did. She said she found herself here, and I guess I feel lost."

"Vanessa, this is about sex and pleasure. It can be a form of therapy for some people, but it doesn't replace it."

Great. Now the gorgeous man thought she was insane. "That isn't what I meant."

"Then maybe you should tell me what you mean. Why don't I begin? I'll tell you why I started in D/s." He continued when she nodded his way. "I was in the military, and when I eventually moved to the private sector, I did so with several members of my former team. We got jobs with a company two of my friends' brother runs, and he has a club somewhat similar to this one, though it has a less confusing name."

Oh, he had a nice sense of humor. It made him all the more dangerous. "Yeah, it took me a while to realize the name of this club is The Club. I thought it was just what people called it. Like I'm going to the store."

His lips kicked up in a heartbreaking grin. "Yeah, my boss would say Julian's so arrogant he couldn't have imagined anyone else starting a club. I think he likes to throw people off. Anyway, one of the perks of working for McKay-Taggart is membership at Sanctum."

She could bet how this story went. "Your friends were all going, so you thought you would give it a try, too?"

"Pretty much. I took the training class, and it changed the way I think about sex and my body. I know I'm a guy and not supposed to think about my body beyond making it as strong as possible, but I didn't realize I could have a relationship with it. I would have made fun of anyone who put it like that, but it's true. I respect my body for what it is, for the scars I have, the age that shows on it. I respect it because it not only houses my soul, but it can bring comfort and pleasure to others. I learned a lot about my sexuality, things I wouldn't have known about myself if I hadn't explored the lifestyle."

She wondered what he'd learned. Her own sexuality was marked by so many outside forces. Her relationship with her body? Pretty much ruined by years and years of people on social media nit-picking every inch of her. She'd been accused of using her body to get everything from a role in a film to money and fame. She was considered a whore by a lot of people out there, and yet she'd never enjoyed sex. Did a whore have to? Or was her body nothing more than a tool she traded for survival?

"Vanessa, if you don't want to do this, you don't have to," he said softly, as though he was worried about scaring her.

Maybe she needed more honesty with him. Maybe she could do what she needed to do and get something out of this for herself, too. "I've never enjoyed sex, and I pretty much hate my body."

"You're beautiful. Why would you hate your body?" Michael asked.

"Because I've been told to, I guess. I worked in an industry that judged me entirely by my looks." She was surprised he hadn't mentioned her former career. For the most part with her more natural hair and in sedate clothes, she could pass someone on the street without comment. Especially when she wore sunglasses. But her eyes always gave her away. They were a vibrant Caribbean blue that most people assumed were contacts. They were a trick of her DNA. It had been her eyes that got her an agent and her first role, and they were the only things about her no one wanted to change.

Sometimes she wore contacts to cover them so she could blend in better, but not today.

"What industry did you work in? Were you a model of some kind?" Michael asked.

She stopped, searching his face, but she didn't see anything there that would lead her to believe he was deceiving her. "I was an actress for a long time."

"Ah, yes. I can see where you would feel judged by that industry," Michael agreed. "Especially if you had any kind of success."

She spent all of her days now trying to go unnoticed. It was perverse that she was irritated by the fact that he didn't recognize her. Still, she wanted to put off the moment when he realized what she was truly famous for. Not the roles she'd played or the people she'd entertained, but for marrying an old man and ruining his family. Oh, she could tell him the truth, but she hadn't met anyone who believed her.

"I made some movies," she replied, her hands coming together on her lap. "Did some TV spots. The constant scrutiny wore me down. I got out, but I still question myself every day. I can't be satisfied with my body because for over a decade it was the only thing anyone cared about when it came to me. Not my talent or who I was deep down. It was all about how I looked."

He nodded again, as though taking in everything she said and weighing the words. "A lot of the training you'll go through with me will be to make you comfortable in your own skin, though again, it's not a replacement for therapy. Have you talked to a professional?"

She'd had to jump through hoops to get to this point. "Of course. I had to talk to a man named Leo Meyer in order to be approved for training. I assure you he can verify my sanity."

He smiled, but there was an odd sympathy behind the expression. "Therapy isn't about sanity. It's about self-care. It's about figuring yourself out. I should know because I've been. For about five years after I left the military, I had weekly appointments with a therapist who helped me work through things I saw and did during my time there. It helped me figure out who I am and what I want."

She liked the fact that he didn't have a problem talking about his therapy. She'd never been because it had seemed like a bad idea. She'd had someone to talk to. She'd had Ashton, and now she worried anyone she did talk to would turn on her. "Then no, I haven't really talked to anyone. I don't trust many people."

He sat back. "All right, one of the conditions for taking you on is to see a therapist twice a week while we're training. I think you should see a woman though."

"I have to go to therapy to be able to go to The Club?" She didn't like the thought of that. No one had mentioned conditions. "You can't make me do that."

Michael had a pen out, marking up the contract she'd been given. "No, I can't. I can require it to work with me, but obviously I can't force you to do anything you don't want to do."

"But if I don't, you'll make Julian find me another Dom and set me back weeks."

"How do you think this is going to work?" Michael asked, one brow rising.

There was the command she'd expected. He was very approachable, but there was a bit of Julian Lodge in the man. "I think you're going to show me around and teach me the rules."

That brow rose to even higher heights. "No, I'm going to be your top. This isn't a training group where we meet up for a few hours a week for class and homework and I pretend to top you. This is an advanced training relationship. I'm your top, and that means I'm responsible for you for the time laid out in that contract. I take my position seriously. Unlike a training class, I'll be taking you into The Club immediately, and that means you behavior will reflect on me. We're both trying to attain a membership here. Your training and progress will be part of my evaluation."

She hadn't thought about that. "So we'll meet more often than club nights?"

"Much more often. I was going to suggest we start at my place tomorrow night, but perhaps you would be more comfortable either here or in a public setting."

"I didn't think we would see each other…" She stopped because he was already iffy about her. Learning that he might not get what he wanted if she didn't comply made the situation much more dangerous to her end goal. Michael was her entryway to where she needed to be, and if he rejected her, it could be weeks before another Dom became available. Or she could be sent to the other club for their training class and not allowed on the dungeon floor here for at least two months. She brought her eyes up, forcing a confidence she didn't feel. "I'm fine coming to your place. Or here, if you prefer. I don't think my place is suitable, Sir. And perhaps having someone to talk to would be good for me."

He stared at her for a moment, a penetrating look that made her want to squirm. "Just like that?"

"When I think about it, it makes sense. And I'm trying to not follow my instincts since they haven't been all that helpful so far." She forced herself to look into his eyes and give the performance of a lifetime. Despite her critics, she thought she was pretty good at acting. "Sir, I'm tired of hating my body. I'm tired of not understanding why some people think sex is important because it doesn't feel important to me. I want to know what my sister knew at the end."

Oh, she meant that. She wanted to know who killed her sister, wanted to see that man before she sent him to jail. Or maybe to Hell, since the system didn't work. At least not for people like her.

For a moment, she thought he would deny her, but then he picked up the contract again.

"Should we go over this?"

She'd been over it, but she knew what he meant. He was asking her to go through the portions where she described her hard and soft limits, whether or not she was willing to open their relationship up to sex.

She nodded.

"Good. I think we should take sex off the table for now. How about we leave intimacy open to a future discussion," Michael offered. "We can take this as slowly as we need to go. I won't go into any interaction with you expecting sex, and any intimate touching will be discussed before the session."

Slow wouldn't help her. Slow meant she wouldn't be allowed in the dungeon. "Like what kind of touching?"

"You said you wanted to explore sex, but I want you to be comfortable with me before you make any decisions regarding how we proceed."

She needed this man on board and quickly. If he decided she was too much trouble, then he would likely ask Julian for a new submissive. Or Julian would decide that all on his own because he was watching her.

She was out of practice. She'd gotten used to not having to play this role. With Dani and the clients she worked with, she could be herself. Or rather a version she preferred. She needed to be someone else in order to get this job done.

It was only a role. It wasn't like the thought of Michael touching her got her heart racing. How long had it been since she'd been touched by a man who had no real idea who she was? Who didn't think she was a celebrity who might bring him some fame? Or a whore who might make him infamous?

Wouldn't it be nice to simply sink into the role laid out in front of her? Did she have to hold her nose and make her way through it? Or could she actually find something out about herself, too?

"I'm not being brave," she said, taking a deep breath and hoping she said the next words with conviction. "Sir, I want to explore this, and while I don't think we should jump into bed, I also don't want to take that off the table. The only thing I have a worse relationship with than my body is my sexuality. Sex has always been something I performed and didn't feel. I'd like to explore the difference with you. You were honest with me. I'll be honest with you. I'm thirty-two years old, and I don't think I've ever had a real orgasm. I've felt some pleasure, but nothing like what my sister described. Not like what other women seem to feel."

He'd gone still, the tiniest bit predatory, and she hated the fact that it did something for her. "You want an orgasm?"

She stared at him for a moment and realized she kind of did. Oh, it probably wouldn't work, but she wished it would. The days seemed so long, and if she could have one thing for herself, wouldn't that make even a few minutes worthwhile? "I do."

She expected him to tell her she would have to earn one with good behavior and that eventually they would get there. She expected him to go back to the contract and go over the details.

"Would you like one now?"

Her brain went a little foggy, and all she could do was stare at him for a moment. She should tell him she needed time, needed some space and wasn't comfortable letting a stranger touch her.

But suddenly she wanted him to. He was exactly her type. Tall, dark, and handsome. Charming and open. Seemingly kind. What would it hurt? It could help her enormously, and in more ways than one.

"Yes."

A slow smile spread across that handsome face. "Why don't you come sit on my lap and we can begin."

Chapter Three

Was she actually going through with this?

She tried to think about the goal she wanted to accomplish, but she couldn't even trick herself into believing she was only doing this to further the mission.

It had been three years since she'd been touched in any way sexually, and that had been more about comfort than pleasure. How long had it been since she'd had this thrill of anticipation running through her veins? Since she felt her body heat at the thought of someone touching her?

This was a huge mistake.

But then she'd read the contract, and Michael's explanations made sense. The Club was about exploring sexuality. Nicki had found herself here. Vanessa didn't expect that, but she might be able to figure out if her body was simply defective or if she could relax long enough to find something other women took for granted.

She glanced at the two-way mirror and was surprised that she'd momentarily forgotten it was there.

Michael was watching her, his eyes like emeralds as he sat back, completely relaxed. "They won't be able to see what I'm doing. It's one of the reasons I sat on this side of the table. They'll be able to hear us, but they won't have a line of sight. It's all right if you're scared, but pushing boundaries is what this is all about."

She took a deep breath, thinking about what he'd said, and then asked the question that truly frightened her. The question that kept her in her seat instead of taking him up on his offer like any sane single hetero woman likely would. "What if I can't?"

"Can't?"

She nodded.

"Vanessa, if you can't say the word, you likely can't do it."

He was frustrating, but he had a point. She wasn't some prissy prude. She'd worked hard not to be what her mother had taught her to be. She'd swung too far the other way, and that hadn't worked out for her either.

"What if I can't come?"

"Do you come when you masturbate?" Michael asked.

"I don't do that…I don't masturbate very often," she admitted. "I find it frustrating, so I don't try."

"I would bet it's hard because you can't turn your brain off. So let's try an exercise, if you want to," he offered. "Or we can go over the contract and talk some more."

She was so tired of being afraid. Afraid of what would happen if she stepped even an inch out of line. Afraid of the press. Afraid she was everything they said she was.

Afraid she was old before her time, and that she would live the next forty or fifty years without any peace at all.

This wouldn't bring her peace, but it might bring her pleasure.

There is power in submission, and I feel strong for once in my fucking life.

Her sister had written those words shortly after she'd begun her training. In her journals, she'd talked about the freedom she'd found in this place and how it had begun with the simple step of giving herself permission to try.

Vanessa stood and moved around the big conference table. Michael pushed back, allowing her to move closer. She wasn't sure exactly what he was going to do, but wasn't that kind of the point?

What if the press found out she was involved in a sex club? She could see that headline play out.

"What are you afraid of now?" Michael asked, every word

patient and kind.

"That people will know," she whispered.

"Will know that you have a top? That he gave you an orgasm? I assure you confidentiality is in that contract, and even if you don't trust me, you can absolutely believe that Julian will murder anyone who breaks it. He'll do it quietly, and no one will ever question him."

That's what Julian would do to her at the end of this, but Michael was right. He wouldn't want his club and his wife linked to her in the press, so she was probably safe.

She moved in, settling herself awkwardly on his lap, one arm around his shoulders to balance her.

Up close she could see the fine lines around his eyes. This was a man who smiled often. She had the sudden urge to run her fingers through his hair to see if it was as soft as it looked. She didn't, remaining still and somewhat stiff as he wrapped an arm around her waist.

"Can we agree this is our first session?" The words were whispered close to her ear.

A shiver of awareness went through her, and she could feel her nipples tighten. "Yes, Sir."

"The first thing I want you to understand is that what happens between us is in your control. If you want me to stop, all you have to do is say the word *red*." His hand moved along her thigh, easing up toward the apex of her legs. "We go as fast or slow as you like today. There will be times when I decide what our pacing is, but you can always stop me. You can withdraw consent at any time, and I mean any. Do you understand?"

It was a day for tears because she was holding them in again. How often had she had any control at all? Consent was something people talked about but the men in her world had seldom followed through on. "You won't be angry if I stop you?"

"I might be disappointed, but anger has no place here," he promised. "This is a training relationship, and it might get quite intimate. I'm here to teach you, and if I'm half the Dom I hope I am, to learn from you, too."

She didn't trust him, but she also couldn't make herself get up and walk away. "Then yes, this is our first session. What do I do?"

"You listen to me. You stop thinking about anything but the

sound of my voice and the feel of my hands on your skin. I want to talk to you about sex. The last time I had good sex was roughly six weeks ago. I was working a job in New York and met a woman in a bar. We spent a couple of nights together. It was vanilla, but good."

Did he have a girlfriend? She stiffened up. "Are you seeing her?"

"No. It was a weekend thing," he said. "I don't have a significant other and haven't for over a year. I don't intend to look for one for the foreseeable future. Like I said, the training relationship can be intense. Would you like it written into the contract that I can't date while we're training? I'm amenable to that change."

God, she did need to relax. "No, it's fine. This is a training relationship, not a romance."

"I would honestly prefer you didn't see anyone," he offered.

"I won't." It was an easy promise to make. She wouldn't be here if she didn't have to be. She would be alone, holed up somewhere hoping she didn't have to see anyone at all.

And how had that worked out for her?

"Good, then we have a few weeks or months where we know we're going to concentrate on this relationship. Now I've told you about the last time I had sex."

A vision of her husband, his sweet face frowning as he turned off the light so she wouldn't see him flashed across her brain. She'd loved him, truly loved him, but that night hadn't been about sex for her. She shook her head. "I can't."

His arm tightened slightly as though he was afraid she would leap up and run away. "Good, then you're setting a boundary for now. I'm going to push it from time to time, but I'm glad you can tell me when you're uncomfortable."

The hand on her thigh stroked from knee to just below her pussy, and she suddenly wished she was wearing a skirt. She'd worn the slacks because she felt like she had to wear heels with a skirt, and she had to walk so much in order to evade potential photographers.

She wanted the choice to be able to run.

"Can I kiss your ear? Play with it a little bit?" he asked.

She nodded because when she felt his breath against her, she forgot what she was thinking about before.

She gasped as he nipped her earlobe.

"I want you to concentrate on me, Vanessa. Stop thinking about anything but me. I'm a selfish bastard, and when I'm giving you pleasure I want every bit of your attention. Normally I would talk to a sub, ask her what she enjoys, but I don't think that's going to work with you. I think you're going to be a mystery, and I'll have to uncover you layer by layer."

His hand was on the buckle of her belt, and she felt him start to release it.

He was going to put his hand down her pants. He was going to touch her. She should be scrambling off him. It wasn't like she hadn't been in this very position before, but now she was in control. This man wasn't threatening her career if she didn't give him what he wanted. He'd offered something to her. Pleasure and control.

She forced away those fleeting moments when she'd felt vulnerable. Was she going to allow those moments to stop her from ever moving forward? Nicki had tried to tell her she couldn't live in the past, that she could learn from it, but she couldn't let it stop her from growing.

Weeks. She could have weeks with him, with a man who was contracted to protect her. That was part of his role. Why shouldn't she take this time?

"So I'll tell you what I like," he murmured. "I like being in control during sex. I like having a sexual partner who trusts me, and I'll work hard to earn that. I like sinking into sex and spending a long time exploring my partner's body. I'll want to study you while you're naked. I'll use my eyes first and take in every inch of your loveliness, including all your scars and imperfections because those make you human."

He worked the button on her slacks.

She had to think to form the words she wanted to say. He had her in a fog of anticipation. "Do I get to see your scars?"

"There are a lot of them, and yes, I'll want you to accept them."

Because he was a military man. Had been. He was a man who worked. He was being offered membership to this club likely because he'd done work for Julian and Julian's partners. He wasn't some overly privileged asshole. He was a real man, and it had been a long time since she'd met one of those. "I will."

Something warm ran along her ear. His tongue. God, he was using his tongue to trace the shell of her ear, and that sensation seemed to go straight to her pussy.

What was this man doing to her?

He eased the zipper of her slacks down. "You might regret that promise. I've got some spectacularly nasty scars, and not only from my time in the Navy. I grew up on a ranch."

He was a cowboy? She could see that. He was being open and honest with her in a way no one had for a long time. It was intoxicating. He didn't know who she was, and he was treating her like a normal woman, like someone he wanted to seduce.

She was starting to think it might not be so bad to be seduced by Michael Malone.

His big palm flattened against her stomach, fingers teasing against the waistband of her undies.

"I'll look at you and then I'll touch you. I'll close my eyes and let my hands stroke against your skin," he whispered. "Like I'm about to do now."

His hand slipped under her cotton panties and toward her pussy. Warmth spread through her as he inched his way closer and closer.

The arm around her found a place right under her breasts, and she was aware of them, too.

"When I'm done touching you, what do you think I'll do?"

The question skimmed over her skin, a warm temptation. "Will you kiss me?"

"Oh, I'll likely kiss you everywhere. This is what I meant by indulging in sex," he replied. "You're thinking about sex, concentrating on how close my fingers are to your clitoris. You're not thinking about work or anything you're worried about. You're letting your body lead the way. And I'm not thinking about how lonely I am. I'm thinking about how good you smell. God, you smell like sex."

She laid her head against his and let him maneuver her into a position where her legs were spread, and she could feel the hard line of his erection against her backside. He was lonely? The words penetrated. His open vulnerability blasted through her walls in that moment, and she gave over. She let her legs fall fully open, her body relax as he found her core and stroked her.

"Yes, that's what I want. That's what I need from you." He nipped her ear again, sending a jagged sensation through her that did nothing to draw her out of the pleasurable fog he'd put her in.

So easily. He'd gotten her here faster than she'd ever gone before. He'd brought out some side of her that she'd thought had vanished forever.

She could feel how wet she was, how his finger slid over her sensitive flesh. Pleasure began to build inside her, and all she had to do was lie back and let him touch her. He was holding her up. She didn't even need to balance herself because Michael was taking care of her.

God, she was so lonely, too.

Her lungs worked overtime, breasts moving against his hand as he rubbed circles over her clitoris and whispered dirty, glorious promises in her ear.

She could have this from him whenever she needed it. He would be her Dom, and her safety and pleasure was his job, and he was so very happy to do his job.

She didn't want him to stop, wanted to stay in this moment for as long as possible, but the wave burst over her, and she couldn't hold it off. Couldn't stop the pleasure that warmed her bones or the cry that came from her mouth.

Her body felt languid as she relaxed against him.

"No worries there, love. You come quite nicely," he said with a chuckle. His hand slid out of her pants. "I barely managed not to come myself. I think we can safely say the chemistry between us is fine."

"Are you really lonely?" All of her walls were down. She would build them back up in a moment, knew better than to walk out of that door without her armor. But sitting here with him, she felt safe and wanted to know the truth.

"I am very lonely, Vanessa," he replied quietly. "I have started to think that I might not have the family I wanted. Want. But you should understand that I'm not using this position to try to build anything more than a friendship right now."

His words soothed her. "Me either, Sir. I'm not ready for any kind of a romantic relationship, but it would be nice to have a friend."

"And a couple of orgasms wouldn't hurt."

"No, they wouldn't, Sir." She started to move, but he held her.

"Sit with me for a while," he commanded, holding her close.

She lay back and let herself enjoy the moment for once.

This could work out.

Hope.

It was the most dangerous emotion of all.

* * * *

Half an hour later, Michael held the door open for Vanessa after hustling to move around the table before she could flee on her own.

Not flee, exactly. It wasn't like she'd run, but it was also clear to him that she wasn't used to the courtesies she would find at The Club.

She stopped, and her eyes came up, looking at him through thick lashes. "I'm sorry. I suppose you're going to be doing all kinds of gentlemanly things."

She was a gorgeous woman, and she'd been hot as hell in his arms. He had to give it to her. The "I've never had an orgasm" act worked well on him. For a hot minute, he'd even believed her.

Vanessa was a dangerous woman, and he had to remember that because she was also a siren. That fragility of hers called to his every protective instinct, and now she looked the part. There was nothing hard about her. She was soft on every level, and it would be easy to forget that the woman knew how to play a man. She'd certainly figured him out quickly.

The whole conversation had been one long circling of two fighters, poking and prodding and looking for weaknesses.

"There are protocols in The Club, and one of them is a Dominant partner shows every courtesy to his or her sub. How we choose to behave in the outside world is up to us, but I would be looked on poorly if I didn't open the door for you. One of my jobs is to make life comfortable for you," he replied. It was true at Sanctum as well, though Sanctum was less rigid about protocol. In some ways Sanctum was a rave and The Club a Victorian tea party with sex on the menu.

"I'll remember that." Her generous lips curled up slightly, and she held the sides of her cardigan together as though she felt vulnerable. "Thank you for an illuminating afternoon, Sir. I look forward to our next session."

"As do I." He watched her walk down the carpeted hallway, studying the sway of her hips. Her whole body seemed to have responded to the physical pleasure he'd brought her. Her shoulders had come down from around her ears, and there was a soft feminine energy about her that had replaced the anxiety he'd sensed before.

Had that anxiety vanished because she'd figured out how to play him? Because she felt comfortable she could control him now?

Or was she exactly what she presented herself to be?

The very fact that he was asking the question gave him pause.

She turned down the hallway that would take her back to the elevators and he could breathe again.

Fuck. He wanted her, and that was something he hadn't expected. He'd known she was attractive, but the actual woman was different than he'd imagined. His cock still ached from her squirming on his lap, from the breathy gasps he'd elicited from her. She could fake both of those things, but not the slick arousal that had coated his fingers as he'd stroked her pussy.

After they'd sat together for a moment, he'd excused himself to clean up while she got her questions together. He'd gone to the bathroom and had to masturbate in order to get his head on straight. He could practically hear Big Tag giving him a lecture for jerking off on the job. That's what he should have done. He should have pictured Big Tag offering him a condom. It was the single unsexiest thing in the world.

It was merely the fact that it had been a while for him. That was what he told himself. It wasn't the woman, merely that he'd reached a level of horniness he hadn't felt in a long time.

Michael moved back into the conference room and picked up the contract they'd both signed. He glanced down, and her signature was neat on the document, her name written in a precise script. That had been a surprise. He'd thought she would sign it like she would a head shot.

"That was unexpected," a deep voice said.

Well, he *had* expected this talk. It was why he hadn't walked her to the elevators himself. He'd known Julian would want a debrief. "I thought it went rather well."

Finn followed his husband in, a grim look on his face. "It depends on what you think *well* means in this situation. She certainly seemed to respond to you."

"Yes, that was what I hadn't expected." Julian unbuttoned his jacket and sank down onto the seat at the head of the table. "I expected her to hold you off, to tease you."

"I told you she's not what you think," Finn said under his breath. He didn't sit down. He paced. "And the way Michael handled her. This could end up hurting her quite badly, and you need to think about this."

"Your opinion is noted, love." Julian's eyes were steady on his partner. "I think it might be best if I left you out of the rest of this. I wouldn't want Danielle to think you had anything to do with it."

Finn sighed and rested his hands on the back of the chair opposite from Julian. "We could sit her down and ask her. Have you thought of that?"

"Why would she tell me the truth?" Julian looked tired as he sat back. "I've gone over this with you. There's money missing, and Chase has reported a couple of incidents of someone attempting to get through our firewalls to sensitive data. I would fire the woman, but the very thought of it upset Danielle. Given that Ms. Jones's sister was one of Danielle's closest friends, I have to prove to her that Vanessa is not Nicki."

"And if she's innocent?" Finn asked.

Julian's expression went blank. "What do you want from me, Finn? Do you want me to ignore all the advice of the people who I pay quite well to keep us and our businesses secure? Do you think our children will be less traumatized by someone plastering their family across magazine covers if it happens because I was trying to be nice? That's where I fear this is going."

Julian hadn't mentioned anything beyond the missing money before. If she was trying to get through Julian's firewalls, she might be doing something worse than stealing some cash. "You think she's looking for dirt?"

Julian frowned. "I'm sorry. Ian knows about someone attempting to get into the part of the system where I keep The Club's records. Obviously it's a sensitive subject, and I would prefer you keep that knowledge to yourself. I've asked Ian that only the tech people are informed."

Because those files contained information on Dallas's elite. On some of the world's elite. If anyone got those files… "You think she wants to blackmail your clients?"

"He thinks she wants to either blackmail us or go to the press,"

Finn said with a long sigh, and he moved toward Julian. "It's why he believes she's pushing to get access to The Club."

"But at least in this case, I have someone watching her, and the contract she signed means I can sue for everything she's worth if she breaks it," Julian replied in a hushed but savage tone. "You have to understand that if she attempts to blackmail me, I will have her quietly disposed of. I rather thought this was a better way to avoid getting blood on my hands, but don't think for a second I won't do it."

He made a mental note to not fuck with Julian Lodge. Of course he sort of worried Julian would shove at least the burial job on McKay-Taggart. "I can figure this out for you, Mr. Lodge."

Finn sank down to the seat beside his partner and covered Julian's hand with his. "I'm sorry, Master. I hadn't thought of it that way, and yes, we need to protect our wife and our kids. Michael's demeanor threw me off, and I have to admit I find this part of the business unsavory."

"Says my bloodsucking lawyer." Julian's palm turned up, and it was quite easy to see that physical contact with Finn had eased the beast within. "I promise you that I have looked at this situation from top to bottom, and this is how I have selected to move forward. If I am wrong, then I've done nothing but allow her access to The Club and given her a training Dom who can walk her through an experience she claims she wants. If she's done nothing wrong, then we can move forward with trust, and once I trust someone, you know I can move mountains for them."

"This is the best way to figure out if she's the one trying to get into the system and why she would want to access that information." He needed to bring Finn in because it was obvious Julian wasn't tough when it came to his guy and his girl. Julian was more of a softie than he'd envisioned, and part of this job was client management. He needed Finn on board for this to work. If Finn went to Danielle, then the whole op could explode, and Tag would be offering him more than his patented lecture on safe sex practices. "I'm going to ask you a question, and I want you to think about it. If this was happening at your law firm, what would you do?"

Finn sat back, his shoulders slumping. "Obviously we would investigate because we would need to see how far the problem went. What we wouldn't do is set the person up to get his or her heart broken. That's what is happening with Vanessa. What the hell was that, Mr. Malone?"

He was the problem? He'd actually changed up his initial plan, which had been to go in as a hard-core top. He'd been kind of nice. "I thought Ms. Jones and I got along well."

"I was talking about how well you played your role." Finn stared at him directly. "Hell, I was half in love with you by the end of it."

Julian's brows came up. "Really?"

"You know what I'm saying," Finn argued. "He could have easily gotten through the first few weeks without touching her sexually. He could have done this without a physical relationship."

"That was very unlikely, and nothing he did was done without her consent," Julian countered. "He was careful about it. I thought he did quite well. After that performance, I would hire him to take trainees through the initial sessions."

"Would she consent if she knew why he was here?" Finn asked.

"She won't ever have to know if she's done nothing wrong." Michael didn't honestly understand the problem. "If she's clean, then I will perform my duties as her training Dom and allow her to explore what she's plainly stated she wants to explore. She'll continue her employment here, and I suspect Julian will change his mind about her. She'll find a powerful ally in him, one she wouldn't have had before. The situation is complex, and my firm investigating her is the best way to handle it. This way Julian gets the information he needs and protects his family, business, and clients. He's protecting Vanessa as well since he doesn't have to dismiss her if she's innocent."

Finn stood, pushing his chair back. "All right. I have to get back to my office. I'll keep my mouth shut and trust in my husband. But Michael, you're playing a dangerous game with her. She's fragile. If you're here to investigate her, then do it, and not simply by reading the headlines. Get to know her for the woman she is, and then I think you'll understand why I'm worried."

Finn nodded and walked away.

"I did not mean to offend your husband." He wasn't sure what had gone wrong. He had Vanessa right where he wanted her. They were going to meet tomorrow for coffee to talk about what he expected from her when they went to play night later in the week.

"I'm afraid he's mostly worried that Danielle is going to get hurt." Julian stared at the doorway Finn had disappeared through. "He also feels for Ms. Ha…Jones. He knows what it's like to have people judge him. He grew up in a small town, and he didn't hide his sexuality as well as some. I think he feels some sympathy for her. I view her differently."

"She's everything we were taught to watch out for." He knew exactly what Julian was saying. They came from the same world, and in this case it wasn't something Finn could understand. "I was raised in a laid-back family for the kind of money we have. My dad preferred to relax by working around the ranch rather than going to hot spots and partying. But I still understood that there was a type of woman who would only be interested in me for my family money and name."

"Did you ever meet such a woman?" Julian asked.

"Oh, yes. Many times. I think the worst was one summer when I was home from college, and my brother and I started dating these two young women we met at a rodeo. JT especially loved to rodeo. I think it called to his cowboy nature. Also, when we were with that crowd almost no one knew who we were. They didn't care. They gave a shit about a man for how hard he could work and how fun he was to have a beer with. So when we met a couple of beautiful sisters, we thought it would be the perfect way to spend a summer."

"And they turned out to be something more, I take it."

He didn't like to think about that summer or how idiotic he'd been. He hadn't even told JT this story, but it was necessary to acknowledge the incident. "I fell for mine. Hard. It was the first time I fell in love, and I was honestly ready to change schools to be close to her. I was going to take a year off and spend time with her and then transfer if we decided to make a go of it. JT wasn't invested, but I was ready to change my whole life for this woman. And then one day I overheard her talking to her sister and complaining about the fact that she should have picked JT instead of me. According to her, I was too intense. Her sister told her it didn't matter because I had just as much money and they couldn't change now. She had to suck it up because money like Malone money would set them up for the rest of their lives."

He'd broken it off with her and told JT he'd simply gotten bored and wanted to go back home to get ready for their senior year. He'd joined the military after he'd graduated and tried to cut himself off from that world. He couldn't entirely, of course, but he'd made a place for himself.

Not that he'd refused the millions his grandparents had left him or the trust his parents had set up for him.

"Yes, I've heard the horror stories." Julian sent him a sympathetic look. "I had an uncle growing up. I rarely saw him. He was a loathsome man. Some of the only advice he ever gave me was that I wasn't a human being. I was a large paycheck, and I should understand that going into any relationship I might have. I should know no woman would truly love me because no woman would be able to see past my money."

"My parents were better than that, but I've certainly experienced people who believed the same as your uncle. I've also seen people of my class think no one without seven figures behind their name is worth speaking to." He wasn't going to fall into the poor rich-boy stereotype. Money had opened many doors for him, but there were drawbacks, too.

Of course, JT had managed to find a woman who adored him and would have been by his side whether or not he was the CEO of a billion-dollar energy company.

Julian sighed, a thoughtful sound. "When I met my Danielle, she told me she would never be special to me. She was ready to walk away because she didn't think she could ever be more than a convenience to a man like me. She was so very wrong. She and Finn…they are the center of my world. I love our children, but I never would have had children if Finn and Danielle hadn't come into my life. I would like to think that I'm a better man than I was back then, that I don't judge people until I know them."

Michael got what Julian was saying, but there were other issues to think about. "And that is all good and well, but you're also the head of your family. Vanessa could be utterly misunderstood. She could be innocent. Or she could be a wolf who figured out how to put on the perfect wool to pass as a lamb. The wolf who studied her prey and knows how to make her way into the house."

"A wolf who could bring my whole house down." Julian turned his way, a grim look in his eyes. "It's funny how children change things. Before we had children, I likely would have viewed all of this as an amusing game. I'm a man who's enjoyed subterfuge from time to time. I would have pitted myself against her with no qualms. But now the consequences of anything going wrong could affect Chloe and Gabriel and John. Life has become complex."

"Then let me make it simpler for you." It was good to remember what was at stake—a whole family. "My firm can watch her outside the office, and our techs can make sure she doesn't do anything she shouldn't inside the office."

"What was your impression?" Julian asked.

"She's lying about something." No matter how much he physically wanted her, he wasn't about to hold back with his client. "I don't think when she sat down that she was truly interested in D/s. Some of what I said made her nervous. I gave her several outs, but she took none of them."

"She sat on your lap pretty quickly," Julian pointed out. "That surprised me. She's not a particularly physically affectionate person, from what I can tell."

Oh, but she'd felt like she needed affection, like she was a sponge and needed to soak it all in. For a moment it had felt like she needed him.

But he knew something was off about her. She was hiding something from him. He'd investigated hundreds of people over his fairly long career, and he knew when someone was holding back.

"I put her in a corner," he admitted. "She was obviously uncomfortable talking about sex."

"An odd thing for a woman who wants to go to a sex club," Julian mused.

"Also an odd thing for a woman who's known for using sex as a weapon," he agreed. "So I put her in a place where she could take what I offered or walk away. I wouldn't have canceled our contract had she walked, but either way I got information."

"What did the encounter tell you?" Julian asked.

"That she's willing to do something she found distasteful in order to keep me happy. Or the distaste I felt from her was acting." He needed to think about it. Coffee with her tomorrow would give him more information. "And she wants me to believe that I'm special, that she doesn't respond to other men the way she does to me. It's a good play. It would work if I believed it."

"Which you don't."

Michael shook his head. "No. I don't believe the ex-Hollywood bombshell only responds to my touch. She also pretended she didn't know who I am. She didn't bring up my last name or ask any questions about my family. I didn't believe that either. I'm meeting with her again tomorrow, and I'll escort her here on Friday night. I'm also going to be putting eyes on her when she's not here at the office. I'd like to know what she does when she's not working. I'll give you a full report on who she sees and where she goes."

"All right." Julian stood and held out a hand. "I'll leave this all to you, Mr. Malone. Find the truth for me. And quickly, if you can. I would like this worry to be put to rest. If Ms. Jones isn't what I think she is, I would like to know."

"I'll take care of it," Michael promised.

And he would take care of her. One way or another.

Chapter Four

Vanessa was still thinking about Michael Malone hours later after she'd managed to make her way back to the house she'd bought for her sister ten years before. It was in a gated neighborhood in North Dallas, and she had to admit that every time she clicked the button for the gate, she breathed a sigh of relief when it opened.

At some point they might decide the best way to keep her out was to simply not let her in at all.

But for tonight, she was inside the house.

Now she would have to find a way to make the hours go by until she could go to work again tomorrow. It was only in her office that she felt somewhat safe.

At least until Julian Lodge figured out what she was doing and had her arrested.

Her cell phone trilled, and Vanessa glanced down at the number before picking it up. "Hey, Dani."

"Hey, I wanted to tell you that Chloe got an A on her creative writing assignment. She told me you helped her work out the plot." Dani's voice was warm and gracious.

Maybe she should change her name and become a tutor. She was an excellent writer for the most part, and she was good at English and history. Though not spectacular, like Chloe's regular tutor. "It was fun. She's got a great imagination and a knack for dialogue. And she used the whole thing as her translation homework for Spanish, so she got double use out of it."

"Yes, David told me he found the story very amusing," Dani replied.

David Hawthorne was a professor at a local university and helped tutor some of the kids in his "family." She used quotes around the word because for the most part David's family didn't share blood. From what she could tell, the super-nice professor was the son of a world-renowned chef who was connected to Julian in some way. Maybe his security firm.

The same one Michael worked at.

She could not get that man out of her head. Though in some ways it was nice to have him rattling around in there. It let her forget her troubles for a few moments at a time. It was way nicer to think about the fact that she would get to see him in leathers on Friday. At least that's what she'd been told the tops at The Club wore.

Shit. What was she going to wear?

"I'm glad I could help," she replied as she walked into the kitchen. She would come up with something for Friday night. She leaned against the bar and glanced around the small room and wondered what she should eat for dinner. It didn't hold much beyond coffee, protein bars she ate for breakfast, and a bunch of frozen meals for one. The cheapest she could find.

Her former personal trainer and nutritionist would die if either saw how she lived now. Of course, they'd dropped her the minute they'd realized she might prove toxic for their careers.

She preferred lunch because she usually ate it with Dani while they worked.

"You ran out of here before I could ask you how the meeting went," Dani prompted.

Vanessa felt herself flush. She'd run because she'd known damn well that Dani would want to talk about what had happened between her and the new Dom. So she went with the least embarrassing part of the meeting with Michael Malone. "He told me I have to see a therapist."

Dani chuckled. "Well, I kind of told you that would be good for you. Though you should know Leo passed you with flying colors. That surprised me a little."

"Gee, thanks."

A huff came over the line. "Let's see. If I told you I had a friend who recently lost her husband, got involved in an inheritance dispute that caused her to get kicked out of her home, lost her sister, and also had her former best friend give a nationwide interview that painted her as a less than honest person…"

"I believe the term you're looking for is money-grubbing whore." She was honest with herself, so why not others?

Dani did not take the bait. "If I asked you if that friend might benefit from talking to someone, what would you say?"

Well, there wasn't any way around it. "Yes, of course. You know why I haven't."

"Yes, money and paranoia," Dani shot back. "But given that your former assistant is the one on all the national talk shows, I can understand it."

"I don't watch TV, so I've only heard about it. How bad has it gotten?" Vanessa couldn't watch live TV. She could watch streaming services when she could afford them. But live TV was a different story. Any break could bring a picture of her face with a nasty headline or some comedian taking potshots at her. She'd been watching a game show she enjoyed once where the host said the contestant had answered as many questions as Vanessa Hale had gone through men.

She couldn't watch that show anymore.

"Honestly, it makes her look petty." Dani's voice had gone sympathetic. "Everyone knows she's doing it for the money. But the point is, you could use someone to talk to."

"I talk to you." It was perverse, but she couldn't admit it was a good idea.

"And I know what that means. Your trust is everything to me," Dani replied. "But you can't talk to me the way you can a therapist. I know you're worried about another leak of your private information, but I assure you we can find a therapist you can trust."

"I already have one. I've got an appointment with her Friday before I go to The Club." Michael had sent her the text confirming the appointment and sending her the address she was supposed to go to.

"She works at someplace called The Ferguson Clinic."

"Oh. I'm surprised he didn't send you to Janine. She usually works with us," Dani explained. "The Ferguson Clinic is good, though. It has an excellent reputation. I guess it makes sense. Michael would have more connections there. His boss helped the clinic in its first days, and it's still located close to Sanctum."

She'd thought a little about this. She knew Michael worked for the security company Julian used, and they had their own club. The Club and Sanctum were rivals. She'd heard some of the other workers talking about how much they looked forward to the annual picnic and the shenanigans Big Tag and Julian got up to. "Why does he need a membership to The Club? I would think he would go to the club his friends probably play at."

"It can be fun to move between clubs." Dani's voice took on the light tone she always got when talking about her club life. "They're different experiences. Julian, Finn, and I have been to Sanctum many times. Also, Michael is doing a favor for us. We don't have the same kind of training program Sanctum does. We usually send new members over there for classes. I didn't think that would be a good idea for you."

She wouldn't have gone to a class. She would have had to find another way. "No, I think it's best I have more private training."

She couldn't handle the gossip, the looks, the way a room would go quiet when she walked in. It would be different in a formal club setting. At least she hoped it would.

"We don't have any Doms who can take on personal training right now," Dani continued. "So he asked Ian Taggart if he had anyone who could take on a new sub for a couple of weeks, and he offered Michael. Was he good with you? He's always seemed like a pleasant man. I know his sister-in-law better than him, and she's lovely."

Michael had been lovely. He'd been generous. "He didn't seem to know who I am. Is that going to be a problem?"

Would he find out who she really was and turn on her? It wouldn't be the first time. After George died, a lot of people had turned on her. The minute they'd realized they had to choose between her and George Jr., they'd left her quickly. She'd found herself in a house that had once been staffed by seven all alone.

Then she'd had no home at all and no money.

"He knows you work for me. I'm not sure what else Julian would have told him. Sometimes it's best for the relationship to develop organically," Dani said.

That was what she'd been afraid of. "He should have been told."

"I don't think he's going to care. If you want to tell him about your past, I think you should, but it doesn't mean anything for the training relationship." Dani went quiet for a moment. "Unless you like him."

Oh, she wasn't going there. "I'm spending at least six weeks with this man."

There was another moment of quiet. "You do like him. You're attracted to him. Oh, honey, I don't know how smart that is. His family situation…it's complex. Maybe I can find another training partner."

She couldn't have that happen. Even if Dani was right. It could take weeks to find another partner, and she'd already wasted a couple of months. The trail was cooling every minute she wasn't in that club. "I don't want another top. I do find him attractive. I'm not looking at this the right way. All the crap with Ashton is affecting me. Rejection hurts, and I worry about it a lot. I know this is a relationship with an end date. I don't need or want anything serious right now."

"He won't reject you," Dani assured her. "And if you're attracted to him and he's attracted to you, there's nothing wrong with exploring. I just don't want you to get hurt."

She wasn't sure she could be hurt anymore. So much of the time she felt numb.

Except for today. Today when she'd sat on his lap and his hands had been on her, she'd felt. When she'd lain back against him, she'd felt a peace flow through her she hadn't had in…maybe never. In that moment she hadn't had to think at all. Her mind was always full of worry, always churning with the worst-case scenario. But in that moment all she'd thought about was how nice it had been to lean on him as her blood thrummed through her system.

She might be able to have more of that if Dani was right and all he wanted was to get access to The Club and have a nice training relationship. Six weeks. She could handle the situation in six weeks.

Maybe Julian would be happy she'd found the dangerous person at his club. Maybe she would be able to stay. Maybe she could find a place for herself in this nice world she'd grown to like.

A shadow moving out of the corner of her eye brought her straight back to reality.

There was a reason she hadn't gone to Julian.

"I know the score," Vanessa promised. "He's a lovely man, and he seems very nice. I think he'll make this training period very comfortable for me."

"And when you're done, I can introduce you to some tops I think might work well for you," Dani began.

She likely wouldn't actually finish the training. She wasn't sure why she'd had that brief moment of positivity, but it was over now because she could hear a quiet knock.

"Dani, I have another call coming through," she said.

"Of course. I'll see you in the morning. We can talk some more then. Good night." Dani hung up.

Vanessa set her phone down and moved back into the living room.

She had most of the lights off for the same reason she always made sure the car was in the garage. She didn't want anyone to know she was home, but this was one visitor she wouldn't keep out. Couldn't really since she still had a key.

She glanced out the curtain covering the window in the door that led to the backyard, and sure enough, there was a slender figure standing there, body covered in leggings and a hoodie, the hint of dark hair coming from under the hood.

She opened the door. "Hey, Ruby. How was your day?"

Ruby Lockwood lived three doors down, and the young woman had formed a friendship with Nicki over the years they'd been neighbors.

Ruby sighed and moved through the open door, her ever-present laptop in her hands. "Same old, same old. Went to class. Came home. Didn't conform to the norms so Mom is silently seething. Fun times, man."

Ruby's homelife wasn't the greatest. "Did you eat dinner?"

She shrugged. "Not all that hungry. Mom's on a no-carbs kick. She told me there was a salad in the fridge if I wanted something, but no actual dressing, so there's that. She's using some kind of oil on it.

Ick."

"I have frozen pizzas." It was terrible health wise, but sometimes calories were calories.

Ruby's eyes lit up. "Pepperoni?"

"Yep." She'd gotten them on sale. "I'll heat it up, and you can tell me all about your day."

"I have some news," Ruby said, hopping on the bar seat.

"Nope. Day first, business later." Ruby didn't seem to have a lot of friends, and her parents were a mess. She needed someone to talk to about the little things. Even when times were the worst, Vanessa had been able to talk to Nicki. Even when they had been fighting, her sister would always answer the phone. "How was your history test?"

Ruby groaned and drew the hood back, and with a sigh started talking.

Twenty minutes and one hot, somewhat plastic-tasting pizza later, she sat at the small bistro table as Ruby got down to business.

"I can't get through that firewall," the teen admitted, her eyes on the screen.

Vanessa felt her stomach threaten to flip. "What firewall are you talking about?"

Ruby's mouth firmed to a mulish frown.

Vanessa was on her feet, pacing back and forth. "I told you to stay away from Lodge Corp. I'll get you the names, and you can investigate from there, but you can't try to get into Lodge's system. It's a crime."

Ruby's chin came up. "And I'm not eighteen. I'm telling you I can do a couple of years in juvie, easy-peasy. My parents wouldn't even notice I was gone."

"When I agreed to let you help me, I had some ground rules."

Ruby's eyes rolled. "You don't know anything about hacking a system, Ness. And if you get caught, you lose everything."

"I already lost everything. I will not have it happen to you." She'd met Ruby when she'd caught her crying in the backyard shortly after Nicki's funeral. She'd been sitting on the porch swing, her long legs curled up to her chest, sobbing so hard she hadn't heard Vanessa come outside.

She hadn't known why this teen was sitting in her backyard, and it hadn't mattered. She'd simply sat down beside her and for the first time since she'd gotten the news her sister was gone, she'd been able to cry. Ruby had looked up, startled, but she seemed to have understood Vanessa meant no harm. So they'd sat there, rocking and crying. Eventually Ruby had gotten up, put a hand on her shoulder, and nodded before jumping the fence and walking away.

It had taken two more crying jags to get the young woman to talk. In the months she'd been here, she'd probably talked more to a sixteen-year-old girl than even Dani.

Was she fucking up Ruby's life, too?

Wasn't that why her mother hadn't allowed her back in the home she'd grown up in? Because she was a poison that infected every person she came into contact with?

"Hey, I'm not losing anything here, Ness." Ruby's expression had lost that eternal rage-against-the-machine look she so often saw there, and concern bled through. "I'm sorry. I wanted to give it a try. I know you said not to. I won't do it again."

"It's dangerous. He's dangerous." How would she feel if Ruby got dragged fully into this? If there was one thing she'd learned, it was getting other people hurt was far worse than taking the pain herself.

"Okay." Ruby nodded, her voice softening as though she knew something would change if she didn't lower the temp in the room. "Like I said, I made a play, and no one even noticed. But I don't have the skills to get in and get a list of names of club members. I did get you some information on the names you gave me last week."

Even having Ruby check out social media profiles and readily available information on the men who went to The Club was risky. "I think you should go."

Ruby stood in front of her. She was a good three inches taller than Vanessa, though she likely weighed twenty pounds less. She had a gawkiness that would fall off her someday and turn her into a gorgeous swan. Or maybe she would keep that adorable weirdness and be okay with it. "If I go, I'll still look for the asshole who killed my friend, and I'll probably do it in new and terrifying ways. I'll end up on *Dateline*. Or they'll do a whole podcast about how they found my body stuffed in a drain somewhere."

That was why she'd given Ruby something to do. Yep. There it was. "Julian would never stuff you in a drainpipe. He would make sure your body was never found." Vanessa sighed. "You have to be careful. I don't think you should be hacking at all."

Ruby's lips curled up. "But I'm so good at it. And usually these kinds of businesses have old dudes watching over the gates. They always think they know how to catch people. I will admit that this security is pretty good. I didn't get far. I got a tiny peek and then I realized someone was coming."

"I thought you said no one knew you were there."

"They knew someone was there, but they couldn't have traced it back to me." Ruby shrugged the concern off with the arrogance of youth. "But I didn't get far enough to get names beyond an employee schedule. Do you know a dude named Kyle Hawthorne?"

Vanessa had to catch her breath and focus. If there was damage, it had already been done. "I know a David Hawthorne. He's Chloe Lodge-Taylor's tutor."

"He and someone named Kyle are on the schedule for what I figured out was the dungeon work list. And chill, because I didn't have to get deep to get it. It was on a low-level employee's calendar that's shared through the system." Ruby sat back down. "From what I can tell, he's only been around for six months, so he should go on our list. They probably both should."

Their list. There weren't many names on the list right now. That was precisely why she was going to The Club. "All right. You can look into him. But only on the surface. You can check his social media."

"Will do," Ruby replied. "And I'll do the same for anyone you want me to. I can find out if any of the new guys had connections to Nicki. I wish she'd put a damn name in her diary."

Vanessa slumped back down to her seat. Nicki hadn't left much to work with. Just initials, and she wasn't sure they corresponded to actual names. "Me, too. I hate to think about how scared she was those last few days."

"She was off the last six months." Ruby shut the laptop screen. "I thought maybe she was doing drugs or something, but it was fear."

"Off, how?" They hadn't talked a lot about Nicki's last months.

Ruby shrugged. "She was paranoid and worried all the time. She thought someone was following her. I knew there was a club involved, but I didn't know what kind. I thought it had to do with her job until I found her diary."

Ruby had been the one to pull the turquoise notebook out of its hiding place. Nicki had given Ruby a key to the house for when she needed to decompress. Her sister had learned that Ruby regularly got kicked out of her house when her mother was drunk and angry, and she'd taken to spending time in the park across the street. At night. Alone.

So Nicki had offered her a place to stay even when she wasn't there. Ruby had been thirteen at the time, and they'd formed a close friendship. Likely because Nicki knew what it was like to be at odds with her mother. Ruby's situation was different, but the result was the same. The teen needed a friend. She also would one day probably need a lawyer because she was good at finding things she shouldn't. Things behind locked doors and secure information.

But she wasn't doing drugs, and she wasn't out in the city vulnerable and alone. She was smart, and she had plans for college, plans Vanessa would make sure happened one way or another.

"I bet that shocked you." Vanessa wasn't sure Nicki had meant for anyone to ever read that diary, but the truth had been spelled out. Someone had stalked her sister.

Someone from The Club had killed her.

"Not really. I mean everyone's got something they're into, right?" Ruby shrugged it off. "The important thing is she knew someone was watching her. I wish she'd left us some names to work with. She did mention an MK, though."

"Yeah. I remember." Her sister's diary had been filled with shorthand. Sometimes she would write out whole names, but mostly it was single letters like D for Dani or MJ for Master Julian, as she consistently called Julian. "We need to figure out if this Kyle person is a top. Is he working on Friday?"

Ruby reached into her jacket pocket. "I printed it off for you. He's working Friday for the whole night. I can't tell who does what, though. He could be bartending, for all I know. The other Hawthorne guy is working Saturday. Do you think they're related?"

"I think we should find out." She certainly hadn't considered the mild-mannered tutor would be a member of The Club. There was nothing about the history professor that told her he was some kind of kinky guy. Then again, she hadn't known about her sister, either.

"I can do that. Once you have any kind of a name to go with MM and E, I'll be all over them. She was having trouble with E, and she turned down someone she referred to as MM," Ruby said. "We all know that guys you turn down can get nasty."

"Yes." She knew that better than almost anyone.

I want a taste of what my father had. Give it to me and maybe I'll let you have a couple million.

She shook off that terrible memory. It had happened after she'd been left alone in that big mansion. When Junior had come to let her know he was going to make her life a living hell.

"Isn't the guy you're supposed to meet with named Michael? He's an M and he's a top, so that's another M."

"But he's new. From what I know, he's never been a member of The Club," Vanessa corrected. Michael was above suspicion in this case, and she was so relieved. She could trust him. Well, as much as she trusted anyone.

"Was it okay meeting him today? Like was he nice and stuff?" Ruby asked.

Nice didn't cover it. He'd been charming, and then he'd been commanding, and both had done something for her. It had been a heady combination.

It might have been the combination she'd needed all of her life.

"He seems like a nice guy. This isn't some love match." She needed to say the words so she didn't forget them. If she was lucky, she wouldn't even make it through the training period. She would find the killer and get back to her…shitty life.

"I think you have to be scared," Ruby said softly.

She was, but not in the way Ruby meant. She was scared she could get in too deep with this man.

There was the sound of glass shattering, and Vanessa stepped in front of Ruby, her arms coming out on pure instinct.

"Assholes." Ruby moved from behind her, her hands in fists at her sides. "How many times have they done this?"

Vanessa let out a breath. It was the same assholes, as usual. "I hoped they would stop when the HOA informed me I had a month to move out. I guess someone wants me gone faster than that. You should go home. I don't want anyone to see you here."

"Let me help you clean up. I'll stay out of the line of sight." Ruby moved to grab the broom and dustpan. "I helped you last time, and it's way faster."

She wanted to say she didn't need the help, but the truth was she did.

A line in her contract came back to her. She was supposed to call Michael if she found herself in need of aid. He was supposed to be there for her while they were training, but surely that didn't mean he showed up every time some asshole threw a brick with the word *whore* written on it through her window.

That would get old fast.

She went into the living room to make sure it was merely the same crime. Sure enough, there was a hole in the window and a rock on the floor. It was one of the smooth rocks lots of people used in their landscaping around here. Anyone could have picked it up and used a Sharpie to write their message on it.

Exhaustion swamped her. She was so tired. Tired of everything.

Tired of life. She was thirty-two, and she felt old.

She stepped outside, looking up and down the block, but there was nothing. A truck she didn't recognize was parked down the street, but the person who'd thrown the rock was long gone.

She walked back in and got to work.

* * * *

The next morning Michael glanced at the clock and realized he still had an hour to kill.

That was a weird way to think of it. He was sitting in his office and had a ton of paperwork to do. He wasn't killing time. He was working, and the event he was waiting on was work, too. It wasn't some date that should make him wish time would speed up so he could get to it.

Coffee with Vanessa. He hadn't chosen lunch or dinner because he needed to play this fairly slowly, let her set the pace in some ways. He'd wanted to see if she was disappointed he hadn't set a more recognizable date with her.

She'd simply smiled and told him she looked forward to it.

There was a knock on his door, and he looked up to see MaeBe standing in his doorway. He gestured her in.

"Hey, I thought you might want to know that someone attempted to get into the Lodge Corp systems yesterday." She strode across the office and sat down in the chair across from his desk. "I got a call from Chase Dawson, who was super annoyed. He's out of town on vacation with his family, and he got the news from the guy who's filling in for him."

He'd met the Dawson brothers many times. They were in charge of security for both Dani and Julian's companies, and the Masters Fund. Both Chase and his twin brother Ben had been trained by Big Tag before taking their positions. "Fill me in. Did they get any information?"

"From what I can tell, whoever it was accessed some emails," MaeBe replied. "And they seemed particularly interested in The Club's work schedule."

Why would Vanessa want a work schedule? He could see her wanting financial records or perhaps even more sensitive data, but a work schedule wasn't something that could help her. Of course he hadn't figured out exactly what scam she was running, so he should keep an open mind. "Can you see everything she accessed?"

A brow rose above MaeBe's eyes. "She? You know for sure it's Vanessa Hale? The time stamp I found was for three thirty. Weren't you with her then?"

"Yes. I can account for her whereabouts from three to around four thirty. And I would be surprised if she had computer skills that run beyond her work duties." Michael sat back, thinking about the situation. "She could have hired a hacker."

"Hackers cost money, and she doesn't have much in her accounts." MaeBe had put together a full view of Vanessa's life as it stood, but she was forgetting a few things.

"We can't be sure she doesn't have accounts we don't know about," Michael mused.

"I was thorough, but yes, there is always the possibility she has offshore accounts. She doesn't have anything on her systems that lead me to believe she's got one, but if she's smart, she would hide it. Of course, she's also involved in a lawsuit that is specifically about money. The lawyer she's up against is smart, and he hires the best. I think he would have found the accounts," MaeBe argued. "So I'm looking for a hacker she hired. I'll talk to some of my connections and see what shakes out, but I thought you would want to know that we have someone creeping on the system. I'll go over there and talk to the techs and see if they picked up anything. If the hacker is halfway decent, we won't get much."

"I'd like to dupe her phone." He hadn't had a chance to do that yesterday. She hadn't brought it with her. She should have it today at the coffee shop. "I'll try to do it today, but if I can't, someone will need to get into her locker on Friday night."

"I believe Tessa knows how to do it. She'll be there at The Club, and she'll have access to the locker room. I'll go down to her office and make sure she's good to go." MaeBe stood up.

"Is there a reason you're not on this op in more than a technical way?" He was curious. He knew it made sense to have Tessa as his physical backup, but she wasn't the only one who could do the job. When he thought about it, MaeBe was the more logical choice since he would need someone who knew all the technical aspects of the job. "I could use a tech in the field. Tessa is an excellent bodyguard, and I would trust her to watch my back anytime, but she doesn't have your skills."

"I can help her, and I'll make sure to be on call whenever she needs me," MaeBe replied.

"But it would be easier to do it yourself."

Her lips pursed before she replied. "I'm not allowed out in the field yet."

He thought she was hedging. Was she worried about going into the field? This wasn't a horribly dangerous op. "I'll talk to Tag. I think this would be an excellent assignment to get you used to fieldwork. I know you've been behind a desk for the last year, but eventually you'll have to go."

Her eyes widened. "Please don't talk to Tag. I already did, and I don't want to push it."

Michael was definitely certain he was missing something. "Tag decided not to send you into the field?"

"Kyle would be the obvious partner for me on this job, and he refused," MaeBe admitted.

"He refused?" He'd thought Kyle liked MaeBe. There were

whole betting pools around the office on when those two finally stopped the pretending and threw down on one of the conference room tables.

"He doesn't think I'm ready, and he doesn't want to go on assignment with someone who could get him in trouble," she answered quietly.

Whoa. "He said that to Tag?"

She shrugged. "I overheard them talking. When Ian brought me in, he said it was because I need more time. He said he wants me to have some more training, but I heard what Kyle said. I can't blame him. I'm not like the rest of you. I didn't go into the military. I don't come from a law enforcement background."

"Yes, but you had to pass the classes Big Tag and Alex require for employees." It included several firearms courses and self-defense certifications. Even the receptionist had to have one of the senior members sign off on her training.

"Yeah, well, I haven't been tested, and that's a big thing for Kyle. So maybe later I can find someone willing to take a chance on me." MaeBe tucked a stray lock of hair behind her right ear. "Let me know if I can help out in some other way."

He had a thought on that. It would be far easier to dupe Vanessa's phone if he had a partner. He could distract the target while MaeBe worked her mojo. "Why don't you shadow my meeting with her today? If you get a chance to dupe her phone, take it. If you get caught, we'll make something up in the field. I'll make sure you get away."

Her eyes lit up. "Are you serious? I would love to do that for you."

He wasn't sure why Kyle was acting like an asshole, but this was his op, and he got to pick his team. MaeBe was smart, and he thought they were underusing her. They didn't have enough female operatives as it was. A young, smart woman should be trained, not forced to sit behind a computer. "Excellent. I need you to dress down, though. You want to be fairly inconspicuous."

A huge smile lit up her face. "I've got workout clothes here. I know the coffee shop you're going to, and it's right beside a yoga studio. No one will even give me a second glance. I'm so excited."

"Hey, don't push it," he advised, happy to give her a shot. "Wait for the right chance. If it doesn't happen, don't move in. Okay? Patience is the name of this game."

It was a good reminder for him, too.

"I totally understand. I won't let you down." She turned toward the door, and her hand lifted in greeting. "Hey, Deke."

Deke Murphy moved to let MaeBe out. "Good morning, MaeBe." He stepped inside Michael's office, watching her go. "She's in a good mood. What's got her so peppy? Not that she's not usually happy."

"She's excited about backing me up this morning. I asked her to help me dupe the target's phone. She wants to go into the field, but Hawthorne's blocking her for some reason." Michael was still thinking about that one.

Deke was a handsome man in his mid-thirties, but Michael had known him when he'd been a kid straight out of the military, working on the same CIA team Michael had. Deke had been a friend for years, and he was the man Michael had called when he needed someone watching Vanessa the night before. "I suspect he's blocking her because he thinks he's protecting her. He doesn't want her out in the field because he's careful when it comes to her. Expect some pushback from him. He gets touchy when it comes to MaeBe."

"But they aren't dating?"

Deke shrugged. "Not in any sense that we would understand, but the ways of the younger generation are strange. I know he's started going to her game nights. MaeBe throws them every Thursday."

He'd heard a bunch of the younger employees gathered at MaeBe's every Thursday for board games. "I don't think he's going to win her over by blocking her from the field."

Deke walked over to the chair MaeBe had recently vacated. "Just know you'll probably hear from him if he finds out you put her in the field. But we have bigger problems. Or rather your target does."

That got him sitting up a bit straighter. "What happened?"

Deke folded his six-foot-three-inch body onto the chair and ran a hand through the dark scruff of his beard. "First off, she's in a gated community. There's no way for me to stay on her block for more than a few hours. The neighbors are nosy, and apparently there's a rule about leaving your car on the street overnight. That was a fun conversation."

"I didn't think about that. How long were you able to keep eyes on her?" He should have thought about the gated aspect of the community.

"Long enough to know that she met with someone, and she doesn't want anyone to know he's there. And I'm not entirely sure it was a *he*, but it's a good bet. He knows how to move. He's tall and slender and likes to jump fences."

"Why would he jump the fence?" Vanessa hadn't mentioned any close friends. She'd stated plainly she didn't have a lover and hadn't for a while. She'd seemed very alone in the world. Of course, she was known to lie.

"I wasn't the only set of eyes on her," Deke admitted. "I managed to get in the gate by slipping in behind a resident, but I watched them turn away two members of the press who tried to get in."

"They know where she is." They hadn't gone into her press situation the day before. She hadn't brought it up, or really anything about her past, so he'd stayed away from it. She knew he worked for a security firm, but she hadn't mentioned she had actual security problems.

Deke nodded. "Yes, and her neighbors aren't happy about it. I think her visitor last night was from the community and didn't want anyone to know he was seeing her."

Anger thrummed through him, a deeply unwanted and unexpected emotion. He shouldn't be emotional at all. He shoved it all down, promising himself he'd examine it later. "How long did he stay?"

"Roughly two hours. He left the way he came, but I couldn't track him back to the house he came from," Deke admitted. "Honestly, it was luck I managed to see him the first time. The light hit, and I happened to be looking in exactly the right spot to see him move over the fence. I wasn't absolutely sure her place was his destination until I saw him in her garage when she had to board up her front window."

Michael frowned. "Why?"

"Because someone threw a rock into it." Deke said the words like it was a perfectly normal thing to have happen.

"What the hell? Someone broke her window on purpose?"

"Yes," Deke replied. "I got the plate number of the car, but I would bet it was someone in that neighborhood. I didn't follow. They stopped in front of her house, threw the rock, and then took off. They knew what they were doing."

"Why would someone break her window?" Michael asked.

"They were sending her a message." Deke pulled out his phone. "I'm forwarding you a link to her homeowner's association message board. It's full of hate for her. It's why they assumed I was a photographer and kicked me out. I thought I probably shouldn't out myself in case someone talked to her and she managed to connect me back to you. I ended up spending the rest of the night watching who came in and out of the community."

He would look through the message board later, but he was still intrigued with the possibility of her having a lover she hadn't mentioned. "Did you get any pictures of the visitor?"

"He stayed back when she opened the garage door," Deke replied. "I couldn't get a good look at him. And again, I can't be sure I'm talking about a male. I'm going off of height and how the target moved. He could be a taller than average she."

He doubted that. If Vanessa was involved in a relationship, it would likely be with a male. "I don't like the thought of her meeting with someone. MaeBe thinks she hired a hacker."

"Whoever jumped her fence last night did have a backpack on," Deke pointed out. "If they wanted to meet in person but keep it as private as possible, it might be a good way to go. There are cameras at the gate, and almost every home has a security system with cameras of some kind."

So this person might not be a lover. He might be working for her. Michael didn't like the fact that he preferred one explanation to another. "I'll get a list of everyone who lives in the neighborhood. I don't like the idea that we can't keep eyes on her. That gate is a problem. I don't suppose there are any homes for rent close to hers."

"Not that I saw," Deke replied. "Unless it was right across the street it wouldn't do much good. It's a small neighborhood. Anyone sitting outside would be noted. And sitting in the park across from the community isn't a good substitute. Too many trees. I can't see the backyard."

His mind started working because he needed to be able to keep eyes on her. "Did she call the police?"

Deke shook his head. "Not that I could tell. At the very least if she called, they didn't come out. I doubt she called it in. I watched her while she was trying to deal with the window, and I would bet this wasn't the first time someone's done it."

"Why would you say that?"

"She had all the materials she needed to board up the window," Deke pointed out. "And she got it done quickly. I wouldn't have said a Hollywood star would know how to do that unless she came from a construction background, which we both know she didn't. She wouldn't have learned it from her mother either, and Dad wasn't in the picture."

What had Vanessa been dealing with? And why the hell would anyone throw a rock through her window? He knew the answer, of course. They wanted her gone, and they were willing to get nasty with her.

He couldn't put a proper tail on her because she was inside a gated space.

"We need to get her out of there. We need her someplace where we can watch her twenty-four seven." A plan was starting to rattle around in his head. There was a clause in their contract about protection. He simply needed to get her to admit there was a problem.

Or maybe give her a bigger problem.

"You have your thinking face on," Deke pointed out.

"I think maybe we can solve a whole bunch of problems." Michael sat back. "I might need you to be a little underhanded, though. She's been good at keeping the wolves out, but I need them in, brother."

"I think I can help with that," Deke promised.

Deke started to talk about their choices when it came to forcing the gorgeous actress into a corner.

A corner only Michael would be able to help her out of.

Chapter Five

Michael felt a thrum of anticipation run through his veins and realized he might be in trouble.

He was going to be honest with himself. He wasn't sitting here in the coffee shop excited about the op starting up. This wasn't the same adrenaline that came from a dangerous situation.

He was excited about seeing her again, and that was a problem.

It was sex. That was all it was. She was gorgeous, and they had serious chemistry, and that was it. He would likely have to fuck her at some point, so that was a good thing.

He hated the fact that the vulnerable act almost worked on him. He watched as she crossed the street, both her hands on the strap of her handbag as though she was protecting the only thing she had left. Wind blew her glossy brown hair to the side, and he couldn't miss the way she moved. Her hips swayed as she jogged the last few steps.

Had the crosswalk light changed? Had she watched it go yellow and hurried so she wouldn't be caught in the street when it went red? The man walking behind her didn't seem to care. He didn't change his gait in any way, but Vanessa hustled.

He wouldn't have expected that from a woman who had the whole world change for her. When she'd been married to George

Benedict, everyone had catered to her. Yet she was trying to make it across the street to please…a light?

She couldn't know he was watching her. Maybe she was more naturally submissive than he thought. He could use that.

She moved toward the coffee shop and stopped, looking up and down the sidewalk. She wore sunglasses over those stunning eyes of hers, and she had on another prissy cardigan covering her chest. She was trying to make sure the press wasn't after her.

There was a little guilt that gnawed at him for what he was about to do. There might be another way.

Had she been nervous the whole walk over? It was a few blocks from the Lodge Corp building to this small coffee shop. He'd selected this shop because it sat next to a bakery owned by a friend of his. Macon Miles used to work at Sean Taggart's restaurant until he'd started his own bakery. Sweet Miles was run by Macon and his wife, Allyson, and they were close to the owner of Perk You Up.

It was in a good central location, and he often had client meetings here if for some reason the client didn't want to go all the way to the McKay-Taggart building.

A young woman slid the Americano he'd ordered in front of him, and the rich scent floated up. "Is there anything else I can get you?"

Vanessa had stopped outside the shop. She probably didn't think he could see her, but he could. She had her back to him, but he could see plainly that she had opened her purse and pulled out a compact. She smoothed down her hair and seemed to stare at her reflection for a moment.

She had to make sure she was ready for the act she was about to play out.

"Why don't you bring us a minis plate?" He wanted to watch her turn the ridiculously decadent platter away. It was all of Sweet Miles's favorite breakfast pastries in mini form. Big Tag could finish a plate himself.

The young woman nodded.

He noticed MaeBe's head had come up, and a frown hit her face. Then her eyes went big and wide, and her lower lip pouted out.

She was going to be so much trouble to some Dom one day.

"Send one to MaeBe's table, too, and put it on my tab," Michael allowed. One of the best reasons to come to Perk You Up was the fact that the owner's brother understood the business. Jolie Lewis was the sister of one of MT's bodyguards.

Jolie put a hand on her hip. "You running an op here, Malone? Is that why MaeBe's sitting at another table trying to look less extra than normal?"

MaeBe did look different. She'd done a good job toning down her goth look. She'd scrubbed off her makeup and put her vibrant hair in a ponytail. Between that and the sweats and sneakers, she looked like any other young woman fresh off her yoga class.

"It's only a meeting," Michael replied and then hedged because he loved her coffee and Jamal could be intimidating, and he wouldn't like it if little sis was upset with him. "I'm duping a phone. That's all. The woman who's about to walk in is the target. Julian Lodge thinks she might be running a scam on his wife."

That seemed to work some magic on Jolie. "On Dani? Okay. I'll hang back. Let me know if you need anything. And I'll feed the goth girl. You might be surprised at the bill. She's a tiny thing, but she can eat."

Jolie started to walk away as the bell over the door rang and Vanessa walked in. Jolie turned back. "Coffee for you?"

"Black, please. Thank you," Vanessa replied. She then turned and smiled his way. "Good morning, Sir."

That *Sir* went straight to his cock, and he actually had to stand up to adjust himself. It was a good thing he was playing the courtly gentleman because it would have been uncomfortable to keep sitting. He held out her chair. "Good morning, Vanessa. How was your evening?"

Thanks to Deke, he knew exactly how her evening had gone, and he was going to be able to tell if she was lying.

"It was fine." Her smile had tightened, and even if he hadn't known the truth, her expression would have told him she was hiding something.

She sat, and he moved back to his seat. He'd carefully placed her so her back was to MaeBe.

"Well, I spent my evening thinking about you and how we should proceed." He relaxed, watching her as she took off her sunglasses and set them on the table beside her purse. He could see the top of her cell phone sticking out of the side pocket. It wouldn't be hard for MaeBe to slip it out, but she couldn't do it if the purse was on the table in clear sight.

Another reason for the platter. The table was a small bistro capable of sitting two comfortably. It was intimate, unlike the longer picnic-style tables that were also available.

"I thought we were going to play night on Friday," she said, those odd, stunning eyes of hers on him. "And I made an appointment with the therapist."

A man could get lost in those eyes if he let himself. If he didn't know the woman behind them was lying to him. "I'm glad. I think you'll like her. I've spent some time at the Ferguson Clinic myself."

"You said you went after you first joined the company you're at now."

"Yes, but that was about ten years ago. I follow up from time to time when I need to. I spent about three months a year and a half ago working through some things. It's good to have a tune-up every now and then," he admitted.

He didn't tell her he'd gone because Big Tag pretty much forced anyone involved in a dangerous op to check in with a therapist afterward. Most jobs weren't. Most involved him going through loads of data and figuring out which employee was most likely to fuck over his or her company. When he had a list of names, the stakeouts began. Those also weren't typically dangerous to anything but his waistline because stakeout food wasn't usually healthy.

But he'd had one go sideways, and he'd been forced to defend himself. Now there was a man out there who couldn't walk because Michael had put a bullet in him. Of course, he'd taken a bullet, too, but sometimes it still haunted him.

They all did. No matter the circumstances.

She nodded, and her hands folded together. "Yeah, I suppose so."

"I thought we would start slow on Friday. We can watch some scenes and then talk about them afterward," he explained. "Until then I would like for us to talk on a daily basis, and I would like to set up some homework for you."

"I got the books you sent over. Thank you for that."

He'd had a few books on the lifestyle sent to her office this morning. It was important to keep up the teaching aspect of his cover. "Are you okay with the reading schedule? I'd like to be able to talk about the texts when we meet up."

"Of course. I assure you I don't have a lot to do in the evenings, so if I'm not working, I can read."

Jolie returned with a cup of black coffee, the platter of minis, and a small plate for each of them. There were cinnamon rolls and tiny croissants with chocolate. The éclairs were particularly good. He reached for one of the lemon mini muffins he never had a chance to try because Big Tag was always too fast when they catered in.

Vanessa stared down at the platter for a moment and then took a sip of her coffee, ignoring the small plate Jolie had set in front of her. She did, however, move her purse, turning so she could sling it over the back of her chair.

Perfect. He caught sight of MaeBe's head coming up out of the book she was reading and knew she'd noted that the target had moved to a more convenient location.

"You should try the éclairs. They're delicious," he offered. "A friend of mine makes them. This coffee shop has a connection to the bakery next door. Macon Miles used to work for my boss's brother. He owns several restaurants. Macon was once his pastry chef."

She didn't look down this time. "Thanks, but I ate earlier. I have a few questions about Friday."

"You know you'll still be gorgeous if you eat the éclair, right?"

Her shoulders straightened. "Mr. Malone, do you know how often I've had my body criticized? I might not have read the books you sent me yet, but I'm pretty sure there's a no-shame clause."

He sat up straighter, surprise going through him. "I wasn't shaming you."

"You were questioning my choices about what I do or don't do when it comes to my body. In this case, I believe you're telling me I'm too skinny."

He frowned her way. "I didn't say that."

"If a male friend of yours was sitting here and told you he was watching his carbs or he was full, would you question him?" Vanessa asked.

"No. I might rib him a little if I knew him well. I wasn't criticizing you."

"You might think you aren't, but we don't know each other well enough to joke, and I can assure you the statement forced me to consider how you perceive my body." She took a long breath. "I'm sensitive. I've spent most of my adult life either being told I'm too skinny and I'm forcing an impossible beauty standard on young women or I'm fat and I'm letting people down."

She'd caught him completely off guard, and he was interested in why she'd had that reaction. "Why would people be let down?"

"Fans, Mr. Malone. I told you I was an actress for a long time. At one point my social media pages had millions of followers, and I spent a good portion of my time photoshopping every single image I put out because all of those followers had a say in what I looked like. I'm sure you didn't mean to make me self-conscious, but you did."

There was the guilt again. Her forthright reaction hit him far harder than any hedging could have. She was right. He wouldn't have said that to a male friend. He would have shrugged and eaten what he wanted himself and moved on. Why had he said it to her? "I apologize. I didn't think about it that way. I wanted to share it with you."

She blinked, and he caught a sheen of tears. "Yeah, well, the sad part is I would love to try it, but I only brought enough cash for the coffee and the tip. But I'm right about the other stuff. Saying things like that makes women self-conscious, and we're already aware every second of the day what we look like."

"You thought I was going to make you pay for your coffee?"

Her shoulders were right back up. "We're in a training relationship. This isn't a date. I pay my way, and coffee is what I can afford."

Something softened inside him, and he reached out for her hand. "Vanessa, this might not be a date, but I never intended for you to pay. I'm the top. It was only a courtesy and the need to share something I enjoy with the woman I'm with. I'm not offering you éclairs in exchange for submission. I promise. Forgive me. I didn't mean to make you feel small."

In that moment, he meant it. He felt her fragility and how much she needed her pride. He didn't understand it. He'd never gone a day in his life without money. It was always there, and he took it for granted. The fact that he had money also made him generous with it. He paid for things because he could, and he never expected his friends to pay him back.

How would it feel if everything he had was taken away and he was left with nothing? Would he understand her then?

Or was he being played again?

She hesitated for a moment, and then her hand covered his. "I'm sensitive about that, too. I need to understand what you know about my past before we move forward. I can't get invested in even a training relationship until you understand what you're taking on."

"I know who you are. After we met, I was curious. I looked up Vanessa Jones and found your stage name. It's not a problem." Now he was the one who was lying, but that was the nature of this particular game.

"You know what they say about me?" Vanessa asked quietly.

"I didn't read anything in depth, but I know about your marriage, and I know you're involved in a dispute over the will of your late husband." This could be good for him. It meant he could talk to her about her past, get her to open up and trust him. Maybe get her to stumble and admit something she shouldn't.

She seemed to relax a bit. "Good. I was worried you didn't know."

"I do, and I will think about everything you've said to me today. But Vanessa, please let me pick up this very small bill. When you have money, I'll let you buy me a beer. This isn't an exchange of anything but comfort and kindness."

"It's hard for me to accept…"

"Don't say charity. It's coffee and a couple of pastries."

She sniffled, but a smile broke over her face. "Okay."

She was facing him when MaeBe eased over and gently pulled the phone out of her bag. Michael held her hand and for a moment wondered what it would be like if he was only her training Dom. How would he handle her if he had no other intentions than to see if they could work as a D/s couple?

He squeezed her hand as MaeBe walked to the bathroom, and the door closed behind her. Then he sat back. It was time for some charm. "So now that we know this is all about sharing an experience I would like to have with you, can I offer you some of my friend's treats? He's a master. In both senses of the word."

Her lips curved up. He was starting to label her smiles. They were all very different. This was her happiest smile, the one she had on her face when she was genuinely amused. “Do you know any vanilla people?”

He thought about that for a moment. Did he? “My parents. And if they’re not, I don’t want to know.”

Vanessa’s laughter rang through the room. “I will give you that. I wouldn’t want to know either.” Her eyes lit as she looked down at the platter. “All right, what’s your favorite?”

“The mini donuts. They are why I work out.” He reached for her plate and started filling it for her.

MaeBe slipped out of the bathroom as Vanessa tried one.

She never saw the phone go back into her bag.

He wished that didn’t make him feel so fucking guilty.

* * * *

She should never have eaten that first donut. It was way too easy to look at the little sucker and tell herself it was perfectly fine to eat because it was so small.

But then so was the éclair she’d eaten, and the muffins, and so on. They’d managed to eat the whole platter while they’d had coffee and talked about what she should expect from The Club.

“So I’ll see actual sex happening on the dungeon floor.” She was still wrapping her head around it. It was a good thing the café was quiet right now. They were having a frank conversation. Luckily the only people sitting around them were a young woman who seemed completely engrossed in the book she was reading and a man who’d walked in fifteen minutes before and had taken a seat close to the restrooms.

His lips kicked up in a grin. “Yes, this is a private club, and I assure you Julian ties up every single member in nondisclosure agreements. Everyone is carefully vetted. You don’t have to worry that you’ll be pressured to do anything you don’t want to do, nor will anyone talk about The Club around non-club members.”

There was one problem she could think of. “But I know most of his employees are also club members.”

“Would it surprise you to know that it’s more usual for a club member to become an employee than the other way around?” Michael asked.

"Really?"

Michael nodded. "Yes, and understand I'm talking about Julian's closest group of employees. Not the guys down in the mailroom. I'm talking about the ones who work in the offices he goes into every day. A lot of them came from The Club. He lives the lifestyle pretty much twenty-four seven. Not in a high-protocol way or anything, but Julian prefers the well-defined boundaries D/s offers. He doesn't want to have to pretend to be vanilla even in the office."

It was one of the things she found intimidating about the man, but she didn't think BDSM was the reason. Julian would be intimidating no matter how he related to his wife. And husband. Julian Lodge didn't let a little thing like thousands of years of societal norms stop him from taking what he wanted.

Hadn't she felt that way once? When she'd started out, she'd felt invincible, like she could fix things, make things easier for the women who came after her. She'd put herself and her career on the line. She'd tried to take the sexpot image she'd gotten from those first ten or so movies and turn it on its head, show everyone she could be sexy and smart.

She'd gotten ground to dust.

Did she have to stay dust?

She used to flirt and have fun with the people around her, and now she didn't trust anyone but Ruby and Dani. She liked the man sitting in front of her. Michael Malone was funny and charming, and he knew who she was. He didn't seem to have a problem with it. The fact that they had an end date made it oddly easier to consider getting closer to him. He could be a baby step into the world again.

Then she would take back her life. She would do what she'd promised George she would do, what she owed Nicki. That work would consume the rest of her life, and she looked forward to it.

But she could have the smallest bit of joy for herself. Couldn't she?

"I would think that would make it weirder. How do you go from The Club to the office?" she asked, not able to quite cover the giggle that came from the vision.

"You think that because you don't take sex seriously," Michael replied. "You see it as something that should be hidden. I'm not saying everyone should have public sex or talk about it at a dinner party, but shouldn't there be places where it's all right to do whatever you want to do? Without judgment?"

"There's always judgment." Now he was the naïve one.

"Is that what you're worried about?" Michael sat up and leaned over, coming closer to her. "You think you'll walk in there and people will talk about you?"

"People always talk about me."

"They won't at The Club. Not in the way you think."

That was where he was wrong. She already caught people talking about her. Sometimes the room she would walk into went silent when the people there realized she'd joined them. It was why she tended to stay in her office. "I assure you they're already talking. I was surprised Julian found someone willing to work with me. The only reason he tolerates me being there at all is because of his wife."

Michael's handsome face turned thoughtful. "I don't think that's the only reason. He liked your sister quite a bit. I've talked to him about her since he thinks you will likely have the same issues."

"Issues?"

"Your sister explored the lifestyle because she had a terrible relationship with her own sexuality," Michael explained and then frowned. "Maybe you should talk to Julian about this."

"I won't." She couldn't see herself sitting in a room with Julian and talking about her sister. Not when she wasn't sure he didn't have something to do with covering up her death. Even then, she wasn't sure she would be able to open up to him. "And I would like to know everything about Nicki. She talked a little with me about it. She said she felt free when she was at The Club. And I know about her struggles. We grew up together. My mother was very religious, and not in a good, happy way. She wasn't the kind of religious person who helped the poor and needy. She thought if you were poor, you probably deserved it. If you were a woman and poor, then you were probably a slut who deserved it. She liked to use that word a lot. And I won't go into her views on any sex that occurred outside of a marriage between one righteous man and one righteous woman."

Michael winced. "Yes, I got that feeling. Your father believed that, too?"

"My father walked out on her to find himself and never came back. I was five and Nicki was eight. Up until then everything was somewhat normal. We went to a regular church and had fun. We had a nice house. When Dad left, we lost the house and moved, and Mom found a crazy-pants church and got old and bitter very quickly." This was something she'd dealt with a long time ago. At least she had on the surface. "She solved every problem we had by telling us to be more modest and to expect less from the world. You can imagine how my announcement that I'd found a modeling agent and was heading out to Hollywood went over."

"Not well, I suspect."

"She told me that if I went out there, I was never to come home again." She could still see her mother standing there in her buttoned-up dress and plain shoes, her hair in a severe bun as though she had to control it the way she did everything in her life—painfully and with no room for movement. "A lot of people say that in the moment, but she meant it. It was five years before I saw my sister again."

"She stayed with your mom after she was out of high school?" Michael asked.

"Mom paid for college but only if Nicki followed the rules. She'd recently started college when I dropped out of high school to pursue my dreams," she admitted. "I was discovered at a modeling competition my mother didn't know I was entered in. I was seventeen, and the agent I was with got me emancipated, and I never talked to my mother again, even though I tried. She died of cancer a few years back, and I was not allowed at her funeral. Nicki wasn't either. By that time, my sister had started working for Dani, and my mother didn't approve."

"I can imagine. You know she found another family at The Club. One that accepted her."

That sounded too good to be true. "Well, my sister was very likable."

"You don't have to be likable." Michael's deep voice was soothing. "Likability is something I've come to view as one of the lesser virtues. It's like being nice. Nice can cover a multitude of sins."

She'd learned that as well. "Kind is better."

"Yeah, kind is definitely better. My boss is one of the single most irritating human beings on the face of the planet," Michael said with a smile. "And he's also one of the kindest men I've ever met."

"Yeah, I know the type. I'll take it over all the polite people who think that taking their swipes behind your back is the height of kindness." Her mother had been polite to everyone and never once kind. "So my sister managed to get over the fire and brimstone approach to sex we were taught?"

"She learned to appreciate her body," Michael explained. "From what I understand, she was shy at first and gained a lot of confidence as she moved through her journey."

Vanessa chuckled, though there was no humor behind the sound. "Well, if being able to show off your body is confidence, then I don't need D/s."

Michael studied her for a moment. "It depends on why you show it off. If you're showing it off because you want to and the attention you get feeds something inside you, then yes. It should give you confidence. If you do it because someone told you it was the only way you could ever get attention, not so much. Did the nudity make you feel confident?"

They were getting deep. She wasn't sure she was ready, but she also didn't want the conversation to end. She liked being around him, and she was feeling comfortable talking to him. After all, they'd signed a contract. Neither of them was allowed to talk about what they did except to people in The Club and any therapist they might see. "In the beginning, yes. It made me feel very confident, like I was free for the first time. I liked acting. I didn't mind the nude scenes, but now I think that was more about giving my mom the finger than actually being okay with myself. When I was starting out, I got a lot of praise. I was working in a small community. When I got bigger jobs, that was when the press started and…you know how you feel when you sit down for a performance review?"

"Like I'm going to want to punch my boss in the face because it's at least half sarcasm," Michael answered.

She was interested in Michael's boss. He sounded like a hoot. Her experience was quite different. "Well, for me that performance review was all day, every day, and public. And more than half the time it wasn't about my skills. It was about my body. No matter how thick your skin is, you feel it."

"Did you feel like your body was no longer your own?"

At least he seemed to understand. "Always. I went from never showing my body because it was supposed to be private and any sexuality I had was to be used to procreate and then be ruthlessly squashed, to every inch of me being under scrutiny. It was my only value to some people. I wasn't a person. I'm still not. I'm a joke, a cautionary tale."

"You won't be at The Club. I think you'll find the D/s community to be very accepting of anyone who comes into it with good intentions. Come in with an open mind and anyone who bothers you will have to deal with me," Michael promised.

It sounded too good to be true, but she'd read what Nicki had written. The Club had become her home. It had been a safe place for her for years. Until a predator had found her.

She wanted to believe everything Michael was telling her.

"I look forward to it," she replied.

"Liar," he accused softly. "But you will. Now I want to give you some homework before we go."

She glanced up and realized it was almost lunchtime. "Oh, I didn't know how late it was. I was supposed to be back in the office thirty minutes ago."

He reached out and put his hand over hers. "I already texted Dani you would be late. She's okay with it, but I'll let you go in one minute."

She relaxed. Dani would be fine as long as she knew where she was. "What's my homework?"

Those emerald eyes suddenly held hers. "I'm going to call you tonight and I'm going to talk you through masturbating. Do you have a vibrator?"

She felt herself flush, and she had to force a reply. She wasn't sure how he easily talked about this. Except that was his point. She needed to be able to talk about sex if she was going to be okay with it. "No. I don't."

"I'm going to send you one."

The gift thing bothered her, and she started to point that out.

His eyes went hard. "I'm your Dom. This part is up to me. I'm sending you a vibrator. You will use it at my request."

It appeared there were some things her top wouldn't be moved on. And it was part of the training. "All right, but I'll buy the coffee next time."

Next time she would be prepared. And she would have gotten

paid. She had to get into a better mindset. Not every man who offered to buy her coffee thought they were paying her for sex. Michael probably didn't have to since she was crazy attracted to him, and she didn't think she would be able to hold out for long.

Even after the crappy night she'd had cleaning up glass and thinking about how everyone in her neighborhood seemed to know how to properly spell the word *whore*, she'd thought about him. After she'd gotten into bed, she hadn't been able to stop thinking about how he'd touched her, how their breath seemed to mingle, and for a moment the world had seemed softer and warmer than it had before.

She wanted to steal this time with him. She knew it wouldn't last, and she feared it made her everything people thought she was, but she was going to do it.

She was going to seduce her training Dom and hope he didn't hate her at the end because he was the best thing that had happened to her in a long time. Even when he'd irritated her earlier, he'd listened and seemed to understand and accept her point of view.

He brought her hand up to his lips and kissed the back briefly. "I'm glad we spent this time together. And thank you for sharing with me. You can absolutely pick up the coffee next time. I'm looking forward to talking to you tonight, Vanessa."

Her heart actually did a flippity-flop, and she'd been pretty sure the thing was dead before. He was dangerous, but she couldn't make herself walk away. "I'm looking forward to it, too, Sir."

He glanced down at his phone and then stood. "I'm going to hit the head before I go. Wait for me, and I'll walk you back to your office."

He was definitely still a Navy man. She nodded and he walked away, leaving her with a warm feeling.

That faded when she saw the man outside the café window. He stood there, a hand over his eyes as though trying to see inside. There was a camera around his neck.

Her heart thudded again but for a completely different reason.

The young woman who'd been sitting at the back of the café had packed up her book and picked up her yoga mat. She walked past Vanessa's table as a second person joined the photographer.

She had to get out of here. Someone had recognized her and called the press in, and where one went there were always two or three more. If she didn't get out now, they would follow her back to Lodge Corp, and then what would she do? They would know where to look for her. Only the damn gate kept them out of her front yard.

Panic threatened, and she could feel adrenaline coursing through her.

She picked up her purse and shoved her sunglasses on. The other woman was moving through the door and the photographer had looked up, his head swerving like a predator scenting prey.

Vanessa moved in behind Yoga Girl. She would slip behind her and get to the alleyway. She'd noticed it as she'd approached the café an hour and a half before. She always tried to find multiple escape routes out of any building she was in. If she'd thought she had time, she would have asked the owner to let her go out the back way, but then the owner might be the very person who'd called the press.

She would take the alley to the next block and try to find a cab, even though she couldn't afford one.

She had to force herself to breathe, to shove the anxiety down. She could freak out later. Right now she needed to get away.

"Hey, what are you doing?" Yoga Girl was staring down the photographer and his friend. And now there was a third person.

Vanessa slipped behind her, keeping her head low. She heard the bell over the door jingle, and someone exiting after her. Michael? She didn't dare look back. She simply moved forward as Yoga Girl started to argue with the photographer, who was asking about whether or not she'd seen Vanessa Hale and explaining the First Amendment to her.

Vanessa jogged the last few steps to the alleyway and turned. She could feel the breath sawing in and out of her chest. She was going to make it. It would be okay.

A hand gripped her elbow, and she was twisted around. She expected to see Michael, but it was a man she'd never met before.

And he had a knife in his free hand.

"Hey!" A woman yelled and then the man let go of Vanessa's arm and turned on the newcomer.

Fear sliced through Vanessa and her first instinct was to run, but the woman from the café was kicking out and trying to fight the man with the knife. She was such a small thing, and the man was a hulking beast, and Vanessa couldn't leave her.

She held her purse in both hands and reared back, bringing it down on the man's neck.

He growled and fell forward, taking the pink-haired woman with him before hopping up and running past Vanessa.

What the hell had happened? Her hands were shaking as she moved to help the young woman up. Her yoga mat had been tossed to the side and she was lying on the ground, a hand over her side.

"Are you okay?" Vanessa reached out.

The woman frowned. "I think I might be stabbed. I'm not sure. I would think it would hurt more."

Her savior pulled her hand away, and there was bright red blood there.

"Yep, definitely stabbed." The young woman's eyes flared.

Vanessa dropped to her knees, all thoughts of fleeing gone. If they took her picture, they took her picture. She pulled her cardigan off and placed it against the woman's wound. "We have to keep pressure on it. Don't move."

With her free hand she called the ambulance and prayed the young woman survived.

Chapter Six

"Can I get you some water? Should you have water?" Vanessa frowned as she looked around the small room they'd put May in.

The woman with the pink hair managed to grin her way. "I think I can drink. That was what the surgery was all about—making sure I don't leak. I was told that as stab wounds go, mine was the best kind."

Her "surgery" had been minor, and she was expected to be able to go home that night. The knife had missed all vital organs and had been classified as a superficial wound.

It hadn't felt superficial. At the time she'd worried this woman would bleed out and die right in front of her.

"She's fine, Vanessa." Michael sat in a chair across the room.

Her training Dom had been the best. He'd come running out, and he'd been the one to find her holding her cardigan over May's body. The woman had identified herself as May and then promptly passed out. Michael had dealt with the ambulance and the police. He'd held Vanessa's hand as she'd given her report and then he'd driven her here to the hospital because she'd wanted so much to make sure the woman who'd saved her was okay.

"Physically, I'm fine," May said. "Mentally, I'm awesome. I like stared down that attacker and remembered all my self-defense moves.

It was very empowering. And now I have a cool scar."

"I have no idea what I would have done." Vanessa had been over it a hundred times. She was pretty sure she would dream about it for the rest of her life. "I thought the guys with the cameras were the threat. You were so brave."

May smiled, a lopsided expression that made the woman look more adorable. "No, I'm just a huge fan of *Terror in Walton Woods.* Couldn't have it play out in real life. Suzy Silk died in the movies. Vanessa Hale wasn't going out on my watch."

Vanessa felt her skin flush. "I didn't think anyone recognized me. You didn't say anything."

May shrugged. "You're a person who was having coffee. You didn't need some crazy fan interrupting. But when I realized the photogs were there, I tried to give you some cover."

"What you did was probably save her life," Michael said. "I would like to point out that I had asked her to wait for me. I was going to walk her back to her office. I would have dealt with the photographers and then no one would have gotten stabbed."

Yeah, she felt guilty about that, too.

He had his phone out, glancing down. She couldn't blame the man since she was the reason he'd missed his workday. She'd tried to explain that she was fine and he could leave, but he wouldn't hear of it.

She kind of thought he was hanging around so he could give her a very long lecture on disobeying direct orders.

Or a spanking. He might want to spank her.

Why, oh why, did that thought not scare her the way it should?

"I didn't want you to have to deal with the press," she said quietly. "I thought…I thought I could sneak behind May and go down the alley and get away. I'm sorry."

May's brows rose. "For what? Girl, I would have run, too. That was weird. I mean, it wasn't as weird as the asshole who stabbed me, but it was weird."

At first she'd thought it had to have been either the café owner or May herself who had tipped the press off, but now she wondered if it hadn't been someone else. Perhaps one of the many customers who'd come in and out while she and Michael had sat talking. Honestly, even if she'd discovered May had been the one, she would forgive the woman almost anything at this point.

There was a knock on the door and then a man walked through. He looked to be in his late twenties or early thirties, but he had one of those youthful faces. Baby face. He wore a T-shirt and jeans and had a Red Vine dangling from his mouth like a cigarette.

"Hey, Hutch." May gave the man a big smile. "I got stabbed."

Hutch looked Vanessa's way, and his eyes went wide. He pulled the Red Vine out of his mouth. "Uh, this is surreal. Okay. Not what I was expecting."

"Michael Malone." Michael stood and held a hand out.

The man named Hutch only hesitated for a second. "Greg Hutchins. My friends call me Hutch. Including this one. Who got stabbed. Who was supposed to be at the office all day."

May frowned. "I lost track of time after my yoga class. But it's cool because I got to save a life."

Michael stepped back. "She really did. I don't know why that man was coming after my…Vanessa, but it was obvious to me what would have happened if May hadn't been there."

Hutch nodded. "Yeah. Okay. I suppose I can understand that. I'm May's boss. You should understand that her other coworkers now know that she's here at the hospital. I thought it would be good if I came and offered her a ride home before the crazies show up."

"Crazies?" Vanessa had asked May what she did and all she'd said was that she worked in tech support.

Hutch nodded. "Yeah, you know every office has at least one. He's the dude who you can't trust to keep a secret or anything. Just goes right off the rails thinking he knows everything. He'll probably show up at some point. Soon. Now, I would like to hear the story of how May came to save…I have to ask…"

She hadn't even introduced herself. "I'm Vanessa Jones. You might know me as Vanessa Hale."

Hutch's grin kicked up, and he looked back at May. "Dude, that is so cool."

May nodded. "I know."

"May was at the same coffee shop Vanessa and I were at. A couple of photographers showed up, and Vanessa got scared and tried to get away. When she did a man followed her into the alley, and that was when your coworker went all warrior princess on his ass,"

Michael said. "Although she let him get away."

Vanessa gasped a little. It was rude. "That was not her fault. She did everything she could."

May grimaced. "I didn't even get a good look at the dude. I got this crazy adrenaline rush, and what I mostly remember was the knife."

"I told the police I thought he might have been in the shop with us," Vanessa explained. "They're going to look at the security tapes. I might recognize him."

May seemed to think about that as a low ping rang through the room.

Michael was staring down at his phone. He looked back up. "I've got to make a call. Vanessa, I need you to stay here. We need to talk about what happened today. I don't want you walking around on your own until we do."

She'd gotten the idea that Michael was worried the attack had been specifically about her. He might be right. It made her gut churn, but she had to consider that the attack hadn't been random. The police didn't seem concerned. They had pointed out the fact that her handbag was a designer bag and worth a lot on its own. "As long as it's okay with May, I'll stay here."

May reached out a hand. "Absolutely. I'm thrilled to have some company. And I promise I won't even ask you three million questions about *Walton Woods*. Even though I have them."

"I think you can ask me pretty much anything," Vanessa replied.

Michael stepped in front of her. "Please don't leave this room."

She nodded. "Okay. I'll wait for you."

It was nice to have someone who cared. He'd been so good to her all throughout. He'd even chased away the photographers. At least she thought he had because they hadn't shown up again.

Her Dom had watched out for her. Maybe there was something to this exchange he talked about. She'd thought it was odd, but wasn't every relationship an exchange of some sort? Perhaps D/s was simply more honest about what was being exchanged.

He walked out of the room as the nurse walked in.

"You know what you're doing?" Hutch asked the question under his breath, and she might not have caught it if she hadn't learned to listen as well as she had.

May gave him a shrug. "You know me, boss. I go with the flow."

Hutch sighed, but when he looked back Vanessa's way he flashed a heart-stopping grin. "So who would want to stab you?"

The question made her sink into the seat by May's bed. "The list is long and mostly undeserved, though I'm sure a lot of people would argue with me."

"Well, that's what happens when you marry an old man for his money and ruin his family." The nurse turned and walked out.

Pure embarrassment flooded her system.

"Hey, that was rude, and if you weren't in control of my pain meds, I would show you how I got here," May shouted.

Hutch stared at the door. "I bet I can get her name. You're going to be laid up for a while. Wanna have some fun?"

May got a steely look in her eyes. "Yeah. I think I do."

"I'm sorry." Vanessa wished she hadn't promised Michael she would stay here. She hadn't considered the fact that her very presence could make things hard on May.

"She's the one who's going to be sorry," Hutch said. "May can be…ruthless when it comes to her friends. And she makes friends pretty fast."

"Well, don't say anything to her. I've found it's best to ignore people who like to comment on my private life," Vanessa said. "They don't know me. I'm not a person to them. I'm a character in a show. I'm the villain."

"Villains have more fun." Hutch offered her a Red Vine. "Want one?"

It wasn't like she was getting lunch. She pulled one out of the container Hutch offered. It was better than smoking at least. "Thanks. If you two want some privacy, I could…"

"Oh, I think you should do what your boyfriend told you to," May said. "He did not look like he was playing. That dude has had too much stimulation for one day. You need to get him home, put a glass of Scotch in his hands, and sit on his lap."

"Oh, he's not my boyfriend." He'd acted like one though. "He's a friend."

"Sure. I mean you might think so, but that guy is twelve kinds of into you." May winced as she settled back. "And he wants you to stay here. Please don't feel bad about the nurse. She has no idea who you are. If it makes you feel better, I get called a whore a lot, too. It's probably the fishnets. They are the most misunderstood of all the hosieries."

"And I get called a nerdling. Always. Stereotypes are awful things," Hutch said with a yawn.

May smiled up at him. "You are a fully grown nerd."

"That's what my wife says." Hutch's smile brightened at the word wife. "Stay with us, Vanessa. You know you want to. We have candy. Besides Red Vines, I brought Skittles, too."

Her phone buzzed in her bag, but she ignored it for the moment. She knew she shouldn't, but she liked May a lot, and Hutch seemed fun. They didn't seem to have turned on her because of the nurse. It had been a long time since she'd clicked with someone as a friend.

Or clicked with a lover. Michael was sending her into new and dangerous territories.

She sat back. "All right then. I guess I'll stay for a while."

May's eyes lit up. "Cool, because I have questions. First of all, what's in the blood they poured all over you when you died in the first *Terror* movie? Also, how did you manage to scream like that?"

She had to smile. It had been a while since someone asked her a fun question. "The blood is a weird mix of corn syrup, water, and dyes. But in that last scene, they were running thin, so the director added ketchup to the mix. Craft services had fries that day so there was a bunch of ketchup. It was gross, and let me tell you it does not come out of your hair so easily."

She sat back, and for the first time in hours, she relaxed.

* * * *

Michael stepped out of MaeBe's hospital room and into the hallway. The text Deke had sent confirmed what Hutch had been subtly telling him. The crazy was here, and it wouldn't matter that he was working an op.

"Get the fuck out of my way, Deke." Kyle Hawthorne stood in Deke's space, his hands in fists at his sides.

Two of the nurses were staring at the men, likely trying to figure out if they should call security. Or the police, since both Deke and Kyle were big muscular guys who could do some serious damage if they got into it.

He'd already had to deal with the police today. He didn't want another run-in. He stalked down the hall because they were in plain view of the room. If Vanessa decided to disobey again, she would probably ask why a member of The Club was trying to fight his way into her savior's room. Kyle wasn't supposed to know the woman Vanessa called May.

This was why Big Tag was always annoyed. He had to deal with shit like this all the time.

"You need to chill, man. You can't go in there," Deke replied, not backing down. "How is it going to look if you walk in and suddenly know the chick who is supposed to be a stranger? MaeBe's fine. Hutch is in there with her now."

"Good, because I have a few things to say to Hutch," Kyle shot back. "MaeBe is supposed to be safe in her fucking cubicle. She was not cleared to go into the field. Hutch should have shut this shit down immediately."

Yep. He was going to have to deal with Kyle. "I cleared her. I made the decision to take her out."

Kyle's head swiveled like a predator scenting prey. "You had no right."

Michael moved into the waiting room, which was blessedly empty at this point. It was a good thing because he didn't think Kyle would care about an audience. "I am a senior investigator. I assure you I have every right to use tech support. All MaeBe was supposed to do was dupe the target's phone."

"Which she managed to do without incident." Deke followed Kyle, sticking close, as if waiting to tackle the fucker if he had to.

He was grateful for Deke's presence. Michael wasn't sure he could handle Kyle all on his own. Kyle could go berserk from time to time.

"Without incident? She took a knife to the gut. Is that not an incident, Deke? What do you consider an incident? Does she have to die for it to be serious for you?" Kyle was right back in Deke's face.

But they were just friends. Sure. He was dealing with a self-delusional powder keg ready to go off at any moment. He also had to remember that this particular powder keg had a Taggart for a stepdad and was vital to the mission at hand. As much as he wanted to knock some sense into Kyle, he had to move with caution around him. "She's fine. Deke is telling you the truth. MaeBe was there to do a technical job. She could have left at any time after she duped the phone, but she stayed until Vanessa was ready to go, and somehow she got caught in the physical op. Deke tipped off some photographers that Vanessa was at the café."

"Why would you do that?" Kyle asked.

"Because she's moving too slowly, and we can't watch her given where she's living." Normally he wouldn't explain himself, but it was obvious that Kyle needed to understand in order to calm down. "Between the photographers and what Deke set up at her house, she'll need a place to stay tonight, and I intend to offer her my guest room. Now I think she genuinely needs someone to watch after her because there's no way that guy was going for her purse. The cops are wrong. He was going after Vanessa."

Michael was surprised at how much that upset him. When he'd realized something had gone wrong, he'd been angry, and then he'd turned down the alley and seen MaeBe on the ground, Vanessa holding her together. He'd realized someone had taken a shot at Vanessa, and he'd felt like he'd gotten kicked in the gut.

She would have stayed in her seat had those fucking photographers not been there. She would have waited for him, and he would have taken care of her attacker. He was responsible for this.

"MaeBe was trying to help. She saw the guy go after Vanessa, and she followed. She would have done it for anyone," Deke pointed out. "She's one of the kindest people I know."

"She shouldn't have been in that position," Kyle argued. "She's supposed to be at the office. I told Ian I didn't want her to have anything to do with this op. If you wanted a tech, you could have asked Hutch."

"Hutch runs the department. I don't ask Hutch to do a simple job any of his employees can do. MaeBe wants to be in the field. And this is my op. You're a bodyguard. You don't have any say in who I use or don't use over the course of my investigation." He was getting irritated. "You know I was running ops when you were still in college, kid."

Kyle shook his head. "I don't care. You don't get to use MaeBe that way."

"She works for McKay-Taggart. I'm not using her. She's doing her job, and you're out of line." He wasn't going to let Kyle's issues fuck with this op. "If you've got a problem with me, feel free to take yourself out of the job, but you don't tell me how to run this show. And I think MaeBe will have something to say about you going behind her back and affecting her job."

Kyle's head shook. "I don't have to go behind her back, man. I'll say it to her front. She's not cut out for this job, and she proved it today. She didn't take out the bad guy. She got hurt. She needs to stay behind a computer screen. Hell, she needs to find another job altogether. Now get out of my way because I'm going to check on her."

Michael stepped in front of him. "You can't. Vanessa is in there."

Kyle's jaw tightened. "Then you should take her home because I'm going to see MaeBe."

"I'll have her out in half an hour," Michael promised. "She's talking to MaeBe. They seem to be getting along."

Kyle's eyes flared. "You're getting her in deeper."

"They're talking. That's all." He didn't see what the problem was. "And you know what? She was good in the field. She didn't panic. She handled the situation, and she protected the target."

"She shouldn't have to protect your target, Michael," Kyle shot back. "She's barely healed from what happened to her when she was kidnapped."

A lightbulb went off in Michael's head. This was what the problem was. MaeBe had been kidnapped by a woman who'd wanted to use her to find Hutch's wife, Noelle LaVigne. She'd been beaten, and Kyle had been there. He'd watched the woman he so obviously loved be hurt, and he couldn't stand the thought of it happening again.

"She's all right. I'm not putting her in any more danger," Michael promised. "She's done what I needed her to do. She'll monitor Vanessa's phone and let me know if anything interesting happens. I didn't mean to put her in danger in the first place."

Kyle let out a long breath and stepped away, pacing across the carpet. "It fucking follows her. I swear. That girl is so much fucking trouble. Only she could walk into a knife."

He could see plainly that MaeBe was trouble for Kyle. "She was a hero today."

"I don't want to hear that shit," Kyle replied. "She could have died."

"But she didn't." Deke sat down, signaling he thought the threat had passed. "She's smart, and she's well trained. Man, it's so clear you're into her, and she's crazy about you. Are you hiding the relationship for some reason? No one cares about office relationships. Obviously. Michael's tanked, but most of them seem good."

He resented the "tanked" comment. It hadn't tanked. It had faded into nothingness. Sometimes he thought he was in the process of disappearing, too. "If he wants a relationship with MaeBe, this isn't the way to go about it. I get that you're scared for her, but she's serious about this job. I don't think she's going anywhere."

Kyle's eyes came up. "She's just a friend. Nothing more. She can't be more."

"Then you back off because you're acting like an angry husband." He had no idea why Kyle wouldn't admit he was crazy about MaeBe. Emphasis on the crazy. All he knew was Kyle's damage was threatening his op, and he couldn't have that.

"You've got thirty minutes to clear your girl out," Kyle said in a flat, done-with-all-this-business tone. "After that, nothing is going to stop me from seeing MaeBe. I'm not leaving the op, but you should understand that I will sacrifice the whole fucking job if MaeBe is in trouble again. You've put her close to the target. There's probably no way to pull her out now, but if she's on the team, then I'm in charge of her."

Kyle strode away.

Deke sighed. "Did Grace beat him as a child? Or lose him in the forest so he was raised by wolves?"

He was getting a headache. "No idea, man, but he is trouble. If I could, I would send him right back to the bodyguard unit. But he's known at The Club. There would be gossip if he wasn't there. And someone took that schedule."

"The one that plainly states Kyle is working this weekend," Deke agreed. "Yeah, you can't get rid of him without tipping off whoever took that schedule."

He wished he could. Kyle was a wild card. "He's right about one thing. MaeBe's part of this now. She and Vanessa clicked."

"I don't get what he's upset about. I mean, I get he doesn't want her hurt, but sometimes that's part of the job." Deke stood up. "She's good. I watched her through the security cameras. She did an excellent job of swiping the phone. She was patient. She got it back quickly."

"You were watching the cameras?"

Deke held a hand up. "Yeah, but I wasn't when the incident happened. When you went to the bathroom, I left the van and got ready to deal with our photographers if I needed to. I got a flash of the guy as he ran back out, but nothing else. As soon as I can, I'll find him on the security cams and get a work-up going for you."

He would feel better when he knew what he was dealing with. "And where are we on the other job?"

"The gate is open and totally broken. They won't get that sucker fixed for weeks," Deke promised. "I already tipped off the paparazzi, so they should be swarming around her house soon. I suggest you offer to drive her home so you're with her when she realizes she can't stay there."

"That's a good plan." Again he felt a kick of guilt, but he shoved it down. Honestly, this was for her own good.

His phone buzzed, and he glanced down. It was Hutch.

Your girl got some bad news. You need to get in here now.

He looked up at Deke. That was interesting timing. "I think she already knows. Figure out who that man is for me. I want to know why he came after her. If all goes well, you'll get to sleep in your own bed tonight."

Deke nodded. "Gotta be better than my car. I'll check in later, and I'll keep an eye on Kyle, too."

At least he had one member of the team watching his back.

If Vanessa knew, then she had someone in the neighborhood she was friendly with. It might explain her late-night visitor. He wanted to ID that guy, too.

He jogged back down the hall and hoped he looked casual as he entered MaeBe's room. He pushed through and stopped at the sight in front of him. Somehow he'd thought she would be angry. Vanessa didn't look mad. She looked completely lost. MaeBe was holding Vanessa's hand, and tears streaked down her face. Her free hand was holding her cell, and she was shaking.

"Hey, she got bad news," MaeBe said. "Something happened at

her house."

Vanessa turned and let go of MaeBe's hand. She seemed to try to shake off the tears. "It's nothing. The gate at my housing development is broken. Some asshole plowed through it. So the press is now outside my house. It's okay. I'll go to a hotel."

That wasn't happening. Not when he'd gone to so much trouble to put her in this very position.

"Where they'll find you again?" He stepped in and reached a hand out. "You're coming home with me. I have a nice guest room. You can hide out for a couple of days. I'll drive you to and from work. And don't tell me no. This is exactly the kind of thing I'm supposed to take care of for you."

She took his hand, and he hauled her close. The minute he wrapped his arms around her, she burst into tears. All of that emotion that she'd kept inside came rolling out.

Or she was acting again.

He didn't think so. She clung to him like he was the last real thing in the world.

He held her as she sobbed, and he felt equal parts hero and villain.

But mostly he knew he was the bad guy.

Chapter Seven

Vanessa stared at the apartment, and a chill went through her. Her senses had started to tingle when she'd realized Michael drove a hundred-thousand-dollar car, but they'd gone on high alert when he'd pulled up to the gorgeous Victory Park apartment building. It wasn't really apartments. There would be no renters here. Everyone in this building would own their place, and they would have spent millions for the pleasure.

But she'd tamped down her suspicions because maybe people who worked for security firms made more than she thought they did. Maybe he was an executive and she didn't understand his situation.

Then he'd taken her up to the penthouse.

She stopped as the door closed behind her. She stood on the marble floors and took in the entryway. It had obviously been "done." There was an elegant mirror and table where Michael stashed his keys. On the opposite wall was a painting she was pretty sure she recognized. It was by a famous contemporary artist. It was probably worth more than his car. "Who are you?"

He turned in the hallway, seeming to understand that she wasn't following him in. A brow rose over his eyes. "I thought we'd gone over this."

She glanced down and noticed he was wearing a different pair of loafers than he'd worn the other day, this one every bit as designer and expensive. "Yes, but now I think we should have gone deeper. You said you were Michael Malone and you worked for a security firm. Do you own it?"

"No. I work for McKay-Taggart. I am neither McKay nor Taggart." He frowned. "What is this about? This place? Vanessa, come inside and we'll talk. You had a rough day."

"Not until I understand who you are."

He seemed to think about that for a moment. "I'm Michael Malone. My parents own Malone Oil and Energy. I have a trust fund that would fund a small country for many years. I don't make a big deal out of it. This place is a good investment. I also like the location. It's close to the office, and more importantly, I share this floor with my favorite cousin and his wife."

"You're wealthy." She didn't say rich. Rich was a different thing. Rich was something a person could become through hard work and a modicum of luck. Michael Malone was something different. He was from generational wealth. The kind that didn't like it when a middle-class girl came sniffing around their sons.

"I have money I did very little to earn. But you should understand that I don't have anything on my father or my twin brother. I left that life a long time ago. I went into the Navy after college and left the family business entirely to my brother. He's the CEO of the company now that my dad retired. JT and his wife run Malone Oil and Energy. I don't take anything from the company. I live off my salary from McKay-Taggart and the interest off my trust fund. I really do work for a security firm."

"But you don't need to work at all." It made her suspicious. Wealthy people didn't work for others. They indulged themselves in art or sport, or some of them worked for charities. She'd found very little in between.

"Everyone needs to work," Michael argued. "I don't understand what's happening here."

How could he not get why she would be upset? Had today taught the man nothing about her life? "I am basically on the run from the press because they think I'm a gold digger."

"I don't think that." He moved toward her, a weariness on his face. "Vanessa, I wasn't trying to deceive you. I'm not sure when I was supposed to show you my bank account. I'm only trying to protect you."

She got a queasy feeling in her gut. He'd done nothing but help her and she was complaining. "I'm sorry. I don't want anyone to think I'm after your money. Maybe I should go to a motel. Or I can call Dani. She said they might have a place in the building I can use."

His gorgeous lips turned down in a frown. "So you think it's better the press potentially finds out you're staying with Julian Lodge than me?"

"I wouldn't be staying with him." But he had a point. It was precisely why she had turned Dani down when she'd offered her one of the rooms in the building.

"Do you think those reporters would care?" Michael challenged. "It's one thing to work for the man. It's another to live in his building. They proved today that they're not going away."

She'd been thinking about that all day. "Someone tipped them off."

"You think they won't do it again? I know a lot of people are scared of Lodge, but you should know that I had some of my techs look around the web. There's talk about a couple of the tabloids offering big money for pictures of you. I think the kind of money out there will be able to tempt even a few of Lodge's employees. The press would love to gossip about you finding another…"

He stopped, but she knew exactly the words he'd been about to use. "Sugar daddy?"

His face fell. "I didn't mean it that way. I was talking about how the press would spin the situation. Please come inside, and we can talk about this. I'm sorry you're disappointed in my living situation, but I truly think this is the best place for you to be. The security here is excellent, and I don't care if someone discovers you're here with me. The press doesn't care about my family. We're boring."

He was being completely naïve. "You won't be if they find out you're associated with me."

"Let me take that risk." He held a hand out. "Please stay here for a few days and let me watch out for you. I've been trying to take care of you all day. I don't care about what the press might say. We know the truth about our relationship. Can we just chill for the rest of the night and deal with this tomorrow?"

He was right. He'd been nothing short of perfect with her all day long. He could have left at any moment. She was an adult who could handle herself. Not that she'd shown him that. She'd mostly cried and clung to him. "I'm sorry this afternoon was rough on you. You shouldn't have to deal with my problems."

He groaned and took her hand. "Vanessa, stop. I wouldn't have been anywhere else."

"Because we signed a contract. I understand that part of the contract talked about protecting me, but that was in the club."

He threaded his fingers through hers. "No. It's everywhere for as long as we're in this relationship. I know it seems odd to you, but for me it's an honest and open way to relate to each other. For the length of our contract I'm going to do what it takes to protect you."

And she was supposed to offer him comfort and submission where she chose to. The contract they'd signed was a flimsy thing, unenforceable in the end. It still relied on goodwill and consent. What it actually did was open a dialogue about wants and needs and how to relate to each other. It required them to negotiate. She could walk away at any time, but he was asking her not to. "I worry that you're going to regret this. Being associated with me could hurt you. I don't know that you should risk that for a training partner."

He moved in closer, looming over her and reminding her how big and strong he was. How safe it felt to be around him. "How about I risk it for a friend? For someone I'm coming to like quite a bit?"

She wanted everything he was offering her in that moment—safety, companionship, and yes, she could feel that he was offering her more. All it would take to bring their lips together was for her to go up on her toes and offer hers to him. She wanted that kiss, and that would be dangerous. Dangerous for her. Dangerous for him.

And she found she couldn't walk away. She squeezed his hand because she also couldn't close that slight distance between them. He was too perfect, and she'd learned that meant he wasn't perfect at all. Or rather what he was offering her wasn't. It would all go to hell, and he would get caught in the crossfire.

She stepped back. "All right. I'll stay for the night and see where things go in the morning."

"Can we compromise?" Michael murmured the question, his

voice low and deep. “Stay with me through the weekend. We’ve got a lot of training to do, and this way you don’t have to worry about getting to and from work or finding a place to stay for a few days. You can take the guest room. My friend will be by in a while to bring you your things.”

Michael had asked a friend of his to stop by her place and grab a few things she would need for the next couple of days. At the time she’d been so overwhelmed by everything that had happened that she’d simply nodded and handed over her keys. She hadn’t even given him her address, but she suspected he could have gotten it from Dani or Julian. “All right.”

She felt his disappointment when she dropped his hand. She felt it too, but her history was between them. If she’d merely been a woman who’d met a man, she likely would have taken that kiss and everything else he’d offered, but the day weighed on her.

He stepped back. “Are you hungry? We skipped lunch.”

She followed him inside, and sure enough, she was in a gorgeous condo with floor-to-ceiling windows overlooking the city. It was quiet, the lights from the buildings around them providing soft illumination to the space.

She moved to the windows. They were a thing of beauty, making her feel like she was high above the city, looking down.

“I’m not hungry.” She felt her aloneness in that moment, felt the loss of her family, of her sister. Of George and Lara. Even Ashton. They’d been friends for so many years she’d felt like family, and her betrayal was like a death.

So much death. She ached inside because she had to wonder if she wasn’t the problem.

He moved in behind her. “I’ll order something for us in case you change your mind. Vanessa, you have to be feeling this. Can I hug you?”

“I don’t know if that’s such a good idea.” If he hugged her, she might feel again, and she wasn’t sure she could handle that tonight. He seemed to warm her when she needed her ice.

“Because you don’t want me to or because you think you don’t deserve it?”

It was obvious he was going to push her. “Because I think the people I care about get hurt, and I like you a lot. Probably too much. I don't trust it."

She'd leaned on him all day, not questioning how easy it was. He'd simply been there, and it had been natural to hold his hand and let him lead the way. All she'd had to do was let him take control and then the chaos hadn't seemed so terrible. But now all of her thoughts and fears were firmly back in place.

"I like you, too. No matter what happens remember that I mean that. You're not what I expected. Can you let me take the risks I'm willing to take? Because honestly, not touching you right now is killing me."

She rested back against him, his arms coming around her and wrapping her up in warmth. Yes, it was every bit as bad/good as she thought it would be. It was so easy to drop her walls around him. She needed to keep them up. "I think I'm too numb to cry."

"You don't have to. You can relax and let me take care of you." His whispered words caressed her skin and warmed her.

She wanted to have the strength to tell him no, but she wanted this warmth he was offering so badly. It had been a truly horrible day, and she didn't have the will to refuse him twice.

"I thought I had some time," she admitted. "When I lost the first court case and they told me the appeal would take a while, I thought at least the press would let up on me. I changed my appearance and lived quietly, and yet here I am."

His cheek rubbed against hers. "People like scandal. Perceived scandal. I live a lot of my life in what most would call an alternative lifestyle. I can't know exactly what you've gone through, but I do know that what some people don't understand, they attack."

"Well, they really didn't understand my marriage."

"It was outside the norm."

To say the least, but in a lot of ways she disagreed. "I loved him. Isn't that the norm for marriage? He was one of the best men I've ever met in my life. I probably shouldn't have married him though. I should have stayed with him and not rocked the boat, but he was so sure of what he wanted."

She felt Michael stiffen behind her and worried she shouldn't have said anything.

"What he wanted was you. Of course," Michael said.

Well, naturally he thought it was all about an old man wanting sex. It had been about more. She moved out of his arms. Maybe they needed to have this conversation. It could change his mind about things, and she'd promised to be open and honest with him. "He wanted comfort and companionship, but mostly he wanted someone who was willing to mourn Lara with him."

Even in the low light, she could see his stare. "Lara?"

"His daughter. She was my director on a couple of the last films I did. She was brilliant and talented and had the biggest heart. By that point, George had stepped back and let Junior take over the business. He'd actually separated his personal wealth from the company, but Junior was angry that he was financing her films. He thought it was a waste of money."

"But it wasn't his money."

"In George Jr.'s mind, it's all his." It was precisely why she was in the situation she was in. He wanted every dime his father had. He'd even fought the charities his father had wanted to give to. "He didn't like his sister getting anything. He thought she should have worked for the corporation and been content with that. I even think he would have been okay if she'd been nothing more than a debutant with a credit card. He would have paid for her designer wear until she found a wealthy husband, but he hated that the money was going to a bunch of art house films."

"What happened to her?" Michael asked. "I don't remember reading anything about a daughter."

Her heart ached when she thought about Lara. "She had problems with drugs. She'd struggled with them off and on her whole life, and it caught up with her one day. We were working on her last film and I was staying with her in this little house outside of Paris. I had gone to bed early, but she'd stayed up with some of the crew. I woke up and I found her on the floor. She'd overdosed, and there was nothing to do. She was gone. I had to tell her dad. I'd gotten close to him. I liked him. He was funny and nice, and he actually listened to me. He said he'd learned that the most important thing to do in life was listen to other people."

She was getting teary again thinking about him.

"I'm sure that was devastating for both of you." He moved over to the big leather sofa and sat down. "But liking the man is a long way from marriage."

"Is it?" She sat on the opposite end of the couch. "I was adrift at the time, and he was safe harbor. It didn't matter that he was older. Way older. In some ways, it helped. I trusted him in a way I didn't trust anyone. I'd had some deeply disappointing relationships by then. George was the first man who made me feel good about myself. I don't regret spending the time I did with him. I don't regret it at all, and the last six months were some of the most beautiful of my life."

She'd felt necessary. He'd been diagnosed with an aggressive form of cancer, and he'd chosen not to fight it. He'd wanted to see his favorite places one last time, and she'd gone with him. She'd listened to his stories and soaked in a life well lived.

Then the storm had begun.

"Not even the lawsuit?" Michael asked.

She shook her head. "I didn't think it would be a problem. I knew Junior was angry, but George changed his will. We were married for three years. Legally Junior shouldn't have had a leg to stand on, and I honestly believed he would back down."

"You had to know his son would be upset the estate was left to you."

She bit back a groan of frustration. "But it wasn't. That's the mistake people make. The tabloids make it sound like I was trying to take the whole estate. That's not how the will was written. I was to be given five percent of George's estate plus the house and my personal property. That does not include the businesses or the property owned by the estate outside of the house. It was five percent, Michael. I know five percent of a billion dollars is a lot of money, but Junior wouldn't have missed it."

His brows had come together in obvious surprise. "I thought it was the whole estate."

She shook her head. "Of course not. I would never have agreed to that. I only agreed to the money George insisted on because of what I want to do with it. I've spent years setting up the Lara Benedict Foundation. It will give grants to researchers and groups studying addiction and new ways to help those who suffer from them. There have been a lot of studies showing the way we treat addicts in this country is hurting their survival rate. I want to see if I can make a difference. It's what George wanted me to do. I've spent everything I personally had fighting for the right to do it."

He was quiet for a moment. "That is certainly not the story I've heard. Why don't you tell it?"

"You think I haven't tried? The reporters who would take the situation seriously don't take *me* seriously. And the tabloids have zero interest in painting me as anything but a gold digger trying to take every dime I can."

"You have plans for this foundation? Why didn't he set it up before he died?" Michael asked.

There was a lot they could have done to work around this situation, but she'd wanted the end of George's life to be about joy and not lawyers. She'd spent all those months traveling and visiting with his old friends. Watching him say good-bye. "We should have, though I worry even if we had Junior would have thrown me out of it and quietly shut it down. He hates me."

"Because you married his dad?"

She sighed, weary because even talking about Junior made her tired. "A lot of reasons. He hates being embarrassed. He didn't even go to his sister's funeral. He said she was a junkie and she deserved what she got. He hated his dad for marrying me and embarrassing the family. Of course he really hated me because I wouldn't sleep with him."

"What?" Michael's eyes narrowed.

"Oh, yeah. After George died, he offered to let me have the money if I slept with him. He was lying. He wouldn't have called off the lawsuit for anything, but he gave it a try," she admitted. "He's a man who paid a doctor to lie about his father's mental faculties. He'll do anything. I have to wonder if he didn't send someone to kill me today. It honestly wouldn't shock me."

"I'm sorry that happened to you. I'm sorry I didn't understand what was going on. I'll be honest. I read a couple of the stories, and I thought I was informed." He moved closer to her. "Has he threatened to hurt you before this?"

"The usual legal threats. Nothing physical. He's an asshole, but I wouldn't have thought he would be violent. Especially since he's winning. Unless I can prove the doctor is lying, I'll probably lose on appeal. I won't be able to go further. The only thing he saves by killing me is some legal fees, and he could get into real trouble. If I die, I'm suddenly interesting as a sympathetic figure."

"I'll look into it. I told you about my friend Deke. He's an investigator where I work. He's good at what he does. He's going to try to get those security tapes so we can figure out who the man who attacked you is."

She shook her head. Maybe the police had been right. They'd pointed out that her Chanel bag would likely make her a target, and there had been several muggings in the area. She'd managed to keep two of her expensive bags. The Chanel was five years old, but it was a classic. "You don't have to do that. Michael, I really am broke. Everything I have is going to the appeal."

"I want to help you," he insisted. "Look, if the contract is bothering you, then we can tear it up, and we'll be nothing more than friends. But everything you've told me makes me want to help you more."

She should tell him why she was really here. The instinct to trust him with her secret was right there. He was looking at her with the most earnest expression on his face, and she wanted this man on her side.

There was a chime, and he sighed. "That'll be Deke with your things."

She reached out and touched his hand. "I don't want to tear up the contract. I think I might need The Club now more than ever."

She was surprised that she meant those words, and not merely for her investigation. She was starting to think that working with Michael could be good for her.

His mouth kicked up in a grin, and he brought her hand to his lips in a gallant gesture. "I'm glad."

He stepped away and turned on the lights before disappearing down the hallway.

She heard the door open and Michael murmuring. Then a tall man was walking into the living room carrying her suitcase. A second even bigger man strode in behind him. He was blond and gorgeous, with wide shoulders and a ready smile. He was also carrying…was that five pizza boxes?

"Vanessa, these are my friends. This is Deke Murphy." Michael gestured to the man holding her suitcase before nodding pizza guy's way. "And this walking gut is Brian Ward, but everyone calls him Boomer. He rode along with Deke and helped him get around the reporters."

"I set off a bunch of fireworks that sounded like gunfire." Boomer was a big hulk of a man with the sweetest smile. "They ran."

Deke frowned his way. "We barely got out of there before the cops showed up."

Boomer shrugged one big shoulder. "I know most of the cops. They have decent sandwiches."

Deke's eyes rolled. "They have bologna. Really, you'll eat anything, won't you?"

"Someone made that sandwich, Deke. It would be rude not to eat it," Boomer replied and then nodded Vanessa's way. "I brought you pizza, Movie Lady."

"It looks like you brought everyone pizza." She had to smile because he had such a sweet energy.

"Nah, I just didn't know what you liked," Boomer replied. "So I got one with everything on it and one with veggies only and one with a bunch of meat and one of those Hawaiian ones and a cheese."

He was a sweetheart. "I'll eat anything, too. Thank you so much for picking up my things."

"I got you everything you need for about five days, and I tossed your makeup in there, too. I found your moisturizer and a razor. I don't think Michael has one." Deke glanced Michael's way. "He's got that constant scruff that lets a person know how cool he is."

"I have a razor," Michael insisted.

Michael did have a sexy scruff, but she was impressed that Deke had managed to pack for her. "Thanks for getting my moisturizer." It had been in the bathroom outside of the rest of her makeup. "You seem to have been very thorough. If you brought me more than one bra, I will thank you forever."

Deke set her case down. "Five outfits. Five complete sets of underwear. Breasts deserve clean clothes, too. I have a lot of sisters. I know how to pack for women. There are also two dresses in case you need to go somewhere nice, and I brought all the shoes."

She had shoes and makeup and clothes. She hugged the big guy. "Thank you."

Deke patted her back. "Oh, you're welcome. I was happy to help you out."

"Hey, if, uh, you're not going to eat all the pizza..." Boomer began.

Michael sighed. "I'll get some plates. Unless Boomer's just going to inhale his."

The boys were off, razzing each other, and she followed them into the kitchen. Her appetite was back.

For a lot of things.

* * * *

Michael tipped back his beer as Deke stood in the middle of his living room.

"Allison, Chris, Eddie, Fiona, Inez, Junie, Leon, Lisa, Lindy, Nick, Paul, Ruthie, Sylvester, Toni, and Tom." He took a bow. "And my youngest sister is pregnant again, so player to be named later."

"You did that alphabetically." Vanessa was smiling again, and Michael was surprised at how relieved he was at that. She'd been so down he'd worried he wouldn't be able to pull her out of it.

"I can list all of my nieces and nephews in several different ways." Deke grinned as he sat back down. "Including birth order and troublesome ratings. Having this big a family, at least one of them is going to jail at some point. I would say Ruthie, but she's so smart she'll be able to cover up her crimes. I'm going with Sylvester. He's a dumbass, and why my sister thought naming a kid after a cartoon cat was a good idea, I have no idea."

Deke and Boomer had kept Vanessa laughing all through dinner. They'd obviously brought her out of the dark place she'd been in.

He couldn't blame her. It had been a rough day all around, and he was responsible for most of it. The guilt he felt was probably what fueled his need to find the man who'd tried to hurt her today. It burned in his gut. He was forcing himself to be patient because there was no way Deke didn't know something. He wouldn't have brought out Boomer and pizza if he didn't want to talk to him. He'd nodded Michael's way when he'd walked in, a sure sign that something was up.

But then they'd had dinner and popped the tops on a couple of beers, and Vanessa had relaxed. He'd decided to be patient.

"You're the only boy?" Vanessa asked.

"Yep, and the youngest," Deke agreed. "My mom was

determined to carry on the family name in a traditional way. So five girls, and she swears she would have gone on for as long as her eggs kept up."

"I have a sister," Boomer offered. "She's older than me, too, but she's only got one kid. That's easy for me to remember because he's a Brian, too."

"Does she live nearby?" Vanessa seemed fascinated by his friends.

Deke picked up his bottle. "I'm going to grab another."

Ah, that was his cue. He stood and gathered the empty plates.

"Nah, my parents are still in my hometown. I'm from Seattle. My mom and dad own a restaurant there. It's a little greasy spoon. My sister, though, makes all kinds of fancy food," Boomer was saying. "She opened her own place recently."

They started talking about his sister's restaurant, and Michael was able to slip away.

"How bad was it at her place?"

Deke put his beer bottle in the recycling bin and turned. "It was bad, and her neighbors are pissed off. Boomer overheard some of them talking about kicking her out."

"They're already trying to force her to move," Michael replied. "So you think it would be hard for her to go back?"

"I think it would be a disaster. They won't be able to fix the gate for days," Deke admitted. "I've got someone watching the neighborhood chat board, and they can't get the parts they need right away. Beyond that, the whole group is planning to up the pressure on Vanessa. There's a lot of pearl clutching going on there. I'm surprised. I thought we were over slut shaming."

Oh, not even close. He'd learned that tonight. He couldn't stop thinking about their conversation before dinner. "They seem to love to do it to Vanessa. Have we heard anything about MaeBe?"

"Beyond Kyle acting like he's already married to her and it's the 1800s?" Deke replied. "She's fine. She's already home. Kyle is sleeping on her couch tonight to make sure no one else stabs her. Or asks her to do a job."

He was probably going to have to deal with Kyle again since Vanessa had made it clear she wanted to reach out to MaeBe to check up on the other woman. He would deal with that problem another day.

He had bigger fish to fry. "Were you able to pull a face for me?"

"Sort of. Those cameras aren't the highest quality. If this had happened at Macon's storefront, it would be easy. We did his security. The coffee shop went cheaper. Hutch is working on enhancing what we've got," Deke replied.

"But you did get something?"

Deke nodded. "I think between Hutch's skill and Adam's software we'll be able to get you a name."

Adam Miles worked two floors down from the main McKay-Taggart office. He and Michael's cousin Simon Weston investigated missing persons with their company, Miles-Dean, Weston, and Murdoch. The company had been started years ago by four couples who had previously worked for McKay-Taggart, but it had been Adam Miles's facial recognition software that had revolutionized the industry. If Hutch could get a face, Adam would be able to find a name.

He heard Vanessa's laughter at something Boomer had said.

"Did the dupe work? She got at least a text from someone who knew about the gate," Michael said.

"The text came from someone named Ruby. No last name in the contacts on her phone. I pulled the number," Deke explained. "It's registered to a woman named Sonja Lockwood. She's got two cell phones in her name. She also has a teenaged daughter. I would bet her name is Ruby. They live three doors down from the house Vanessa is staying in. I think she might be her visitor from the other night. I found some of her social media. She's tall. She could have been the one in the hoodie."

So no lover, just a friend. "I'd like a report on her and how she might know Vanessa. Since MaeBe's sidelined for a couple of days, is someone monitoring Vanessa's phone?"

"I'm on it." Deke leaned against the island. "I've read through her email and her texts and reviewed what she's been looking up on her phone. She's interested in Julian."

That made his gut twist. "What has she been looking up?"

"She's done several searches on him, and she's got notes on her phone about things he's said or done. Mostly about The Club. She could be simply curious," Deke said in that way that made Michael think he didn't quite believe the words.

He didn't either. "Or she could be studying him for some reason. I'm going to keep an eye on her for the next few days. I'll watch her while she's not at work."

"And I'll shadow her if she leaves the office. Does Julian have eyes on her while she's there?" Deke asked.

"Yes." He'd made sure that Wolf Meyer would be watching whenever he could, and they were monitoring all of Vanessa's tech.

Had she been lying about her relationship with her husband? She'd seemed so sincere when she talked about the man. The truth was it was hard to think about her with that old guy. He'd been old enough to be her grandfather. He could understand her caring for him, but love?

He would get a copy of that will tomorrow and transcripts of the case. He'd been going off media reports, and that had been a mistake. He certainly couldn't trust the tabloids, but he wasn't sure he could trust her either.

He'd connected with her today, felt for her. Briefly he'd even thought maybe he was wrong about her.

But he wasn't particularly smart when it came to women. Even when he found a good partner, something wasn't right about it.

"I'll get some sleep then," Deke said. "And I'll take Boomer with me so you've got alone time with her. Be careful, brother."

He shook Deke's hand. "I'm being very careful around her."

"No, I think you should be careful with her." Deke placed careful emphasis on the word *with*. "I watched her all day. I watched her when she thought no one was watching. I think she's more fragile than she looks, and I don't think it's an act. I know she's the target, but someone tried to hurt her today."

"And I'll make sure no one tries again." He didn't admit that he was worried Deke was right. Something about Vanessa called to him, but he didn't trust his instincts.

Maybe he simply didn't trust himself.

He would take care of her, but she was a job. That was all she could be to him at this point.

Deke walked out, and Michael grabbed another beer for himself and took the bottle of Pinot Noir he'd opened for Vanessa. She'd sipped her glass as they'd eaten, and Boomer had told stories about babysitting the Taggart kids. That night had ended in blood and tears and more pizza for Boomer.

But it was a good story.

"Did you honestly think the worst thing about that night was a dirty diaper?" Vanessa had the sweetest smile on her face as she sat back after he'd locked the door behind Boomer and Deke fifteen minutes later.

He shuddered because even though that night had been years before, he could sometimes still smell that kid's pants. "It was the worst thing I've ever smelled. Something was wrong with him."

Vanessa sat back, her glass in hand. She looked completely relaxed, and he was glad Deke had brought Boomer. There was something about the big guy that lit up any room he walked into.

"Your friends are nice. I can't believe Boomer ate two whole pizzas. He must work out a lot." She stood and picked up the last of the beer bottles, starting for the kitchen.

He wished she was nothing more than a date. Just a normal woman he was trying to get to know. He would follow her in there and slide in behind her. He would brush her hair off her shoulders, revealing the nape of her neck. He would run his fingers over that part of her spine, caressing the soft skin he found right before he dropped a kiss there.

Of course if they were a couple simply exploring their connection, he wouldn't feel so shitty about how her day had gone.

"It's getting late. Should I go to bed?" Vanessa asked. "Or did you want to talk some more? Are we going to have a training session tomorrow? I'll be honest. I don't want to go into The Club without any training at all. I'd like to know how you expect me to behave."

He looked up at her and made a decision.

He could figure her out for Julian. If she was clean, she didn't have to know he'd ever investigated her at all. Then maybe they could explore the attraction between them. He couldn't deny he wanted her in a way he hadn't in a very long time.

Perhaps if it had just been sex, he could have turned her away, but there was something warm and real about the woman in front of him that drew him in, made him want to try again.

"First, when we're in The Club and we're in the lounge section, talking to friends, you should be sitting on my lap or at my side at all times." He did need to start training. He wanted her comfortable and confident while they were there.

If she was who she said she was, doing nothing wrong, there was no reason they couldn't have a D/s relationship. Maybe that was the only kind of relationship that would work for him. He wasn't going to get the marriage and kids thing. That was obvious, but he could have companionship.

It went through his brain that this wasn't a woman he could take home to his parents and brother, but he brushed that aside. They could keep it to The Club, to a contract, and it might work.

She started to sink to her knees, but he stopped her.

"I would rather you sat on my lap tonight."

She let him guide her down, settling on his lap. "It's been a while since I was this close to anyone. It's nice."

Her head rested on his shoulder.

He liked having her close, too. There was something deeply intimate about holding her now that everyone else was gone. She filled a spot that had been empty for a long time. "It is nice. Tomorrow I'll take you to work and pick you up. Before we come back here, we'll do a walk-through of the dungeon so you can get familiar with the space."

She yawned. "Yes, that sounds good. What should I plan on wearing on Friday? I've got a couple of miniskirts and a bustier."

"I get to pick your fet wear. It's in the contract." He expected her to argue, but she simply cuddled against him.

"All right."

"Your clothes for the night will be in the locker they assign to you," he explained.

"That sounds good."

"No arguing?"

"It's a costume," she replied. "It's theater, right? You need a proper costume to play the role. I'm used to that. I don't know much about it, so I'm letting you lead the way."

"It's not a role you're playing."

She looked at him through thick lashes. "Isn't it? It's not who I would be in the everyday world. We all play roles all day long. We just don't label it that way. Aren't you a slightly different Michael when you're around your friends than you are your family?"

He didn't think about it that way, but she was right. "I suppose."

"We all do it. I call it a role I'm playing. You would call it your work personality or adapting to your surroundings. It's all the same. It's all me, but not the same me. Having the right costume will get me in a good headspace to explore the character."

He wasn't sure he liked her referring to herself as the character. "It's another side to yourself. It's real."

"So is a character," she replied quietly, as though she wasn't sure how honest she wanted to be. "When I act, there's always a piece of myself in the character, some place I explore. That's what I get out of it. I get to figure some small part of myself out. It can make me understand other people more."

"What part of yourself did you find in the horror movies?" From what he could tell those scream queen slasher films were what she was best known for. And being the bombshell in raunch coms. He wasn't sure what she'd learned from those except that her boobs made teenaged boys lose their minds.

She went still, and for a moment he worried she could read his mind. "I learned how afraid I can be. I learned how I can try to tell myself something's okay when it's not. There's this stupid scene in the first movie where one of the guys comes on to my character, and he's very rude and sexist about it. He demeans my character, and she flirts back and acts like it's no big deal. I realized I'd done that a lot in my life. I'd shrugged off something that hurt me because it was easier to pretend it didn't than to fight for myself. I realized I was willing to internalize that pain rather than have everyone think I was a bitch. That's what I got from that role."

He hadn't been expecting that. "Did it change how you behaved?"

"I became more okay with being a bitch," she replied. "At first it was empowering. I stood up for myself, and I got some of the things I wanted. And then I was labeled difficult for the same behavior that was considered confident and forthright in my male colleagues. I started to lose jobs. That was when I worked with female directors. That was a good place for me."

And then her friend had died and she'd been left alone. Was it wrong to pretend? To put herself into a role in order to explore that aspect of her personality? He was fairly certain any therapist would tell him no, that it was healthy and necessary.

He didn't like the idea of her playing a character around him. He wasn't playing a character with her. He was keeping a secret, but that was a necessary thing.

Everything else was the real him. Wasn't it?

"Why do you like being a top?"

Such a simple question, and yet he wanted to avoid it. There was the answer that came right in his head. "Because I like to be in charge during sex. I find it does something for me."

"What do you mean by *something*?"

Yes, there was the reason he hadn't wanted to answer her. He didn't particularly want to look deeper. He could make something up, but he was lying enough to the woman in his arms. He wanted her to know something real about him. "I think I've felt out of control most of my life. I know that sounds weird because I had pretty much anything a person can have, but when I was born my future was laid out. My parents were—are—great. But I felt like I followed my brother all through our childhood."

"He's your twin, right?"

"Yes. He's older than me by a couple of minutes, but my brother is kind of a force of nature. He's a good guy. He really is, but he's a lot like our dad. Larger than life. I was JT's shadow."

"Is that why you went into the military?"

"Yes. I didn't even tell my family until I was leaving for training." How was this tied up in his sexuality? He knew he was talking too much, but there was a thread there. "It was the first time I surprised them. That time in the military was a revelation. I wasn't David Malone's kid. I wasn't JT's brother. I got to be me. When I left and followed a bunch of my friends and my cousin to work at McKay-Taggart, that was when I got into the lifestyle. I suppose in the beginning I did it because I was curious, but I found something there. I found an honesty there. I found a willingness to explore in a fascinating way. I'd never thought of sex as anything but something to do with a girlfriend. I didn't see it as this huge part of myself, but it was and it is."

Maybe he still wasn't through exploring.

"You've had subs before?"

She was full of questions. Questions that made him want to squirm a little. But he'd asked her the questions yesterday, so it felt fair to answer. This process couldn't work if they both weren't open to it. "I've only had one who wore my collar. She took it off when we canceled our engagement."

"You were engaged?"

He didn't want to talk about this, but she deserved an answer. "Yes. We broke it off a little over a year ago, and it was perfectly amicable. I've actually never had a bad breakup. I think that might be my problem. Every relationship I've had has been pleasant but not passionate. I don't know if I'm capable of that level of emotion, but I can be a good Dom."

She sat up, and her hands found the sides of his face as though she needed him to focus on her. "Of course you can. You are. You took such good care of me today. You were a wonderful top, Sir."

Damn, but she was sweet. He knew it was dumb, but those words of praise went straight to his soul. "I'm glad. It felt good to help you. I felt necessary for the first time in a long time."

Not a lie. He had. He'd liked the way she'd clung to him, how she'd looked to him to take care of things.

And that was why he liked D/s. He'd never thought about it. It was sex and fun, but there was a base level to D/s that made him more than a cock and the relationship about more than pleasure.

In a D/s relationship he had a place. There was no question about what he should do or how he should act. It was all written out and discussed. He was necessary in a D/s relationship.

Could he be necessary to this woman?

"I want to kiss you, Vanessa." He'd touched her, brought her to pleasure, but he hadn't kissed her. He wasn't sure he'd ever meant to kiss her. A kiss wasn't required, but suddenly he wanted one. He wanted to put that particular act on the table.

She hesitated for a moment, but he gave it to her. He'd gotten to know her a bit, and she was careful. It would be easy to step back and not allow her to make the decision, to take offense that she hadn't agreed immediately, but that wasn't what she needed. She needed patience and time to decide what she wanted. She needed to understand that if she didn't agree with him, he wouldn't walk away.

"I think I might want that, too. But it's been a long time since I kissed anyone."

"I'll go slow." Anticipation thrummed through him. "You can

stop me whenever you like. And when I'm done, we'll talk some more. There's no sex on the table tonight. I want you to have time to decide if you're willing to connect that way with me."

She was staring at him like she was memorizing his face.

He brought her hand up, shifting his until they were palm to palm, looking each other in the eyes. Connection. That was the word that mattered. He was connecting with her in a way he hadn't ever before. "But you should know that I thought about you all last night. I think you're gorgeous and sexy, and getting to know you better only makes you more lovely to me."

"I thought about you, too. I want to touch you the way you touched me."

Fuck. His cock hardened painfully. "I don't think that's a good idea."

He was on edge after a rough day. He wouldn't last long if she squeezed him in that soft hand of hers.

She bit her bottom lip, and then a challenging look came into those crystal eyes of hers. "Then we should negotiate. You want a kiss, and I want the same chance you had. I want to see if I can make you come."

"There is zero doubt in my mind that you can make me come." And then it hit him. There was doubt in hers. This gorgeous woman sitting on his lap was unsure of herself.

Or she was playing him, but he wasn't sure she was capable of that tonight. She was tired, and the day had been hard on her. What if she wanted to give him something? What if she needed to feel like she was necessary, too?

"I want my kiss first because I'll probably come in your hand and then you're going to think it's gross and then my kiss gets lost."

All of her hesitancy evaporated, and she was the aggressive one now. It was a good thing. He wasn't the kind of top who had to be in control every second of every experience. He'd seen nothing that told him she was anything but submissive during sex. She wanted him, and she felt comfortable enough with him to take it from him.

She wanted to give, but in giving she would take something for herself. She would get a little of her confidence back.

She kissed him, her lips brushing over his, and a wildfire lit in his system.

This was where he'd wanted to be all fucking day. He'd wanted to shut the world out and take it all down to just the two of them. In this moment her past didn't matter. His job didn't matter. All the things that came between them were gone, and all that mattered was this electricity that happened when they focused on each other.

He let her explore for a moment, soft lips rubbing across his as her hands found his shoulders.

The minute he felt the tentative touch of her tongue, he almost lost control. He had to force himself to stay still because his first instinct was to flip her over and get between her legs. He wanted to press her back against the couch and rub his cock against her.

But he'd promised to give her time. He was sure she'd had a hundred guys who got inside her the minute they could. He wanted to be the guy who drew her in, the one she begged for, and not the other way around.

Still, he couldn't resist the call of her. When her tongue breached his lips, he followed her lead and deepened the kiss.

He wrapped his arms around her, bringing them chest to chest. Her breasts crushed against him as she tightened her hold, and the kiss threatened to go incendiary.

He kissed her for the longest time, losing himself in the feel of her body against his. She was so soft, her every curve calling to him, tempting him to go further. Instead he let himself indulge in the simple act of kissing. He gently took the lead, and she followed him with perfect ease. Every rolling caress of her tongue felt right and good, like they'd been doing this forever. They didn't need that awkward time when they figured each other out physically. They simply fit together.

When she moved up, her eyes were lit with satisfaction as though she'd found the kiss every bit as fulfilling as he had. And there was an impish glow to her expression he hadn't seen before.

"Is it my turn, Sir?"

She wanted this. He could see it plainly. She wanted to see if she could affect him the way he had affected her. He liked this playful side of her. It contrasted with the soulful shy side and made him wonder what other parts of Vanessa he hadn't seen yet.

"Ease off my lap. I want you on your knees next to me."

Her smile amped up as she did as he'd asked. She slid that silky goddess body of hers down to the floor, not sparing him a moment. She stayed close, letting him feel her breasts brush against him. She wasn't wearing the concealing cardigans she always seemed to have on. It had been left behind today, and he hoped Deke had remembered to bring her a couple because they were her armor. But now she was in nothing more than her slacks and a thin blouse that gaped open, revealing her skin and the tops of her breasts. They were gorgeous, and he felt ashamed he'd told Tessa they weren't real. She'd been right. It didn't matter where they'd come from. They were beautiful on her. They were a part of her she'd chosen.

"God, you're gorgeous."

Her chest was against his leg, and she looked so right clinging to him. This was how they would look in The Club. A benevolent Dom and his way too stunning for him sub.

"You make me feel that way," she admitted. "I'll be honest, Sir. I've been so tired for the last few years, and you make me feel pretty again, young again. I'm enjoying this time together. I truly am."

He put a hand on her head, smoothing back her hair, her words going straight to his soul. "I've been tired, too. Lonely and fucking tired. I'm glad you're here."

"So what can I do for you, Sir? You were so good yesterday at telling me what you were going to do. I thought you might have some suggestions."

She wanted him to walk her through this? Or rather command her. He could do that. "First I want you to undo the top two buttons on your blouse. I want to look at your breasts while you stroke me."

She brought her hands up, undoing the buttons that left her lacy bra on display. It was a cream color, and he could see her nipples were hard against the cups.

"Unbuckle my belt." He might not survive this experience. "And then unzip my slacks. Be careful. I'm painfully hard."

"I'm so sorry about that, Sir," she said with a smile that let him know she was sorry not sorry.

"That's what happens when a gorgeous woman sits right on top of it." He would have to be careful or he might come the minute she laid a hand on him.

She eased the belt out of its buckle, and he went still as she unbuttoned his slacks and brought the zipper down. His cock strained at the material of his boxers. It was easy for Vanessa to draw the waistband down and free it.

She stared for a moment, and he watched as her eyes widened and she looked like she could eat him up.

How long had it really been for her? She didn't have a lover here if everything he'd heard was true. The mysterious visitor from the previous night hadn't turned out to be a boyfriend. Did she need physical affection as much as he did?

Then he wasn't thinking at all because her hand encircled him, and he forgot to breathe.

She stroked him, drawing him out and exposing his cock to the cool air. It was a stunning contrast. Cool air and warm hand. Her head was down, studying him. He joined her, watching how her hand moved up and down on his cock.

"That feels so good." He practically groaned around the words. "Tighter. Grip me a little tighter."

She followed his instructions, closing her fist slightly.

He wanted to tell her to open those lips of hers and take him inside, but they weren't there yet. He could imagine watching her head bent over, tongue whirling around and around his cock.

She would suck him deep, and he wouldn't hold back. He would come right in her mouth, and she would swallow him down.

The very image made his worst fears come true, and he held on to the cushions of the couch as he came.

She was grinning when she looked back up at him.

He winced. "Yeah, I told you that would happen. Damn, that did not make a great argument for you going further with me. You're going to call me Minute Malone."

That smile of hers lit up the night. "Never, Sir."

She offered him her lips, and he took them, kissing her again.

"Now let's clean up, and maybe we can watch a movie before we go to bed," he said, not wanting the moment to be over.

She fell asleep in his arms half an hour later, and Michael was left to consider the fact that the woman was a mystery.

And he had to solve her. No matter what.

Chapter Eight

Vanessa stepped inside the locker room and heard the door whish closed behind. It had been a heavy door, ornate and traditional looking, so there had to be some technical magic to keep it from closing with a *thunk*. But then the world seemed to reorder itself to Julian Lodge's whims. Everything about The Club appeared perfect, from the red carpet that didn't show a single stain to the way the lights seemed to make the world a little softer here.

So why did she feel like she'd been locked in a cage and she might not be let out?

She wished Michael was here with her. She might not feel so alone if Michael was here.

Or Dani. The way they'd planned this first evening, Dani should have been here in the locker room waiting to show her around. Instead she was meeting Tessa, who had been described as a long-time submissive. She was David Hawthorne's fiancée. They'd met briefly, but she didn't know the woman well.

She'd actually noticed that Michael had an invitation to their wedding that he hadn't responded to. It was sitting on the table in the entryway where Michael put his wallet and keys when he walked in. He took most of the mail to his desk, but that invite was still sitting there. She probably shouldn't have opened it, but she'd been curious about the pretty invitation.

Three days in to practically living with the man and she found herself falling into all of his traps. She'd woken up that first day and realized he'd carried her to the guest bedroom and tucked her in, and the sweetness of the gesture had pierced through her. So much so that she'd held herself back the rest of the week. She'd agreed that she couldn't go home, but she also couldn't play house with him.

So she went to work during the day, and she'd had her first session with the therapist. It turned out it was kind of nice to be able to talk to someone who had no judgments to make. Then she came home with Michael, and they trained in the evening, with him teaching her the ins and outs of how to behave in a club, teaching her form and the practicalities, but there had been no more soulful kisses or deep talks. He'd made sure she was familiar with the types of play she might see and the various "toys" used in scenes, but they hadn't tried them out. She could sense his frustration, but she wasn't ready for how he made her feel when they were truly in synch.

Like everything was right with the world. Like she could breathe again.

"I do not understand how you walk in those shoes." A pretty woman in tiny shorts and a sheer T-shirt that barely covered her breasts was walking down the hallway. She was petite and barefoot.

Her friend was not. Her friend wore five-inch stilettos that Vanessa would bet had some slick red soles. The woman wore a miniskirt and blinged-out corset, her shiny dark hair curling over her shoulders. "I have to or I only come to Wolf's chest. Leo's the tiniest bit shorter. I should have picked smaller men if I didn't want to be in heels for the rest of my life."

Shelley Meyer. She hadn't met the woman, but she had met one of her husbands. Leo was The Club's resident therapist.

"I've even stopped putting my heroines in heels. I'm a kinder, gentler author. Seriously, though, I can't do it. I don't know why, but having four kids has ruined my arches," the other woman said. She had to be Lexi O'Malley. Dani talked about the woman a lot. She was a romance author, and a lot of Dani's employees read her.

Shelley shrugged. "I have a kid. I can be a mom and fashionable. If having more than one means I only wear flats, then we're done.

They'll take my Louboutins out of my cold, dead hands."

Lexi's nose wrinkled. "But having a bunch can be fun. I mean when they're not causing me to have a heart attack."

"I might try for one more, but she better be a girl. I've seen what boys can do when they're in a pack," Shelley said with a chuckle. She seemed to realize they weren't alone. "Oh, hi. You must be the new girl." She grimaced a little. "Sorry. It's weird because this should be the part where I introduce myself and then you do, but I already know your name and stuff."

Vanessa held out a hand. "And I think I know yours. Shelley? And Lexi?"

Shelley shook her hand, but Lexi was studying her.

"You're shockingly normal," Lexi said, reaching out a hand.

Vanessa shook it. "Expected me to have a couple of heads?"

Lexi's lips curled up. "And a backpack so you can shove the money you steal into it. Maybe a couple of knives to backstab with."

Shelley gasped.

But Vanessa knew a joke when she heard one. There was something about the other woman's eyes that told her she wasn't accusing. "I am knife free for now. I used my last one. I need another sugar daddy so I can buy more."

Shelley's eyes had gone wide. "I'm so sorry. She didn't mean anything. She wasn't trying to be rude. She doesn't understand."

Lexi raised a brow and looked her friend's way. "Are you serious? You do know that my mom suffered through a whole lot of that crap. She got run out of town over gossip and rumors. I know a lot about it, too. I live in Deer Run, Texas, and I'm married to two men who kiss each other in public."

"And yet you also seem shockingly normal." She understood what Lexi was doing and agreed wholeheartedly. "Slut?"

Lexi chuckled. "Slut. Skank. All of the above." She sobered. "I thought it was best to get it out in the open. I know who you are and what they say about you. I won't talk behind your back, and I won't consider anything the press says to be true. They're writing stories, and you make a good character."

"Yeah, I'm the villain." She was owning that these days.

"Oh, but I happen to know that it's all about POV. Sometimes the villains are the best characters of all," Lexi said. "If you need anything, even a friend to talk to, let me know. Are you a hugger?"

She was already half in love with this woman. No one—no one—simply said the truth, acknowledged what she was going through in a forthright way. They smiled and talked behind their hands. They pretended the elephant wasn't there. Or they were rude and asked her to leave.

She opened her arms and hugged the other woman, blinking back tears.

"Welcome to The Club, Vanessa," Lexi whispered. "You get to be whoever you want to be here. Don't forget it. And if anybody gives you trouble, I'll sic my boys on them."

She stepped back. "Thank you."

Shelley leaned closer to Lexi. "Do you mean Aidan and Lucas or your mob of chaos and destruction?"

Lexi winked Vanessa's way and then started for the door. "Definitely the boys. Lucas doesn't fight so much anymore, and his face is too pretty to risk. And don't count my daughter out. Daphne can be mean when she wants to be."

She watched as they walked out of the locker room.

"Vanessa." A stunning woman with dark hair and a brilliant smile strode up to her. She was dressed in a miniskirt and a white corset that set off her tan skin and toned arms. Tessa Santiago worked at the same company Michael did.

The same company as Kyle Hawthorne, her soon-to-be brother-in-law.

That little fact brought Vanessa back to reality. She'd floated along for days, thinking of nothing but Michael Malone and how it felt to be in his arms. She was reminded that she had a job to do, and it didn't matter that she so wanted to make friends. "Hello. Thanks for coming in early to show me around. I'm sorry. Dani was supposed to do it, but she got held up."

Tessa nodded. "Yeah. I heard her youngest caught a bug, and she had to pick him up from school."

"And now Finn's down, too." She'd talked to Dani earlier, and it sounded like the stomach bug was going to make its way through the whole Lodge-Taylor household. Well, with the exception of Julian. She doubted a stomach bug would ever dare to attack him. "I offered to cancel tonight and help her out, but she insisted."

"I talked to her, too. She said something about you meeting with a big client, and she didn't want you to look like death warmed over." Tessa shook her head. "All of this makes me happy David and I are taking some time before we discuss the whole kids thing. The good news is my mother-in-law still has teenagers at home, so she's not pushing. Now my mom, on the other hand, is a totally different story. You know how moms are."

Mean. Cold. Unwavering.

You're such a disappointment. I don't care how much money you made. I'm ashamed to be your mother.

Vanessa forced a smile. "Sure. Anyway, thanks again. Michael said someone had already stocked my locker. He bought me some fet wear."

Though he hadn't shown it to her. He'd said he wanted it to be a surprise.

Tessa turned and started down the hall. "Of course. Michael has some very specific likes when it comes to fet wear. I think you'll find all of the tops do. Nothing too crazy, but it could take some time to get used to a corset."

"Oh, I've worn plenty. I did a couple of historicals. Spent at least a year of my life in one of those suckers." She wasn't going to mention the raunch com she'd done where she'd played an actual hooker who had to save a bunch of idiot bachelor party guys from the mob. Although it had been a funny film. But she'd learned people respected her more when she talked about the two period pieces she'd done.

"Oh, yeah. You were in that movie about life as one of Anne Boleyn's ladies-in-waiting. David loved it, though you should know he can point out all the historical inaccuracies," Tessa said as she walked along. "I wouldn't mention the *Robin Hood* thing you did."

"It wasn't meant to be historically accurate. It was supposed to be fun," she replied. Maybe the history professor would prefer the raunch com.

"Yeah, history is a serious thing for my guy. He started in on a lecture when they brought out the repeating arrow guns," Tessa explained. "I thought they were cool, but apparently they aren't even a thing today. This is where all the ladies get ready. I think you'll find it's got pretty much everything you could want in here. There are showers in the back and vanities with all kinds of dryers and flat and curling irons. You'll find your own locker stocked with things you requested."

"That's easy. I didn't request anything. I brought some makeup with me and my brush." She could use whatever soap they had in the showers. She'd run into a drugstore and replaced some of what she'd left behind when she'd been forced to stay at Michael's. Deke had done a great job, but he'd still forgotten some things she needed.

Tessa stopped at a tall locker, holding a small silver key in her hand. "Here you go. I think you'll find Michael ensured you have some special products."

She nearly winced because she wasn't sure what that meant. Lube? Some weird sexual things she would have to wear?

She opened the door and nearly sighed because what Michael had left for her was deeply sensual, but it wasn't some sexual aid. There was a tray of some of the world's most expensive, indulgent skin care and makeup. Chanel and La Mer and Lancôme. Products she hadn't come close to in the last year. She brushed her fingers over them, even the containers bringing her a comfort she hadn't realized she'd missed.

"I think Dani helped him out with those," Tessa said quietly. "But I know he wanted you to have a treat. There's a shower caddy with some amazing shampoo and conditioner. I'm a little jealous."

"I'll share," she said quickly. She should turn it down, but it would only make him feel bad. He'd tried to buy her some things she'd been missing, but she'd insisted on getting them on her own. She'd made the deal to accept his gifts while they were here in The Club. Outside of it, she had to be Vanessa. Outside The Club she had to deal with reality, but here she could play the part of Michael's sub, and it was obvious her training Dom wanted to take care of his pet.

Wasn't that a nice thing to be? She'd loved their training sessions. He always started by talking about what he wanted to go over, answering her every question, and ended with a long hug that she sank into. She knew every night that the hug was Michael's way of offering her affection and the ability to go further if she wanted to. All she would have to do is tilt her chin up and Michael would press their lips together.

She'd kept her head down and gone to her own bedroom.

"That's so sweet of you. I might take you up on that La Mer. I've wanted to try some, but I shouldn't get addicted. My fiancé is serious about his crappy paying career, and throwing your body in front of bullets doesn't pay as much as you would think it does," Tessa said with a smile.

It was a good opening. "You're a bodyguard? I know you work at McKay-Taggart like Michael, but not in the same department, right?"

"Not at all. We're not even on the same floor. He's been there for a long time and is considered one of the top guys." Tessa sat down on the long bench. The locker room was quiet, but Vanessa could hear one of the showers running and low talk from the other rooms. "I don't have much to do with his unit. I'm down in the man cave with the other bodyguards. The big boss is awesome but also kind of a dick. He calls us the full douche. He says that's what a group of bodyguards is called. Like a pack of dogs or a murder of crows. I'm pretty sure he made that up."

She couldn't help but chuckle. "He sounds like a colorful guy."

"Oh, he is. Trust me. I thought long and hard about the fact that he's kind of my fiancé's uncle."

"Kind of?"

"David's mom is Grace Taggart," Tessa explained. "She's married to Ian's brother, Sean."

"The chef? I've never heard of Ian, but I totally know Sean Taggart. The Viking chef." She loved cooking shows. "I saw him on *Top Chef Masters*."

"That is my soon-to-be stepfather-in-law. I don't know. It gets weird with all the step stuff, but the Taggarts don't need blood to claim you as family. They're also super nosy, even though they seem like they wouldn't be. Ian looks like he should be an assassin in some Nordic mafia, but deep inside he's a grandma who wants all his kids married and happy."

Michael had told her his boss was an odd man. But she wanted to know more about another Taggart relation. "Your fiancé is Kyle's brother, right?"

Tessa's head dropped back, and she groaned. "Yes, and he's never leaving my house. I was almost happy when his girlfriend got…" She brought her head up, face flushing slightly. "She's not really his girlfriend. She's a girl who's a friend and she was in an accident the other day. Anyway, he's been hanging out at her apartment, which means he's not at our place. He's been home for eight months, and he still hasn't found his own place. I think he likes the cat. I know it's not the food because David can't cook, and I don't."

Eight months? She did some quick math. It still worked though. Barely. "Where was he before?"

"The Navy," Tessa replied. "He was in for almost a decade. According to David, the family thought he would go the full twenty. Not at first. The way I've heard it, he had some problems to work through, and the Navy offered him some discipline."

Oh, she would love to know what those problems were. Had he been violent and the Navy had refined his rage? Taught him how to cover his tendencies? How to stalk his prey? Nicki had written that the man was new at The Club. They would have overlapped by roughly four months. That was more than long enough for a man to get obsessed. "Is it weird to play in the same club as your brother-in-law?"

"Nah." Tessa waved off the thought. "Kyle honestly doesn't play a lot. He works mostly now."

"Now?"

"Well, I don't know a lot about it because Kyle isn't a big talker, but I've heard he played a lot in the beginning, and then he met a woman, and well, he's a weirdo who doesn't admit when he's mad crazy about a woman. She doesn't play here. He got to know her a couple of months ago, and he doesn't show a lot of interest in any of the subs here now."

She had to be careful about how she questioned Tessa. The last thing she needed was her mentioning to her almost brother-in-law how interested she was in him. But she needed to start figuring out a few things. Maybe a little lie could help open up the conversation a bit. "My sister mentioned him a couple of times."

Tessa's face went grave. "Nicki? I knew her. She was a nice lady. I was so sorry when she passed."

"She liked it here." She thought Tessa was sincere. She'd liked Nicki, though Vanessa would bet they hadn't been close. "I'm sorry, but she never mentioned you. Not that we talked all that much. She was distracted the last few months of her life. Were you friends?"

"We were friendly, but I wouldn't call us friends. We met a couple of times at work-related events. Up until I met David I played at Sanctum. David and Kyle play here because their mom still goes to Sanctum."

She could see how that would be…unsettling. "That makes sense then. Nicki played here for years. I don't remember her having a specific top though. Like I said, she mentioned Kyle a couple of times."

"Oh, they probably played. I would have to ask him, but I'm pretty sure he played around a lot." She frowned suddenly. "You know that doesn't necessarily mean sex, right? From what I understand, Nicki was what we would call a club sub. She didn't have a permanent top. She liked to play around. Okay, that sounds bad, too."

Vanessa held up a hand. She knew this much. "She enjoyed D/s activities. It doesn't mean she had sex with every man who topped her."

Something about the way Tessa's eyes widened slightly let Vanessa know her sister had blown way past vanilla.

"Or woman," Vanessa corrected with a smile. "She didn't talk about that, but it doesn't bother me. I'm glad my sister was happy here."

"I know she played with some of the married tops. Again, not in any sexual way, but they all found what they needed," Tessa offered. "I hope you find that, too."

The sentiment was sweet, but Vanessa doubted she would find anything beyond who killed her sister. And she would start with Kyle Hawthorne. Still, she knew how to play this game. She smiled. "Me, too. In a couple of months, I'll be out of training and on my own."

Tessa paused. "You don't like Michael?"

She liked him far too much. She kind of thought he was perfect. "I didn't say that. He's a great guy. He's going to be a magnificent Dom for someone."

"But not you?" Tessa stared at her as though trying to figure her out.

Normally she would hedge on a question like that, but she'd recently had that magnificent interaction with Lexi O'Malley, and it made her want to be honest. "I…I like him a lot, but I'm not the kind of girl who would be welcome in his family. Not that he would ever want to bring me home with him. We're not a couple like that. We're good training partners, that's all."

"I've found that good training partners often leads to a good D/s relationship," Tessa offered.

"That's all it could ever be, though. I'm not looking for that. I'm honestly not looking for anything at all. I'm good on my own. I think I'll be like my sister. If I like this kind of thing, I'll be a club sub. I'll play around." She wouldn't. She was rapidly coming to the conclusion that she liked the lifestyle, liked the idea of spending hours devoted to giving and receiving physical affection, but she was pretty sure it was about the man, too.

She was worried it might be all about the man.

Julian hadn't understood, but he'd fucked her over by pairing her with Michael. She felt guilt at lying to him, worry that she was screwing up something that could be good for her.

But how could it? She hadn't lied to Tessa. He would never be able to take her home to his family. She would always be his dirty secret, and she couldn't live that way. She knew that beyond a shadow of a doubt.

Lately, though, she'd started to wonder if it actually was dirty. If they could have a relationship and it would simply be private.

She brushed the idea away because it couldn't work. He would want a woman he could show to the world, take to his family.

"Well, I'm sure that's what Julian is hoping for. We have more single tops than we do subs. A well-meaning sub tends to get swept up pretty fast around here." Tessa said the words in an even tone, but there was something about her expression that made Vanessa feel like the other woman was almost disappointed in her answer.

She wasn't sure why she would be. And she certainly couldn't tell Tessa that she wouldn't be here for long, and she wasn't what Julian would call a well-meaning sub. She was lying to everyone and starting to wonder if it would even work.

"It was why everyone loved your sister so much. They all got to really know her," Tessa continued. "She helped out everyone. Like I said, I'm not sure, but she probably helped out Kyle. He was kind of fucked up after he came home. Not in a scary way. He's just very intense."

Yes, that was the way Nicki described the man she referred to as MK. Intense. She'd claimed he'd watched her with burning eyes, that she could feel him watching her always.

"Nicki was intense in her own way." She needed to work her way into a friendship with the Hawthorne clan. It would be far easier to decide if Kyle was the one her sister had talked about if she spent some time with him.

She could do it, could play the friend. Or more likely she would end up liking Tessa and feeling for her and her family.

She steeled herself because the truth of the matter was she had no family. Neither had Nicki. They'd only had each other, and in so many ways they'd failed each other in real life. They'd let things that didn't matter come between them, allowed themselves to believe they had the luxury of time to make it right. She was the only one who could bring her sister any justice now.

"I know everyone around here adored her," Tessa said with a fond smile. She stood up. "Let's get you dressed and ready to go. I know David was planning on sticking pretty close to Michael tonight. Julian asked us to show you around."

Was Julian being kind? Or did he worry she might see something she shouldn't? "I appreciate it. And thanks for the help. I know enough about corsets to know I can't get myself into one."

She pulled out the stunning blue corset. It was sleek and would accentuate her every curve. It would also contrast beautifully with her eyes. Every costumer she'd ever worked with loved her in blue. It appeared Michael did, too.

She liked yellow. A sunny, happy color that made her feel vibrant. She never wore it now because it also attracted the eye. She preferred dark colors, or rather she wore them because she could hide more easily. She would never choose this peacock blue even though it would look good on her. Looking good was no longer her goal.

But this was all one big act, and she shouldn't forget it.

She should forget how good it felt to be close to him, how safe she was when he was around, how things seemed possible when Michael held her hand.

If she chose him she was being everything her mother had accused her of, everything the world labeled her. Selfish. Narcissistic. Uncaring.

Tessa started to loosen the laces of the corset, and Vanessa went to work on her clothes. She didn't even think about the fact that she was getting naked in a locker room. She'd done it hundreds of times.

Her mind was on the night ahead. She had to focus on the mission. But maybe the smart play would be to simply take it all in, to pretend to be what she was supposed to be—a curious sub with a gorgeous, indulgent Dom.

If she got a chance to ask questions, she would, but she needed to be careful.

Tessa continued to chat, but all Vanessa could think about was Michael and the fact that their time was running out.

* * * *

Michael stood in the hallway that connected the men's locker room with the women's and waited for Vanessa to walk out.

He had a meeting later tonight. Deke was coming up to The Club to talk to him about something, but after the play session was over.

He got to play with her tonight. *Play* was a silly word for what he wanted to do with that woman.

"Everything going okay?" David Hawthorne leaned against the wall, obviously waiting for Tessa, who would be coming out with Vanessa.

"Besides the hiccup with Dani? Yeah, it's okay. It probably works out better this way. I'd like Tessa's take on her."

"I don't know if you will. She's not happy about this particular assignment." David kept his voice down, his eyes on the door across the hall. "Not that she won't do her best, but if it was up to her she would be direct with the woman."

Tessa was almost always direct. It was why she was a bodyguard and not an operative, why she'd been a soldier and not a spy. But he wasn't going to point that out to David. "She's made it clear how she feels, but this is my job, and I have to do it my way. I genuinely believe I'm conducting this investigation in the way I feel best serves my client and Vanessa. I know it seems harsh, but she's the one who wanted a training Dom. She'll get the training she wants, and if she's innocent, she never has to know Julian doubted her. Once I've ascertained what she's doing here, if she's clean, she'll discover

Julian is a good boss. Once he can trust her, Julian will likely be incredibly generous."

"So she has to be above reproach," David mused. "Like Caesar's wife."

Michael raised a brow. "Sorry, Professor. I studied business in school."

And then he'd studied the fine art of espionage. He was not well versed in Roman emperors' wives.

"Her name was Pompeia. Caesar divorced her because she wasn't quite above suspicion," David explained.

He managed to not roll his eyes because David obviously didn't read the tabloids. "It's a totally different scenario. Vanessa has a reputation for doing exactly what Julian is afraid of. Whether it was earned or not," Michael pointed out. "I'm not trying to hurt her. I know this side of the business can seem harsh. What Tessa normally does is much simpler."

"And what you do can be necessary." David looked utterly changed in leathers. Normally the man wore khaki slacks and button-downs, the occasional tweed jacket thrown in as though to prove the stereotype. But he looked like a Dom in a leather vest, pants, and boots. "Sorry. I can put my nose in where it doesn't belong at times. Like I said, Tessa will do her job. You'll have more trouble with my brother. He's not happy that MaeBe's still talking to Vanessa. She called yesterday to check up on her, and they talked for a long time."

Michael nodded. "Yes, I heard about the conversation."

MaeBe had written up a report. It had been a glowing, cheery thing that talked mostly about how awesome Vanessa was, and she didn't seem at all like the type of woman who was trying to play an angle. But she had gotten one good piece of information. Vanessa had talked about him, and she'd mentioned that his family was a drawback. MaeBe had gotten her talking in a way he couldn't. MaeBe was one of those women whose kind soul drew people in.

Kyle had also filed a report. It contained all sorts of threats if MaeBe wasn't allowed to recuperate in peace.

Ian had made a quick phone call to MaeBe, who'd talked about how cool it was to be a spy, and then he'd promptly deleted Kyle's report.

"MaeBe wants to do the job."

David sighed. "I know. Kyle is fucking up with her, and when it all goes to hell, I don't know how he'll handle it. He's obviously in love with her but he can't admit it. I think he's afraid."

"Afraid of loving her?"

"Afraid of losing her. Afraid of being the reason why she gets hurt," David murmured. "I don't know. My brother talks to me about a lot of things, but not his past, and I think that's what's holding him back."

Kyle's past was a mystery everyone was curious about. "His time in the Navy?"

"Yes, and I know everyone suspects he did some work for the CIA. I do, too, but he won't admit it. I also think there was a woman, but again, he won't talk about it, won't even acknowledge she exists. Or existed." David straightened up. "Hell, sometimes I think about hiring a firm to investigate my brother."

"That's not a good idea." Kyle was a potential powder keg. "Look, I know you're worried about him, but if he thinks you're getting into his business, you could lose him. He'll talk when he's ready to talk. All you can do until then is let him know you're there. I should know. I was Kyle at one point. Not for the same reasons, but I pretty much ran away from my family for a while. I needed that time. Kyle needs this time. Despite his irrational relationship with MaeBe, he's good at his job."

"I worry about him."

"I understand. And my brother worried about me. He was patient, and that's probably why we have a great relationship now." He felt for David. He knew what it meant to be worried about a brother. He also knew what it meant to be the one who had everyone worried. "We all watch out for Kyle."

"Thanks. I appreciate it," David said. "I'm glad we can talk, Michael. You're a good guy."

Michael had to smile a little. "Yeah. Tess and I had the world's most amicable breakup. I doubt you would get the same treatment. She would come after you and hard."

David's lips curled up. "I would go after her, too. That woman isn't getting away from me. Ahh, there she is."

The door opened, and he suddenly wasn't thinking about David or Kyle or MaeBe at all.

His whole world was Vanessa.

He knew somewhere in the back of his mind that she wasn't alone, but every bit of his focus was on her and how fucking gorgeous she was.

He prayed he wasn't actually drooling.

She wore exactly what he'd left for her. He'd selected the corset and boy shorts, and he'd thought she would look great in them, but she eclipsed his wildest dreams.

His most erotic dreams. This was the woman who commanded the silver screen, who had millions of men dreaming of getting their hands on her.

Long legs that led to hips he could hold on to while he fucked her. A waist that flowed in, making the sexiest hourglass. The corset caressed her and showcased her breasts and all that creamy skin. The blue of the corset almost perfectly matched those eyes of hers. Caribbean blue. Clear and true. He sometimes found himself getting lost in those eyes.

"So she looks pretty good, huh?" a familiar voice asked. Tessa's tone was tinged with a wry humor.

"You look great, too, baby," a deeper voice replied.

He'd forgotten David Hawthorne was waiting beside him. He'd definitely forgotten Tessa would be coming out with Vanessa. He'd forgotten everything but Vanessa.

He heard Tessa chuckle and noticed out of the corner of his eye that David had taken her hand and drawn her in.

And he still couldn't take his eyes off Vanessa.

He should say something or he would seem like a weirdo who stared at her like she was a work of art and not a living, breathing woman. "You look stunning, sweetheart."

They'd agreed when they were playing that he could use affectionate names with her. He'd taken advantage of it, calling her *sweetheart* and *baby* when they were training. He had to remind himself not to when they weren't. Since that first night she'd stayed with him, she'd pulled back, placing a careful distance between them that he found deeply frustrating.

They'd been close that night when she'd wrapped her hand around his cock and stroked him to the most pleasure he'd had in years. She'd fallen asleep on his lap, and he'd thought they'd made a real breakthrough.

But she'd been back to her skittish self the next morning, and the only time he could get her to truly relax was during training. She seemed to sink into the role, and only then could she allow herself to be open to him.

He had her all night, and he meant to make some serious progress with her. He'd studied her for days, and he thought he might know how to get to her.

"Thank you. The colors are good on me, Sir." She said the words evenly, but there was a sweet flush on her cheeks.

"Can you turn around for me? I'd like to see how the shorts fit."

Her lips curled up. "They don't, and I think that was the point."

Saucy, but he allowed it because she turned and showed him how perfectly the shorts fit her luscious backside. Her cheeks peeked out from under the hem, and they were tight enough that he could see the whole outline of the round globes of her ass. "They're perfect, and so are you."

She turned again, and there was a light in her eyes that had been missing for days.

It might be the time and the place to push her again.

He moved into her space. As he'd requested, she'd left her hair down. He took advantage of it by sliding his hand across the back of her neck and sinking his fingers into all that silk. He tugged her head back and stared down into those kick-him-in-the-gut eyes of hers. "Tell me I can kiss you while we're here. Tell me I can touch you when I want to."

It was a request, and he'd gone over this with her during their training sessions. He would command, and she could shut him down if she chose. The command was all part of the play. It was something he'd done a thousand times, but commanding Vanessa did something to him. It had him growling, some primal urge making his dick twitch.

"Yes, Sir. I think in this club it's all right. In this club, I can be your submissive."

Not out of it, though. It would have to do for now. It wasn't like he was going to turn her down. He'd had days of thinking about kissing her again, getting his hands on her. He'd had restless nights of imagining she was in bed with him, of the sighs she would give him when he'd tired her out.

He dragged her against him and didn't pretend to be a gentleman. That was what he was known as. A gentlemanly top. He was always polite and rarely possessive.

He wanted to possess her.

He fused their mouths together, his free arm wrapping around her waist and dragging her against his chest. Her mouth opened, allowing him in, and he took the territory like the invader he was. His tongue dominated hers, rubbing and tasting and exploring. He didn't care that they had an audience and that the audience included his ex-fiancée and her new fiancé. He wasn't thinking about them or anything at all. All that mattered was Vanessa was soft and submissive in his arms. She was giving him everything he'd dreamed of all week.

He could do this whole mission without fucking her. She'd made it plain she was all right with a simple training relationship, but he wasn't going to do it. He was going to have her. He was getting in this woman's bed, and he didn't care how he had to do it.

She'd told him he could touch her, so he did what he'd been dying to do. He let his hand run down her back and onto her ass, cupping one cheek.

Her chest rubbed against his, her pelvis, too, as though she was seeking out his heat.

"Are they going to do it here? I thought we were at least supposed to wait until we got to the dungeon."

Vanessa pulled back, and Michael thought seriously about punching the newcomer, but then lots of people wanted to punch Kyle. His own brother mentioned it a lot.

Vanessa's mouth was slightly open, her face flushed pink from arousal and now likely some modicum of embarrassment. "I'm sorry. I got carried away."

Tessa was staring at him like he had grown an extra head. "Yes, I can see that. Master Michael looks like he's going to be a passionate top."

He felt his face drop, but Tessa smiled at him. It was the little half smile she gave him when something came up about their relationship, the one that let him know it was okay, that they were better friends than lovers, and that was perfectly fine with her.

"I think that's a wonderful thing to be," she said quietly.

"I'm glad to hear that, baby." David took his fiancée's hand and dragged her close. "I think the professor is having office hours this evening. I hope you did your homework."

Tessa gasped and bit her bottom lip. "Oh, Professor, I forgot all about it. How can I make up the grade? I don't want to fail."

Michael threaded his fingers through Vanessa's. He didn't like not having a hand on her. Like he was afraid she would get away if he didn't keep her close. She moved readily into his space, leaning against him.

Kyle made a barfing sound. "Now they'll do that all night long. I walked into the house the other day, and she was wearing pigtails and a school uniform. It's gross."

Tessa laughed, but David fixed his brother with a stare that might freeze fire. "You're free to move out at any time."

Kyle frowned. "But I just got settled in. And I'm used to the cat."

Tessa's eyes rolled, but the smile on her face told Michael how happy she was. "Brothers. They're the same everywhere. Let me know if you need anything, Vanessa. I think the Master will probably take care of you, though. See you later."

Kyle and David were still bickering as they walked toward the dungeon.

Vanessa dropped his hand. "That was his brother? David's brother?"

She was staring as the Hawthornes walked down the hall.

"Yes. His name is Kyle. I work with him. Tessa, too." He wasn't about to mention that he'd done far more than work with Tessa once. It didn't matter. He didn't have those feelings for her anymore. He was starting to think he'd never had strong feelings for the woman he'd asked to marry him. They'd been together for over a year, and he'd never felt the feelings he had for Vanessa.

It was primal attraction. She was gorgeous and a challenge. That was all. The tenderness he felt for her was just the Dom in him. She needed protection, and he was a sucker for that.

She stared at Kyle.

Kyle, who was younger than him. Kyle, who had that dangerous predator thing women found hot down.

Jealousy curled through him, but then she was smiling as though she hadn't been watching the other man like she couldn't take her eyes off him.

"What shall we do first, Sir?" She grinned up at him, the intense expression so completely gone that he almost wondered if it had been there at all.

He was being ridiculous. There was nothing to be jealous of. They weren't a couple. They were training partners who were going to have sex. That was all it would be. He didn't need to feel this crazy thirst for her. It would be gone once he'd had her. He would be good to her in bed, and if he found out she was doing something that might incur Julian's wrath, he would deal with it. He would handle the problem for her and set her on the proper path. Hell, if she needed money, she could have some of his.

He'd been going about this all wrong. He didn't have to be the bad guy. He could be the guy who helped her out and shielded her from the storm Julian could bring into her life.

Yeah, that was what he would do. He didn't need to be jealous at all. He needed to get her in bed and then he would be able to think straight.

"Let's start by watching some scenes, and then I'd like to introduce you to some impact play." He'd planned the evening carefully. It would end exactly how he hoped.

With him getting what he wanted. And setting himself up to help her out.

Then he could move on with a clear conscience. At least that was what he told himself.

Chapter Nine

Vanessa watched as the big Dom used a paddle on his submissive. Wolf Meyer was a huge man, his body corded with muscles. Like many of the members of The Club, he was a man with an obviously open mind since he wasn't the only Dom topping this particular sub. His brother, Leo, was also married to Shelley, she'd been told. At first she'd been worried about Shelley Meyer. She was so small compared to her two husbands. The first scene they'd watched had been between two men, and it had been sexy and beautiful. Then they'd moved to the main stage, and she'd gotten a little antsy when Shelley had taken the stage and sank to her knees before those two gorgeous men. All she could see was size and the disparity of physical strength between them.

But it was blatantly obvious that Shelley could handle her men. She'd stopped her husband in the middle of the scene because he wasn't going "hard enough," as she'd put it.

Then he'd gone super hard, and Shelley had grinned the whole time. Until her other husband had declared she was bratty and decided her mouth needed something to occupy it, and that something had been his very large penis.

She was watching sex. Watching it right in front of her, and it was doing something for her. It wasn't that she'd never watched porn. She had, and it could be arousing, but nothing like seeing the real and deep connection between a woman and the two men who loved her.

"Are you okay?"

Michael stood right beside her, as he'd been all night long. He'd kept a hand on her, either tangled with her own or wrapped around her hip as they'd watched the scenes and talked to the other couples.

Other couples. She was starting to think of them as a couple. It was probably because except for sleeping together, they'd been behaving like one for days. She'd woken up that first morning at his place and made breakfast and coffee. He'd driven her to work and picked her up, and then they had dinner together and trained.

She liked it far too much.

"I'm fine, Sir."

He tugged on her hand, easing her out of the crowd. All around them scenes were going on in the public portions of the very private club. The Meyers were on the main stage, but there were others. A pretty woman with light brown hair was being tortured in a medical scene to Vanessa's left. Tortured was the right word, though she was certain the woman liked what was happening to her. She was begging and pleading, and not for the man with the violet wand to stop.

All around her people were happily exploring and indulging. They didn't hide their bodies or their pleasure.

This was what Michael meant by taking sex seriously. It wasn't some grim analyzation. It was a celebration of what their bodies could do, what they'd been made to do. Give and receive pleasure. She'd been taught her body wasn't her own. Her mother had taught her it should belong to some amorphous religious figure who'd created pleasure but withheld it from all but a few. Hollywood had taught her that her body belonged to the world, to be worshipped and denigrated at the public's whim.

George had taught her that her body could be a comfort, could be used to express affection and find solace.

What if Michael could teach her that her body was an instrument that could play the sweetest of songs?

"I don't like that word," Michael said when he'd gotten them free of the crowd. "Fine. It tells me you're not fine."

How did she ask for what she wanted? She didn't even know she had the right to ask, but she didn't want to live the rest of her life not knowing what it felt like to be dominated by this man.

She'd had sex before. For the right reasons. For the wrong reasons. She wanted to have sex simply because it felt good to connect with another human being, because she cared about him, and he cared about her.

She cared way too much about him. It would be smarter to keep her distance, but she was tired of sitting up at night knowing he was one room over, and all it would take was a little bravery to be in his arms.

"I'm sorry, Sir. Fine is one of those words I use when I'm not sure how to express what I'm feeling. I suppose I think it's polite, but the truth is everyone knows fine means not fine. It's passive aggressive."

She expected him to start a stern lecture, but his face softened, and he stared down at her.

"Why are you not fine, sweetheart?" His hand reached up to brush his thumb over her cheek. "Do you find the scenes upsetting?"

She was so tired of holding back with him. She'd recently decided that she'd been playing a role in her real life—the wounded heroine. She'd gone into a shell, and only now did she see how much that shell had held her back. She didn't feel the pain the way she used to—but there was no joy here either. She'd been grieving for so long, and she wanted the tiniest bit of sunshine in her life.

It might be selfish, but it wasn't like Michael was madly in love with her. And he'd made it clear he wouldn't mind having a physical relationship during this training period. He'd explained to her that many tops and subs played around while they were training. It was practically expected that they do so.

"The scene did make me uncomfortable."

He immediately backed off, his hands coming to his sides. "All right. We should talk about that. Come with me. I have a private room reserved for us." He started to turn but seemed to think better of it. "Unless you would be more comfortable in the lounge. Or leaving the club altogether. We could have a late dinner and talk in a public place."

He was so careful with her. It made it too easy to forget why she was here. She'd watched Kyle Hawthorne for a while, but he'd been working, walking the dungeon and monitoring the place with a careful eye. She'd tried to listen in, hoping to hear any gossip, but she'd gotten caught up in the scenes.

It wouldn't hurt to indulge for one night. She knew she was on a slippery slope, but she couldn't stop herself from sliding.

"The privacy room is fine, Sir. I'm not afraid of you, if that's what you're worried about." Fear was the last thing she felt for him. Hunger. Tenderness. Hope. Those were all in there, but no fear past the recognition that she would inevitably get her heart broken when he had to walk away from her.

Her whole body felt antsy. As she walked behind him, she could feel the air brushing her skin, the way her nipples rubbed against the inside of the corset. He'd left her feet bare, and she could feel the hard wood against the soles. Everything he'd chosen for her seemed selected to force awareness of her body. The slightly too-tight boy shorts had ridden up, and she could feel the silky fabric sliding against her as she walked.

She watched him as he moved ahead of her, one hand in hers, guiding her through the crowd. He was so big and gorgeous it sometimes hurt to look at him. He wasn't movie-star gorgeous. She'd worked with some of the most beautiful men in the world, but they didn't hold a candle to Michael. There was something about the man that spoke of safety. He was a protector. She'd seen it in how he treated all the women around him.

She was safe with him. She could explore with him, and he wouldn't sell her out to some tabloid, wouldn't show up on the cover of a magazine to talk about his wild night with Vanessa Hale.

He liked Vanessa Jones.

Kyle Hawthorne stood at the desk at the beginning of a hallway. The low illumination and red sheen from the dungeon cast the man in eerie shadows. He was attractive, but there was something dark and dangerous about him that couldn't be denied.

Had her sister given in to the temptation he offered only to realize he was more dangerous than he seemed? Or had she known from the start to stay away, and that was what had set him off?

"Kyle." Michael held out his free hand. "I reserved a room."

Or maybe the man was completely innocent. He wasn't the only top whose name started with a K. There was also a Kevin and a Kirk, according to what Ruby had been able to find. Probably more, since she'd only been able to see who was on the work schedule list.

Kyle shook his hand and nodded toward the hallway. "Of course, Michael. I stocked it myself. Welcome to The Club. Let me know if you need anything, and I hope we can talk sometime later. Perhaps I can give you a guided tour of the facilities."

"I think I know where everything is, but thank you."

"Oh, there are some tricks to things around here," Kyle insisted. "And The Club always gives McKay-Taggart guys shit. I'll be sure to find you later."

Kyle held Michael's hand for what she would consider one second too many, but then he seemed like a kind of intense guy.

"Of course," Michael said and then pulled away.

"You're in room three." Kyle turned her way, and that darkness seemed to flee for a moment. He grinned. "Hi, Ms. Jones. It's a pleasure to have you here. Please let me know if you need anything at all."

So he could turn on the charm when he wanted to. When he smiled like that there was a boyish look about him that made her want to smile, too. "Thank you so much, Master Kyle. I appreciate the warm welcome I've been given. Your brother and Tessa have been lovely."

"I'm glad to hear it. I hope you'll be here on a night when I'm not working," Kyle said. "I would love to buy you a drink and ask you twelve million questions about working with Jason Fray. I love all his films."

"Sure," she offered, a little viciousness bubbling up. She didn't lie about this stuff anymore. "I can tell you a lot of stories about what a massive dick he is. Good director. Hates anyone who questions him, especially women."

Kyle's smile dimmed. "Yeah, I had heard that. Maybe we can talk about what it's like to work with appliances that turn into robots."

It sucked, but she would do it. She would talk to him and get a feel for what his relationship had been with her sister. "I'll take you up on that."

"I'm sure we'll find some time later." Michael's hand tightened slightly around her own, and then he started down the hall.

She followed, grateful she wasn't in heels because he had a long stride, and the plush carpet under her feet would have been hard to jog on. He was suddenly tense, and she wondered if he was angry she'd disrupted his plan. He'd wanted to watch some more scenes before they came back here.

He closed the door after she'd made it inside, and then she was alone with him.

He turned on her, his jaw tight. "Have you changed your mind? We can go to the lounge. I think Kyle's shift ends at midnight."

"Why would I do that?" She stared at him for a moment. She'd never seen him this way. He was always calm.

"You've been loo…" He stopped and took a long breath.

Surprise rushed through her. "Are you jealous?"

His eyes closed, and he seemed to take control of himself. "Viciously, and I'm not used to the emotion. I'm not this guy."

He seemed so sincere, so confused, and she couldn't help but move toward him, reaching out. "I'm not interested in him. I liked Tessa and David. He's David's brother. I was being polite."

"You were watching him earlier."

He was obviously paying close attention to her. "I was curious. I still am. I read in my sister's diary that she'd spent some time with him."

Michael frowned. "I didn't know that. You found her diary?"

She nodded, feeling a flush steal across her skin. "She kept a pretty detailed journal. I found it and wanted to feel close to her. We weren't for a lot of years. That was starting to change. So yes, I read it. I wasn't trying to come on to Kyle."

He let out a long sigh, and his head dropped down, bringing his forehead to rest against hers. "I'm sorry I was jealous. He's younger than me."

Her Dom was feeling his age? She could fix that. "He's not hotter than you, Sir. He's not the one who makes me want to close the door and see what all this play is about."

He stilled. "You said you were uncomfortable."

"Horniness makes me uncomfortable. I think we should negotiate." Wasn't that what she should say? They had a contract, and it allowed for sex, but he'd taken it off the table.

She wanted it back on.

His head came up, and he straightened, looming over her, and his eyes had heated. "Are you asking for what I think you're asking?"

"Probably." She thought he'd figured it out since she was standing very close to him, and either his dick was engaged or he suddenly had something hard in his leathers.

His hand came up, sliding over her neck and burying itself in her hair. It was a move he used regularly, and it never failed to send a bolt of desire through her. He tugged on her hair. "Say it, Vanessa. Say you want sex."

"I want you." She wasn't going to hide. She didn't merely want sex. She wanted sex with him. "I know it's probably a mistake because you're being so nice to let me have a place to stay. I'm working on finding an apartment. Dani says she might have something for me."

"Dani needs to stay out of it." He got in close. "I don't want you to leave. Stay with me until the training period is over."

"That's weeks, Michael." She couldn't stay that long. If she stayed, she wouldn't want to leave.

"Only a couple. You can keep your room. It's your space, but that doesn't mean you can't crawl into bed with me. Let me take care of you for a few weeks, Vanessa. Let me be your Dom. I'll help you find a place that's secure, and I'll help you move in. We can start looking tomorrow."

It was everything she needed, and in that moment she didn't care that it wasn't smart to say yes. She didn't care that giving in to him would make the ache worse later. At least she would have had the joy. "All right. I'll stay with you. I'll let you help me."

He brushed his lips over hers. "And we'll play as often as we can."

He nearly kissed the breath from her body. "Yes, Sir."

"Then let's begin," he whispered against her lips.

She let everything else fall away. She was ready.

* * * *

His dick was definitely ready.

He'd almost lost it when she'd turned that gorgeous smile Kyle's way. He'd been able to see her with the other man. They would make a beautiful couple. He knew Kyle was hung up on MaeBe, but it didn't matter because what man could ever turn down the goddess Vanessa was?

All night long he'd been dealing with this feeling in his gut. The one that reminded him he wouldn't be her top forever if he couldn't figure out how to keep her. The one that had him thinking about how to do his job and keep the woman for at least a couple of weeks. A month, perhaps. That had to be long enough to get her out of his system.

"Find your position." He forced himself to back away. He wanted nothing more than to throw her down on the bed in the middle of the room, but he had to stay in control. He needed to show her how good this could be between them.

If the sex was mind-blowingly good, perhaps she would stay even if she found out all the shit he'd done to her.

Vanessa stepped back, and there was a charming awkwardness to her as she sank to her knees, slowly splaying them wide.

He was going to see her naked. He was going to see every inch of her gorgeous skin.

She turned her hands over, palms up, resting on the tops of her thighs, and she looked up. "Like this, right?"

She was sheer perfection, and the hint of nerves in her tone did nothing to detract from it. "Yes, that's exactly what I want."

He moved in, planting his boots about a half a foot from where her knees were. "What did you like about the scenes we watched?"

His close proximity to her forced her to bring her head up in order to look at him. Her chin tipped back, and he could see the graceful line of her throat. "I liked how connected they seemed. Don't get me wrong, I liked watching them play, but I loved how they seemed to flow together, how the Dom seemed to know what the sub needed."

"We watched scenes with long-time couples and trios. They didn't start out that way. They had to talk and explore and be honest about what works for them and what doesn't."

"It's a journey. That's what I've figured out," she replied, staring up at him. "It's not something to fumble through and hope it happens. We have to work on it."

Practice made perfect. Practice would build that connection she was talking about. Practice would bind them together. "I agree. We've waded into the pool. It's time to start swimming. You have to talk to me. To be honest with me. You can't think about hurting my feelings. If something isn't right, we need to adjust."

She nodded. "All right. I'll tell you if I don't like something. You want to please me, and I want to please you, and that's how it works."

Good. She understood. It only worked if they understood what was at the core of the mission. Pleasing each other. "I want to spank you. I want to try some impact play and see how you enjoy it, but before that I need you to do something for me. I'm so hard, I can't think straight. How do you feel about putting your mouth on me?"

He was ready for her to say no and then he would either go to the bathroom and rub one out, or if she wanted to watch, he could do it here. He just knew he couldn't breathe, much less give her what she needed without some relief.

Her lips curled up. "It's been a while, Sir, but I enjoy giving a blow job."

His cock tightened to the point of pain, but he merely groaned. "What do you like about it?"

One shoulder shrugged slightly. "With the right person, it makes me feel powerful."

He liked that answer. Sex could be about far more than mere pleasure. But there was a dark side to it as well. "And with the wrong one?"

She stared at him with clear eyes. "It can make me feel cheap."

He put a hand on her hair, her honesty going straight to his soul. "That is the last thing I want for you. I think you're the most gorgeous woman I've ever seen, and I will worship you. That's what the session after will be about. Me worshipping and appreciating your body. I'm glad you're here with me, Vanessa."

Her eyes suddenly shone in the low light. "I'm glad to be here with you, Sir."

He let go of all the worries of the night. All that mattered was being here with her. He would deal with everything else later. He would concentrate on her now. He let his hands fall to his side, ready to allow her to take care of him. "Untie my leathers."

He felt her anticipation as she brought her hands up and started to work the ties of his leathers with her manicured fingers. She bit that plump bottom lip of hers and let the sides fall away. He wore no underwear, wouldn't ever in a club. His cock was thick and hard, standing upright as she reached for it and took it in her soft palm.

Fuck. He wasn't going to last long. He hadn't lasted long the other day when she'd stroked him to release. How the hell would he hold out when she put that mouth on him?

He steeled himself as she began to stroke his cock. Her palm was soft around him, but she firmed up her grip gradually.

"I like this, Sir. I enjoy focusing on you."

"What makes you feel powerful?" He knew the answer, but he wanted to get her used to talking about sex, to being open about how she liked to please a lover and how it made her feel.

She leaned forward, and her tongue came out, a long, luscious swipe over his cockhead.

He groaned, his breath catching.

"That makes me feel powerful, Sir." She winked up at him, a playful expression that he hadn't seen from her before. "Watching how you respond to me. Knowing I'm the one who's bringing you this pleasure, and you trust me to do it. Trust is important to me."

She always seemed so serious, but he was starting to break down her walls, starting to see the impish side of Vanessa. In the beginning he'd seen exactly what the world had told him to see, but now he understood how complex this woman was. She had so many more sides for him to explore, but he couldn't think about that right now. All he could think of was the fact that she was laying soft kisses all along his cock.

She was going to kill him. He clenched his jaw, watching her as she played with his cock. He wanted to tell her to get on with it, that he couldn't stand the soft touches, the gentle kisses. He needed her to get serious.

But he couldn't. She was enjoying herself, and that made him happy. He would let her play until he dropped over the edge.

This was what he'd been missing since she'd started staying with him. He liked spending time with her, but they needed this intimacy. He didn't want to be her roommate. He didn't want to be the guy investigating her. He wanted to be her Dom.

They had time. She'd agreed to stay with him, and he had to believe he could convince her not to sleep in her own bed. He wanted to get this first release out of the way so he could do exactly what he'd promised—worship her. Fuck her with his fingers and tongue and cock after he'd initiated her into some impact play.

He watched and bit back a groan as she suckled his cockhead, drawing him behind her lips. Pure fire licked along his skin as she began to work his cock. She teased him with light passes before opening her mouth wide and going deep.

His eyes nearly rolled to the back of his head, the pleasure was so great. It kept building and building with every pass.

He couldn't hold back a second longer. He had to touch her. His hands found her hair, sinking his fingers in and twisting lightly.

Her eyes had come up, staring at him as she continued to suck his cock. She was watching him, wanting to see how she affected him.

"You feel so fucking good, sweetheart." He gave her all the praise she deserved. "Do you have any idea how long it's been since I wanted anything the way I want you?"

She didn't speak, couldn't because she didn't stop her work, but there was a light in her eyes that let him know he said what she needed to hear.

She worked him, one hand coming up to play with his balls. Fuck, that nearly undid him. He wanted the orgasm that was one or two passes away, but he also didn't want her to stop. She was right. There was a connection between them like nothing he'd felt before. He could sense it in a way he never had. Now he realized that he'd always focused on the technical aspects of a scene and not this crazy, wild emotion that ran through him.

He let it sink in. He didn't fight it. He felt for this woman. He had no idea how they would make it work. There were tons of obstacles facing them, but he didn't want to think about those right now.

Then he couldn't think of anything but the way pleasure exploded through his body. She drew him in deep, soft heat surrounding his cock, and she sucked hard, forcing him over the edge.

He pumped into her mouth, trying to draw out the moment, but he couldn't last forever, and a sweet languor pulsed through him as she drank down the last of his orgasm. She licked his cock clean and then sat back, a satisfied smile on her face.

A woman who knew she was powerful in that moment.

He took a long breath and then tucked himself back in. He wasn't finished with her, would get inside her again this evening.

But now it was her turn.

He felt a fierce smile cross his face. "Strip for me, and then we'll begin."

Chapter Ten

She could still taste him. She licked her lips and was surprised she didn't feel the usual letdown that came over her when she realized she'd done something spontaneous. This was normally the time when her insecurities would wash over her, but they didn't now.

Because it hadn't been spontaneous at all. Because they'd been on a road since the moment they met, and they hadn't truly played around. They'd talked about sex and what they wanted. He wasn't some douchebag she'd met who wanted to fuck her simply to say he had. He wasn't looking for fast sex.

He liked her. She liked him. They would be kind to each other.

He leaned over and took her chin in his hand, tilting her head up and brushing his lips over hers. "Thank you, sweetheart. I've been dying for that for days and days. Now let me help you out of that corset because the other thing I've been dying to do is see you naked."

"I can send you to several streaming services for that." She wasn't sure why that popped out of her mouth. She hadn't been this jokey about her past in years. Her past seemed like a millstone around her neck, but she was starting to understand it was okay to find that part of herself again with him.

He moved his hand down, taking hers and letting her balance

against him as she stood. When she was solidly on her feet, he brought her hand to his lips. "It's not the same, and you know it. I don't want to see some character. I want to see you. I want Vanessa Jones. Vanessa Hale is gorgeous and talented, but Vanessa Jones is the woman I want to know, and she's definitely the woman I want to see naked."

And that was why she didn't need the worry and shame that always threatened. It didn't have a place with this man because he was safe. He was honest with her so she could trust him, and that made it easy to indulge herself.

She turned and allowed him access to the laces of her corset. Big hands covered her shoulders, sending a bolt of heat through her. He moved in behind her, letting her feel how small her body was against his.

"Remember that you can stop me at any time. We're exploring. I'd like to get you on that spanking bench and have some fun figuring out what you like and what you don't. Can we play that way, sweetheart?"

She loved how he always asked her what she wanted. "I would like that, Sir. I'll tell you if I'm uncomfortable with something, but I want to give it all a try. And can we both understand that unless we choose to change our minds, this session can end with you inside me?"

One arm wrapped around her waist, pulling her against him, and she could feel the heat of his breath against her ear. "There is nothing I want more. You won't regret trusting me. I'm going to take care of you. No matter what happens, remember that."

She believed him, and it made her let go of all of her inhibitions. She wanted him to see her, wanted to be naked in front of this man. Definitely wanted to wrap herself around him and revel in everything he could give her. "I will."

If he thought she was worried he wouldn't be good in bed, he was out of his mind. Even if he didn't last as long as he needed to, she rather thought he was the kind of man who would find another way to take care of her. He would be a generous lover. She would bet her life on it.

He stepped back and started in on her laces. In moments she was free of the corset. He'd moved away and she turned, allowing him to see her breasts before she eased off the boy shorts and stood in front of him naked.

"Damn, you're gorgeous."

She felt that way with his eyes warm on her. She had a lot of body issues. She'd gained weight since her acting days. The camera really did add pounds, so she'd been underweight to try to look perfect. She'd been praised for how she'd looked then. She was healthier now, and the tabloids called her fat.

But she felt sexy standing here with him. She felt good in her skin.

"One day we're going to do a scene, and you're going to be naked for me in front of everyone here in The Club," he promised. "I'll show them all how gorgeous my sub is."

She would have told him that she wouldn't ever be naked in public again, but it was all right here. This was one of the reasons her sister had felt free in The Club. No one would judge her. They were all on the same journey. "I'll be happy to scene with you."

It might be the only way she ever performed again. Private performances where she knew the audience would be warm and inviting. Where she knew her partner would take care of her.

"I want you on the bench. Do you remember how to place yourself on it?" Michael asked.

She was a quick learner. The bench he had at his place was slightly different, but she could do it. She eased down, allowing her breasts to rest on either side. The end of the bench was slightly elevated, putting her ass in the air and her pussy on display.

She breathed in, trying to take in the moment. This was different than the practice.

"How are you feeling?"

She could see his boots. "I'm fine, Sir. I feel vulnerable, but there's something sexy about it."

She'd thought the bench was weird in the beginning, but now she got how being physically vulnerable could be sexy. It wouldn't with another man, but with Michael, a certain thrill went through her because he could do whatever he wanted with her. He could tie her up and force himself back into her mouth. He could shove his cock into her pussy or thrust himself into her ass.

He could do anything. It made her heart race, and she could smell her own arousal.

His boots moved, and then she felt a big hand on her back. Warmth suffused her as he started to stroke down her skin.

He moved slowly, and she felt the anticipation building.

Where would he touch her? How would it feel? She wasn't thinking about how she looked or what he was thinking. She was wholly focused on her body and this moment.

It was perfect.

She breathed in as he cupped her cheeks. The way the spanking bench was built it kept her legs open, tilting her ass up and giving him access to her pussy. He continued his long, slow exploration of her skin, skimming over her pussy and making her groan with anticipation.

But he moved on to her legs and then her feet, where he surprised her by tickling her.

She nearly came off the bench.

A sharp crack split the air, and she gasped at the shock of pain that slammed on her skin.

"No moving, sweetheart," he said with a chuckle. "I don't want to have to tie you down. I want to be able to move you quickly and easily when the time comes."

When the time came to fuck her. There was a comfy-looking bed across the room. He wanted to be able to pick her up and throw her on the bed when he was ready to fuck.

She went still because she wanted that, too.

The pain had morphed quickly into heat.

Michael rubbed a hand over where he'd spanked her. "Your skin is pretty. I think it will be even prettier when it's hot and pink."

He smacked her cheek again, and she let out a squeal.

"That's what I like to hear." He said it on the sexiest sigh. He spanked her again. "I love this. I love how you tense and release. I love how it feels to put my hands on you. But let's see what you like. We'll start with my hand and move on to some more interesting toys."

She held on to the bench as he took her on a tour.

He spanked her with his hands first. Thirty slaps that he peppered across her ass and thighs. Some were soft, and others made her bite back a cry. Every single one of them sank into her skin and seemed to transform from something she barely noticed to something she felt at the center of her being.

After he spanked her with his hand, he moved over to the closet. She watched in the mirror as he pulled out the leather bag he'd brought with him. At some point one of the monitors must have placed it up here.

The Club was full service. A one-stop luxury sex shop. He turned, and she had to catch her breath. No man had ever been as sexy as Michael Malone in a set of leathers. He was so big and broad and masculine.

He set the kit down out of her line of sight. That, she'd figured out, was all a part of the game. He didn't want her to know what was coming for her. He wanted her on edge, wondering what he would do to her next.

She liked it. She thought she wouldn't, thought that uncertainty was the last thing she would want, but there was a thrill that came with not knowing what came next.

Something soft brushed over her. It started at the nape of her neck and slowly worked its way down her spine, making her shiver and sigh. She looked at the mirror that dominated the wall across from her and liked the picture she saw. A sub being worshipped by her Dom. They were erotic partners.

She was starting to think they were just flat-out good partners in everything.

There was a big white feather in his hand, brushing over the skin he'd spanked.

"That feels good." She let her eyes close so she could focus on the light strokes over her skin.

"The pain enhances the pleasure," he murmured. "Though I don't think it was all that painful."

"It wasn't. I liked the spanking, Sir. I liked that it hurt at first and then it felt good."

"I'm not the Dom who would spank you as punishment," Michael explained. "This is all play between us. Any relationship we have outside of sex, we're going to have to sit down and talk about."

"How about we agree that we'll try to take each other into consideration when we make decisions that can affect us both." She liked the fact that he was talking about them having a relationship outside of sex. She wasn't sure how it would work, but she was starting to think she could maybe try with him.

He drew the feather along the seam of her ass, and she bit her bottom lip. He'd sensitized her so much with the spanking that she could truly feel the lightness of the feather, how it brushed over her softly.

He tickled down her legs, and that sadist rubbed it gently over her feet, which made her jump and whimper.

"Oh, baby. I told you to be still. I guess we're done with the feather," he said in a silky tone.

She gritted her teeth because she didn't think he would simply put the feather aside.

Something hard smacked her ass, sending her body jumping.

"This is a paddle. I have several, and we'll get around to using them all when you're a naughty sub."

"I thought you didn't do punishment." She knew what his answer would be, but she enjoyed this part of the game, too. Nothing he'd done actually caused her any damage. Even the hard smacks that had her groaning and biting back a cry did something for her.

She liked it. Getting spanked by Michael aroused her in a way she'd never been before.

He brought the paddle down on her ass. "This isn't punishment. This is something you'll feel all day tomorrow and remember everything I did to you. This is something you'll beg me to do again and again because you'll know exactly where it leads to."

"Where does it lead, Sir?"

His hand moved on the back of her thigh, stroking up to her core. She held her breath as his fingers skimmed over her pussy. She was wet. There was no denying that her pussy was soaking wet and desperate for attention.

"You know exactly where it leads." He gently stroked her, his fingers playing in the arousal he found there.

Her fingers curled around the bench, holding on because she got the feeling if she moved against his hand he would go back to the not-punishment thing, and they might have to start over. This was why the rat-fink gorgeous bastard had requested the blow job. So he could torture her and not have his cock go completely insane. The way her pussy was right now.

She wanted to shove back and force him to fuck her with his

fingers. She would take anything in that moment. His hands, his mouth, his cock. She so wanted his cock. But honestly, if he let her hump his leg, she would do it.

He had her panting after him. Somewhere in the back of her head a warning signal was going off, but she ignored it totally. She didn't need a warning with Michael. For the first time in years she was going to follow her instincts, and every one of them told her this was the guy. The right man.

"You're being exceptionally good, sweetheart." His deep voice was like another hand stroking over her flesh.

She held on as he moved back and forth between hard smacks and soft touches. She didn't move at all, not wanting to give him any reason to start this torture all over again.

She wanted him. She wanted sex, and that felt good. For most of her life sex had been something to either get through or a way to attain the physical affection she craved. She'd had some good sex, but she'd never gone near crazy with pure desire. That was the place Michael was driving her toward. She would go insane if he didn't take her soon.

She gritted her teeth, determined to take whatever he was willing to give her. To take the torture because she firmly believed this man would reward her for her effort. He wouldn't leave her wanting.

A big finger teased inside her, taunting and tempting her to take more, but she wasn't going to do it. She was going to be Michael's good submissive this first time around. Later on they could play and explore and test some boundaries, but tonight was about showing him everything she'd learned over the course of their week together.

"Fuck, you're so tight, baby. Do you have any idea how good it's going to feel to get inside you?" He stretched her, adding another big finger while his thumb skimmed over her clitoris, forcing her to clamp down hard on the arms to keep from coming off the bench.

"I think it's going to feel like I'm impaled on a monster cock, Sir." She could talk dirty. This was a role she could sink in to and have fun with because it was all a part of her personality. She'd just never been able to be so free with a man before.

That earned her a stronger stroke, and she could feel how close she was to the edge. It wouldn't take much at all to send her right over.

"Monster cock? I'll take that as a compliment. But I think you'll find you can handle me with ease. You were born to take me. But I'm going to be honest, even though you did a marvelous job taking the edge off, I'm still not sure I'll be able to last as long as I'd like, so I think I'll have to make sure you get what you need first."

His hand was suddenly gone, but she didn't have time to mourn it because he hauled her up like she didn't weigh a thing. One minute she was on the bench and the next she was in his arms, and he was stalking toward the bed. She got the briefest glimpse of his face—tight jaw, fierce look in his eyes. He was a hungry Master, and she got the feeling she was about to be made a meal of.

He tossed her on the bed, and she felt the soft comforter on her back right before he took her ankles in hand and dragged her to the edge. She didn't fight him, let him spread her legs wide.

He dropped to his knees, holding her legs open.

Instead of the arms of the bench, she fisted that comforter as she felt the heat of his mouth on her most sensitive flesh. This time he didn't tease or torment. He simply put his mouth on her and feasted.

He fucked her with his tongue, and his thumb found her clit. He pressed and rotated, and she couldn't hold back a second longer.

Pleasure flowed through her, and it felt like all the tension in the world released in that second.

"I need you. I need you so fucking much." He was on his feet again, his mouth still glistening with her arousal.

He pulled something out of his pocket. Condom. Thank god he was thinking straight because she wouldn't have stopped him. She was too far gone to think about protection. All that mattered was being with him.

He tore at the ties of his leathers, shoving them down. She watched as he rolled the condom on, big hand stroking that cock of his. She'd loved having it in her hands, in her mouth. She'd loved having that power over him, and now she loved being in his power.

He stroked himself one more time before he stepped between her legs, and she could feel that big dick poised at her pussy. "This means something to me, Vanessa."

Her heart threatened to melt. She wasn't capable of holding out on him a second longer. "It means something to me, too. I care about you."

"I care about you, too. Don't forget that." He dragged her leg up, hooking it around his waist as he held her opposite hip and started to push inside.

Fuck, he was big, but the stretch felt good. She brought her other leg up, wrapping them both around his lean waist as he worked his way inside her.

He stared down, holding himself still against her. "We're together for now. We don't go backward."

She didn't want to. "I want to be with you for as long as I can."

"For a long time. We'll make it work." Before she could reply, he dragged his cock out and then slammed back home.

Then she couldn't think of anything to say because her whole being was focused on the feel of him, his heat and muscle and that cock pounding inside her. He was gorgeous as he worked over her, shifting his hips until he hit the spot inside her that had her panting.

She didn't think she would be able to come again so soon, but Michael proved her wrong. His jaw had tightened, hips moving faster, and it sent her careening into pleasure again.

Michael's body tightened above hers, and he pumped into her before falling on the bed beside her. His arms came out, resettling them on the bed, holding her close.

She liked this too. It was unexpected, this tenderness. She lay there, listening to the sound of him breathing in and out as her heartbeat ticked down.

"As far as scenes go, that one was spectacular," he whispered, and she saw his lips curl into a grin. "I think we've proven ourselves more than compatible."

She put a hand on his chest. "I would say so, Sir."

He was quiet for a moment. "I'm glad you're staying with me."

"Me, too." She cuddled close and knew time was running out. She would give herself a few more days and then she would have to tell him what she was really doing.

And she prayed he could forgive her.

* * * *

"What do you mean someone was at her house last night? The same person from before? That girl?" Michael sought his memory as he stood in the men's locker room at The Club. It was a refined space with none of the modern amenities of Sanctum. There was no massive TV dominating the wall and a bunch of ridiculous loungers where the guys would sit and watch sports. The lockers and showers were decadent, but Michael missed the easiness of Sanctum.

What he truly missed was being in that quiet room with Vanessa. He should have stayed there, should have ignored Deke's texts. Normally he wouldn't carry his cell on the dungeon floor, but he was working so he'd silenced it. Next time he would trash the fucker and spend all night with her.

Deke sat on the bench that separated the lockers. He was dressed in jeans and a T-shirt, his sunglasses poking out of the pocket of his shirt. "Ruby?"

Michael nodded. He would give Deke a long talking to if this was about the high school kid who liked to spend time away from her own house. He had a file on Ruby Lockwood, and she certainly wasn't a threat to anyone except perhaps Vanessa's refrigerator. Deke had put together the file himself and learned that Ruby had spent a lot of time with Vanessa's sister and after she'd died, she'd transferred that affection to Vanessa. It seemed like a relationship the kid needed, and he liked the fact that Vanessa gave her some time.

"No. It was definitely not Ruby," Deke replied. "This guy was much bigger, and he obviously didn't know where Vanessa keeps the spare key."

"She keeps a fucking spare key?" He would have such a long talk with her. He hadn't spanked her nearly enough if she was hiding an extra key in the flower bed or some shit. It was a good thing she was going to be safe at his place.

Deke waved a hand. "It's a figure of speech, man. Chill. She's not careless, but I'm pretty sure Ruby can get into the house, and this guy had to break in. I pulled it off the security cameras. The sister had several, but Vanessa didn't have them turned on. I suspect she didn't have the money to have them monitored so she didn't bother with them, and she obviously didn't understand that McKay-Taggart built and monitored that system."

He hadn't known that either. "Why didn't we turn it on at the beginning?"

"I think this is a case of the company growing too big. I didn't think to look in our records, and the guys who run that team weren't exactly given her name. Also, it wasn't under Nicki's name. It was paid for by Dani's company. It was only installed a few months before she died," Deke explained, handing him a folder. "I figured out the house had a system when I was watching Vanessa, but I wasn't sure if we could turn it on, and then she moved in with you. Anyway, I ran by her place the day after she was attacked and took another look. I went in as a realtor and I found the system. It's custom done. Lots of small cameras on the inside. I mean lots. It's kind of weird. There are only three outside. It's like Nicki Jones was way more concerned with what happened inside the house than anyone getting in."

That was odd, but not unheard of. He opened the folder and looked through the original work order. It was fairly routine. Cameras on both doors and the garage. Cameras in every room. He didn't feel like he needed a camera in his bedroom or bathroom, but apparently Nicki had gone for coverage. He glanced at the date. Eight months before. It had been turned off after she died at Danielle's request.

Dani had been the executor of Nicki's will, not Vanessa. Dani had been her emergency contact on every form. It wasn't a surprise that she had handled the security system. "So you turned it back on?"

Deke nodded. "I turned it on the day after Vanessa left. I was curious, and I wanted to see if Ruby came back. I'm starting to suspect she might be our hacker. Like I said, whoever broke in last night definitely wasn't the girl. I've sent you a copy of what the cam caught, but this guy's a pro. He came in from the back around three a.m. Jumped the fence and then cut the glass on the back door."

"I thought she had an alarm."

Deke stared at him like the answer should be obvious. "I didn't turn that back on. Dani would get a notice if the alarm was suddenly monitored again, and I was told not to make her suspicious. I could turn the cameras on and send them to my phone without anyone but Hutch picking up on it."

Michael closed the folder. He wasn't thinking because that answer should have been clear. But then his brain was still foggy. All he wanted to do was cuddle up with Vanessa, not remember that she was potentially planning something criminal. She was, at the very least, involved in something unsavory, and he needed a clear head to deal with it. "What did he do? Do you think it's the same guy who attacked her?"

Deke shook his head. "No. He's taller and better built than the guy who attacked her the other day. I don't think we'll have any luck ID'ing this guy. He wore a balaclava and even black out around his eyes. Gloves on his hands. I don't know what color his skin is. He moves like he's military. Probably ex."

"Was he there to steal something?"

"If he was, he didn't find anything interesting." Deke leaned back against the lockers behind him. "He moved around the house, rifled through the desk in the office. That was where he spent most of his time. And in the bedroom. He was looking for something, but I have no idea what it was. He was interested in paperwork. But he left something behind, too."

Now Michael's interest was piqued. "Did you grab it?"

Deke huffed as though insulted at the very question. "Of course. I'm afraid it doesn't make your girl look good, but that was likely this fucker's point. He got on the computer in the office and uploaded some photographs. I sent those to your phone, too."

He pulled up his email and brought up the pictures. The first was of Vanessa getting out of her car, but it wasn't the restrained Vanessa he knew now. She was wearing vibrant colors, her hair a pretty honey blonde. She looked good either way, but this Vanessa had a secretive smile on her face, a coy look in her eyes. She was sexy as hell, and she knew it.

The second shot showed where she was. In a motel parking lot. She was walking up the stairs, and there was a man standing in the doorway. Whoever was taking the pictures had managed to get the sign on the motel's front in the shot. It clearly stated *Welcome Village Creek Golfers*.

That was there to give a time. It would be easy to find out when the golf tournament occurred.

"Do we know who the guy in front of the door is?" He didn't want to keep going, but he forced himself to. He forced himself to click through the pictures that showed Vanessa's luscious backside as she greeted the middle-aged man wearing a suit.

Was that her stepson? His stomach rolled at the thought.

"You're not going to like it." Deke's words didn't give him hope.

"It's her stepson." Now he could see the man fully, and he recognized him. He also recognized that he had his hand on her ass as he kissed her and welcomed her inside. He forced down his anger. So much for her telling him the truth. He couldn't show how fucking much seeing her like that hurt. "Is he trying to blackmail her?"

"Keep going," Deke said with a sigh.

That was when he got to the emails. They were from Vanessa to George Jr. dated two weeks before. Vanessa demanded twenty million or she would release the photos to George Jr.'s wife.

He stared at it for a moment. "So this wasn't on her computer until the man put it there?"

"From what I can tell, no, it wasn't." Deke had a grim expression on his face.

"So there's a chance the pictures are fake, too."

"They look real to me, but we both know all it takes is a dude with a computer and the right software to alter a photo," Deke replied.

"Get Hutch on it." He hated those pictures because they forced all of his doubt to creep right back in. He knew this was some kind of a setup, but the doubt was still there. He had to ask the questions. Had she lied when she'd told him she'd had no relationship with her stepson? She was so gorgeous there was no way the fucker hadn't tried. She'd told him as much.

"You think someone's setting her up?" Deke asked.

"I would say the stepson, but this makes him look bad."

Deke shrugged. "Bad is relative. It might be worth it if it means he wins the appeal on his father's estate case. The truth is even if it was real and it came out, he wouldn't be the one held accountable, and you know it."

Vanessa would be the one to pay the price. She would be seen as the seductress who tore a family apart. George would be able to apologize and tell the story of how she'd tricked him into bed, how she'd played on his emotions. How she'd turned to his father when she realized it wouldn't work with him.

He would say she'd then tried to blackmail him, and look, the proof is on her computer. "He's setting her up. Likely he'll call the cops in right before the appeal. Those photos are fake. She's done a ton of photo shoots. I would bet the first one is real and the others are of someone he hired to play Vanessa. You don't see her face after the first one. It would have been easy to dress someone else up. Tell Hutch he's looking for differences between the first photo and the others."

A brow had risen over Deke's eyes. "You done doubting her?"

"I am on this. I don't know about the rest of it. I don't think for a second that woman would blackmail someone. Even someone she hates. I don't want to move on this. You got everything off her system, so we've got some time," he replied. "There's still the matter of the money that's gone missing. We've verified it was moved from the computer she uses at work. She's the only one who knows her password."

"But there's a master password on all Lodge Corp systems," Deke pointed out.

"And it's only known by people who are above reproach. I seriously doubt that Dani would need to hide fifty thousand dollars from Julian. Finn wouldn't either. The only other people who know that code are Ben and Chase Dawson. Believe me. I've checked, and I haven't found another explanation." Michael wanted to believe her.

But the money was gone, and he could see her thinking Julian wouldn't miss it. But then why wasn't she spending it? She'd only had enough for coffee the other day.

Or she's playing you and wants you to see her as fragile to bring out your protective instincts. No one else would be on her computer at work.

It didn't matter because he would figure out what she was doing, and then he would pay Julian back.

Then he would make sure she stayed out of public life, and eventually the press would relent. He might even be able to get her to drop the lawsuit. He could take care of her financially. He could give her the life she wanted even if he had to do it quietly for a while.

Once she was out of the limelight and things died down, he could introduce her to his family, and maybe things would work out.

"You know you could put the evidence in front of her and ask her what she knows," Deke offered. "I'm well aware that's not what the client wants, but if you're into her, it might be your only shot at keeping her around after she finds out."

"Who says she has to? Look, if I find irrefutable proof that she's taking the money, then I'll confront her." And he would offer her a way out. She wouldn't leave him then. She would cling to him. He halfway wanted that scenario to be true. It would make things easier if he had the upper hand. "If she's done nothing wrong, there's no need for her to find out I was ever anything but her training Dom and eventually her formal Dom. She doesn't have to know I was brought in to investigate her."

She wouldn't have to know he was the one who'd put her in a corner and left her nowhere else to go.

Deke frowned his way. "I don't know what world you're living in, but in this one, there is one truth. They always find out. Always."

Michael had to pray that Deke was wrong.

Chapter Eleven

Vanessa yawned and turned in bed, expecting to find what she'd found the last eight days of her life—Michael's warm body next to hers.

It was Sunday morning, and she was looking forward to waking up the same way she had yesterday. Michael took his time in the mornings. There wasn't a ton of play, but there was a long, slow exploration of her body that inevitably led to her wrapped around him, sighing out his name.

His side of the bed was empty, and she heard someone moving around in the bathroom.

She sat up because he didn't usually get out of bed without waking her up.

Of course her use of the word *usually* was only based on a little more than a week, but it had been an awesome week.

After that first night at The Club, they'd come back to Michael's place, and she hadn't even thought about going to the guest room. It wasn't like she had a ton of stuff, so it had been easy to move it into here. They'd played every night after he picked her up from work and they'd shared dinner. They used his private playroom, and then they'd spent Friday and Saturday night at The Club. Her ass was still a bit sore from their scene the night before, but she'd found she even liked that ache.

There was a little voice inside her head screaming that she was moving too fast, that he was way too good to be true, but she wasn't listening. She'd talked about her fears at her therapy appointment this week and found a compromise. Her therapist had talked about how it was okay sometimes to live in the moment, and Vanessa was going with it. She would think about all of this later. It was too nice to sink into this lovely place and let herself simply be for a few days.

There would be a reckoning. Whether that came down to Michael realizing she wouldn't fit in with his family or something more mundane, she was fairly certain this relationship couldn't work the way she wanted it to, but she'd started to wonder if they couldn't have a few months together.

"Hey, gorgeous." Michael stepped out of the bathroom dressed in slacks and a button-down shirt.

She sat up in bed, pulling the sheet around her breasts. "Are you going in to the office?"

He held out a hand, his eyes going to the sheet, and he didn't have to tell her what he wanted. She let the sheet fall away and took his hand, allowing him to help her to her knees. He stood beside the bed, his eyes roaming her body as his hands did the same. They stroked over her.

"No, it's much worse. I've got to meet my mother for brunch. She's got something she wants to talk to me about," he said, leaning over and kissing her softly. "She called at the last minute and said it was a family matter."

She knew what he was trying to do. He was trying to make it not sting that he wasn't taking her with him. "No problem. I suspect I can entertain myself."

Even if she wasn't a lightning rod for controversy, she wouldn't expect to be introduced to his mother at this point. They'd just started a relationship.

He lowered his forehead to hers. "I'm sorry. I'll get back as soon as I can. Maybe I should bring in a bodyguard."

He was such a sweetheart. He'd been the most attentive Dom a sub could ask for. Since they'd moved their relationship forward, he'd spent every night with her. Even when he'd needed to work late one night, he'd arranged for her to have some company. Her new friend

May had shown up. They'd spent the night watching movies and eating popcorn. Vanessa had felt like she'd really fit with May.

She didn't want Michael to have to give up his Sunday, and she didn't want him to go to a bunch of trouble to bring in one of his friends.

"I'm fine here," she promised. "You don't need to bring in a guard."

He sighed and his hands skimmed over her hips. "Are you sure? The building is secure. No one can get up here without security calling to let them up. You have control over who has access to this floor."

"And I won't let anyone in." She was perfectly fine with that. "I could use some time to myself."

He kissed her again. "All right. Then I should be back sometime this afternoon." He stepped away and seemed to remember something. "My cousin and his wife…they stop by every now and then. We share the top floor with them, so they don't have to be buzzed up."

She hadn't met Simon or Chelsea Weston, but Michael had talked about them. "If they show up, I'll let them know where you are."

There was a picture of the couple and their adorable little girl on the mantel above the fireplace. She would know them by sight.

"Only them," he said, his eyes steady on her. "Or your friend, if you want some company."

"I'm having lunch with May on Tuesday. I think I'll catch up on some work. I also got the stuff to bake cookies. I might do that. I don't know." She felt her lips curl up. "Without my Dom here, I might go wild and spend the day reading in that monstrosity of a bathtub."

His whole face lit up. "You do that, baby. I'll see you in a couple of hours, and I have my cell on me."

One more kiss and he walked out. She let herself fall back to the bed, warmth flooding her system.

She could fall for this man.

So do it. Don't let this world hold you back. I know it's hard and it feels like the right thing to do is to retreat, but you only get one life.

He'd never actually said those words to her, but she could hear

George in her head. He'd wanted her to fly as high as she could.

Now all she wanted was to honor his legacy and live a nice, normal life with a man she loved.

Michael Malone was not going to be that man. He couldn't be. His family would be horrified by her, and the press would lose their minds if they knew she was dating another wealthy man.

Were they dating? It felt like they were. It felt serious to her.

She heard the door close and the security system come on.

She felt safe here.

She got up and showered, forcing all those nasty thoughts out of her head. She was living in the moment, and the moment included a glorious shower and no need to get dressed in anything but yoga pants and a T-shirt, something easy to get out of since the minute her Dom came home he would have her naked.

She loved sitting on his lap every evening. She cuddled up to him, naked and warm under a blanket. She'd even gotten okay with watching the news with him, though mostly she just breathed him in and let her mind float.

Her creativity was starting to come back, and she'd had some thoughts about stories and ideas for little scenes.

Not that she would do anything. But it was good to be able to think about the stories and characters that had always been in her head.

She was pouring her first cup of coffee when her cell phone rang. She glanced down and guilt filled her. Ruby.

Yeah, she'd spent so much time rubbing herself against Michael that she hadn't paid much attention to her investigation. She'd put Ruby on trying to figure out if Kyle Hawthorne had any other connections to her sister and then had her fun.

She was starting to think that maybe her sister had been wrong. Nicki could be a little on the paranoid side.

Or she wanted so badly for things to be as good as they seemed.

She slid her finger across the screen to answer. "Hey, Ruby. How are you doing?"

There was a pause over the line. "I'm okay. When are you coming back?"

More guilt. "I don't know, sweetie. Michael is convinced someone tried to hurt me, and honestly, it's hard for me to be in that house." First Ruby had lost Nicki, and now she herself was gone. "Why don't we have dinner later on this week? Do you think you could? I'd like for you to meet Michael."

"Are you serious?" Ruby asked.

"Of course. And I'm coming to your play later this month. How are rehearsals going?" Vanessa had been the one to convince Ruby to try out for her high school's musical. The kid had a hell of a voice, but she was too shy to share it. Or she had been before Vanessa had worked with her and she'd managed to get a key part in the show.

"They're good. I like it a lot. More than I thought I would," Ruby admitted, and now Vanessa could hear a smile in her voice. "I'm getting to be pretty good friends with a couple of girls from the set. They're cool."

"I'm so happy to hear that." She'd known all Ruby needed was opportunity.

"And I'd love to have dinner, but we have rehearsals." She hesitated for a moment and then her voice was quieter. "Maybe we could go out after the show."

"Of course." She'd always planned to go. She even had a wig, and she would sit in the back so she didn't bring any attention to herself. "I would love to."

Ruby's mom didn't attend school functions, and her father didn't call enough to know what Ruby was doing.

"Awesome. I'm going to pick someplace fun like Cheesecake Factory," Ruby vowed.

She hoped the wig worked there. "Sounds perfect."

"All right. Now on to weirder news. I've been looking into this Hawthorne guy, and I've hit a wall," Ruby admitted. "I'm almost sure something else is here, but I can't find it."

"What do you mean?" She moved to the fridge and pulled out a yogurt. Michael had taken her to the store to stock up. She'd loved how normal and domestic it felt to shop for groceries with someone.

"I mean it's like his whole military life is classified. Not really. There's nothing that says it's classified, but his records don't make sense to me. Some of these records say he's in places he couldn't have been in at the time. I've talked to a couple of my contacts online, and they think the government is trying to hide what this guy was doing."

She put down the yogurt. "Ruby, please tell me you didn't hack into military records."

A huff came over the line. "Well, I had to since they wouldn't let me in the normal way."

How far had this gone? "You have to stop. I never meant for you to get into the kind of trouble you could get into with the military."

"Hey, it's cool. They can't trace it back to me." Ruby sounded so self-assured. "But I do think it could get rough if I go deeper."

"Don't. I want you out of this," Vanessa replied. "Concentrate on the play. I'll handle everything else. I'm starting to think that maybe I was wrong. Maybe the accident was nothing more than an accident."

"I don't think so. I remember how scared she was at the end. But I think you need to consider telling this Michael guy. You said he was an investigator, right?"

"He works for a security firm. But he also works with Kyle Hawthorne, and Kyle is Michael's boss's nephew." She'd seriously considered telling Michael. She'd gone over how she could present her case to him in a way that wouldn't cost her the relationship. He was a reasonable guy, but this would potentially put him at conflict with a coworker. She needed real evidence before she went to him.

"Yeah, I don't like the sound of that," Ruby said with a sigh. "I've gone over and over that police report, and I've got nothing. There's one video of Nicki's car about half a mile from where she crashed, and none of the cars that follow her are suspicious."

She knew. They'd spent an evening painstakingly going over the grainy video footage they'd managed to get their hands on, taking down every license plate number and then researching each one. None of the cars who could have reached her in time to cause the accident had been taken to a shop or seen with any damage. Vanessa should know because she'd tracked them all down.

According to the police report there had been no signs that Nicki had been forced off the road. But she'd been afraid of MK. MK, Nicki had been sure, was going to kill her.

"I want to take a couple of days to try to figure out what to do next," Vanessa said. "Let the stuff with Kyle Hawthorne go. I can ask around The Club and see what I can find out, but I do not want you to get in trouble."

Ruby was quiet for a moment. "All right. I do need to spend more time on this report I'm writing. I've started to think about maybe applying to some colleges."

That was the best news she'd heard in a long time. When they'd first met, Ruby had told her there wasn't a reason to go to college. She knew everything she needed to know, and all she'd cared about was getting out of the house. The one thing her parents had done right was start a college fund, but at that point Ruby had planned to use it to move out.

"I'm glad to hear that." She took a deep breath, feeling better about the situation. She needed a couple of days to reflect and maybe change direction. Tessa had invited her and Michael to dinner next weekend. Kyle lived with her and David. Maybe she could even talk to the man and try to ascertain if her sister had any reason to be afraid of him.

Or she had the wrong Master, and she would have to start again.

There was a chiming that told her someone was at the door.

"Ruby, someone's here. I have to go."

"I'll talk to you later." The line went dead.

Vanessa strode across the living room to the entryway. She glanced at the display on the security system. Michael had a state-of-the-art system, with cameras all along the hallway.

Chelsea Weston stood outside along with three kids, and she did not look like she was having a good day. She held a baby in her arms, a diaper bag slung over her shoulder. Sophy Weston had a backpack emblazoned with a blinged-out unicorn. She wore a set of denim overalls, a purple T-shirt, and sneakers. The toddler boy had on shorts and a T-shirt, but it was inside out. And his shoes were on the wrong feet.

Oh, she should not open that door. She knew that desperate look in Chelsea Weston's eyes. Vanessa quickly put some things together, a deep protective instinct taking control. That was the look of a woman who was about to foist off a bunch of kids on another unsuspecting woman.

Chelsea pushed the button again, and the chime sounded through the condo. That chime sounded so calm. Like there wasn't a tornado on the other side of the door.

Chelsea had her hair up in a ponytail and looked very unlike the put-together woman in the picture Michael kept. She cursed under her breath and looked around like someone might show up to help her.

When she turned back to the camera, there was a single tear on Chelsea's cheek.

And that was when Vanessa gave up the fight. She turned off the alarm and threw the door open.

Chelsea's eyes went wide with hope. "Hey. Hi. I'm looking for Michael. I'm his…"

"Cousin's wife. Yes. He's told me all about you and Simon. I'm so sorry. He's not here. He went out to lunch with his mom."

Chelsea's shoulders drooped as she moved the baby to her other shoulder. "And his brother, apparently. They didn't tell me they were going out with Michael. They dropped these guys off and said they would be back later."

Vanessa gave her a smile. "I'm Vanessa. I could call him for you."

"It would be too late." Chelsea obviously sized her up. "You're the new sub. Si told me Michael had taken…I mean met…a new friend. Do you like the world the way it is, Vanessa?"

"Uh, mostly," she admitted. "There are definitely some things I would change."

"Mommy needs to save the world. The weird man is back. His name always changes, but Uncle Ian just calls him asshole," Sophy said.

"Sophy," her mother hissed. "We don't talk about Mr. Brown or Mr. Pink or whatever he's calling himself this week. And you do not repeat anything your Uncle Ian says. And don't start that fake crying."

Sophy, who'd looked like she was on the verge of tears, suddenly shrugged. "Uncle Ian's funny."

"Uncle Ian is also too far away to help me right now," Chelsea said with a sniffle. "I never cried before I had kids. I was the best. I was feared throughout cyberspace, and now I'm just a mom who everyone leaves their kids with, and this morning Mr. Brown shows up and he says I'm the only one who can help, and I started to fix the problem, but Jasper likes to climb on everything, and he didn't mean to push that button."

Whoa. Okay, so according to Michael, Chelsea was some kind of coding wunderkind, and she'd worked with the government when they needed her help in a time of crisis. Now she wondered which agency.

She'd done a movie about CIA agents in love, and while it had been criticized for being not realistic—the rival agents managed to have sex in the shower in the middle of a gun battle—the male lead had called himself Mr. Black because that's what CIA agents did to conceal their real names.

"I didn't mean to make the world go boom." Jasper started to cry.

"Please help my mummy save the world." Sophy had tears in her eyes again. And a British accent that she hadn't had before.

Oh, she was fucked. "I can watch the kids. I'm good with kids."

She hoped.

Chelsea didn't even wait a second. She passed that chunky, adorable baby over. "This is Ryder. He will sleep if you give him a bottle and hum the theme song to *Gunsmoke*. I know it's weird. You'll have to meet his grandfather someday. Jasper will climb on all surfaces, and he is not immune to gravity. Also, he's not big into clothes. Sophy will help you with everything. My number is in the bag, but honestly, I won't be able to answer until I fix the problem. We should know something in…" She glanced down at her watch and then a weird laugh came out of her mouth. "An hour. If that timer was right. Okay."

She turned and sprinted down the hall.

"What's *Gunsmoke*?" Vanessa looked to Sophy, who was leading the kids inside.

"Some weird old show," Sophy replied, entering like she'd been here a million times. "Do you have any cookies?"

The baby was patting her face, the sweetest toothless grin coming out.

"I like cookies." Jasper ran down the hallway, and that was when she noticed he'd already ditched his pants. They were lying on the floor. He'd already started taking off his shirt and was screaming something about being Spiderman.

She was in so much trouble.

* * * *

The minute he realized his brother was sitting with their mom, Michael knew he was in trouble.

His mother was sitting at a table in the private dining room of one of Uptown's most exclusive restaurants. The table was right beside the big windows that overlooked the city, skyscrapers rising all around them. Ava Malone was a lovely woman, and she'd been the best mom he could have hoped for. She was smart and kind and fierce when it came to her family.

His twin sat beside her, a coffee mug near his hand and a concerned look on his face.

The last time he'd seen JT so concerned had been when Michael had joined a CIA team. Of course, he hadn't exactly told JT that was what he was doing, but his brother was smarter than he looked.

He thought seriously about turning and walking out because this had all the hallmarks of an…intervention. The only thing lacking was his father.

He sighed and wished he'd told his mom he was busy. Of course then she would have shown up at his doorstep, and Vanessa would have gotten involved.

Though the fact that his mom and brother were here made him a little nervous that Vanessa was already involved. He'd noticed a photographer lurking around the Lodge Corp building. It was only a matter of time.

Or this was about his dad.

His heart threatened to seize. His dad was in his seventies, and he'd given up the daily running of Malone Oil to JT and JT's wife, Nina, who'd rebranded it as Malone Oil and Energy. His dad seemed to be happy and healthy, but anything could happen.

Now there was no thought of leaving. He followed the server to the table. JT stood and held out a hand.

"Hey, brother," JT said.

"Is everything okay?" He shook his brother's hand, holding it because if this was bad news, he would need JT to hold on to.

JT's brows rose, and then he seemed to understand. "Dad's great. No, this isn't about Dad or the kids or Mom. Everyone's fine."

He hugged his brother and breathed a sigh of relief. "Good."

His mom was standing, a hand on his arm. She spoke to him in that crisp upper-crust British accent she'd never lost despite living the majority of her life here in the States. "Darling, I'm sorry you thought that for a moment. No. Your dad is perfectly fit. His cholesterol is down, and he's running around the house like a kid, playing with Jasper and Ryder. He's so happy."

His father lit up every time he looked at his grandsons.

What would his kids with Vanessa look like?

Not that he was having kids with Vanessa.

He shoved that thought aside and sank down to his seat. "All right. Everyone's good, so what is up with the command performance?"

From the tight set of his mother's jaw he figured he'd been right in the first place.

JT called over a server. "We're going to need something stronger than coffee. Could you bring a pitcher of sangria and two beers?"

Well, at least he knew why he was here. "You know about Vanessa."

The server strode away, and his mother pulled a folder out of her bag. "We're worried about you and yes, we know that you have some sort of connection with Vanessa Hale."

"Her name is Vanessa Jones." He felt the necessity to correct them. "She doesn't go by her stage name."

If his mother heard him, she didn't acknowledge it. "I was given this report a few days ago. I don't know much about George Jr., but I did know his father. He was a good man. He didn't deserve what happened to him."

"What happened to him, Momma?" JT frowned their mother's way. "He got to spend the last years of his life with a gorgeous woman who by all accounts was good to him."

"She wasn't his wife. I knew his wife. Martha Benedict was a lovely woman," his mother said. "Vanessa was fifty years younger than him. She could have been his granddaughter."

"His wife died. He'd been a widower for twenty years when he married Vanessa," JT argued.

What the hell was going on? Was his brother defending him? It wasn't like JT wouldn't protect him physically. If someone attacked him, JT would be right there throwing punches. They were brothers. But when it came to their parents, JT tended to side with them. When Michael had chosen to go into the Navy, JT had fought him on it. It had been a year before his brother had talked to him again. JT had helped his mom take down his entire CIA team when they were just forming. It hadn't endeared him to the others.

Though Boomer had been won over with his mom's brisket.

"Twenty years alone, and he lost his daughter, too," JT was saying. "He had every right to spend time with whoever he wanted."

"Well, she was obviously after his money, and I've got the proof," his mother returned.

It was pretty much everything he'd feared.

"What's in the folder?" He wasn't ready to ask JT how he knew so much about this. It seemed like this was well-worn territory for his mother and brother.

His mom's hand was still on that unmarked manila folder. "This is a report from a private investigator."

Michael felt his eyes narrow and his blood pressure tick up. "You hired an investigator?"

JT's hands came up in that way that let Michael know he was likely overreacting. Except he was pretty sure he wasn't. "No. We did no such thing. We didn't even realize you were dating her until that asshole showed up at Momma's club two days ago."

His mother was active at a Fort Worth country club. It was exactly the sort of place where George Benedict Jr. would feel comfortable. He wouldn't hesitate to walk right in and spread his lies. "Are we talking about Junior? The man who's trying to cheat Vanessa out of her inheritance?"

His mother's fists tightened. She looked far younger than her years in her designer shirt and tailored slacks. "The way he explained it, it's the other way around."

"She's not trying to screw anyone. Certainly not out of the entire estate. Her husband left her five percent and the house in Houston so she wouldn't be homeless." That fact always got lost when the press wrote about the case. "Everything else was left to Junior."

JT sat up straighter. "Are you serious?"

"I'm sure that's what she's told you," his mother began.

His mom was a deeply kind woman, but she'd been raised wealthy. She'd been born into a family with ties to British royalty. She'd married an American who'd also been born into generational wealth, and they'd both been taught to watch out for that money and keep themselves safe from people who would use them for it. He needed to chill the fuck out and deal with the situation. She wasn't some crazy woman who thought everyone without a second home was money hungry. "I know all of these things for a fact. I don't care what Junior's investigators found. I assure you he paid them to push his narrative."

"Why would he do that?" his mother asked.

"Because he obviously hates her," JT replied.

Yes, that was obvious to him, too. "I need you to understand that my relationship with Vanessa started out as an investigation. I assure you I've got a copy of the actual will, and MT's legal department has gone over it. It was five percent and the house. She wasn't ever going to touch the company, and according to all of the court documents, she's never asked for more than what the will provided."

"But there's an article in here about how she was threatening to take it all down," his mother said with a frown.

"What do you mean you were investigating her?" JT asked, and the expression was so similar. They both might look like their dad, but that frown was pure Momma.

Michael glanced around to make sure no one was listening in. The dining room he'd walked through had been loud and crowded, but they were the only ones here. "I mean my company has a client who was worried about her potentially influencing his wife. I was hired to make sure her intentions are pure. I had the same suspicions you did because I read the same articles and listened to that interview with her ex-friend. Ashton Banks is being paid quite well for that. Seventy-five thousand for the last TV interview. She's made a whole career of talking about Vanessa."

"I mentioned that, Momma," JT pointed out. "You know how this goes." He turned Michael's way. "I'm here to make sure she doesn't alienate you. She means well, but she can't think straight when it comes to her family. George Jr. cornered her and put all kinds of thoughts in her head. She's not some snob who won't let anyone without a million dollars get close. You know that. Nina didn't have any money and yet Momma accepted her fully."

"Well, Nina is lovely. She certainly didn't have any of these rumors hanging about her." There were tears in his mother's eyes.

Michael was seriously thinking about ending George Jr.

"No, but the press did write about her when we first got engaged," JT reminded her. "And they wrote about me, too. They wrote about how I might have been involved in Dana's disappearance."

Michael's heart constricted. Dana had been a dear friend, and she'd gone missing when they were in college. She'd never been found. No amount of money could fix the problem. She'd disappeared off the face of the earth, and they'd all had to deal with it. Given her close connections to the Malone family, they'd all come under scrutiny. They still did from time to time when some true crime podcast brought the case up again.

Now his mother's tears fell on her cheek, and she reached out for JT's hand. "They were quite terrible." She released his hand and dabbed at her eyes with her napkin, and then that stubborn British will was right back in her eyes. "That doesn't mean this Vanessa person isn't after Michael's money."

"Michael is too smart to let that happen." JT's mouth shut the minute the server returned with the drinks.

Michael happily took his beer. He hadn't driven. The restaurant was only two blocks from his place, so he could have a few and still walk home. Where Vanessa was probably lying naked in a bathtub, reading a book.

She would have no idea he was discussing her intentions with his family.

The server took their orders and left.

"Why isn't Dad here for this interrogation?" Michael asked when they were alone again.

"It's not an interrogation." His mother sat back, her shoulders straight and a regal look in her eyes.

"Dad said you're a grown-ass man, and if you want to sleep with a gorgeous woman with a past, you should do it." JT's tone had deepened, mimicking their dad's. "He said George Sr. had obviously had it good, and then he and Momma had a big old fight, and he's sleeping at the camp. Momma took those words to mean he's looking for his own young hottie."

"I certainly did not," she replied. "But he was obnoxious about the whole incident. Called me meddling for wanting to protect my son."

The camp was one of the many small cabins that dotted their sprawling ranch. They were meant to provide shelter in case one of the hands got caught in a storm or out on the range overnight. And yes, over the years they'd also provided shelter for their dad when he and Momma fought.

"I don't need protection, and she's not what you think," Michael replied.

This answered one of his questions. His family would lose their shit if he brought Vanessa home. And he had to tell them something he never intended for Vanessa to know. He'd believed the photos Deke had found were fake, and Hutch had proven it. That first photo had been lifted from a photo shoot when she was barely twenty years old. That meant the rest had likely not been Vanessa at all.

So now he had to figure out who had written the blackmail letters and why they'd planted them on Vanessa's machine. He didn't believe for a second Vanessa had sent those letters. He thought it was Junior himself, but Ian had pointed out that Ashton Banks—Vanessa's former friend—could have done it, too.

But none of it would matter because if he brought her home, he put them all in the line of fire. The press would go wild. He might be able to keep it all quiet for a while, but they would find out, and it could hurt his family.

"Apparently not, since I thought she was a girlfriend." JT was staring at him in that big-brother-knows-best way of his. "She's a…what would you call her?"

He would call her beautiful inside and out. He would call her sweet and kind. He would call her the most complex thing that had happened to him in forever. He was starting to think she might be very good for him. "She was the…is the target of an investigation."

"Then you're not dating her." JT liked to poke and prod. "But she's staying at your place."

What he meant was *You're not sleeping with her*. Michael wanted to lie, but it was hard to lie to the man he'd shared a womb with. "It was necessary to get close to her."

JT's head shook, and Michael knew he'd shifted back into his normal disapproving role. "I hate the spy shit. You couldn't be honest with her?"

"You're lying to her?" His mother was staring, too.

"I can't tell her I'm investigating her." They had never approved of his job. Not even once. They hadn't liked him going into the Navy, and they'd hated him working for the Agency. It had gotten better when he'd hired on at MT, but he still got the feeling they would rather he'd followed his brother into the family business. "That would defeat the purpose of the investigation."

"She's staying at your place," his mother pointed out. "That's what George Jr. told me. He said that was exactly how she'd gotten to his father."

He bet Junior had put the situation in the worst possible light. "She's staying at my place because someone tried to kill her, and the house she lived in became too dangerous to stay in. The press won't leave her alone, and someone likes to throw rocks through her window. Of course they write on the rocks. They call her a whore. Did Junior tell you that? Did he offer you a rock to throw at her?"

"I would never do that." His mother had gone slightly pale. "I have the right to ask questions. I did not mean to make this a fight, Michael. You have to know that I would accept and love any person you bring home. But I have worries about this."

"You don't have to worry because I had no intention of bringing her home," he stated flatly.

"Because she's nothing but a means to an end." JT took a swig of his beer.

Frustration welled. "I didn't say that."

"You said she's not your girlfriend and you have no intention of making her your girlfriend. So she's nothing but a target," JT challenged.

"Well, I don't like the sound of that. Unless you truly think she's done all these things. I'll be honest. I didn't like that man. I did like George, and I talked to him after he married that girl. He seemed happy. We didn't specifically talk about her, and I've never met her, but he seemed happy." His mother pushed the folder his way. "You should look into this. One of the things he accused her of was blackmailing him. He said he had an affair with her when she was married to his father."

No wonder his mom thought Vanessa was the devil. He quickly looked through the folder and verified it was the same photos the intruder had uploaded on Vanessa's laptop, which was now safely at the MT building with Hutch and MaeBe. "I've already seen these, and my tech guy proved they're fake. Now I know where they came from.

Junior is trying to make sure she's in the worst position possible before they go back to court. She's not who he said she is. She's a nice woman."

"Who you're lying to since she's nothing more than a target." JT seemed to need to push him.

"She's my sub, and I'll take care of her," Michael shot back to shut his brother up. Fuck. He hadn't meant to say that. He hadn't meant to let JT know they had a D/s relationship because his brother would know what that meant to him.

The minute JT's lips curled up, he knew he'd made a mistake. "See, Momma, I was right. I told you this whole thing would have started as some kind of spy game and he would get in deep. I told you if she's in his condo, he's got real feelings for her."

"I believe it was Nina who first thought this was probably a job," his mother murmured. "You should know that Nina's already a supporter of Vanessa's. She doesn't like how the press treated her. If she wasn't out of town, she would be right here telling me she told me so."

Nina didn't hold back. But then Nina had fit in from day one. So had Tessa. His ex-fiancée had immediately been accepted, and it kind of pissed him off that Vanessa wouldn't get the same treatment. She wouldn't get a chance to make a first impression because the press had already made it for her. She wouldn't get to walk in and show how sweet and smart she was. "You would like her. If you gave her the chance, you would like her. She's intelligent and creative. She's kind to the people around her. She got a reputation for being difficult for doing things men would be called assertive and confident for. She stood up for herself, and it cost her a career she enjoyed. She's been betrayed by pretty much every person she ever cared about because she lived in a cutthroat world. Yet she's still capable of kindness. Her mother wouldn't even speak to her because she didn't like her choice of career. Not that I think she was much of a mother to begin with. All Vanessa wants in the world is to do some good and live her life. She's not fighting for the money because she wants to spend it. She's fighting for it because she promised her husband that she would build a foundation to help people with addiction issues. People like the daughter he adored, the one he lost. So believe what you want to believe, but you're missing out if you don't give her a chance."

He started to stand, but his brother put a hand out. “Michael, please stay. I should have asked you if you had feelings for her, but I kind of thought you wouldn’t tell me the truth.”

“I don’t make it a habit to lie to you,” Michael replied.

“No, but you can lie to yourself,” JT pointed out. “I think what just came out of your mouth is the complete truth. You like her.”

Damn it. His brother was right. “I like her a lot. I’m hoping I can prove she’s innocent and then she doesn’t have to know I was investigating her at all.”

JT snorted. “Sure. That’s going to work out fine.”

Yeah, he’d heard that a lot, but he was smarter than people gave him credit for.

Their mom sent JT one of her patented mom stares, the kind that made JT sit up and stop laughing. She then turned back to Michael. “Don’t go, son. Tell me more about her. That awful man got me all upset. And honestly, it’s something I’ve worried about since you were a young man. You deserve all the love in the world, and I want that for you.”

Now he felt like he’d oversold the situation. “It’s not that serious.”

“Are you or are you not planning on seeing her when all of this is over?” JT asked.

His brother was forcing him to be honest with himself. It was something JT had always been able to do. “Yeah, I want to, but I worry that it could put my family in a rough position. I care about her a lot. But the press…”

“Can bite my ass,” JT said. “Nina would say the same. She’s been hankering for a good throwdown since she left the bodyguard business. You do what you want, brother. I’ll handle the press.”

“And I’ll take them all down if they come for my family,” his mother vowed. She reached out and put a hand over his. “I’m sorry, darling. I was worried, and there was a better way to handle this. I trust you. Please forgive me, and let us have a lovely brunch. After all, I’m going to have to go home and apologize to your father, so I would like to have a pleasant time with my sons.”

JT snorted. “Yeah, because Dad’s going to make it so hard on you.”

His parents had been married for fifty years, and they were still madly in love. His father would grouse, but all his mother would have to do was apologize and give him a kiss and all would be forgiven.

Could he have that with Vanessa?

Would she forgive him if he paid off her debts and got her out of trouble with Julian Lodge? The money was the trouble. He could prove her innocent of everything but the money.

But in a lot of ways the money was the most forgivable thing.

Of course, he also needed to prove she wasn't behind the hack. He could certainly prove she didn't do it herself, but there was the problem of her young hacker friend.

"Well, if he is, I'll sic Jasper on him, and he'll forgive me if only to get me to take him back," his mother was saying.

JT chuckled. "That kid is going to be the death of me. Michael, you need to have a couple of girls to balance out all the boys. Nina says she's done."

"Where are the kids?" Michael finally took a sip of beer, relaxing because he might have been wrong about all of this. If his family accepted Vanessa, everything could work out. He might be able to keep her.

At least for a while.

JT sat back. "Chelsea's got them. We dropped them off before we came here. We kind of tiptoed down the hall so you wouldn't know we were there. They're fine. We can take our time. Chelsea can handle anything."

Chelsea hadn't been left alone with Climbing Jasper. Still, she'd held the balance of the world in her hands a couple of times. Surely she could handle JT's boys, and her own daughter was old enough to help.

Michael sat back as the server brought out a whole basket of cinnamon rolls and fruit and yogurt. It was the kind of thing Vanessa would love.

His mom and brother started telling stories of how often Jasper had nearly died while scaling something he shouldn't.

Michael listened in, but his mind was on the woman he'd left at home.

Chapter Twelve

The elevator doors opened, but Michael was on the wrong side of the building. The top floor of the high-rise he'd lived in for ten plus years was split into two large penthouse condos. It was far more room than he needed, but he'd convinced himself it was an investment. He owned one of them and his cousin, Simon, the other. Simon actually owned the whole building, but then he'd had to put that good old British royal wealth to use here in the States.

"Thank you for coming by to see the boys," his mother was saying as they walked out of the elevator. There was a hallway that led to his place, and the temptation was right there to walk down and invite Vanessa to join him. They'd spent the majority of the afternoon talking about her, after all.

But he couldn't. Despite what his mother had said, there were still massive walls to scale when it came to Vanessa.

That missing money being the worst of it. Although the fact that Junior was trying to set her up wasn't helping. He would have to find a way out of that trap. He could prove the photos weren't real, and he could prove someone else uploaded them with the security footage they had, but it might not be enough for some people. He thought he had some time when it came to the photos and blackmail scam. Junior would need to spring that trap closer to the trial.

"They miss their Uncle Michael." JT strode across the hall.

"Only because I let Jasper climb me like a jungle gym." He adored his nephew, but he only saw him a few times a year. JT's family lived out on the ranch, and it was an hour and a half away. Three hours round trip. Not that there wasn't space for him out there. His parents kept a room for him, but he always found a reason to make the trip back to Dallas. Probably because waking up and having breakfast with JT and Nina and the kids made him realize his life was flying by without any of the passion he'd thought he'd find.

Until Vanessa.

His mother knocked on the door. "Well, I'm sure our darling Chelsea will be happy to drop the boys right back in our laps. I'm going to offer to bring Sophy back with us so she and Simon have a bit of time alone. He's been working on some case, of course, and she's always busy. Everyone's busy. Nina's off at one of our satellite offices, and poor JT works all the time. Such industrious children."

They were all still kids to his mom.

"Well, we have to be since Dad opted for the lazy life," JT snarked.

His mother shook her finger JT's way. "Don't you say that around him. I just convinced him to retire. He gets to enjoy his golden years."

Dad would enjoy them when he wasn't pissing off his wife and getting sent out to the camp. Michael was smart enough not to say that. He usually knew how to handle his mom. Agree with her. She was almost always right.

Except about Vanessa, though she'd thawed considerably.

His mother frowned because it had been a while since she'd rung. She pressed the bell again, hearing it chime behind the door. "I hope Chelsea's all right."

JT grimaced. "Me, too. The boys can be a lot."

The door opened, and Chelsea stood there, a slightly wild look in her eyes. She stared for a moment and then seemed to remember she could speak. "Hey, Aunt Ava. Uhm, a little something came up, and I needed some help with the kids."

"Are they okay?" JT's brow had furrowed, and he was trying to get a glimpse behind Chelsea into the condo where his kids were supposed to be.

"The kids?" Chelsea nodded. "Oh, I'm sure they are for now. I mean, I totally fixed that one problem, but you know how these things are. It's like whack-a-mole. I should get back to my computer. I'm not cut out for this anymore. It used to be a fun game, and now all I can see is bombs potentially going off and countries going to war. I got out of this life, damn it." She started to turn but stopped. "Oh, the kids are with Michael's new girlfriend. I legit didn't have another choice. She seems nice. Familiar, though. It was weird. I've seen her somewhere. Anyway, they're down the hall, and nothing's blown up yet. Well, nothing's blown up here."

Oh, fuck. The boys could be so much trouble, and Sophy could do her own damage. She spent a lot of time with the Taggart kids, so she had skills kids shouldn't have. Skills Vanessa wasn't ready for. Vanessa had never even mentioned liking kids, and she'd been left to deal with his nephews?

"Well, my darling, we shall handle everything." If his mother had picked up on Chelsea's end-of-the-world vibe, she didn't show it. "I'll get the boys from Vanessa and take Sophy with me. She can stay out at the ranch for a few days."

Chelsea's eyes widened, and then she threw her arms around his mother. "I love you, Aunt Ava."

He would have witnessed more of his cousin-in-law's gratitude, but he took off down the hall because someone had to save Vanessa.

JT was right behind him. "What does your girl know about kids?"

"No idea," he admitted, pulling his key out of his pocket as they approached his door.

He heard a strangled scream, and his heart threatened to stop.

"Get in there." JT was practically pressing against the door. "Someone's hurt."

He got the door open and raced down the hallway.

"I don't see 'em, Captain," a familiar voice said in a completely unfamiliar accent. It was Vanessa, but she was affecting a deep, harsh tone. "I think that last harpoon did the trick."

All of the cushions of his couch were on the ground, lined up like a platform. Vanessa was crouching down at one end, Ryder wrapped around her in a sling. The baby was giggling like mad at the antics. Sophy stood at the other end of the cushions, a paper hat on her head, and she seemed to be steering an imaginary wheel.

"You can never tell with the Jasper shark," Sophy shouted. "He's still out there. We can't let down our guard!"

The whole place smelled like cookie dough and grilled cheese. Vanessa's hair was pulled back in a high ponytail, and she was throwing herself into the role with gusto. She pointed into the dining room. "Yer right, Cap'n. He's off our bow right now!"

Jasper was crawling on the floor, and for once the kid had some clothes on. There was a triangular piece of paper taped to the back of his shirt, and he was playing the role of shark to the hilt.

"I think your girl has this covered," JT said quietly. "Damn. That was smart. She figured out how to keep him from climbing."

"Should we take out the shark, First Mate Ryder?" Vanessa was grinning down at the baby in her arms, who bounced against her hip in obvious glee.

"Well, that's charming." His mother strode in.

Vanessa gasped as she realized they were no longer alone. Her eyes went wide, and she stepped off the cushions.

"Nana!" Sophy jumped off and ran toward her grandmother. "Nana, we had so much fun."

"I'm a shark!" Jasper was on his feet, pointing to his back. "Nessa gave me a fin, and I'm the terror of the seas."

JT smiled broadly as he got to one knee to inspect his son's fin. "Now that is a great fin. I'm glad you had a good time. And it looks like Ryder's in love."

Ryder wasn't paying his father any attention at all. He was staring up at Vanessa, his hands on her shoulders.

Vanessa looked slightly panicked. "I'm so sorry. I should have thought about the cushions but we were deep into the storyline and…"

"Cushions can be replaced," his mother said. "Although these look fine. What can't be replaced is a good old-fashioned adventure. My boys were worried the children had taken you down, but it's obvious to me you're made of sterner stuff than that. I'm Ava Malone. You must be Vanessa. Michael's been telling us all about you."

"He has?" Vanessa asked, her eyes wide.

His mother nodded. "He has. Now hand off Ryder to one of my lads and I'll make us some tea."

His mother was already on her way to the kitchen.

Vanessa simply stood there like she might get out of this if she didn't move.

She was adorable standing there in her bare feet with a baby squishing her face in his chunky little hands. There was still a bit of what looked like flour on her shirt. She'd expected a quiet afternoon and gotten the storm, which she'd turned around and made into something delightful for the kids.

Michael moved in.

"I didn't know what *Gunsmoke* was so I couldn't get Ryder to go to sleep, and then Jasper tried to climb the bookcase in your office, and I had to do something," she whispered. "And now your mom is here."

He eased Ryder out of the sling and passed him off to JT. Sophy had already disappeared, following after her grandmother.

Vanessa was still standing there when he turned back around. He followed his instincts and pulled her close. "You did a magnificent job, baby. The kids loved you."

And he was starting to think he might, too.

He kissed her, a sweet brush of his lips across hers.

"Your mom is here," she whispered again.

He nodded. "She is, and she tends to get what she wants, and she obviously wants a little time with you. But I promise she doesn't bite."

"Does she know?"

His heart threatened to break because he understood what she was asking. How hard was it to always have to ask if the people she met knew who she was? Like she needed to put her shame out there for everyone to see so it didn't surprise anyone. Like she had to apologize for existing. He pulled her close, letting her feel him standing there with her. "Yes, she does. She's a good woman. She might ask you questions, but she won't judge you. I promise. She's my mom."

If someone had told him this morning that he would be standing here praying that Vanessa got along with his mom, he would have told them they were insane. But here he was, hoping it all went well because he was crazy about her.

Vanessa nodded. "Okay. I can have tea."

"I'm JT." His brother was holding Ryder, and Jasper was attached to his leg. JT was grinning like a loon.

Vanessa smiled and held out a hand. "Vanessa Jones."

"She bakes the best cookies, and she can do all kinds of voices," Jasper said. "And she makes awesome shark fins."

JT shook her hand. "And she also makes your Uncle Michael happy, apparently. It's good to meet you, and I hope we haven't scared you off."

"Not at all." She seemed to steady herself. "Your boys are wonderful. We had a good time. It's very nice to meet you."

JT kept grinning. "You, too."

She turned to go and got to the kitchen before she pivoted, looking back his way. "Hey, does anyone know if Chelsea managed to save the world?"

Michael shrugged. "Hasn't blown up yet." Chelsea saved the world one keystroke at a time. She had her own business, one she co-owned with a group of former MT agents. But the CIA still came calling from time to time. Especially in an emergency. "I think we can assume everything is fine."

Vanessa nodded. "Good to know."

She disappeared into the kitchen.

JT's free hand came up to pat him on the shoulder. "You're in trouble, brother. The best kind. Come on. Let's clean your place up and let Momma work her magic."

Michael sighed as Jasper started to play shark again.

He was definitely in trouble because he was almost certain he was falling in love with that woman.

* * * *

Vanessa had stared down some scary things before. A coked-up director who thought a death scene needed a little more realism. The press outside George's funeral. The tiger she'd been told absolutely wouldn't eat her but then sounded like he wanted to. That tiger had been a good actor.

She'd pretty much never been more intimidated by anything than that one petite woman.

Ava Malone had a kettle on, proving she was more than

comfortable in her son's kitchen. She already had a tin of tea leaves out and a pretty ceramic pot.

Sophy was happily munching on the chocolate chip cookies they'd made after she'd served them all lunch. The little girl was smart and helpful and would likely be a hell of an actress someday.

"Then Vanessa came up with the idea to play sea captain versus shark," Sophy was saying. "And she told Jasper that if he was the shark, he could only swim."

Ava's laughter rang out through the kitchen, and she looked up, catching sight of Vanessa. "That was clever of you, dear. You managed to keep Jasper from scaling the furniture without tying him down somewhere."

"I wouldn't do that. I promise." She still wasn't sure how this could go well. Michael…well, she honestly hadn't expected him to even mention her to his mother much less introduce them.

"Oh, you only say that because you don't have any of your own yet," Ava said with a smile. "They can't all be as perfect as our Sophy. But then I could have told you that any son of JT's was likely to be hell on wheels, as my husband would say. Jasper will probably inherit the ranch. He'll need all that energy. JT was always running as a child. Michael was the quiet one."

She wanted to ask a thousand questions, but she was nervous. If she asked questions, then Ava would likely feel comfortable asking her own.

When was the last time she had to meet someone's family? Even most of her friends didn't introduce her to their moms. Not that she had any.

The last time she'd been to a family gathering she'd been accused of flirting with a cousin's husband, and she'd had to leave.

"That doesn't mean he wasn't a delightful child," Ava was saying. "He was simply less outrageous than his brother. He liked puzzles. JT would run wild across the range during the summers. Sophy's father, Simon, would come and visit, and they would both ride and play, and I would find Michael working a puzzle inside or reading a book. It can be hard to not fit in."

"My dad wears suits. It's weird to see my dad in a cowboy hat," Sophy said.

"And yet he wore one every single summer." Ava leaned over

and kissed the top of Sophy's head. "Run along, darling. I'm sure your uncle is making a perfect hash of taking care of the boys."

"Well, they're all boys, aren't they?" Sophy asked, snatching a cookie as she skipped out of the kitchen.

"She's a helpful girl," Ava said, turning back to her kettle. "I worried when Chelsea said she was only having one. It can be lonely, especially when your parents are as intellectual as hers. But then I realized their family isn't like others."

"What do you mean?"

"That company my son works for is another family. I know a lot of places say they have a work family, but it's different for the McKay-Taggart people. So many of them didn't have a place to go, didn't have family who loved them or truly understood them. They made their own. I've found that for some that lasts for a few years, but it's been over a decade. They'll be family all of their lives, and it's given their children something they wouldn't have had without them. Sophy has grown up with sisters and brothers. They simply aren't blood. I often wonder if Michael feels more at home with them than he does with us."

It was said with a wistfulness that made Vanessa's heart ache. "He talks about you a lot. You and your husband and JT."

Ava's lips turned up but not quite in the same high wattage as before. "I'm glad. He's been distant lately."

"I think that's more about his wedding falling apart than anything." She'd put a few things together over the last week. Michael didn't talk about his ex-fiancée, but he did talk about calling off the wedding. He told her it had been for the best, but the way he said it made her think. It was also there in the way he talked about his twin brother and his family. "I think it bothers him that JT has a family of his own and it hasn't happened for him. I know he made choices that made their paths diverge, but he loves his brother."

"You've made a study of him. That's very astute of you."

She wasn't sure that was a good thing. Ava might think she was making a study of her son so she could take him for everything he had. It might be best to be upfront about their relationship and herself. It was likely why Ava had sent Sophy out. She was about to get a very polite warning off from this lovely woman in front of her. "I'm not interested in your son for his money. I didn't realize he had money when I met him, and honestly, the money is something I would like to stay away from."

"The money is a part of who Michael is." The kettle started to sing, and Ava shut off the stove, transferring the water into the teapot.

"He's more than money. I was surprised when I found out his family was wealthy. He's a very hard worker." She felt herself flush. She shouldn't have put it that way. "Not that wealthy people don't work hard. Many of them do."

"And many of them don't," Ava replied in her crisp British accent. "I wasn't implying Michael is dependent on his family's money. I was saying he comes from it, and it's part of who he is. I grew up in a wealthy world. I've found we tend to come in two types. My parents were the first. Money was everything to them. Money, and more importantly, their place in society. Meeting my husband was a revelation. He didn't care at all what a person's family history was. He cared about the person in front of him. He judged a man or woman on their character and not how closely placed they were to a throne. My husband's family has had money since the 1800s. He never wanted for anything, but he also understood that the money he was surrounded by didn't make him better or worse than any other person, merely luckier in some ways since he hadn't been the one to make the money. He taught me to become a caretaker of the wealth we've been given. Part of caretaking is giving away a decent portion of it."

"Michael told me you do a lot of charity work."

"I do. I find it very satisfying, and not merely in a fund-raising way," Ava explained. "I like to donate time as well. I live in a rural community. Getting out and helping is a part of the way of life out there."

"I used to love working in this soup kitchen in inner-city LA. It made me feel good to get in there and actually help." Right up to the moment she realized her presence was doing harm because the press would follow her inside.

Ava put a teacup and saucer in front of her. "You would like to do some work with addiction, right? Michael mentioned something about your plans. Could you tell me about them?"

This felt far too good to be true, and there was a part of her that wanted to push and prod until she got this nice bubble to burst.

Because it would.

But she thought about the fact that Michael was right outside, and he'd brought his mom back here. He'd kissed her in front of his brother. He wasn't hiding their relationship.

"I know it's not something that's typically considered a charity," she began. "It's more of a research group. It would fund intriguing new studies on how to handle this country's addiction problem. Just say no doesn't work."

She shouldn't have said that. The woman in front of her might have had legit ties to Nancy Reagan.

Ava poured the tea with an elegant hand, something she'd likely practiced a thousand times.

When she was growing up tea was something her mom kept in a pitcher in the fridge and put way too much sugar in.

"Obviously," Ava agreed. "I've found the people who tell others to say no have usually said yes at some point. It's not so simple, is it? This isn't a subject I know much about, though I did lose some family members to addiction. It doesn't seem to care if you're rich or poor."

"No, it doesn't. It cares if you're lonely, if you have an empty place inside you." Vanessa leaned forward, warming to her subject. "There is a biological component, and many people are studying that, but I want to specifically research how community affects addiction. There are some incredible studies out of Portugal that show promise in significantly reducing relapse by encouraging recovering addicts to engage in community projects."

"Well, that sounds intriguing." Ava poured her own cup. "Tell me more. I'd like to hear all about it. How did you get involved?"

She sounded so sincere, and no one ever wanted to talk about Lara since George died. "I had a very good friend. She was a director, the best director I ever had."

She started to talk, getting comfortable, her passion coming out for the first time in a long while.

Chapter Thirteen

"I still don't quite understand what happened. I walked in and Drake was sitting in my living room and both he and Chelsea looked exhausted and they'd gone through half a bottle of Scotch."

Two mornings later, Simon shook his head and stared out the window of Michael's office.

"Seriously? She won't tell you what happened?" Michael sat back. It was a rainy morning, and his mind was still on Vanessa and how they'd spent the weekend.

Apparently Simon had spent a portion of his with the man they knew as Drake. He was the CIA operative tasked to handle Chelsea Weston, and he'd had several interactions with McKay-Taggart.

Simon shook his head. "She said it was beyond classified, and it was better I didn't know. I swear I wanted to throttle Drake. Why can't the bloody Agency leave her alone?"

"Because she's still the best hacker in the world," Michael pointed out. "I know I feel safer when Chelsea's behind the keyboard. How is she today?"

Simon shrugged. "Back at work like nothing happened. I think it would have been far worse if she'd had to deal with the children. She wants to take Vanessa out to dinner sometime this week as a way to thank her. I think she also wants to get to know her because Sophy's talked so much about her. According to our daughter, Vanessa is very cool. I thought we could make it a double date. Sophy's spending next weekend out at the lake house with Erin and Theo. She's spending a lot of time with Devi since they started playing on the same football team."

Over a decade in the States and his cousin still called soccer football.

"Sure. That sounds great." He would pick a place that had private dining rooms and a discreet entrance. Lucky for him Top had both, and if reporters showed up, the kitchen was full of ex-military men and women who didn't mind kicking a little ass. "It would be good for her to get out and spend some time with friends."

Simon turned. "I hear she's making quite a few. She seems to have charmed Aunt Ava."

His mom had sat and talked with Vanessa so long he and JT had been forced to order pizza to feed the kids. They'd all sat around his usually empty dining room table and eaten dinner together, and he'd been shocked at how emotional the whole evening had made him.

It had felt right to sit across from Vanessa and spend time with his family. He'd felt like he fit in a way he hadn't in a very long time.

Because she's the right woman for you.

"They got along very well. Better than I expected them to," he admitted.

"Does she understand the situation?" Simon asked. "Aunt Ava, I mean."

"I told her the relationship began as part of an investigation."

"Began?" A brow rose over his cousin's eyes.

"I'm not even trying to fool myself anymore. I want this relationship to continue. Even if I find out she stole that money, I want her."

Simon's brows rose. "You still think she did it?"

He'd talked to Si about the investigation when he'd brought in Phoebe Murdoch to do some financial investigation for him. "I don't see who else would have gotten on her computer to move money around. Phoebe says she thinks she's got something for me, but she got hung up at her kids' school. I'm meeting with her later this afternoon."

"And if you find out she did steal from Julian's company?" Si prompted.

"It was Dani's," Michael corrected.

Si chuckled. "I assure you no matter whose name is on the company, it's all Julian's. Are you planning on paying him back?"

"I'll handle it for her, and I'll make sure she's never again in a position where she needs to steal from anyone." He would protect her. "If she took the money, she had a good reason. She needed it."

She might be using it to pay her attorney fees. The lawyers wouldn't keep working if they didn't get paid. He would take care of that, too.

"I don't think that will mean anything to Julian," Si pointed out. "He's not known for his kind heart when it comes to people who fuck him over."

"I'll make sure he understands." He could handle Julian. At least he hoped he could. If the situation upset Dani, Julian would be completely unreasonable, and Michael would have to protect her from his wrath.

He would do whatever he had to do to make sure she was safe. Even if it meant convincing her to give up on the lawsuit.

"You're serious about her," Si said softly.

"I am." He'd known he was through fooling himself when he'd seen her with the kids. He couldn't pretend she was nothing more than a good lay. His heart was involved, and that meant things had gotten very complicated. "I have to decide how to handle the investigation. My first instinct is to hide the fact that I had different intentions."

"It always comes out," Si replied. "Whether you tell her now or she finds out later, she will find out."

Yeah, that seemed to be the general consensus.

"Then she should hear it from me." He'd been thinking about it for days, his gut in knots. Except when he was in bed with her. When he was making love to Vanessa, he forgot about everything but her. In those moments the world fell away, and he was content.

Was he about to lose her?

"She should," Si agreed. "You need to make her understand that the feelings you have are real even if they started out as something else."

"I don't think that will matter as much as me being the one who called the press down on her head so she would need a place to go." He wasn't proud of that now.

Si's eyes widened. "Bloody hell. I'm glad I'm out of this business. Finding missing persons is so much cleaner a job. I don't miss the days of subterfuge. You might not tell her that part of the story until you've been married a couple of years."

Maybe she'd forgive him if they had a couple of babies. She would have to, right?

He was thinking of marrying her. Not thinking. He was planning on marrying her.

There was a knock on his door and then Deke was walking through.

Deke had a laptop in his hands and a frown on his face. "I have something I need to show you."

Simon took that as his cue. "I'll be down in my office if you need anything. And we'll plan that dinner."

Michael nodded and then turned to Deke after the door closed behind his cousin. "What's going on?"

"I've got movement on a couple of fronts." Deke settled into the chair across from him. "First, you should know that I've identified the PI who wrote the report Junior sent your mother. He's your usual investigator. Mostly works divorces and insurance scams. I believe he's still following Vanessa around."

"Yeah, I picked up a tail a couple of days ago." He'd thought it was probably press, but he hadn't wanted to worry Vanessa. "He's been following me after I drop Vanessa off. I started taking her into the parking garage instead of dropping her at the front door. I'm using the rain as an excuse, but I won't be able to forever."

"I can go talk to the man," Deke offered. "Try to get a feel for how long this harassment is going to continue."

"Excellent." It was time to start protecting her. "Take one of the lawyers with you. I want him to understand Junior isn't the only person with an interest in Vanessa. What else do you have?"

"I think it's safe to say that Ruby was our hacker," Deke continued. "I've been watching the kid to see what she does when she's not around Vanessa. MaeBe's been on some of the same boards, posing as a high school hacker, and she's gotten Ruby to talk a little. You won't fucking believe who she's looking into now."

He didn't want to guess. "Julian?"

Deke shook his head. "Kyle."

"Why would she look into Kyle?" Michael couldn't help but remember how Vanessa had studied Kyle that first night at The Club. She'd been fascinated with the younger man. Was Ruby doing some background on her friend's secret crush?

He hated the jealousy that curled inside of him, a snake waiting to strike.

"Ruby seems to think Kyle might have had a relationship with Nicki Jones," Deke explained.

That didn't make any sense to him at all. "What kind of relationship?"

"Romantic was the vibe MaeBe got," Deke explained.

"Was Kyle even at The Club when Nicki was there?" He tried to piece together the timeline in his head. It felt random to him that Kyle would be her target. Kyle had pretty much walked into MT, seen MaeBe Vaughn, and not looked at another woman since. At least that was how it appeared to Michael. Kyle could play deep games.

"Yes, they would have both been there for a few months before she died. Do you feel comfortable with me asking him?" Deke asked.

"Of course, why wouldn't I?"

Deke shrugged. "We didn't ask Vanessa."

He groaned, his head falling back. "It's not the same."

"I wanted to check with you before I asked him. I'm not sure how he fits into this," Deke admitted.

"I'm not either. Vanessa talks about her sister a lot, but I've never heard her mention Kyle's name. If she had questions about her sister's relationship with him, why wouldn't she simply ask him? What would make her send a hacker after him?" Another thought struck him. "Do we know if Ruby's been looking into him? Like more than asking questions."

"That's what MaeBe is worried about," Deke replied. "She said Ruby was asking about hacking into military records. She told the girl not to, but she wasn't sure how seriously Ruby took the warning."

"Well, we're about to find out how good she is." Michael sat back.

"We also might find out if the rumors are correct." Deke shrugged. "I mean, come on, man. Aren't you curious?"

He knew the rest of the office was, but he didn't need to be. "No. I can tell you unequivocally that Kyle was an Agency operative. I might not have proof, but I know the signs. So if Ruby started poking that beast, she's going to be in trouble very quickly." He'd hoped he would have more time to make this decision. Or rather time to figure out the best way to tell Vanessa. "Tell MaeBe to monitor the situation and let me know if anything else happens. I have to figure out how to help my girlfriend's friend not get arrested by the CIA. I will go and talk to Kyle and try to figure out why Vanessa's worried about him."

She wasn't interested in him. If she was sending her friend out to investigate Kyle, it was because she was worried about something. Any other explanation that ran through his head was pure jealousy. He started to push his chair back.

Deke held a hand up. "I'm not done. Hutch managed to pull a face off the video feed."

Now this he was very interested in. They'd been trying to figure out who'd attacked Vanessa for days. "Did you get a name?"

"John Smith of Colorado. Not much information on the guy, but he's done some time for petty theft," Deke explained.

"All right, let's send that to the police." If this had truly been a crime of convenience, he would sleep a little easier at night. His phone rang, and he glanced down at the number. "This is Phoebe. I need to take this. She said she's figured out where the money is going."

Deke closed the laptop. "All right. I'll meet you back here around lunch?"

He nodded and answered the phone. "Hey, Phoebe. What do you have for me?"

Hopefully he could have this whole thing wrapped up by then and he could deal with Julian and get on with being what he wanted to be—Vanessa's man.

* * * *

"Did you get what you needed?" Vanessa settled back onto her seat as Dani moved around her desk. The rain was coming down lightly. It had been raining for two days, and Michael had been the sweetest. He'd insisted on dropping her off inside the parking garage instead of the front door despite the fact that it was only a few steps from the car to the door. She'd gotten the feeling he would get out and hold a damn umbrella over her head if she argued with him, so she hadn't.

She could get used to the kind of attention and care Michael Malone gave his sub.

What would he give a girlfriend? Or a wife?

"That should be the end of it. At least on the financial end." Dani sighed. "Thank you for letting me use your system. I know I should tell Julian, but he can be unreasonable about some things, and this is one of them."

She didn't mind. Vanessa understood that family could cause problems. Some things were better left quiet.

"All right, then, I'm going to hop on a call with some suppliers. Let me know if you need anything," Dani said, giving her a wave.

"Will do."

Vanessa turned back to her system. She had a full day of placing orders and checking in on contractors. The party was coming up, and she wanted everything to run smoothly. She'd already had the florist cancel on her.

Maybe she should call Ava Malone. The woman threw a lot of parties. It might be good to get her advice.

Or she might be fooling herself. She'd loved spending time with Michael's family. She couldn't remember the last time she'd felt so welcome in a place. Between the adorable kids and Ava's obvious maternal love for her boys, that night had been pleasant, and she'd never wanted it to end.

Would it be so wrong to ask Michael for his mom's number? Would he be horrified?

She was about to text him when her cell trilled. She glanced down at the number and answered, a little worry gnawing at her. "Ruby? Shouldn't you be in school?"

A sniffling sound came over the line. "Uhm, I was. And that was when the cops came. They hauled me out in front of everyone. In handcuffs. It honestly would have been pretty cool except I cried like a baby. I thought I was scared of them. Then the dude in the suit showed up and made them look like nice guys."

"What?" She stood, grabbing her purse. "Where are you?"

"I'm fine. I'm home," Ruby said. "They let me go. I think my hysterical crying made them feel like I'd learned my lesson. Which I have. I'm okay, but I don't think I'll be hacking into the US military again any time soon."

"You did what?" She was fairly certain she screeched the question. She glanced around, but everyone seemed wrapped up in their own work, luckily.

"I went looking for Kyle Hawthorne's records, and that's where they were. I'd been talking to some people online, and I figured out how to do it. I should have listened to that one chick. She told me this would happen. Look, I'm sorry, but I have to stop. My mom is freaked out. She took my laptop. I wanted to call you before she takes my phone. I'm so sorry, Vanessa. I think it was him, and all the security around him proves it."

She wasn't sure it proved anything except that she'd gone too far. "I'm sorry for getting you involved."

"You need to stay away from him, Ness." Ruby's voice went low as though she was terrified she might be overheard. "He's bad news. I got the tiniest glimpse at one of his boss's evaluations of him. He's a killer."

Vanessa's stomach knotted, guilt flowing through her. She'd done this. She'd gotten Ruby in trouble because she'd been too scared to tackle the problem head on. "I'll do what I should have done in the first place. Ruby, you call me if you need any help. I'll talk to your mom if I need to."

"I think that would make things worse. I'm sorry I couldn't find the proof." There was the sound of a woman yelling in the background. "I gotta go. I think I'm grounded for the rest of my life."

The line went dead.

And Vanessa made a decision. The scariest one of her life.

She picked up the few things she'd left on her desk and placed them in her bag. It wasn't much. Some hand cream. A picture of her and Nicki. A couple of protein bars. It was sad, really. The computer here belonged to the company. She logged off and closed the lid before heading for the elevator. She rode it up six floors to the Lodge Corp floor and marched straight to Julian Lodge's office, right past his stern-looking secretary who stood and started to come after her.

That let her know she was on the right track, and the man was definitely in his office. She opened the door and there was Julian staring at his laptop screen. A brow arched over his eyes, a regal expression.

"Mr. Lodge, I'm so sorry. She walked right past me," the assistant said.

"I need to talk to you." She wasn't about to turn around now. She was about to find out if she was making the worst mistake of her life. She had no idea what this man would do to her if she was wrong and he was actively involved with what had happened to her sister.

She wanted Michael here. She would feel safer if he was here, but she had to put this in someone else's hands, and she didn't want it to be his. She'd already gotten one person she cared about in serious trouble.

"Gwendolyn, I don't think you could have stopped her. She looks very intent. Please don't worry about it. Close the door on your way out. I'll handle this." Lodge nodded, and she found herself alone with him. "What did you wish to talk to me about, Vanessa?"

She was about to blow up her whole life. Again. "I lied to you."

Lodge's expression didn't change at all. He merely held out a hand to offer her a chair. There were two wingback chairs across from his desk. Like everything around Julian Lodge, they were expensive and elegant and felt the slightest bit sinister. "About what? Why you took the job Danielle offered you? Why you claimed to want a membership at my club when it was obvious you found the idea distasteful in the beginning?"

She felt bile creep up her throat, but she forced it back down. Maybe she hadn't been so good at this. She sat down in front of him, clutching her purse like a lifeline. She wouldn't be able to go back to her little desk. She would be escorted out, and she had to hope Michael didn't hate her after this or she would have nowhere to go. "Both."

Lodge sat back, his fingers steepling in front of his chest. "I'm listening."

She hadn't thought this through. She'd forced herself to come down here before she could talk herself out of it, but now she had to make him understand. "When my sister died and I moved into the house, I found her journal. She mostly wrote down little things. Thoughts. She drew some pictures. But the last few pages were more like a real diary. She was seeing a man at your club, and she was terrified of him. I don't think her accident was an accident at all. I think that man stalked her and killed her, and I took the job to get to the club so I could find him."

The placid expression was gone, and his hand was on the phone, pulling it to his ear. He pushed a single button and she expected to hear him calling for security. "Danielle, darling, I need you down here in my office now. Yes. It's rather an emergency. I've done something, and you need to be here when I confess."

What? He hung the phone up and leaned toward her, his whole expression softening. "Vanessa, I need you to understand that I felt like you were lying to me, and I was worried. I'm a cautious man."

"What's happening?"

He shook his head. "I would rather wait for Danielle. So you found your sister's journal. Did she say who was stalking her?"

He seemed to be taking her seriously. She relaxed slightly. He wasn't throwing her out or threatening her. If Julian could help her, this might work out all right. "She called him MK. Since she spoke directly about The Club and meeting him there, I assumed the M stood for Master and his first name would be K. Like some people call Michael Master M. I believe she might have been talking about Kyle Hawthorne. I think he could be very dangerous. He seems to have ties to military intelligence."

Julian paled. "Please tell me you didn't look into him. I know a bit about our Mr. Hawthorne, and I think anyone looking into his military history could find themselves being visited by our government."

She wished she'd known that last week. It could have saved Ruby a rough morning. "Yes, that's why I'm here. I had a friend who went a little too far. You have to know I did not want her hacking into military records. She's fine, but this has gotten too dangerous. I can't go deeper without hurting people I care about."

"I understand. And honestly, I also understand why you didn't immediately come to me with your concerns. I wasn't warm and welcoming. I'm sorry. That's not my way. Let me know if I should make some phone calls on your friend's behalf." Julian looked up as the door came open, relief plain on his face. "Danielle, please come here, love. Vanessa has just told me she's been investigating Kyle Hawthorne."

Dani strode into the room. "Why would she do that? What did Kyle do? Vanessa, what's going on?"

There was a surprising amount of relief in the full-on knowledge that Dani hadn't been any part of what happened to her sister. "I'm sorry. As I was telling your husband, I took this job because of something I read in my sister's journal. She was being stalked by a Dom here at The Club."

Dani gasped and looked to Julian.

"You have to tell her," Julian said softly, sitting back down. "I think it's best coming from you. She believes Kyle is the man who was stalking her sister. She thinks he was the reason for her accident. I know you talked about this with Nicki, but she has to know now."

"Know what?" Vanessa looked up at her boss, whose eyes were now shining with tears. She had the sudden feeling that she didn't truly understand what was happening.

Again, she so wished Michael was here with her.

Dani sank down to the seat beside her and reached for her hand. "Sweetie, there was no stalker." Dani sniffled and seemed to think about how to continue. "There are things about your sister that you don't know. Things she didn't want you to know. She was paranoid in her last days. She thought there was always someone after her, and she would sometimes see things that weren't there."

"Why?" She didn't understand.

"Because she had a very aggressive brain tumor," Dani said quietly. "She found out four months before the accident. She went to the doctor because she was having episodes. She had these terrible headaches, but even worse, she was seeing frightening things. She would see red eyes in the dark and think a demon was after her. She had a whole conversation with someone who wasn't there. We were all worried about her. She thought she was going crazy."

Vanessa shook her head as the implications washed over her. Her sister had been sick. Deathly ill, and she'd never said a word? "No. She would have told me."

But would she? They'd talked on the phone, but Nicki hadn't come to support her during the trial. She hadn't come down when George had died. She'd made Dani the executor of her will.

Why would a thirty-five-year-old woman need a will unless she'd known she was dying?

"She didn't want anyone to know. Even here at the office, she kept it quiet," Dani replied. "She said there wasn't anything you could do so to tell you would have hurt you."

"Or it would have let me say good-bye to her. It would have given me the chance to stand by her." But her sister hadn't wanted that. She hadn't wanted Vanessa at her side. Tears fell as everything slid into place. "She knew I would bring my problems with me, and she didn't want me around."

It was one thing to talk to her on the phone, quite another to have a real relationship with her.

"She loved you, but anything surrounding you was complex for her." Dani seemed to weigh every word carefully. "It was the same with your mother. Your whole family, really. I think she thought she had more time. The tumor was inoperable, but the doctors said she could live a year or so. I had the cameras installed inside the house so she could be monitored. She didn't want to go into assisted living. We made a plan. Eventually we would have paid for around the clock nursing so she could stay in her home. It didn't turn out that way. We believe the tumor affected her driving that night."

"I should have given her a driver." Julian's eyes were grim, his skin somewhat pale in the low light.

"She didn't want one. She wanted to be independent for as long as she could," Dani argued.

"There wasn't a stalker?" She could barely wrap her head around the idea. For months she'd lived with this secret. A secret that was nothing more than an illusion.

"No. I don't even think she spent more than a few minutes with Kyle. They didn't spend time in the same circles. He was in training most of the time they were both in The Club. I'm sorry you found those writings. I thought I'd taken all of the journals she kept. I must have missed one. The others were quite disturbing," Dani admitted. "I'm so sorry you found out this way."

She took the tissue Julian offered her and dabbed at her eyes. "I'm…I don't know what I'm feeling. Stupid, I guess. I should have seen this. I'm sorry I took the job under false pretenses. If it helps, I ended up liking it here. I'll miss it."

Dani's eyes went wide. "Why would you miss it?"

"I told you. I lied."

Dani's hand squeezed hers. "And I kept the truth from you. You are one hundred percent forgiven. I understand why you lied. I don't have any intention of firing you. I'll pretty much do anything to get you to stay."

She wasn't fired? She could stay? She looked to Julian.

"I think you should hear me out before you make any decisions." Julian frowned. "Now I understand why you had someone attempting to hack into The Club's records. But that doesn't change the fact that Danielle's accounts are down over fifty thousand dollars, and each transaction was made from your system. I also have a report that details a blackmail scheme that was found on your system at your home. I'm willing to listen to explanations, Vanessa."

She drew her hand back because part of that wasn't her story to tell, and she was left reeling from what Julian had revealed. "Blackmail? On the computer at Nicki's place? I haven't been back in over a week. How would you know what's on her system?"

Dani stood, facing her husband. "I moved that money, Julian. I used Vanessa's system because I didn't want to tip you off. It seems I didn't do a good job."

"Why would you do that?" Julian asked, his brows coming together.

"Because you're very stubborn about certain things, my sister being one of them," Dani replied. "Because she was about to lose her house, and it's not about Val. It's about my nieces. I can't let them be homeless."

"You sent Val money?" Julian asked. "Fifty thousand dollars?"

Vanessa knew the story. Dani had explained that her sister was a terrible person who Julian and Finn both loathed. But she had two small girls Dani adored, and she couldn't turn her back on them. She'd thought Julian wouldn't notice the money being gone.

It seemed like Julian knew a lot of things he shouldn't.

Dani started to argue, but all Vanessa could think about was how Julian would know what was on the rat-trap computer she'd left behind when she couldn't go back. Deke hadn't brought it with him.

Deke, who had a key to her place because he was "checking" up on things.

Deke, who worked for a security firm. Who did investigations. The same firm Michael worked for.

"Danielle, anything I have is yours." Julian had moved into his wife's space, his hands on her hips as he stared down at her. "If you want to buy your sister's mortgage out, you can. I only ask that…"

"Well, I didn't put it in her name," Dani shot back. "I know her too well. She would sell the whole thing and come back to me after she spent the money. I own the house. She lives in it."

Vanessa's brain was still working, still putting together pieces that fit into a nasty puzzle. Michael was an investigator. He didn't attend The Club. He had his own club. He'd given her some excuse on why he wanted to explore, but the logical explanation was that Julian had known she was lying, and he needed someone to figure out why.

"Forgive me, Danielle. I should have come to you in the beginning." Julian had his forehead resting against his wife's, their intimacy plain for anyone who was watching. "Let's call Finn and take the afternoon off so we can talk. Wolf can get the children from school, and we'll go down to The Club like we used to."

There was so much love between them. Dani had two men who adored her, a whole family who craved her attention. She took care of a sister who apparently didn't deserve it.

Vanessa was always the one who didn't deserve care. She wasn't sure why, but the world told her that again and again and again.

Her own sister hadn't wanted her love and attention when she was dying.

"I would like that, Master," Dani said softly.

Julian would do anything to protect Dani. Even hire someone to investigate her new "friend."

She wouldn't have trusted anyone who worked for him or who'd been in The Club for a long time. "It was smart to go with the training Dom. He even told me what he did, and I never suspected him."

She should have.

"What?" Dani had turned her way.

She knew this wasn't Dani's fault, but she didn't have the bandwidth to deal with it right now. She merely needed confirmation of what she knew had to be true. She kept her eyes on Julian. "Michael Malone is investigating me, isn't he?"

She'd made it easy on him. She'd fallen right into his hands the first time they'd met. Julian had watched to make sure his plan was going to work.

"Vanessa, all I knew was…" Julian began.

"What do you mean Michael is investigating you?" Dani had stepped back. "Honey, he's your training Dom. I know he works for McKay-Taggart, but no one would try to trick you like that."

"What is the blackmail he found on the system at my sister's?" She ignored Dani's explanation. It was obvious she didn't know what her husband had done. She tried her best to go cold. She didn't want him to see her cry. She wanted him to confirm that she'd been sleeping with a man who had hopped into her bed in order to prove what a criminal she was.

Julian sighed and ran a hand over his head, smoothing back his dark hair. "It was something about you sleeping with your stepson. I'm not sure if you were the one being blackmailed or the blackmailer. I thought perhaps it was why you took the money. Vanessa, I'm sorry. I didn't understand what was going on."

"You could have asked her." Dani was suddenly looking like she didn't want to take that trip down to the dungeon. "Julian, she's sleeping with him. She's in love with him."

"And I didn't mean for that to happen. We don't know that Michael doesn't have real feelings for her. It certainly wasn't my intention to do anything more than find out what she was doing." For the first time since she'd met the man, Julian didn't seem to be in control of the world.

They began to argue, but it didn't matter. An odd numbness descended. It wasn't like this was the first time she'd been betrayed. But it might be the time that truly taught her. She was a moron who kept getting kicked over and over and still thought someone out there might be able to love her.

She stood and quietly left. She walked out of the building, and the rain started to hit her.

Someone shouted for her to stop, but she knew exactly where she was going.

Chapter Fourteen

Michael sat in the conference room as his boss went over the report he'd turned in.

"What the fuck?" Ian looked up. "Did he honestly believe no one would figure out these pictures were from a photo shoot?"

"I think he didn't care." MaeBe sat across from Michael, Kyle at her side. She'd come back into the office yesterday, and Kyle had been hovering ever since. "I've gone through this a couple of times, and I think what he truly intends to do is leak this to the press."

"She's been studying Junior," Kyle explained. "I actually think she's got a pretty good handle on him."

"He's nasty." MaeBe shuddered as though even thinking about the man was distasteful. "Everyone who works for him hates the guy. Also I'm pretty sure he's heading for divorce number three. It's all in my report."

"You know she could have sent her report in." Kyle frowned Ian's way. "She shouldn't be up here. She shouldn't be working at all."

MaeBe's jaw clenched. "I feel fine. The doctors cleared me."

"Well, Ian shouldn't have," Kyle said under his breath. "You should be on leave."

"The doctor did clear her, and she's visiting with a therapist to follow up." Ian's eyes had gone stony as though he was sick of this argument. "I'm treating her like I would treat any of my employees. I won't treat her like a child because she has a vagina. Do you think her having a vagina makes her less tough, Kyle?"

MaeBe had blushed when Ian had said the word vagina, but then she'd turned as though brushing right past her boss's mention of genitalia and clinging to the opening he'd given her. "Yeah, do you have a problem with my vagina, Kyle?"

"I don't have a problem with your…" Kyle groaned. "I'm worried that you're pushing yourself too hard. You got stabbed. That's all."

"I'm fine. I need to work." MaeBe turned back to Ian. "Like I was saying, I don't think this easily holds up, though the police would likely investigate. They might even arrest her."

Ian nodded Michael's way. "You okay with your girl getting interrogated by the police? Is that why you haven't dealt with this yet?"

His boss could be so judgmental. "I needed to make sure it wasn't real. I believed it, but I wanted proof. I haven't warned Vanessa about the blackmail scheme because I don't want to worry her. I want to have a plan in place when I tell her what's going on. I believe that Junior intends to use it to put out negative press before the appeal. He doesn't need her in jail. He only needs the story out there. He'll sit on it until the time is right."

Would Vanessa view that as him treating her like a child who needed to be protected from the big bad world? The trouble was her world really was big and bad and threatening to eat her alive.

"And if you're wrong about the timing?" Kyle seemed far happier pointing out all of Michael's flaws. "This is a bomb that could explode at any moment."

"I don't think so, but that's why we're talking today." Michael sat back. "I want to be able to tell Vanessa what we're going to do about it. Then she won't have to worry."

"We wouldn't want the target to worry her pretty head over anything," Taggart said with a snort.

Michael barely managed not to roll his eyes. "So Hutch is busy putting together a report that will lay out the whole scheme to the police. He thinks he can have it together tonight. I'll present it to Vanessa tomorrow, and we'll go from there."

"Okay, can we talk about the fact that I got a call from military intelligence last night?" Kyle had straightened up. "Someone is looking into my military records."

MaeBe turned his way. "I told you. She's just a kid."

Ian put a hand to his head. "Yeah, I've already had a call about it. I'm afraid Ms. Lockwood's age isn't going to stop the feds from visiting her. It should happen at some point in time today. The good news is she didn't get far. She did, however, read a couple of performance reviews. Should we be worried about those?"

It was Kyle's turn to shrug and act nonchalant. "Depends on which ones she reads. If they're from my early days, she'll likely find out I'm good at keeping my bunk clean and I follow orders well."

"And if it's not?" Ian asked.

A savage smile crossed Kyle's face. "Then she'll find out I'm good at other things."

MaeBe sent Kyle a nasty stare. "Don't you threaten that poor girl."

"Why would she be looking into you?" It was one of the things he couldn't figure out. He knew damn well she wasn't interested in Kyle in a romantic fashion. So why was her friend investigating him?

The door opened, and the receptionist poked her head in. Yasmin Tahan was in her mid-twenties. She'd been with the firm for less than a year, one of the new hires who made him wonder if he'd ever been that young. "Mr. Malone, you have a call."

He'd stopped trying to get her to call him Michael. "Please take a message and I'll call him back."

She nodded and strode away.

"I don't know," Kyle replied. "Unless she's not what she seems and she's working for another group."

"She's a kid," MaeBe argued. "She thinks she's invincible. I know exactly where she is and how she thinks because I used to be her. Can we stop the feds from going after her?"

"That is above my pay grade. The feds do what the feds do." Ian pulled his cell out of his pocket. "Let's not jump to conclusions. Maybe they won't visit her." He looked down at the screen. "I've got to take this. Michael, did you get Phoebe's report?"

He'd gotten it and practically jumped up and down. That report meant the last of the walls between them had been smashed. "Dani's hiding money from Julian. She bought the mortgage on her sister's house. Sister was in arrears, and the bank was about to foreclose."

Ian held his cell up. "Yeah, I get to tell Julian all about that. Your girl's clean on the money front. That doesn't answer all my questions, though. Figure out why she's got a hard-on for Kyle here and you can wrap this up." He put the phone to his ear, starting for the conference room door. "Julian, I've got good news and I've got bad news."

"So Vanessa didn't take the money." MaeBe nodded as though she'd always known it.

"I suspect she's been helping Dani hide it from Julian." That had been Phoebe's opinion, and it was his, too. "I need to go down and talk to Julian. I need him to call off the investigation so I can start protecting Vanessa." Michael stood. He needed to head over to Lodge Corp. Deke walked in as Michael picked up his tablet. "Hey, we're going to get the report from Hutch in a few hours and wrap this case up. I'm going to talk to Julian if you want to come with me."

"It's about time," Deke said. "I'll take care of the PI, and you sit her down for a long talk. Be careful with her. You've got to ask her what she's afraid of because I think this all comes down to fear. I think that's why she's been looking into members of The Club. It probably has something to do with her sister since she was a member before she died. She might want to make sure her sister wasn't abused. You know how outsiders can see us sometimes. She was probably shocked her sister was involved in the lifestyle."

Michael started out of the conference room. She might have been shocked in the beginning, but she'd taken to the lifestyle beautifully. He wasn't a twenty-four seven top, but he deeply enjoyed the nightly rituals they'd fallen into. He liked picking her up and making sure she was safe, enjoyed helping her cook dinner and cleaning up afterward.

God, he loved the fact that he was going to be with her.

He had a lot to do if he was going to talk to Vanessa tonight, and it started with going over and talking to Julian. His boss would fill the client in on what was happening with the money, but it was up to Michael to convince Julian to drop the investigation entirely.

"Whatever reason she has, it's not to hurt someone." MaeBe followed him and Deke out. "She's a good person."

Kyle was frowning as they made it to the lobby. "Why would she have a hard-on for me? I barely know the chick."

"I thought you killed my sister, but it turns out a brain tumor did it."

He stopped because he knew that voice. He turned, and Vanessa stood in the corner, her hair wet and plastered around her shoulders, her mascara ruined. She held her purse in both hands, and he could see from the empty look in her eyes that something had gone terribly wrong.

"Hey, sweetheart." He started to move toward her, his hands coming out to reach for her. "What's going on? Are you okay?"

"Don't touch me." Her eyes shifted to where MaeBe stood. "I should have guessed that. The funny thing was I was about to call you to see if I could stay at your place for the night."

MaeBe had paled, and Kyle moved in front of her like Vanessa was going to attack.

What the hell had happened? Why was Vanessa here? "We should go to my office to talk."

"I'm not going anywhere with you." Her voice sounded flat, all the emotion gone. "I needed to see it, to make sure it was real. I didn't know May was in on it, but it seems like you all are. I suppose Tessa and David were watching me, too."

Fuck. Michael's gut rolled. "Vanessa, if you come to my office, I can explain everything."

"I think I have it." She backed away from him. "Julian was worried I was sketchy because everyone told him I was. He didn't want to risk his precious wife getting infected by me so he brought you in to make sure I didn't hurt her. He decided the best way to watch me was to fuck me over, and that's where you came in."

"I can understand how it sounds that way." He had to tamp down his panic. Something had gone wrong, and she'd found out.

She looked at MaeBe. "Him I can understand. He's a rich prick who thinks a woman like me is something to use and toss out the minute he's done. But I thought you were different. I guess the goth crap is there to hide the fact that you're just like the rest of them. Feminism to you is all about being able to be one of the guys. You get to join in on fucking a chick over, huh?"

"That's not what I meant to do." Tears rolled down MaeBe's

cheeks.

"Hey, she was trying to protect you." Kyle took a step toward Vanessa.

That was not happening. "Leave her be."

"Yeah, she protected me all right. She helped shove me into bed with him." Her chin came up in a stubborn expression. "I want to know everything you did to me. It seems awfully coincidental that I wouldn't be able to go home at the precise moment you needed me close to watch me." She turned to Deke. "Did you have something to do with that? Did I actually hand over my keys to the man who called the press down on me?"

"Well, fuck," a deep voice said. "That was Julian calling to tell me we might have an avenging angel on the way over. Guess Michael should have answered his phone. Ms. Jones, I'm Ian Taggart, part owner of the company I hope you don't decide to sue. Why don't you come into my office and we can talk?"

Ian stood in the doorway that led back to the offices, a fierce frown on his face.

"She's coming with me, and we're going to talk this out." He wasn't about to let Ian get in the middle of this. Vanessa was his. Ian wasn't going to take over, and Michael sure as hell wasn't going to allow his boss to throw him under a bus to protect the company.

"I'm not going with either of you." Vanessa stood her ground. "I want to know if you're the one who called the press that day. When we had coffee, you kept me there for longer than we'd agreed. Is that because you were waiting for the press to show up?"

"It's because I didn't want the date to end," he replied.

Her eyes rolled. "Sure."

"Vanessa, I told you that no matter what happened, you should know that I care about you. I meant that." He could get control of this situation. She'd had a hard truth hit her, one he could have softened if he'd been the one to tell her, but he could turn this around.

"Did you or did you not call the press?" Her eyes were steady on him.

"I did." He wasn't going to lie to her again. "At the time all I knew was money was missing. A lot of it. And I knew someone was attempting to hack the systems at Lodge Corp. I wanted you close for a lot of reasons. Baby, I might have started this relationship out the wrong way, but I want it. I want you."

She turned to Ian. "Mr. Taggart, I assume your investigation of me is over, correct?"

"Yes." Ian's expression softened marginally. "I believe you will find that Mr. Lodge regrets any discomfort he's cost you."

Vanessa crossed her arms over her chest, a protective gesture. "Sure. I could almost forgive him knowing there was money missing, but then I remember that he set me up with a man he had to know was going to lie to me to get me in bed. After all, he designed the contract and then stood outside the room watching to make sure Michael was able to get into my panties the first time I met him."

"It wasn't like that," Michael protested. Except he knew it was.

"So I think Julian Lodge can fuck himself," she replied righteously.

"You can rage against that machine, Ms. Jones, or you can look at your options and play this smart." Ian moved to the receptionist desk where Yasmin sat watching the whole scene play out with wide eyes.

"I haven't shown myself to be smart in any way," Vanessa said with an unamused chuckle.

"Then let me show you how to play this to your best advantage," Ian replied. "Julian is currently in the doghouse. It's not a position the man is used to. He's also not used to feeling guilty. Let me broker a truce for you. You have enemies, one in particular. You can't scare or intimidate your stepson, but I assure you Julian can. I can. You want that man out of your life forever, let us take care of him."

Vanessa hesitated. "In exchange for what?"

"In exchange for nothing," Michael assured her. "I'll help you. I'll hire Ian to help you. Baby, that was always my plan. I knew very shortly in that you were innocent."

She ignored him. "In exchange for what, Mr. Taggart?"

"Well, there's the not suing me part," Ian began. "You go back to working for Dani. She's very angry at the thought of losing you."

"I don't know that I can." But it was easy to see she was starting to waver.

"And you give Michael a chance," Ian finished. "Look, I've been dealing with numbskull operatives for over twenty years, and I can tell you how this goes. You can punish him for a while or you can let him grovel and get it over with so you can move on. Unless you didn't care about him, and then he's going to have to live with that for the rest of his life because he's the dumbass who didn't confess fast enough."

"I was going to tell her tonight." His boss was going to make this worse. "I wanted the plan from Hutch and then I was going to tell her. I also needed that report from Phoebe. If she'd taken the money, I was going to pay it back to Julian and get her out of trouble."

"That's where you made your mistake." Ian shook his head. "You got sidetracked. Now, why don't we find Ms. Jones some clean clothes, cater in some lunch, and talk about how to get everything she possibly can out of Julian before he forgets he's human and fallible again. A twenty-five percent raise is only the beginning."

For a second, he thought she would take Ian up on his offer. Her expression lost the blankness, and he saw a longing there. She wanted to forgive him and go on. She wanted everything he'd offered her before she'd found out what a shit he was.

"I don't care about Michael. He was a means to an end." Every word that came out of her mouth was steady and cold. Calculating. "I quite like having rich men around. If you think I can get Mr. Lodge to help me with my stepson, then I don't need to sleep with Michael anymore. I find D/s distasteful. I agree to your other terms."

Liar. She responded beautifully to D/s, and the instinct to prove that to her and everyone around them rode him hard. He might have if he'd thought for a second she meant a word of it. But he knew when she'd taken on a role. She was playing to type, pulling on the jaded, bombshell seductress like armor around her. She was trying to go to a place where nothing could touch her.

"Vanessa, you don't have to do this." He wasn't going to get pulled into this scene. "I know you, and despite the fact that I've been a massive asshole, you know me. You are not this woman. You did not use me. You opened yourself up to me, and now that feels like a mistake. But I promise you, we'll get through this. And I won't hide you. I'll stand right beside you. My whole family will. I'm so sorry I wasn't smart enough to lay my heart down the minute we met. It's what I should have done, but I've been hurt before, and you were way too good to be true."

"Yes, far too good to be true." Bitterness dripped from her tone.

"Because what you always wanted was a societal outcast. You were desperate for a woman you can't bring home with you."

"My mother is crazy about you." She'd called him twice since the day she'd met Vanessa, asking when he would bring her out to the ranch. "I told you. My family won't care about your past, but they will fight for our future."

"We don't have a future." She huffed and turned. "Mr. Taggart, I'm ready to talk."

"Are you sure? Because I've been through this enough to know that you're only putting off the inevitable. Not that I don't think you should make him beg. Like go for it, girl. But I know how these things go, and someone's going to show up with a gun at some point, and it's easier if the two of you have your shit together," Ian said.

She stared at him.

"Hard way it is." Ian stopped, his jaw tightening. "What's that about?"

Michael followed his boss's line of sight and watched as a familiar face got off the elevator. Derek Brighton wore a suit and tie, a lanyard with his badge and ID around his neck. Derek was a high-ranking member of Dallas police and a member of Sanctum. He was escorted by two uniformed officers.

Michael moved in front of Vanessa and prayed he hadn't been wrong about Junior's timing.

Except George Benedict Jr. was the final person who walked off the elevator. Michael knew the man from the numerous reports he'd read. Junior was in his late fifties, and his vices were starting to show. He wore an expensive suit, but the light color emphasized the ruddiness of his cheeks, and it was slightly too tight, as though the man who wore it refused to accept his middle-aged spread. "That's her, Captain Brighton. I told you my investigators saw her come this way. She was trying to get to her new boyfriend, who obviously has no idea who she really is. Mr. Malone, I'm so sorry you had to find out this way. I tried to warn your mother. We have to stick together against these…types of women."

"We are not a *we*, you and I." Michael felt the need to make that plain. "And she's come to the right place because if you think I'm going to let you hurt her, you've severely misunderstood what's going on between Vanessa and me."

"What's happening? Why is he here?" Vanessa moved in behind him, and for a moment he could feel her hand brush against his.

He leapt on the chance, threading their fingers together and giving her all of his focus. "Whatever happens, I'm going to deal with it. I will not leave you alone. Do you understand? You don't say a thing to anyone. I'll have an attorney for you in thirty minutes, and I'll show the police everything we've discovered about this plot of Junior's."

"Ian, I came down myself when I found out who the warrant was for." Derek looked around the room, assessing the situation. "We originally thought we were going to pick her up at Lodge Corp. I thought someone senior should be dealing with Julian."

"Whatever that man has told you, he's lying," MaeBe said, pointing Junior's way. "If this is about that stupid blackmail thing he had someone try to plant on her computer, I can prove he manipulated the whole thing."

"I certainly did not." Junior waved that off. "I'm the victim here."

"Blackmail? The stuff Julian was talking about?" Vanessa pulled away. "He said something, but I didn't ask him to explain. I thought Junior was trying to blackmail me."

"You know exactly what you've done." Junior's lips curled in distaste. "I have the proof, and I've taken it to the police."

His timing had been off. Michael had been so sure he had weeks to deal with this, but obviously Junior had other plans.

"I'm sorry. He does have evidence. I have to take her into custody." Derek nodded and the uniformed officers moved in on her.

Michael moved in their way. He wasn't about to let them take her. "She didn't do this. Any evidence he has, I can refute. Derek, we've been working on this for days. I know exactly what he's trying to pass off as evidence."

"Then we can discuss it down at the station." Derek's jaw was a tight line. He'd obviously not enjoyed his work today. "I've got a warrant, and you should know there are detectives going to her house with a search warrant. I suggest Ms. Jones gets her attorney out there as soon as possible."

"I don't have that kind of attorney." Vanessa sounded small, like she couldn't quite believe what was going on. "I only have one who specializes in inheritance. And she's in Houston."

"Mitch, I'm giving you an address, and I want you to get out to it and give the police hell." Big Tag was already talking into his cell phone. "You watch everything they do."

"Come on, man," Derek said. "They're only doing their jobs. I meant she should have representation. You don't have to send your battering ram."

He would feel so much better with Mitch there. Mitchell Bradford was the attorney of record for McKay-Taggart. "And get someone down to the station for Vanessa."

Tag talked into his cell while those officers stepped in, staring him down.

"Derek, let me bring her in." He couldn't stand the thought of her being hauled out in handcuffs. "We'll surrender, but don't take her in like this. You know he's probably tipped off reporters. This is exactly what he wants. He wants to put her in the worst light possible. Why is he even here?"

"He's got some pull with brass," Derek said. "And I have my orders. I can't let you bring her in. I'm sorry. I'll take her myself. I promise I'll take her out as quietly as possible, but you know I have protocols to follow."

Derek was caught between a rock and a Taggart.

"I'll go with you." Vanessa stepped out from behind him. "I don't want to cause a scene."

A scene was exactly what Junior wanted. It was the whole point. All Junior had to do was put the story out there, and then it wouldn't matter if it was true. The press would leap on it, and then even when they proved the whole story wrong, it would have caused the damage Junior wanted it to.

"I think we can wait to put the cuffs on her until we get to the car." Derek put a hand on her arm, and Michael was overcome with the urge to punch the guy. Anger thrummed through his system because even though Derek was a friend, Vanessa was his woman. Derek sent him a stare. "Hey, man, I'm going to make sure she's fine. If what you say is true, she won't be there for long. You can stop growling at me."

He'd growled?

"Dude, you got crazy eyes." Kyle was frowning his way. "She'll be okay. I happen to have been recently arrested by DPD, and I came out of it all right. And I was an asshole. They'll be gentler with her. Vanessa, do not let them bring you food. That's the real torture."

He could punch Kyle, but he was panicking that she was being led toward the door. "Let me go with her."

Vanessa looked back at him. "I'll handle this. It's my problem, not yours."

"I can't let you go with her, and you know I can't." Derek opened the door. "I'm taking her downtown. You can meet us there."

"I hope it was worth it to you, Vanessa." George Jr. sneered her way. "I know I'm ashamed of everything we did behind my father's back, but I won't allow you to blackmail me. You wouldn't take no for an answer, and I'm just a man. I couldn't resist. You've brought enough shame to my family. I'm not letting you get away with anything else."

Michael saw red and heard someone scream. He wasn't sure what had happened but suddenly he was on the ground with two cops on top of him, and Junior was crying in the corner, holding his nose.

His arm was wrenched behind his back, and he felt the cuffs go on.

"Well, that's one way to go with her." Big Tag stood over him, shaking his head. "Derek, I'll send someone down to make bail for them both. Kyle, get the crew ready. We're going to the station house. It's another fun day. And someone get the crying billionaire off my floor. Preferably someone large and cranky. I think Boomer had to skip lunch."

"I'll handle the fucker," Deke promised. "Mr. Benedict, let me help you out of the building."

"Captain!" Junior yelled.

But Derek was busy holding the elevator doors open for Vanessa. Michael caught a glimpse of her pale face as he was hauled up to standing.

"Thank you, Deke," Derek called out. "I've obviously got my hands full. Boys, I'll take Ms. Jones. You handle Malone."

The elevator doors closed, and his heart sank.

He had to hope the doors hadn't closed forever.

* * * *

Five hours later, Vanessa was brought into the interview room. Once she'd played the girlfriend of a crazed killer on a police procedural show, and now she realized they'd gotten the set pretty right. It was utilitarian and chilly. The chair they led her to wasn't meant to be comfortable for long periods of time, though she was sure she would be here for hours.

How had her life fallen apart so quickly? She'd woken up this morning looking forward to the rest of the week, looking forward to the weekend and going to The Club with her Dom.

Her awful, horrible, lying Dom.

She'd had most of the day to think this through. She could almost forgive Julian. He'd been trying to protect Danielle. He'd read about his wife's new friend and seen what the world wanted him to see, and he'd reacted. He didn't know her, and the stories about her were awful enough to make anyone worry, much less a paranoid billionaire.

It was harder to forgive Michael.

Michael hadn't had to sleep with her. He could have investigated her without humiliating her. Michael had gotten to know her. She'd been more open with him than she'd been with anyone in years. Emotionally. Physically.

She'd been falling in love with the man, and he'd been using her to further his career.

So why had she nearly run back to him? Why had she reached out for his hand when she'd realized everything was going bad? She'd wanted him with her, wanted him to protect her.

She was an idiot.

The door opened, and she was surprised to see the big blond guy from Michael's office walk in followed by Deke Murphy. Kyle Hawthorne brought up the rear.

She felt herself flush. She'd basically accused the man of murder. And stalking. And lots of other things. She'd sent out people to gather information on him.

"Ms. Jones, how have they treated you?" Taggart slid into the chair across from her.

"Did you eat the bologna?" Kyle sat down beside his boss. And uncle of some kind.

Deke hovered in the background.

She hadn't been offered food. She also hadn't been taken to lockup. "I've been in Captain Brighton's office, and then someone came to take me here. He brought me some coffee and a towel, and then they let me change out of my wet clothes."

As police interactions went, it had been shockingly polite. Captain Brighton had put her in the back of his car and then he'd taken her into his office. She hadn't seen him again. A female officer had brought her the bag of clothes someone had packed for her.

"MaeBe ran by your place and grabbed you some clean clothes," Kyle said. "She's worried about you."

She wasn't sure what to say to that. She definitely wasn't ready to forgive the woman she'd been starting to like. She could forgive the people behind the scenes much faster. They'd been doing their jobs, not breaking her heart and her trust. "Thank her for me, please."

"She's in with the detectives, showing them what she's found," Kyle said. "She's been working on your case for days, and she's been your biggest defender."

"I didn't know I needed a defender. No one told me what was happening." She was still confused. "How was I supposed to be blackmailing Junior?"

It was ridiculous to call an almost sixty-year-old man Junior, but she wasn't about to call him George. He didn't deserve the name. He was nothing like his father. He was a selfish prick who would stop at nothing to get one more dollar out of the world. He would cut anyone's throat to get the tiniest bit further.

"He faked photographs of the two of you meeting at a seedy motel and had someone write an email demanding cash or you would turn over everything to the press," Deke began.

She felt herself flush. "I didn't…"

"MaeBe and Hutch can prove that the photos are fakes, and we have video of the man Junior hired uploading those files to the system at your sister's house," Taggart continued. "I would like to point out that had my employees not been dipshits doing shady things, you would very likely be in a cell right now waiting for an attorney you can't afford because it would take the police a while to figure this out."

"I turned on the cameras inside your sister's house," Deke admitted. "I was watching to see if anyone showed up. When you had a late-night visitor, I investigated. We can prove you weren't behind this ploy of Junior's."

She didn't care that Michael's schemes had worked in her favor. She didn't. She cared that he was one more lying asshole who'd used her.

"I still can't afford a lawyer," she said quietly. "So I'm not sure they'll listen. And I certainly can't afford your services."

"I wouldn't worry about that," Taggart replied. "I've already explained that I'm willing to deal with your case in exchange for the whole not suing us thing. And we do enough work for DPD that they will listen to us. As of ten minutes ago the police agreed this was all a misunderstanding. You won't be charged with anything."

"I haven't been able to prove that Junior was behind it." Deke leaned against the wall. "All I've got is some asshole sneaking in to upload the data to your computer. He sent the email to Junior."

Taggart shrugged. "We all know Junior did it. It's just going to take time to prove it. And I told you we would take care of the attorney. Lea Stone handles our dealings with the police. She's already gotten this incident taken care of, and she's trying to get Michael out on bond. It's surprising how fast a judge can work when you're the son of a billionaire."

"Or the girlfriend of a son of a billionaire," Kyle pointed out. "They didn't even book her from what I heard. Michael got booked real fast. I hope he avoided the bologna, too. I'm serious. They put something in it as punishment."

"I'm not his girlfriend." But she wanted to see him. Her stupid heart was so battered it should be broken beyond repair, but when she'd seen him on the ground with two police officers on top of him…

She wasn't giving in. She couldn't. Of course, she also had nowhere to go.

Taggart sighed as though that was what he'd expected to hear, but it still disappointed him.

She stared the big guy's way. "What am I supposed to do? He lied to me. He used me. I'm almost certain he did something to the gate at my housing community so I couldn't go back. Hell, maybe he was the one sending the rocks through my window."

Deke straightened up. "No, that wasn't any of us. You know that old lady across the street with all the cats?"

She gasped. "Mrs. Tillmon? That nice lady? I helped her with her groceries."

Deke shrugged. "She's real active on the community boards, and she's very judgmental about everything. She calls the cops on kids who are playing too loud, and she hates you. She's also got a surprisingly strong arm for an eighty-five-year-old."

"But it was you who fucked with the gate." She normally knew a guilty man when she saw one. She'd just gotten flustered by how gorgeous Michael was.

She'd seen what she'd wanted to see. She'd wanted desperately to be cared for, to have someone. She'd been alone for so long. That was why she'd fallen for Michael's lies.

"I did." Deke's shoulders went straight. "At the time we thought it was important to watch you carefully. We had every reason to suspect you were the one who took the money, and we believed you were working with someone to hack into Lodge Corp's systems. I know you feel what Michael and I did was wrong, but we truly believed something was going on. The way you believed Kyle was sketchy."

Kyle sat back with a sigh. "I don't blame her. I am pretty sketchy. And hey, she didn't try to trick me into a romantic relationship."

At least he got it.

Taggart turned to stare his way. "Really? Do I need to remind you that Deke and Michael are on your team?"

Kyle shrugged. "Doesn't mean they don't do bad shit. I don't think sleeping with a woman for information is good for the soul. And they were wrong to bring in MaeBe. She can't do this part of the job. She's been crying all day because she likes Vanessa and she can't stand the idea that she hurt her friend."

"She's not..." Vanessa frowned. She was saying that a lot. "I wish she'd been upfront with me. I do get why Mr. Lodge was worried about what was happening. I wish he'd asked me, but I also get it. Why would I tell him the truth? But what Michael did..."

Taggart pointed her way. "Michael did what all my idiot employees do and fell for the client. Trust me. I've seen it a thousand times. Operative walks in, thinks he's the big man and the bad girl will give up all her secrets because his dick is so special. But let me tell you, special dick always gives it up for a magical pussy. Or that one asshole that fits perfectly for my gay brothers. Or when the scissoring works just right between two chicks. Gay, straight, bi, it's all the same. Suddenly big bad operative is all *The bad girl isn't so bad and if she did something wrong, my penis will fix it.*"

Kyle's mouth was hanging open. "Why do they let you around clients?"

Taggart shrugged. "Clients love my sparkling personality. And my honesty. Deke, was Michael still planning on turning Vanessa over?"

Deke shook his head. "Nope. He was going to pay off all her debts, spank her, and then make sure she didn't get in trouble again. He wasn't actually planning on letting her find her own place. He was going to make excuses for her to stay until one day she'd been there long enough it made sense to call his place home. You know where it goes from there."

"Yeah, south, man. That leads to kids and dogs who pee when they're happy or scared. Or awake. Invest in potty pads." Taggart's expression went earnest. "Ms. Jones, I know you're pissed at Michael and your instinct is to get as far away from him as possible, but he's got an excellent plan to fix your situation. He's had a couple of hours to think."

She didn't want to know what Michael wanted. "I thought you already fixed my situation."

"I meant your situation with the press," Taggart replied. "I've had a long talk with Julian, and he's willing to provide you with a PR firm that specializes in crisis management."

She wanted to tell him to fuck himself. She didn't need this.

But she did. The press had made her life a living hell, and she wasn't sure she could survive this new scandal. "What's the catch?"

"The catch is you have to stay at Michael's for a while. You'll go to work as normal. You'll be provided with a bodyguard," Taggart explained.

Kyle held up his hand. "As long as you're not scared of him. By him, I mean me."

Ruby had talked about him being a killer, but she was young and she likely didn't understand what it meant to be a soldier. If there was one person Vanessa owed a second chance, it was Kyle. "I would appreciate it. But I don't understand why I can't stay at Lodge Corp. Dani offered me an apartment there."

"Because then you don't have access to our ace in the hole." Taggart pushed back from the table. "She should be waiting for us. Kyle, go bring the car around. Deke and I will escort them out. I don't trust you not to kill someone."

Kyle's grin was slightly sinister as he walked to the door. "It's been a while. Fine. I'll get the car, but with that crush, I can't promise not to roll over someone."

Taggart groaned. "I need more insurance. The younger generation is going to kill me. I swear. I've turned into the old man who looks at all the shitty times of long ago like they were some golden age."

Deke held the door open. "Ms. Jones, if you'll follow me."

"Where am I going?" It was a little surreal. She'd expected to spend a few days here before she could figure out how to get out on bond.

"Back to Michael's." Taggart was on his feet. "He's being released, too. The press already has the story that he beat the shit out of Junior when Junior tried to falsely accuse you of blackmailing him. I think you'll find they've also gotten a press release detailing how he hired someone to falsify those photos."

Her head was reeling. "But you said you couldn't prove it."

"Not to the police," Taggart admitted. "The press is a whole other animal. I know you've been told to keep your mouth shut and that staying silent will make them go away, but they won't as long as Junior feeds them."

"So we feed them something new," Deke finished. "And we send Junior a very specific message. He thinks you don't have a single person who'll protect you. Let's give him a fucking tiger to deal with."

She looked up ahead, and standing at the opposite end of the hall was a petite figure wearing a fabulous designer suit, her hair in a chic bob. She was the queen even in the gloom of the precinct house.

"Ava?" Was she here to pick up Michael?

Ava Malone turned, and her face immediately went sympathetic. She quickly crossed the space between them, her arms opening as she came Vanessa's way. "My darling girl, I'm so sorry I didn't get here sooner. Come here and let me look at you. Did that disgusting man get his hands on you?"

She found herself wrapped in the older woman's arms.

Like a mom would wrap up a beloved daughter. Like she was cared for and protected. Tears blurred her eyes, and she found herself holding on. It wasn't a good idea. Ava wasn't her mom. Her mom would have left her here and told the press she belonged in jail.

"I'm okay. Where's Michael?" He had to be here somewhere. Why else would Ava be here?

"He's almost through. He's going to join us in a moment." Ava stepped back, looking her over like she was checking to make sure she wasn't damaged. Her hands came up to smooth back Vanessa's hair. "I know you don't want to see him, but I'm asking you to just get through the next hour or so and you can properly yell at him when we're safely behind closed doors. That's how this family works, love. We show a united front to the outside world and hash it all out in private. Trust me. I have a few choice words for him as well. We have to understand that men are not as intelligent as we are. They're missing a chromosome and it shows."

She was so confused. "Why do I have to go back to Michael's?"

"He's ready, and the car's in place." Taggart had his cell to his ear. "Deke, go meet up with Michael. He's coming out now. I've also got security at Michael's building. The press is there, too, but we've got a back way in."

Deke jogged down the hall.

The thought of facing the press made her physically ill. "Can't we find a back way out?"

Ava's lips firmed. "I'm sorry. We can't. We need them to see us all together. We need them to understand that from now on if they come for you, they come for all the Malones."

Oh, that trap was sprung. "Mrs. Malone, I can't ask you to do that."

"Of course you can. Sweet girl, I think my son is in love with you. He obviously screwed up. But whether you ever forgive him or not, he wants to do this for you, and this is something he's never done for another woman. He doesn't ask anything of us, but he begged for this. So let him…let us do this for you. It doesn't have to be forever."

"Ava has talked to the PR expert," Taggart explained. "They

believe this is the best way to move forward and to start to change public perception of you. It could help your appeal."

So she had to choose her pride or the promises she'd made to the only person who'd ever really cared about her.

Up ahead she saw Michael come into sight. He was unkempt, his shirt untucked and hair ruffled. He looked weary, and for a second she wanted to hug him.

What she truly wanted to do was turn back time so it was morning and she was waking up in his arms. All she'd worried about was what to make for breakfast. He'd kissed her awake and made love to her before carrying her to the shower.

The world had seemed so warm this morning. Now it was cold.

He turned slightly, and his eyes found hers, and she felt like there were miles between them. Miles they would never be able to cross. She could take what he was offering. He felt guilty now that he knew she was innocent. She could let his money and family power restore some part of her reputation and then they could be done.

"All right. I'll do it."

Ava's lips curled up. "Excellent. We should begin then. But you should know that I'm going to change your mind about him. I'm going to bring you in, Vanessa, because I think the two of you are good for each other."

Michael might not be the truly dangerous one.

Vanessa forced herself to walk down the hall, toward the man who'd betrayed her.

Toward the man who might save her.

Chapter Fifteen

"You look worse for the wear, brother." Deke shook his head as he looked Michael over.

"Well, lockup isn't great on a grooming routine." Michael tried to straighten out his shirt, but it had gotten wrinkled between his fistfight with Junior, the cops who'd tackled him, and being thrown into a cell with a bunch of high schoolers who'd had a turf war over a soccer game.

God, he was going to make sure his kids never got that entitled.

Of course he was never going to have kids because the one woman he loved wouldn't ever touch him again.

"How is she?" He'd been everything Tag said he was. A moron. Arrogant. Short sighted. He should have talked to her the minute he knew he cared about her. The minute he'd thought they might have a chance, he should have sat her down and told her everything and figured it out together. Now he was well aware he was completely in love with the woman, and he'd lost her trust.

Deke's expression sobered. "She's in shock. She doesn't know what to think. Your mom showing up seems to have thrown her for a loop, but in a good way. I think she's going to go for the plan."

"She doesn't have any other choice," Michael replied. "She

hasn't since the day she met me."

He'd been thinking about it all afternoon. He'd convinced himself that she'd had a choice, that she was doing what she did with him because she was attracted to him, because they were good together.

She'd gotten close to him because he'd forced her to. He'd manipulated her into basically moving in with him, and now he was doing it again.

But if he didn't he would lose her.

He had to wonder if he already hadn't. He knew how he'd felt when he'd believed all his choices had been made for him. He'd basically upended his whole life and alienated himself from his family for years. Why shouldn't she want to do the same? And with no real ties between them, she wouldn't come back.

He'd killed the light in her eyes. Maybe he didn't deserve another chance.

"That is defeatist thinking," Deke replied. "You need to shove that out. Do not turn into Morose Mike. You always do this when you feel guilty. Don't give in to that useless emotion. It's more about you than her. I need Magic Mike. Not Morose Mike."

He frowned his friend's way. "Excuse me? You think I should strip for her?"

Deke shrugged. "I think you should use all your assets to convince her to give you a second chance. Do you honestly believe you can't come back from this? That you can't care about her enough to make her overlook how you met? Because if you can't, then we should rethink this plan. We can still take her to Julian's."

Julian hated being in the public eye. It could hurt him and his family. The Malones were bulletproof, for the most part. Oh, the press could dredge up old crap, but the kids were young enough, they wouldn't notice it, and it would go away. His parents and brother would make sure of it. Julian's kids were at a delicate age when public perception and the critical lens of the press could wreck them.

But even if they hadn't been, Vanessa was his responsibility. He owed Vanessa.

He still wanted her so very badly.

Was he the best thing for her? Deke was right. He'd been mired in his own guilt for the last few hours. He'd fucked up, but he could make things good between them again. He would stand beside her, give her the support she needed.

She was alone in the world, and he was a nasty, ruthless bastard because he was going to offer her the one thing she didn't have. A family.

All she had to do was find a way to forgive him. Or she could take on the role of his partner in this endeavor and nothing more. She was capable of doing that. She could stay with him just long enough to get what she needed. She might even get back into bed with him. It would be sex and pleasure and a little bit of revenge since he intended to let her know exactly how he felt.

He would take that risk. She was worth it. Hell, even if he knew one hundred percent that she would never forgive him, he would still do this. He wanted her to be happy more than he wanted her to be his.

But he really, really wanted her to be his.

"She's not going to Julian's." He was set on his course. "I've got a plan in place. Is the press here?"

He hated exposing her again, but it was necessary. He had to reboot the narrative.

"Yes, everything's in place. Tag has it handled. He's with Vanessa and your mom," Deke said. "You should know Tag is in full bloom when it comes to your situation. He did not hold back."

Tag would never let it go, but then that was all part of who the man was. And he'd been right. That was the problem. Big Tag was an asshole, but he was almost always right. "Please tell me he didn't talk about healing penises and magical vaginas."

Deke sighed. "I would love to tell you that, but I'm not supposed to lie."

Damn it. He turned and looked down the hall and there she was. His heart threatened to catch. Vanessa stood beside his mother, dressed in fresh clothes, but her hair had dried wavy, and she'd washed off her makeup.

He wanted to scoop her up and take her out to the ranch.

That was one choice he could give her. She walked down the hallway, her chin up in a way that let him know she was going to be stubborn. That was okay. He would give her time.

"Are you all right?" His mother looked him over.

"Yeah, I think it's safe to say you should see the other guy," he replied, his eyes still on Vanessa.

Junior had barely punched back. He'd mostly tried to get away.

"I did." Deke seemed to be way more comfortable than anyone else. "He will be visiting a plastic surgeon. That nose isn't going to work the same way again."

"Good." Vanessa's eyes met Michael's. "I can't say I'm unhappy you punched him. I've slapped the man before, but he laughed at me."

At least he'd done one thing right. "I won't let him treat you badly. I promise you won't have to put up with him."

"But I have to put up with you," she countered.

There was the fire he was hoping she would have after all this shit had gone down. He'd feared she'd retreat to the shutdown woman he'd met that first day. She'd come to life over the weeks they'd spent together, and he'd prayed today hadn't snuffed that flame. "Unless you have another plan, baby."

"Don't call me that." Her lips turned down.

"Okay. I'll try." It was hard because she was his baby. His sweetheart. His love. "Did they fill you in on what we're going to do?"

"I'm your pretend girlfriend," she replied. "Emphasis on pretend. If I stay with you, Julian will pay for my publicist and Mr. Taggart will provide security."

"Don't forget the bloodsucking lawyers," Tag added. "They can be very helpful right up until you get the bill. Which Michael will be paying."

Well, of course he would. Big Tag hadn't gotten rich by throwing money around. "I'll take care of it."

"And Michael and I will work as hard as we can to prove that Junior set you up," Deke promised. "We're also going to go through your court case to see if we can find anything Junior did that we can challenge."

"And that second part is going to happen no matter what." He was going to give her the only choice he could. "I will find a way to prove what that man did to you. But if you don't want to stay at my place, my mom will take you out the back way and to our ranch. It's isolated, and I assure you the press won't be able to get to you there."

She glanced toward the hallway that would lead them to the front of the station house. "I wouldn't have to see them?"

He shook his head. "No. And you can stay there as long as you like."

"Consider it a sanctuary," his mother confirmed. "But, darling, you need to think about this. Michael is offering you a way to stay safe now."

"But if the publicity team can turn this around, I wouldn't need to run anymore." She stared up at him, her hands on her hips. "I won't stay with you. Not for one minute beyond what it takes to get the press off me. The minute that happens, I'll leave."

A fierce satisfaction ran through him. "I'll take the chance."

She shook her head. "There's no chance, Michael. I won't ever trust you again. We can spend the next year together and I'll still walk out at the end."

But she did trust him on some level. She trusted that he would do what he said he would. She trusted that he would let her go when it was time.

Deke was right. His guilt wouldn't fix the problem, but his love might.

He moved into her space. "I want them all to understand that I'll protect you whether or not you stay with me. If you leave, all you have to do is call and I'll be there. But for now, you have a role to play. Know that I won't be acting at all. This is the role I want for the rest of my life."

"We should move out." Big Tag took a post to Vanessa's left. "Kyle's here. Ava, you need to be the one to talk to the press. I want Michael to keep his mouth shut since he's already got a court appearance to deal with. Vanessa, not a word from you. All you have to do is hold Michael's hand and look as vulnerable as you do right now."

Her hands went to her cheeks. "I should put on some makeup."

"You are perfect." Michael loomed over her, wanting her to feel his strength. It was all for her. "You're perfect when you're a blonde and you're perfect when you're a brunette. With your hair up or down. With bombshell makeup or a clean face. Your body was perfect before you had your breasts done and they're perfect now. Every scar and little line is gorgeous, so no, you don't need to do a thing. You need to let them see this side of you, too."

She went still for a moment and then she frowned. "Maybe I

should go to the ranch."

He didn't want to lose her now. "Or you can play this role. You can do it. It's nothing more than another movie role. You don't have to feel anything. You're my girlfriend, and I'm going to protect you. All you have to do is let me walk you out and put you in the car and then you can go right back to hating me. I'll let you yell at me all night."

He didn't fear her yelling. He could handle it. Hell, he wanted the fight because the fight meant she thought there was something worth fighting over. He feared her silence.

She looked to his mom. "I won't stay with him, Mrs. Malone. You're a lovely lady. I don't want to disappoint you, but I won't be able to forgive him. I don't know why you would want to be invested in this relationship, but it's not going to work, and you should know that up front."

His mom moved in front of her. "You let me worry about that. If there's one thing I've learned over the years it's that loving someone, really loving someone, isn't something to ever regret. You might regret the outcome or the pain, but never the love. The love we feel makes us better people."

"Even when it's not real?" Vanessa's voice wavered.

"It's always real. What you feel is always real. What you have to decide is whether what he felt was real and whether he's worth taking that risk on again," his mom said. "But all you have to do right now is face down a pack of wolves who want to tear you apart. You can figure out the rest later. I'm going to stay with you tonight. You don't have to worry that Michael will do anything he shouldn't with his mother there."

Now that was something he hadn't planned on. "Uh, I only have one guest bedroom."

"Not a problem, love," his mother cooed. "I'll take yours and you can have that lovely couch. Unless Vanessa would like your room. I don't know if she wants to sleep in the bed where you misrepresented yourself, dearest."

Well, it was good to know his mom was one hundred percent Team Vanessa. Though her words did make Vanessa's lips tug up slightly.

She turned back to him, and the smile was gone. "All right. Let's do this."

Her hand slipped into his, and he watched her mask go on.

He loved the feeling of her hand in his.

"We're a go. You should understand it's a mob out there. I don't think DPD was ready for this, though it could work in our favor. At least we'll know the big news stations aren't going to ignore this." Big Tag nodded to the uniformed officers at the end of the hall and then took a place beside Ava Malone. "Derek has already given the press a statement clarifying that you were never technically arrested and the matter has been satisfactorily concluded with no charges being sought."

"Please thank him for me. I know they don't like to admit they were wrong." She walked along beside him, his mother and Tag in front of them.

He stopped as they reached the glass doors, and he was confronted with a mob. Shock slammed into him because it was like something out of a movie set. A horror movie. There had to be two hundred people pressing against the police barricades. The instant the doors came open, they all turned, like a flock of predators scenting a long-denied meal.

She glanced up at him. "Didn't expect so many, huh?"

She wasn't surprised at all. No. She'd known exactly what she would be facing, and he'd brought her to this.

"I'm so sorry, bab…" He stopped himself. "I'm sorry."

She didn't look up, merely started to make her way out.

The press mobbed them, but DPD was there, holding the line, and Tag snarled at anyone who got too close. He could feel Deke at his back, knew they were protected, but he curled an arm around her anyway. It was so much. The lights. The shouted questions. The focus and the attention.

"Have you got another rich man on the hook, Vanessa?"

"Did you blackmail your stepson?"

"Mrs. Malone! Mrs. Malone, are you worried Vanessa Hale is going to use your son to get to your husband?"

His mother stopped at that one.

"I think we should keep moving." Tag pointed to the big SUV with Kyle behind the wheel.

"I speak for the whole Malone family when I say Vanessa would be a lovely addition to our family should she decide she can put up with my son Michael," his mother declared. "And she's not guilty of blackmailing anyone. If you print that she is, well, our lawyers know how to handle a libel suit. Good evening."

Tag put his big body between Michael's mom and a camera. "Keep pushing, buddy. I've got five kids, and three of them are teenage girls. Do you think I don't want to punch someone? Because I do."

One of the cops was shouting, trying to get the crowd back.

"I love you, Vanessa!"

Michael was shocked by the thin man who reached out, trying to grab for her.

Ian punched the man in the face, and he dissolved back into the crowd.

Was this what she went through? This was fucking madness.

Her eyes were on the SUV ahead of them, focused on her goal. Deke had moved in front of Michael's mother, with Ian on her side. Vanessa stayed close to the group, seemingly unaffected by the madness around her. The reporters were shouting questions her way, and the "fans" were screaming alongside them.

One minute she was walking close to him, and the next she was pulled from his side. She shouted out.

Someone had gotten a hand on her hair and was pulling her toward them. Michael caught sight of an older woman, her gray hair askew on her head. She had a hand in Vanessa's dark hair, and she twisted, yelling something Michael couldn't make out. Vanessa brought her arm up hard, breaking the hold, but the woman was trying to go over the top of the barricade, trying to get to her again.

Michael picked her up and shoved his way to the SUV where Deke was handing his mother up. Vanessa's arms clutched him, wrapping around his neck hard, but he didn't care. He was probably holding her so tightly she couldn't breathe.

They would tear her apart if he let them. Literally tear her apart. What the fuck had she done to make strangers act this way? His anger was only tempered by his need to see her to safety.

He set her on her feet and helped her into the car and then turned, looking back at the gauntlet they'd run through. It was waiting there to swallow her up, to pull her into the anger and chaos.

He wanted to eradicate the whole fucking lot.

A hand reached out. "Please, Michael. We need to go."

Vanessa sat next to his mother, holding her hand. They held on to each other, neither giving away a thing with their blank expressions.

"I'll handle the cleanup." Big Tag stepped back. Deke was already in the front seat.

Michael forced his body inside, getting into the far back. The minute Tag slammed the door shut, Kyle took off.

"That was intense. Ms. Jones, your job sucks," Kyle said.

"It's all right, love," his mother said quietly. "We'll get to Michael's and I'll make us some tea."

His mother thought tea could fix anything.

"Are you all right?" Michael asked. It was a stupid question. She wasn't all right. She had to be devastated.

"I'm fine. Thank you for getting me out of there." Vanessa sniffled but she took a deep breath and seemed to shove all that pain down.

Kyle pulled onto the main road and sped off, taking them away from all that madness.

But did distance truly take Vanessa away from it? She'd been in that craziness for years, and it had taken a toll. No wonder she'd fallen for a man who could protect her. Even if he'd been old enough to be her grandfather. She'd never had one. Not a grandfather or a father. From what he could tell, she'd never really had a mother either. She'd had a warden, and then she'd had nothing at all.

"I'm sorry." He whispered the words and he meant them.

"It was part of the story," she said flatly. "It was necessary."

He intended to make sure she never went through that again. He would wrap her up and protect her and give her the family she deserved.

And maybe then, she would find a way to forgive him.

* * * *

Vanessa felt like the walking dead. Except they were probably happier.

A numbness had settled over her. Since the moment she'd seen the crowd outside the police station, she hadn't been able to feel anything. It was like a wall had sprung up around her and nothing could touch her.

Well, except the insane woman who'd tried to pull her hair out. She'd screamed at Vanessa, telling her how she would go to hell for all the things she'd done. Her scalp still hurt, but it was a weak reminder of the fact that her whole world had fallen apart. Again.

She stared out over the balcony at the lights below. They were high enough that it was quiet up here. Michael's balcony was bigger than some of the apartments she'd lived in while growing up.

It was so odd to think of how far she'd come. She'd gone from sharing a bedroom with her sister in a seven hundred square foot apartment to living in a mansion, and none of it had made her happy. Not until she'd found this place, and that had all been a lie.

It had been good to be reminded of what her world was really like. She couldn't escape it.

She glanced back inside the condo. The lights were all on inside, and the place was full. They were all in there. Michael was standing at his dining room table like a general laying out battle plans. Deke was at his side, and MaeBe had shown up with her laptop. She was typing furiously as they all spoke to some other investigators over the speaker phone. Or the cops. She wasn't sure. She'd realized quickly she wasn't necessary. Not that she wanted to be.

She wanted to be free. She wanted to be one of those people twenty floors below walking the streets and living their lives without cameras in their faces.

"You want a beer?"

She gasped and turned to see Kyle Hawthorne standing there, two bottles in his hands.

Kyle grimaced. "Sorry. I didn't mean to scare you. I'm afraid I'm pretty quiet. It's a habit. I thought I'd come out here for some peace and quiet."

"With two beers?"

One big shoulder shrugged. "I also prefer a certain precision of movement. Two hands. Two beers. Less walking through that place and listening to some chick from New York talk about narratives and spinning things. She's very interested in spinning things."

"Yes, when I was in there she was telling everyone she's got a list of things for me to do that she thinks will help rehab my image."

She hadn't been able to breathe in there. She felt so fucking numb. "I don't want to have an image."

He held out the beer. "It's not even poisoned. Promise." He frowned. "Unless you don't like beer. I can go get you a Coke or something."

She reached for the bottle. It was cold, one of Michael's. He tended to sit with her on the balcony after work and drink a single beer while she had a glass of wine. "I'll take what I can get. Again, I'm sorry about the whole I-thought-you-killed-my-sister thing."

"How about I forgive you if you can find a way to forgive MaeBe?"

Ah, that was why he was out here. "I can forgive her, but I'll be honest, it would be hard to trust her again."

"Then why bother to forgive at all?" He said the words softly, as though they were of no real consequence to him. He turned and stared out at the city. "It's pretty up here. Sometimes I forget how nice it is to see things from a different perspective. It's hard to imagine how peaceful things can be when you're that ant on the ground running around like there's no tomorrow. When you're down there it feels like you're the most important creature in the world. You have to get up high to realize you're nothing but a cog in the machine, and you're replaceable."

Good. He was in a mood. She was, too. "I'd love for someone to replace me."

"Would you? You want someone else to have to deal with all the shit you have to deal with?"

Would she put someone else in her place? Would she put someone else through this life she found herself in? "I don't know. Some days, I'm sure I would trade in a heartbeat. Other days I know I wouldn't wish this on my worst enemy. It doesn't matter because someone will, of course. There's always a woman waiting in the wings who thinks she can beat the system, who thinks because she has good intentions that the system won't touch her. But it's random in a way. There are actresses who've behaved far worse than me who are held up as sweethearts. Somehow you get shoved into a mold and never allowed to take any other shape."

"I can understand that. I was in the military. It's decided pretty early on who's who—who will be cannon fodder and who will move the chess pieces around."

"Which one were you?"

A ghost of a smile twisted his lips up. "That's what everyone wants to know. I suppose I was something in between. Now I'm trying to be someone new. Someone better. I'm curious. Why did you think I was involved with your sister? I wasn't. I only met her a couple of times, though she seemed like a very nice lady."

"I misinterpreted something my sister wrote." She quickly ran through her thought process and how she and Ruby decided it must have been him. She confessed that Ruby had taken things a bit too far. "So now my friend is in trouble with the military, and I've proven I shouldn't be trusted with high schoolers. I'm sure that will come out at some point in time. Vanessa Hale, defiler of old men and leading America's children into sin."

She could see that headline already.

"I suspect the real problem will come for her in a couple of years," he replied. "If she managed to get through to my records, she's beyond good. Someone will be following her through college. They'll have a job for her."

Vanessa frowned at the thought. "Are you saying the military will recruit her? I don't think Ruby would make a good soldier."

"Not a soldier. And not exactly the military." He took a long drink. "If she's deep into the hacking world, there are a couple of places she can end up. Some of them aren't so good. The Agency is a viable alternative to jail or getting caught up in some criminal organization. They recruit hackers, too, but the benefits aren't as good."

"Or she can just stop." She didn't like the thought of Ruby being involved in that world.

Kyle's head shook, a sharp negative. "I've found hackers have a real problem stopping. It's an addiction for the true hackers. Like all addictions, it has to be managed or it can ruin your life. Sometimes the hacker gets lucky and finds a mentor who gives a shit, and they end up in a decent job surrounded by people who don't let them fuck up."

"I take it you're talking about May? I mean MaeBe." She'd been told the woman she knew as May went by the nickname. Kyle seemed determined to force her to see the woman in a different light.

"Yeah. She got that same visit as your friend, though she was fourteen at the time," Kyle explained.

"What was she hacking into at fourteen?"

"NASA. She was very interested in space travel. So she gets into something she shouldn't have and her parents lose their shit and she doesn't see a computer for three years. Naturally she gets to college and goes right back to work. Lucky for her the company we both now work for was on a job at the time. They were infiltrating a syndicate, the same syndicate that was days away from recruiting MaeBe. Of course she didn't realize she was being groomed. Hutch did. He talked to her, mentored her, and convinced her to go to grad school, and then when she was ready, he offered her a job. She's brilliant, and she gets to put all that skill and intellect into doing some good for the world. It might be helpful for her to talk to Ruby."

There was the trap. She should have known it would be sprung at some time. "But only if I forgive her."

"No. MaeBe would never make a deal like that. It wouldn't matter if you refused to ever speak to her again. She would still help your friend. That's who she is, who she's still able to be because she didn't go down that dark road." He turned her way. "I'm not MaeBe. What I'll offer you is one hundred percent dependent on you being nice to her."

Ah, there was the ruthless man she'd seen from the beginning. He could be charming, but there was a predator beneath his good looks. "And what are you offering me?"

"I'll make sure Ruby's situation is fixed," he promised. "No one will contact her again. I'll have them scrub her name off all their lists."

"What makes you think you could do that?" It was one of those too good to be true things. It was far too simple.

"Because I've been Ruby, though my skill wasn't hacking. It was something a bit more visceral." He looked at her, and in the low light his eyes seemed almost black. Like he was a gorgeous demon standing in front of her, offering her a deal. "I was technically military, but I worked for some people who would love for me to do the occasional odd job. My openness to future employment will make them amenable to my suggestions that Ruby Lockwood be deemed off limits. Couple that with MaeBe befriending her, and your friend should be on the right path."

She owed Ruby so much, and there was a recklessness to the kid that worried Vanessa. She needed a mentor, a strong presence in her life who could help her along. "What makes you think MaeBe would even like her? You haven't met her."

"MaeBe likes everyone. MaeBe sees the good in everyone. Even when she shouldn't." He glanced back into the living room. It was a warm, inviting place, a place where family gathered, and perhaps that was why she hadn't felt comfortable there. "You should know that I pretty much threatened to kick Michael's ass for putting her out in the field. I knew this would happen. I knew she would get hurt."

"I didn't hurt her." She was getting a little angry. "Everyone here expects me to forget what you all put me through. Could I have a day or two?"

"Not in my experience. Things move fast. So do we have a deal?"

He was a bastard. "Fine. I'll be nice to MaeBe. I'm a good actress."

"And she's not good at telling when someone's lying to her. I should know all about that. I've been lying to her for a long time." He finished off his beer. "I'll handle the situation. Now would you like some advice?"

"No. I'd like a new bodyguard." She was pretty sure this wasn't going to work out. Any guilt she'd felt for mistaking his relationship with her sister was gone.

"Good luck with that," he returned. "Now, I think we're very similar people, Vanessa."

"I don't see how." She was as far from Kyle as she could be.

"We've both suffered betrayals that cut so deep we'll never recover from them. Or at least we think we can't."

"Is that why you don't make a move on MaeBe? Because some other woman betrayed you?" She could ask questions, too.

"Oh, there are a myriad of reasons I can't touch MaeBe, but that's in there. I'm damaged in a way that would likely kill her if she ever found out. If she knew the things I've done…well, the crazy thing is she would forgive me for all of it and try to help me be a better person. She wouldn't see that there's something rotten in my soul."

"I don't think I'm rotten, Kyle." And she resented him for saying she was. He'd said they were alike. She hadn't become what she could have. She hadn't become bitter and angry.

"No, you think you're unlucky," Kyle countered. "There's a voice in your head that tells you that even when you got everything you wanted, it fell apart. Your dream turned into a fucking nightmare. Man, if what happened at the station is what you go through every day, I have no idea why anyone would want fame."

She didn't either. Not now that she'd tasted it and it had turned so bitter on her tongue. "I wanted to feel seen. I spent my whole life as this poor girl no one looked at twice until I got boobs, and then I was something to be used and thrown out with the trash. My sister was the smart one. I was told I was the pretty one, and then I found acting classes. I had to do it behind my mom's back because she thought most movies and plays were low forms of entertainment. She thought movies gave people unrealistic expectations. She was a big believer in realistic expectations."

"And what should one expect, according to your mother?" Kyle asked.

"That we all suffer and die, and that's how to get to heaven."

"And my mother believes there is nothing we can't get through as long as we love each other." He set the bottle down. "I guess we're going to find out which mom was right."

She knew the answer. "Yours. That's why you're here, right? You left whatever you were doing and came home because she engrained that belief in you. That she loved you so much, you could get through anything. You're not as damaged as you think you are."

He chuckled, an unamused sound. "Oh, don't underestimate how deep my wounds go. But you're probably right on why I chose to come back here. I could have gone anywhere, gotten a job somewhere my uncle doesn't work. Sometimes I think the greatest gift my mother ever gave me was this weird family she married into. Oh, I will swear it's the opposite after a long talk with Big Tag, but they took us in, made us theirs. It's important to belong to someone. I know that sounds…old fashioned, but for me, it's true."

"My own sister didn't want me to take care of her." She'd managed to forget that fun fact for a while, but it had crept back in, that truth sliding over her soul.

"Or she was scared you wouldn't want to at all. You can't know what she was thinking."

Oh, but she was fairly certain. Her sister had found a life she loved, and there wasn't room in it for anyone from her old life. "I think she had her new family. I think she loved them."

"And what did she leave you?" Kyle asked.

"She left me her house."

"And her job," Kyle pointed out.

"She couldn't know that I would take over her job."

"And yet it happened. She knew you would likely need a place to live. She knew Dani would need help. She might not have known for sure what would happen, but she set up those dominoes knowing how they could fall. What she truly gave you was a chance at finding your place in the family she loved."

"Well, that family she loved decided I was a thief." Her sister hadn't wanted her around, and there was a chance she'd been right.

"No, a very paranoid dude figured out something was wrong, and you were the best suspect," Kyle pointed out. "And you were doing something shady. So was Dani. Maybe Julian should have handled it differently, but this is who Julian is, and the minute he realized you weren't what he thought you were, he told you the truth. He offered a way to fix many of your problems. You should understand that Michael had already decided he didn't care if you stole that money. He was going to pay it back and ensure Julian didn't prosecute you. I know he didn't tell you why he was fucking you. I think he didn't know, but he does now. He was fucking you because he couldn't not fuck you."

She wasn't sure she believed him. "It doesn't matter."

"It should. You could make it matter," Kyle insisted. "You do understand that it would be far easier for Michael to walk away at this point. He could have foisted you right back at Julian and not worried about you again. Ask yourself why he didn't do that. Why he put his own family in harm's way for you."

The answer was clear to her. "Because he feels bad."

"Because at some point in all of this madness, you became part of his family. It's the only reason he would ever do this. So you get to make the decision. Are you going to listen to your mother? Are you going to finally admit she was right? Or are you going to do what I think you've been doing for a long time—look for another one. Look for a whole other family, one that loves you. You got dealt a shit hand, Jones. Several of them. I've found there are two types of people. The ones who get out of the game and never play again. Or the ones who ask for a new hand and start the fuck over again. I'm trying to be the second one."

"This isn't my second time around, Kyle. Do you have any idea how many times I've been tossed to the ground?"

"A lot. And you had to do a whole lot of it in front of a camera with the whole world watching. It sucks. I wouldn't blame you if you decided to never even try again. But there's this thing my dad used to say. It's stuck with me even during the bad times. It's the little things, you know. When everything seems dark and you don't think you can pull through, it's always the little things that give you something to hold on to. He used to say the tragedy isn't in getting your ass kicked. That's life. The tragedy is when you don't get back up. You couldn't control the ass kicking. That was going to happen no matter what you did. But you control whether or not you let it kill a piece of you." He pushed back from the railing. "I'm going to hit the sack. I'll escort you and Michael to work in the morning. You're safe at Lodge Corp, but if you need to leave for any reason, you call me. You don't leave that building without me or Michael. And don't forget to have that talk with MaeBe. You don't have to forgive her in your heart, but if you want me to help your friend, you better do it with your mouth. And make her believe."

He turned and walked away.

Make her believe.

She watched as Kyle joined the rest of the group. Michael's head came up, his eyes searching for her.

Was it guilt that was pushing him? Or something else?

It didn't matter. She wasn't going to think about that tonight. The truth was they were inside making decisions that should be hers.

She was on the ground again, her face in the dirt. This was the moment when her mother gave up, choosing to spend her days holding her misery close as if it was a shield against anything that could hurt her. Her mother had chosen to hurt herself first. Self-inflicted wounds that she somehow tried to turn into badges of honor.

Her mother hated herself. That was the core problem of her life.

She was so like her mother. It was right there, the instinct to internalize all the blame. Why was she standing on this balcony? She'd had a choice. She could leave it all behind or she could try to salvage something. But instead of forging ahead, she was letting Michael make the choices.

Like she'd allowed George to guide her. Like she'd let her agents talk her into things she shouldn't have done.

She'd stood up for herself back then. She'd made a stand to get what she deserved, and she'd gotten the shit kicked out of her for it.

So the fuck what? She'd gotten kicked and bruised and battered and then she turned around and let everyone else decide for her because it was easier? Because she was afraid?

What did she want? She was at a crossroads, and Kyle was right. There wasn't time to sit here and mourn what she'd never really had.

She had a unique opportunity. It didn't matter why she had it. What mattered was what she did with it.

Some of the numbness had started to melt, and she was surprised at what took its place. She'd expected sorrow, and it was in there. Mourning for her sister and the relationship they could have had. Heartache that Michael hadn't been the man she'd thought he was.

But there was a fire inside, too. A good and righteous anger that she might be able to stoke into fuel.

She could sit here and cry or she could take back her fucking life for good or bad.

She'd left home at the age of seventeen to build a life for herself. She'd stood up for herself, tried to make her life and career better and gotten labeled difficult, and that had begun the slide that led her here.

Because she'd given up on being difficult. Because she'd wanted comfort and had forgotten to fight.

She'd been so tired and so alone. Even with George. She'd been his companion, but they'd always known there was no future for them. They'd cared for each other during a time of deep mourning.

If the last weeks with Michael had taught her anything, it was that she wanted to be alive again. She wanted to stop living in the moment and start working toward a future.

Her future was inside that condo. Whether she could ever find a way to forgive Michael didn't matter. She could not continue to exist in this space where she floated through life, praying no one noticed her.

It was time to be difficult again.

She took a deep breath and walked in. "I'm sorry. I needed a moment. Could we go over the plan one more time? I have some thoughts."

"Uh, sure." The woman on the computer screen was a lovely blonde who wore a designer suit despite the fact that it was almost eleven o'clock on the East Coast. "Michael was telling me he thought you wouldn't want to do any interviews, but I…"

"Get me a big one." She hadn't done an interview in years. She avoided all press like the plague, but maybe that had been a mistake.

The publicist nodded. "I think it's the way to go. In the morning I'll start looking for the right venue."

"Are you sure?" MaeBe was looking at her with worried eyes.

"I am." She noticed Kyle was hanging around the hallway, lurking. "I'll need to do some prep work though. If you don't mind, you could help me."

MaeBe's eyes lit up. "Absolutely. Anything you need."

It might not be so hard to forgive the young woman. There was an infectious light around MaeBe Vaughn. Light to Kyle's pitch black.

"All right." Vanessa pulled a chair up. "Let's get to work."

She caught the faintest hint of a smile on Michael's face as he sat back, giving the meeting over to her.

She didn't want to think about how nice it was to have a team around her, watching her back.

To have a family.

The publicist started talking, and Vanessa forced herself to focus.

Chapter Sixteen

Michael couldn't sleep. His mother hadn't even gone through with her threat to take over his room, but he still couldn't sleep.

His father had come out to pick his mom up, and he'd met Vanessa. His father's big booming presence had lightened the mood briefly, but the gloom had come roaring back after everyone had gone and he and Vanessa had been left alone for the first time since the world exploded.

She hadn't said a word to him, merely turned and walked into the guest room.

He hadn't been able to tell her how proud he'd been of the way she'd handled herself today, hadn't told her how angry he'd been at the way she was treated, how he'd wanted to kill the woman who'd hurt her.

The person he wanted to murder was Junior. That fucker had done some serious damage. Michael had caught the late news, and Vanessa had been all over it.

He walked out on the balcony. He couldn't stay in his own fucking room because now the bed was too big without her in it. He couldn't close his eyes without seeing her face and how hurt she'd been.

His gut had been in a never-ending roll, and he wasn't sure how he would face her in the morning.

He stepped outside, cool night air brushing over his skin. He'd bought this place already furnished. The big wrought-iron couch and firepit had been here along with the grill and outdoor kitchen.

He'd probably been out here a handful of times over the years until Vanessa had started staying with him. She liked to sit out here and drink coffee in the mornings, letting the sun warm her face.

She likely wouldn't sit out here with him again.

"Can't sleep?"

He turned and she was curled up on the sofa, her feet tucked underneath her. She'd changed into pajama pants and a tank top, a robe around her body. Her hair was loose, and she'd scrubbed her face clean.

She was the most stunning woman he'd ever seen.

"No. I can't, but I'll leave you be," he said, turning to go.

"I wish you wouldn't. Alone isn't working for me tonight."

He stopped and made his way around the sofa. Hope lit inside him. If she was willing to be around him, maybe they could get through this. "Do you want to talk?"

"Not really. I talked enough."

She'd taken over with the publicist, and when that meeting had finished, she'd spent some time with MaeBe going over her investigation. She'd been polite, but there was a coldness that had settled between them. "Well, I didn't. I didn't get to tell you how sorry I am."

"You did." She turned back to stare off into the distance. "Several times."

"But you don't believe me."

"I don't know what to believe. And honestly, it doesn't matter."

He hated how cold she sounded. Vanessa was always warm. "It does. It matters so fucking much to me. Vanessa, you have to know that I never meant to hurt you."

"Why would I have to know that?" She turned to him, one brow cocked over her eyes.

It was the first spark of emotion he'd seen in her since she'd been arrested. "Because I think I've made it plain how I feel about you."

"You've made it plain that you don't mind sleeping with

someone you're actively investigating, and you planned to do it. You planned to get intimate with me before you'd ever met me."

That hadn't been the way it had gone. "I knew it was a possibility, but I didn't set out to get you in bed. The training relationship was in place so I could get close to you. I never had to sleep with you."

"And yet you got your hand down my panties within an hour of meeting me."

"Yes," he agreed. "I did. I did it because I couldn't help myself. I did it because the minute you walked in the door I wanted you."

"Do you know how many times I've heard that from a man? *I wanted you the moment I saw you.*"

How could he make her understand? "I did. I'll be honest—the whole Hollywood star thing didn't do it for me. I wasn't attracted to your image. I was attracted to Vanessa Jones. Not Vanessa Hale."

She pointed his way like he'd made her point. "Yes, you made it clear you barely knew who Vanessa Hale was. That was a lie. You knew all about me. You had your opinions. Did you think it might be fun to bring me down a notch or two?"

"No. I didn't." But hadn't he? He'd promised not to lie to her again. "I don't know. When I was first handed the assignment, I was in a bad place. My engagement had ended, and it felt like I was going to be that guy who never got his shit together. I had pretty much decided I wasn't capable of truly loving a woman. So yeah, the thought of spending time with someone who was known for being mercenary was a little thrill. I wouldn't have to look at you and wonder why I couldn't feel for you, why my soul didn't move. I thought I could probably have sex with you and not worry for a second that I would hurt you because you couldn't be hurt. And I was so fucking wrong."

"You were just like everyone else."

"I was." He hated that he'd been so closed-minded. He'd read the stories about her and hadn't once considered she might be different. He should have known better. "I had an image in my head of who you would be when you walked in the door. But then I talked to you. I got to know you, and I fell in love with the woman you really are."

She huffed, a frustrated sound. "You fell in love with a woman you thought you could save. And I wouldn't call it love. If you loved me, you would have told me the truth."

"The way you told me?" He wasn't the only one who'd lied. She hadn't told him why she wanted access to The Club.

"I never said I loved you."

That was a kick in the gut. But it was also true. She'd never even come close to saying the words.

She stared at him for a moment, her eyes softening as though she was going to take the words back. Instead she took a deep breath. "Kyle told me you were going to pay off Julian."

At least she wasn't walking away. "I was. I knew you weren't trying to hurt anyone. But I couldn't figure out the money until earlier today. I thought you needed it maybe to pay off your lawyers. It's important for you to keep fighting. So I was going to pay off Julian and offer to take over the legal fees."

"I wouldn't steal from my employer even if I was going to be homeless," she replied with a sigh. "Much less pay off my lawyers. I might have asked for a loan, but I didn't even do that. Why not ask me? I understand why Julian didn't. I can even understand why you wouldn't ask in the beginning. But if you fell in love with me, why would you leave me in the dark?"

"I didn't want it to be over. I have reveled in these days with you. I've felt like a different man. I didn't want to lose you." He hated that she was right in front of him and yet there were miles between them. "I knew you might be able to forgive me for lying. But I didn't think you could forgive me for what happened to you at the café. I put you in danger. I never thought you would leave without me."

Her arms crossed over her chest. "So you did that because you wanted me to turn to you?"

He was going to tell her everything. "I duped your phone that day."

"Of course you did." She sighed, her head shaking. "Hope you enjoyed my many calls to Dani. Ah, that's what MaeBe was doing in the café. She was good. I never suspected a thing."

"She was only doing her job. And she wasn't supposed to follow you. She was worried about that man," he pointed out.

"I'm sorry she got hurt." The thought seemed to settle her a bit. "I don't suppose you know anything further about that."

"We have a name, but we haven't been able to track him down

yet."

She shrugged. "It could be a lot of people. I don't know if you remember this evening, but I think I proved how much people hate me."

"I heard some people out there to support you, too."

"They're not supporters. They're stalkers. Anyone who makes their way to a police station to shout *I love you* to a woman they've never met before isn't exactly normal. It might be different if I'd had a career that didn't consist of horror films and raunchy comedies. Those men who were shouting their 'support' didn't watch the indie films I made where I actually acted and kept my clothes on."

"There's nothing wrong with horror films. Or any of your films."

"No, but it's not like they were out there because I touched their lives with my art," she replied. "Those people tend to be lovely. They write letters or quietly talk to me if we happen to meet. The people who scream like that…they want a piece of me. And there aren't many pieces left."

His heart ached at the thought. "I won't let them take another thing from you."

"No, you want every piece for yourself. Until you wake up and realize being with me is hard. You'll revel in the sex and the danger and playing the white knight for a while. But this life will get old."

There was a scenario she wasn't considering. "Or you'll settle down with me and we'll be boring as fuck. We'll work and go to clubs and have dinner with my parents. We'll have a regular life, and after the trial is over, no one will care enough to follow you."

"What am I supposed to do in this world you've built in your head?" she asked.

"Whatever you want to do. If you want to act, we'll make it happen. If you want to work with Dani, keep your job. If you want to run the charity you and George talked about, then go for it. All I care about is your happiness."

She shook her head. "It won't work like that. I don't get to walk away. The best I can hope for is the scandal to die down and I end up writing *bons mots* on social media like Monica Lewinsky. I'll always be the gold digger. And you being in the picture won't help that. If you want to help me rehab my image, how about finding me a fake boyfriend who doesn't have a trust fund? Let the press think I'm fucking Deke."

He felt his blood pressure tick up. "The only man you'll be fucking is me."

Her arms came down, and a savage smile twisted her lips up. "You think I'll spread my legs because you were kind enough to save me from the big bad wolf?"

That fierce look on her face set off alarm bells, but they seemed a distant thing. He knew he was falling into a trap, but he couldn't help himself. "Junior isn't a wolf. He's a wasp who stings you. You want to know who the wolf is in this scenario? That would be me, and maybe I'm going about this the wrong way. I'm begging and pleading. Maybe what I should do is show you who the boss is."

She didn't back away. Not a single inch. "You are not my boss. You are not my boyfriend. You're not my friend or even someone I care about at this point."

"I don't see you walking away."

"Where would I go?" She huffed the question. "You've put me in the box you wanted me in and left me with no real way out."

"There's a simple one. Call Julian and he'll send a limo to pick you up. He'll do all the things I'm doing. With one exception." He was starting to understand what she'd been doing out here. The very same thing he had. Wishing things were different. Wishing they could start the day over and end it properly.

He could. He could apologize and beg for forgiveness, and he would happily hop back into bed like nothing happened.

She couldn't. She'd had her world ripped up and she ached inside, but she couldn't trust him again. Not yet. She wanted the one thing she could believe in. She wanted the pleasure he could give her. Now that he knew her, he believed every word she'd told him that first day.

I'm thirty-two years old, and I don't think I've ever had a real orgasm.

He'd been the man to give her that pleasure, and she needed it now. She needed the comfort of his body against hers, inside hers, but she couldn't ask for it. She couldn't accept his tenderness.

But she might find some comfort in his dominance.

He was taking the chance that she would hate him for it in the morning.

"What's that? What won't Julian do for me?"

"He won't fuck you. He won't take you in hand and make you scream out his name. I'm going to do that tonight, Vanessa." His body had started to hum. His dick didn't care that this was probably a bad idea. All his dick cared about was getting inside her again.

"What makes you think I would let you fuck me?"

"The fact that you haven't walked away." He didn't mention that her nipples were hard. They pressed against the thin material of her shirt. Her robe had come open, and she didn't pull it back around her. "You told me you didn't want to talk and that you didn't want to be alone. If you want me to hold you I will. I would love to be gentle with you, but I don't think you can accept that from me right now."

"I won't accept it from you ever again," she vowed.

If he truly believed that he would want to howl. But he'd told her exactly what she could do if she didn't want to stay with him. She could have everything he'd promised her, and she didn't have to be his girlfriend. She could easily explain that they'd broken up and she was alone again. He could do his investigation from afar. Julian could handle the rest.

But she was here. She hadn't been able to sleep without him.

She needed him. She wanted him. She didn't want to need or want him.

Luckily he had a very easy way to stay close to her. She could hate him right this second, but if he was in her bed for weeks and weeks, he could change her mind. He could be the man she'd thought he was.

"We still have a contract, Vanessa."

She went perfectly still. "I think you broke that contract. I believe there was something in it about protecting me."

Guilt twisted inside him, but he couldn't let it win. "And I failed, but I won't again. I will honor that contract for as long as you will allow me to. I'll protect you from everything that might hurt you. Everyone who might hurt you. Everyone but me."

"You can't hurt me now."

"Then you've got nothing to worry about."

Her shoulders straightened, chin coming up in a stubborn expression. "I'm not going to lie to you. I want to scene. I want to play and forget this whole day. I don't think I can live here with you without falling into bed. So I want to go in with my eyes wide open this time. I will not stay with you. I will fuck you. I'll let you fuck me. I'll let you top me in the bedroom. I might even fall back into old habits, and our days together might seem good. But you should understand that no matter how much I end up feeling for you, I'll leave in the end. When this is done and it's safe, I'll go."

She would punish him. That was what she was saying. She would take everything he had to give her and then she would leave him.

He might deserve it. If he had a single ounce of self-preservation, he would tell her to go to Julian's.

He didn't. He would take the bet. He would bet that time could soften her heart, that he could show her how much he loved her.

"Drop the robe."

She frowned. "I told you what's going to happen."

"And I promised to give you what you need. So drop the robe. We're playing, and I'm in charge until you use your safe word. It's red." He hardened his tone, settling into his role. He was giving her what she needed. He wouldn't get what he needed. He wouldn't get her saying how much she cared about him. But if this was all she would accept from him, he would take it.

Her robe dropped, and her chin came up. "I'm using you, Michael. I want to play to get out of my head for a while."

"And I want to worship your body. I want to touch you and feel like I didn't fuck up for two seconds." Blood started to pump through him, his cock beginning to twitch. "Take off your top. I want to see your breasts."

Her hands moved, tugging the shirt off. She wasn't wearing a bra, but he'd known that. She didn't like to wear them unless she was going out somewhere or they had people over. It made it easy for him to slide his hand over and play with her nipples. "You didn't fuck up. Like you said. You were only doing your job."

"I never said that. You weren't merely a job." He moved in, looming over her. Even in the gloom of the night, her eyes shone. "You became everything."

She shook her head. "No. I don't want to listen to that shit."

"And I don't want to be the dick you ride so you don't have to feel anything. Guess neither of us is getting what we want. Take off the bottoms and the underwear and understand that I don't want to see it again. I don't care if you wear it to work, but the minute you get here, those panties come off."

"Changing the rules?" The challenge was there in her tone. She kicked off the pajama bottoms but left the underwear on.

"If you want a hard-core Dom, you'll get one."

"You think you can be hard-core? I think you're a liar. I never asked. Are you even a Dom? Or did you take a quick class so you could fool the idiot actress?"

Oh, she was about to find out who he was as a Dom. He leaned over and picked her up, tossing her over his shoulder. Though the balcony was private, he didn't trust that there wouldn't be someone in one of the surrounding buildings watching them. He didn't give a shit, but she would. At this point all they could possibly have seen was the beginnings of intimacy between two people who should be intimate.

But what he was about to do would shock anyone watching.

"Hey, put me down. What are you doing?"

"I'm proving to you that I know how to deal with an angry little brat." He strode to his bedroom where his kit was. He was obviously going to need some tools to get this job done.

He knew damn well she was pushing him, but she needed it. She needed to spew some bile and needed the discipline he was about to give her.

He kicked open the door and moved to the closet.

"Let me down, asshole," she snarled, her feet kicking at his torso.

He tightened his hold. She was petite in his arms and absolutely no problem for him physically. He could carry her weight all day and not notice the difference. She was easy to manhandle, so he didn't have to put her down to grab his kit. "Asshole isn't your safe word."

"No, but it describes you."

The fact that she didn't spit out her safe word reenforced his belief that she needed this. That safe word was magical. It meant they could work this out the way they needed to. She could yell at him and release all her anger while getting the attention she also needed. They could play out this scene that might help them process the emotions they brought out in each other in a safe way. She could tell him no, let him feel all the negativity the day brought out without really pushing him away because that one word would stop everything.

"I'm sure it does, but I'm still your Dom, and you're going to show me some respect when we're playing."

"I'm not playing with you," she argued.

"Then what exactly do you think we're doing?"

"I'm using you the way you used me."

Is that what she thought she was doing? That was almost certainly what she thought he'd done. He had this time to prove her wrong, to be the Dom she needed him to be. "Then I'll have to make sure you get what you need."

He used his free hand to slide the zipper of his kit open and extract the first item he would need.

Handcuffs.

"You can't give me anything but an orgasm," she replied.

He intended to give her so much more. He set her on her feet, and before she had the chance to step back, he had her wrists in his hands and the cuffs clicked on in a heartbeat. "I assure you, I'll give you more than one."

He gripped the chain that connected the cuffs and tugged.

"Are we going to the playroom?" She only resisted a bit, as though she had to show him how she felt in every movement of her body.

There were still things she didn't know about this place she'd lived in for the last two weeks. "I don't have to. I can take care of you wherever we go. You should know I'll always find a way."

He brought her to one corner of the room. It was a seemingly empty space, but he touched a button and a lever sprang from the wall. It had been professionally done so it could hold her weight. If anyone else looked at it, they might see a holder for a hanging plant.

But it was all about restraining a sub. He'd measured and recalibrated it for Vanessa's height, though they hadn't played with it yet. They'd spent their time in this room in bed, fucking for hours and exploring each other's bodies.

"What the hell is that?" Vanessa seemed determined to put a curse word in every sentence.

He brought her hands up and hooked them over her head. He'd gotten that height perfect because she was on her toes. He wanted her on the edge of discomfort, to have to dance around to keep her balance. What it did for him was place her whole body on gorgeous display. He put his hand around her neck. "That is the way I keep you where I want you. You look gorgeous."

"I don't give a damn what you think." Those glorious eyes flashed fire.

At least she wasn't quiet. He could take her anger, but not her silence. "You don't have to care, but you do have to obey. I gave you an order and you did not comply. Before we can start, you have to accept your punishment."

"I don't have to accept anything from you." But her eyes stayed on him.

And she still wasn't close to her safe word.

He slapped her ass. Not an easy slap. She didn't need that from him. She needed dominance. She needed to get through this first night and reset in the morning. He smacked her ass again.

"Fuck." She gritted her teeth, tears in her eyes. "Do it again."

"You don't tell me what to do in this space. In any other space you can direct everything we do, but here, I'm the king." He pulled at the back of her panties, tugging them between the cheeks of her ass and drawing them high. It forced her right on her toes. "I told you to take these off. I told you not to wear them when you're in our home."

"It's not my fucking home, Michael."

He tugged on the panties, knowing damn well when he manipulated them the fabric rubbed against her clit. He could already smell her arousal. "That little place in the suburbs isn't your home."

"I don't fucking have one. I never did." She practically snarled the words.

Ah, they were getting somewhere. But he was smart enough not to push her. "Fine. When you're in this space, you don't wear panties. You don't put anything between my cock and your pussy. Am I understood?"

She twisted, obviously trying to find her footing. "Yes. I understand. You want to fuck me."

"I want to do a lot of things to you. With you. Fucking is only part of it, but I think it's all you'll allow me right now." He moved in behind her, his fingers still twisted around her thong. "But you should know that I'm fucking you because I've never felt more like me than when I'm inside you. You are everything I've looked for in life."

"Yeah, because what you wanted was a money-grubbing whore."

He wasn't about to put up with that. He knew why she'd said it.

She was pushing him, needed to see if he would break. But he couldn't let her get away with it. He reached around and twisted her nipple as he tugged on the thong.

The little squeal that came out of her throat let him know he'd hit the right spots.

"Don't you ever let me hear those words come out of your mouth again," he growled in her ear. "I'm not fucking joking. I won't put up with that, and you will not like the spanking that comes from it."

"I'm only saying what everyone says. What you thought when you met me." The words came out in a breathless rush.

"I thought you might be a little mercenary. Would it shock you to know I don't have any disdain for a woman or man who makes money off sex? Sex is nothing to be ashamed of. Intimacy of some kind is necessary to be happy and whole, and if a prostitute is happy, good for fucking them. If a woman marries a man because he can take care of her and she can meet his needs too, good for them. Same goes for a man marrying a woman for the same reasons."

"But you had disdain for me. You didn't like the fact that I married an old man."

"I didn't care in the beginning, and then I was fucking jealous of anyone who ever touched you before." He let the thong go, though it stayed there between her cheeks. He moved around her, glancing down and seeing that the panties had bunched up and split her pussy, hiding between the lips. That fabric was also soaking wet. "I know I'm the villain in this piece, but I wasn't the only one who stereotyped the other. The minute you found out my family had money, you thought I was suspicious."

"And I was right about you. You were using me. Just like everyone else does."

"I'm not like anyone else in your life. I will lay everything I have at your feet," he promised. "You keep me in that box. I will bust out. But for tonight, I'll be your bad guy, baby. I'll be the man who makes you cry because you need it."

"I don't need anything from you."

Still not her safe word. He turned to his kit and prayed she didn't mean what she'd said.

* * * *

The bastard knew what he was doing. Her thong was caught, and every time she moved it slid against her clit. Just enough to make her desperate for more.

She, on the other hand, had no fucking idea why she was here. She'd gone outside because she couldn't breathe. She hadn't been looking for Michael. So why hadn't she walked away the minute she'd seen him?

Instead her heart had thudded in her chest when she'd watched that big body walk out onto the balcony.

She'd realized there was no way she didn't fall back into bed with him. And what was wrong with that? She wanted him. He wanted her.

She would still leave in the end. Why shouldn't she take everything he was willing to give? As long as she was honest, anything that happened was no fault of hers.

You are everything I've looked for in life.

She wished he would shut up and fuck her. Every stupid word that came out of his mouth threatened to melt her ice, and she needed her ice.

But she'd found something she needed far more and that was pleasure. She needed to fuck him out of her system so she could move on with her life when this was over. No man had ever moved her the way this one had. Both physically and emotionally.

She'd learned, though, that a man who could take her to the highest heights could also slam her into hell.

He was too dangerous. In this moment, he thought he wanted her, but his guilt would dissipate, and he would realize she wasn't the right woman for him. The trouble she would bring him would ensure they couldn't work in the long run.

Michael turned, a crop in his hand. "You don't need anything? Are you sure about that? Because you look pretty needy to me, baby."

She wished she didn't love the way he called her baby. She'd wanted to be his baby. When she'd thought he was real, she'd felt all the warmth of that endearment.

"What I need I could get from any man. You just happen to be here." One hundred percent lie, but she couldn't tell him the truth. She couldn't tell him that she'd come to crave this time she spent with him, that she'd found herself with him.

The tip of the crop touched her ankle and started to brush up her leg. "Any man? That hurts, baby, but I think that was the point. You want to push me to hurt you." The leather tip kept moving up, sliding up her thigh.

She wasn't honestly certain what she wanted, but she knew she wanted him. And yes, she wanted what he could give her. If he'd insisted on talking, she could have walked away, but he'd given her a place where she could hate him and have him, too.

He was giving her a place where it was safe to process all the shit she'd felt today. A few hours ago she would have sworn she would never feel anything again, but mere moments with Michael and her emotions were threatening to crash over her.

Deep inside she knew that was a good thing. Not that she was going to admit it to him.

"You want to be able to take all the pleasure I can give you and still think of me as the bad guy," Michael said, the crop between her legs. He tapped her thighs one after the other. "Spread your legs. If you want me to play the bad guy, you have to be a good girl and obey me."

Or she didn't have to admit anything. Michael already understood what was going on in her head because he knew her deep down. Somehow they'd connected in a way she never had before. When she was with Michael, she felt him, felt that he was with her even when they weren't talking.

How could she have lost him?

She forced her legs apart, dancing on her toes. It took concentration. She had to focus on her body. Yes, that was what she needed. She wanted to know what he would do with that crop. She would concentrate on the physical.

He moved around so she couldn't see him, and then she heard a smack. Pain flared across her backside. She'd heard the crack of the crop seconds before she felt the sting. It hurt and then seemed to pulse out, sending a pleasant sensation across her skin. It made her gasp as her body tightened.

"Wider," he said in a soft growl.

He was a bastard. Her legs were wide enough apart, and it would be hard to get them wider because he had her arms up so high. Of course, that was his point. "I can't."

Another crack, this one louder. The pain and the sweet heat that came after were stronger, too. "You can. You can do anything."

She made a vomiting sound. "Sure I can."

"I knew there was a major brat under there somewhere. I knew that the minute you felt comfortable enough she would show up." Another slap, and then she felt his hand on one of her cheeks, squeezing hard. "Spread your legs wider or I'll do it for you. I've got a spreader bar somewhere around here. I'll strap you in and then you won't be able to move at all. Is that what you want?"

That didn't sound good because it would take far too long. She forced her legs apart another inch, the movement sending every muscle in her body taut. She had to stay on her toes to keep the position.

This was the way her life was. Always having to focus or it would fall apart. And then it fell apart anyway no matter how hard she tried.

The world went blurry.

"Stay with me." Michael had hold of her thong again, pulling it up and bringing her back to the here and now. "All you have to think about is obeying me. Nothing else matters. Stay still. I want to play. If you move too much, you'll get the crop."

He was behind her, whispering in her ear, his breath warm on her skin. She could feel the hard line of his erection against her ass.

She wanted that cock.

She stayed as still as she could, and one big hand came around to cup her breast. He rolled her nipple between his thumb and forefinger to just the point of pain. It made her grit her teeth because that sensation went right to her pussy.

"That's my sweet sub," he whispered.

She couldn't handle his tenderness. "I'm not fucking sweet."

He let her nipple go, palming her breast again. This time the touch was soft. "You are sweet. I know the world keeps telling you you're not, but they don't matter. What people say doesn't matter. All that matters is what's between us, what you want. I know exactly what I want and that's to prove how fucking sweet you are."

He stepped back, and suddenly the crop came down again, smacking over her ass and the backs of her thighs. Then he tossed the crop away, and she felt his fingers slide under the strings of her thong. The delicate material ripped, and he tossed it away, too.

"That wasn't cheap, Michael."

"It doesn't matter since you don't need it now." He moved around her again, pulling his T-shirt off to reveal his chest. He was so broad and masculine. She loved how big he was compared to her, loved how muscular he was. She definitely loved the hungry look in his eyes. When he looked at her like that it wasn't hard to believe he truly wanted her, and for more than just sex. She'd had many men look at her as a sexual object, but something about Michael's hunger went deeper.

"You can't make me not wear underwear. Even here." It was perverse, but she couldn't stop arguing with him.

"I think you'll learn when I rip every pair up and you're left with none." His eyes seemed to burn through her. "Now do you want to argue with me or do you want me to get on my knees and eat your pussy until you scream?"

She went quiet because there was no reason to argue about that. If his mouth was on her, he couldn't keep talking. And when she had her orgasm, when he got up and started to fuck her, when his cock was so hard he couldn't breathe, she would say her safe word and walk away.

She would use him like he'd used her.

He crowded her, one hand going to the back of her neck, and then his mouth was on hers. His tongue dominated hers.

She would use him.

"That's better." His forehead touched hers. "But know every second I'm with you is the best part of my day. Every second I'm with you I'm a better person. I'm in love with you, and that will not change. Not tomorrow. Not the day after. Not ever. I've been with a woman who I thought I would spend my life with, and now I know I was wrong. I would have been so wrong to have married her because it's you, Vanessa. It's always going to be you."

Before she could argue he dropped down and gripped her legs, pulling them up over his shoulders.

She was completely dependent on him, his strength holding her up. He didn't play with her or tease her. He gripped her ass and shoved his tongue up her cunt.

Her eyes threatened to roll to the back of her head. His tongue was silky heaven against her pussy. He nipped at her, lapped at her, laved affection all over.

Yes, she would use him and walk away.

He sucked her clit, and the orgasm hit her like a shockwave. Her body shook as she came, Michael stroking her with his tongue over and over again.

He eased her feet to the floor and then stood, unhooking the cuffs and hauling her up into his arms. He strode across the room to the bed.

"I told you how sweet you were." He settled her on the bed and had her hands out of the cuffs in no time at all. "See how sweet you taste to me."

He kissed her, offering back her arousal to her. She could taste herself on his tongue and lips.

She wouldn't listen to his sweet words, wouldn't trust him again. She would punish him. She would tell him she was done.

He stepped back and shoved his pants down, releasing his cock.

Now was the time to tell him. Tell him he could go, that she had everything she wanted from him. Tell him he didn't need that condom he was rolling on his cock because she wasn't going to let him close again.

"I know you don't believe me." He climbed on the bed with her. "But I'll show you. I fucked up, baby. I can't make it up to you. I can't take back what I put you through, and I can't promise you there won't be more hard times. But I will be with you. I will not let you down again."

Somehow her mouth didn't open. Those words didn't come out.

Her arms went around him as he thrust inside, joining them together. He held himself still, staring down at her. One hand came out to brush over her cheek.

"It's okay. You can cry. You should cry."

His eyes shone in the low light, and she realized he was on the verge, too. He was emotional, and he was always in control.

What if he wasn't lying to her?

She was stupid. So stupid. She was still a little girl wondering why her mother couldn't love her the way other mothers seemed to love their kids. She was still a teen wanting to find a place where she could belong.

Michael moved over her, fucking her even as he held her eyes.

It had been the worst day. It had been so horrible and yet she felt like she wasn't alone. He was here with her.

His betrayal had been the worst part of the day. His betrayal had damn near killed her.

A second wave of pleasure hit her, and she held on to him as she rode the wave. The pleasure mixed with the emotions swirling inside her, and she cried even as she came. Michael went stiff above her, finding his own release.

He collapsed on top of her, kissing her over and over. He held her as she cried. He didn't talk, didn't use the moment to push his claims. He simply held her and let her cry.

She should push him away.

She shouldn't listen to that little voice inside her that begged her to try again, to let him in because life would mean nothing if she didn't keep her heart open.

She should get up and go to her own room.

After a while she was cried out, and Michael slipped out of bed. She heard him in the bathroom. It was time to make her exit, but she was so tired. She'd been tired all day, but her brain kept going. Now she felt a bone-deep weariness.

She could sleep.

Michael turned off the light and climbed into bed, drawing the covers over them both. He was warm and naked, spooning her.

"I don't..." she started.

He held her close, kissing her cheek. "Punish me tomorrow. Sleep tonight. Let me take care of you. I owe you that. Sleep, baby. You're safe. You can go right back to hating me tomorrow. I promise."

Bastard. She did want to sleep. And he was warm. So warm.

Tomorrow she would put up her wall again.

She hoped she had the strength to.

She fell asleep with his arms around her.

Chapter Seventeen

One week later, Vanessa still wasn't sure how she felt. She stood in the kitchen, the smell of coffee surrounding her as the morning news played in the background.

"Darling, how was the meeting with Lane? Did she think the interview went well?" Ava placed a mug in front of her.

Her mother-in-…whoa. Nope. That was not how she was going to feel. She was not starting to think of Ava Malone as her family because that would mean that all the days Michael had spent being the absolute greatest boyfriend/bastard in the world were working. And she couldn't let them work.

Since that first night when she'd allowed herself to sleep in his arms, their days had taken on a rhythm. They got up and had breakfast. They were never alone for breakfast because Kyle or one of the other bodyguards showed up. The fact that she hadn't been alone with Michael had led her to not fight with him that first morning. She'd made some breakfast, and the conversation had been stilted but pleasant. She'd gone to work and been surprised at the lack of press waiting there. Julian had done something to prevent them from showing up, though he wouldn't tell her what. She'd had a nice workday, and after dinner, she'd pushed Michael until he'd taken her into the playroom, spanked her until she cried, fucked her until she screamed out his name, and then carried her to bed. Then they started the whole process all over again.

Ava had been true to her word, taking her to NorthPark Mall the Saturday before to let the press take pictures of them shopping like she was one of the family. Michael's sister-in-law, Nina, had joined them, and when the press wasn't around, it felt like…she belonged. She had lunch with Ava and Nina and laughed over stories of Michael and JT as kids.

Then the rest of the family had shown up, and they'd all had dinner at Top in a private dining room. She'd spent time with Michael's father, who was over the top and funny.

She loved Michael's family. She was pretty sure she loved Michael.

She wasn't sure she could forgive him. She also didn't know if she could bring his family further into her hellscape of a life. It only seemed quiet right now. At some point the press would come roaring back like a rogue wave threatening to drown them all.

She picked up the mug. "She said she thought it went well." The publicist had set up an interview with one of the national magazines. The reporter had been out three days before along with a photographer. She'd talked to Vanessa and Michael, and they'd looked like a happy couple. "She's read the story and it's got a positive spin on it. I like Lane. She seems to know what she's doing, and she was right about how quickly the blackmail story would fade. Apart from last Saturday, they've left me alone. There was only one photographer waiting for us when we got home last night."

Home. That was a word she shouldn't think either. This gorgeous condo wasn't her home. It was her asylum for the moment. And she wasn't making love with Michael every night. She was using him to help her process her emotions. That was all.

Sure it was. She was already softening toward the man. He glanced over from where he was buttering his toast, and she couldn't help the fact that her heart skipped a beat.

"I think having the police release the full report helped." Michael put another two slices in the toaster. "DPD made it clear you were the victim. Couple that with the fact that you were almost stabbed and now the press is starting to look at Junior as the bad guy."

Lane Hannon was worth her weight in gold. The New York-based crisis handler had worked wonders to turn the narrative around. There had even been a spot on one of the national morning shows where they discussed if the press had been fair to Vanessa Hale.

It was a start.

In a few weeks, maybe a month, she would be able to quietly move out of Michael's place. She'd already talked to Dani about taking a small apartment in the Lodge Corp building. It would be a good place to start over. And The Club was right downstairs. She had definitely decided that she wasn't giving The Club up. D/s had been her haven for the last week. When she was in the playroom or The Club, she'd been able to let go and allow herself to feel every emotion inside her. She didn't have to hold it all in. It was her safe place, a place where she could be herself fully.

Michael had given her that place.

She'd started to wonder if maybe they could continue a straight-up D/s relationship. She would only see him on club nights, and they wouldn't pretend that it was an emotional thing.

And she gave that two days before she ended up with him in her bed or her in his.

She was going to have so much trouble quitting this man.

Was she going to quit him?

"I want to take Vanessa to the country club next week," Ava was saying. "We're having a charity luncheon that would be the perfect time to introduce her to our friends."

Oh, that sounded like a terrible idea. It kind of panicked her. "Why would you do that?"

Ava was wearing a designer suit and a killer Chanel necklace, her hair perfectly done. She'd stayed with them the night before because she had an early meeting in Dallas and hadn't wanted to fight her way through traffic.

Vanessa hoped she hadn't heard them in the playroom last night. She'd thought about pretending she wasn't sleeping in Michael's room. Ava would have gone to Simon and Chelsea's and stayed in their guest room. But then she wouldn't have talked to Ava, wouldn't have gotten her impressions of how things were going, wouldn't have felt the other woman's deep approval of how she was dealing with Michael. It had felt good to sit and have dinner with Michael and Ava, to have Ava kiss her cheek and wish her good night.

And she hadn't been willing to give up even a single night in the playroom. There were so few of them left.

Ava sipped her own coffee. "Because it's important they get to know you, of course. It's a show of family unity. I wouldn't bring anyone Michael wasn't serious about to the club. Out of all the women he's dated over the years, I've only brought one. It's not scary. It's nothing more than a group of women I've known for decades who like to help out their community. And there might be a tiny spot of wine involved. Nina will come, too."

"It's good for you to get out there," Michael murmured, setting two pieces of toast in front of her. "Lane said she wanted you to show your face around town or you'll give the impression you've got something to hide."

She was sick of impressions and honestly, hiding was an underappreciated activity. "I would think the country club wouldn't want the kind of exposure that comes with hosting someone like me."

Ava waved that off. "Darling, these are bored wealthy women who watch far too much *Real Housewives*. Now their families would never allow them to actually star in one of those, but a day in the spotlight would make them all feel very scandalous and important. The minute I tell them you're coming with me, they'll all make Botox appointments."

"There won't be a single expression in the whole place." Michael's lips quirked up in a grin. "Even if they were upset, you wouldn't be able to tell."

Ava frowned her son's way. "I still have plenty of expression, I promise. When skillfully done, it simply keeps one a bit smoother. And I assure you even if I had far too much, I could make you understand my emotional state."

Michael grimaced. "Yes, Mom."

A chime rang, signaling someone was at the door. Probably Kyle. She'd gotten used to the quiet, somewhat mysterious man. Deke watched her sometimes. He was much more talkative, but he usually talked about how awesome Michael was. It was obvious he was trying to help his buddy out.

"I'll get it." Ava walked out of the kitchen.

Michael passed her the strawberry preserves. "Did you sleep

okay?"

She nodded. She was surprised how well she slept now. She'd expected nightmares and anxiety, and instead she was so exhausted she slept like a log.

How would she sleep when he wasn't around to push her boundaries? To give her so much pleasure she couldn't think of anything except him?

"I was up half the night staring at the ceiling." He covered a yawn.

"Why?" Now that she really looked at him, she could see the weariness in his eyes. "Everything's going well. I haven't even had a nasty voice mail from Junior in a week."

He stared right at her, a grim look on his face. "Yes, and that makes me think you're planning to leave me as soon as possible."

She didn't like how her heart ached at the hollowness of his words. "I told you I would."

"I know," he whispered. "I also know I deserve it, but I can't stand the thought of being here without you. I've lived in this condo for ten years, and now I cannot imagine it without you."

"Don't." They'd stayed far away from emotional discussions. Even when she broke down and cried her eyes out, he'd simply held her. He hadn't pushed her in this way.

"I have to say it because I'll regret it if I don't try," he replied. "Vanessa, I love you. Just stay with me for another month or so and see how you feel at the end of it."

Stay with him. Sleep with him. Get used to how lovely he could make life. Spend time with his family. Fall in love with them so it would hurt if she didn't see them.

She was already in love with his family. She adored his nephews and brother and dad, and she so loved his mother. It was like having a real mom for the first time in her life.

"I don't know." Maybe it was time to be honest instead of pissed off. "I'm having a hard time forgiving you, but I'm also struggling to figure out what the world looks like without you."

"I want you to know that if you choose to walk away from me, you won't lose the people you've met." Michael put a hand over hers, warming her. "You won't lose the friends you've made. You've started to put together a group of people you can count on, and I need you to understand that you not accepting me won't change that."

Those stupid tears that always seemed so close to the surface were back again. Since he'd pushed her to cry that first night she'd never managed to get the numb iciness she'd come to rely on back. She'd tried to build it up, and every single night she was reminded of how much nicer it was to be warm.

She knew she wouldn't lose Dani. She hadn't honestly made many other friends. They all kept her at arm's length. Or maybe she was the one who didn't know how to connect after everything she'd been through. "Somehow I don't see your mom paying much attention to me if I walk away."

Michael huffed. "You don't know my mom then." He kissed her cheek and stepped back. "I want you to know that I'll do anything I can to make your life easier. Even if I'm not in it. I'll be right back. I'm sure that was Kyle, and we should leave for work soon."

He walked off, and she had to force herself not to go after him. It was hard to be in this odd limbo. She was with Michael but she wasn't. She'd made a decision but she truly hadn't.

Was she fighting the inevitable?

Her cell buzzed, a short sound that let her know she had a text coming in.

She flipped it over and quickly read the text Lane had sent.

I'm in a meeting but I thought I should let you know that I've got rumblings of an interview about you coming out later today. More details to follow. Don't panic.

Oh, she was definitely going to panic. Who was doing an interview about her? Junior? He was the most likely one, but any interview about her would likely lead to questions about his involvement with the busted blackmail scheme. Junior wasn't usually the kind to leave himself open. Right now they didn't have the evidence they needed to charge him, but if he opened that door, Michael and Deke would take apart everything he revealed, and they wouldn't stop until they'd made sure they left no crumb unturned.

So who could give an explosive interview about her?

Ashton. Of course. Her ex-friend would want to jump on the bandwagon. But it wouldn't be anything the other woman hadn't said before. She would come out with all the old *Vanessa didn't know a good thing when she had it. Vanessa always wanted more and didn't care who she hurt. Vanessa was aggressive and mean to poor directors who just wanted her to give up every moral she had to fuel their own egos.*

She wouldn't put it like that, of course, but it was the truth.

Ava walked back in, followed by Tessa Santiago soon-to-be Hawthorne.

The lovely young woman looked different outside The Club. Vanessa had only ever seen her in fet wear, looking sexy and submissive. Today she wore slacks, a button-down, and sensible shoes, her long hair in a bun. This was work Tessa, the Tessa who'd been in the military and now protected her clients.

"Hey, Vanessa." She set her backpack at the end of the bar and moved into the kitchen. "Kyle had a little emergency this morning. He's trying to buy a car, and something went wrong with the loan, so he's working that out. I told him I'd take his shift today if that's all right with you. If not I can have someone else over here in an hour or two. I was the easiest replacement."

She sounded slightly tentative, as though she expected pushback.

Tessa had only been doing her job. Like the rest of them. The days had even softened her toward MaeBe. The young woman had already talked to Ruby about her choices and how she could take her love of computers and find a great career. MaeBe was already proving to be a positive influence on Ruby.

She wasn't going to balk because Tessa had watched her at The Club. "Sure. I'll warn you it's going to be a boring day. I did my walk-through yesterday with the florists and the caterers for the party next Friday. The rest of my week is a whole lot of me staring at a computer screen."

Tessa gave her a smile and opened the cabinet to grab a mug. She poured herself a cup of coffee. "Excellent. I've got a book to read, so you stare as long as you like."

Ava shook her head. "You shouldn't be reading one of those murder books you love. You need to be picking out floral arrangements. Your wedding is six weeks away, darling."

Tessa found the creamer and sugar. She looked at Ava, wrinkling her nose. "I'm not good at that, and you should know. I'm letting my mom and Grace handle all the things. I'm going to show up and smile and say whatever I have to in order to stay with that man for the rest of my life. The wedding is for our families. Now the honeymoon…I had a lot to say about that."

"Where are you going?" Ava asked with a smile.

"Ten days in Bora Bora without a library in sight." Tessa's pleasure shone through. "We're at a resort that has not an ounce of history attached to it. Just me and David." She grinned Vanessa's way. "I had to carefully plan this. If I take us anywhere with an interesting history, the professor will go right down the rabbit hole, and I'll end up on the beach while he's taking notes somewhere. And honestly, that's not usually bad. I'm cool with it. But for this trip I want his focus entirely on me."

"Of course you do," Ava replied.

Michael was almost always focused on her. From the very beginning. She could excuse the first part of their relationship as he was a man doing his job, but the last week? He'd been so careful around her, giving her what she needed, taking her insults and bile with grace. She'd said terrible things to him, accused him of all manner of crimes, and he'd merely apologized for hurting her and promised not to do it again.

What did he gain at this point? She wasn't his target anymore. He was putting himself and his family on the line for her.

If this was about feeling guilty, shouldn't that go away soon?

"Well, *this* wedding is actually going to happen," Tessa promised. "I'm not going to let all my future mother-in-law's hard work go to waste this time. I did apologize for that, right?"

Ava waved her off. "Darling, you and Michael did the right thing, as evidenced so beautifully by you and David. And this one, if I can convince her to give my son another chance. Oh, Tessa, you can help me out. Tell our dearest Vanessa that the country club ladies are nothing to be afraid of. I'm trying to get her to come with me to charity day."

Tessa snorted and said something, but Vanessa was still caught on what she'd said previously.

"Why would you apologize to Ava?" Vanessa asked, not wanting to make that leap of logic.

Though it was odd that a coworker Michael didn't seem to have much in common with knew exactly where everything was in his kitchen. And Tessa had been surprised Vanessa accepted her so readily as Kyle's replacement. As though Vanessa would have a reason to reject her.

Because who wanted to be guarded by their boyfriend's ex-fiancée?

"Oh, I apologize often." Tessa's eyes had gone wide, and she nodded. "Ava and my mom planned that wedding for a good year, and Michael and I blew it all to hell with two months to go. Deposits were lost, if you know what I mean."

"Tessa," Ava began, her eyes on Vanessa.

Tessa flushed slightly. "Oh, hey, that doesn't mean Michael isn't an awesome guy. My mom still adores him. I mean she loves David, but she's still very friendly with Michael. As breakups go, ours was like the best."

"Dear, I don't think Michael mentioned the two of you were previously engaged," Ava said quietly. "Vanessa, I'm so sorry. I wouldn't have joked if I thought for a second you didn't know. It was a long time ago. They've both moved on. They were right to end their relationship because there wasn't passion between them."

"He didn't tell you?" Tessa's question was tinged with outrage.

Vanessa shook her head. "No. And you must still work well together since he had you spy on me."

"I was watching you," Tessa corrected, her skin flushing slightly. "And honestly, I was there to protect you, too. Look. Michael is obviously a dumbass."

"Why am I a dumbass?" Michael asked. He'd put on a sport coat and looked so gorgeous it hurt. "I mean, this time, that is. I am obviously a dumbass, but I usually have a reason."

Ava frowned at her son. "You didn't bother to mention to Vanessa that you used to be engaged."

"Of course I did." Michael looked to her, a clearly confused expression on his face. "I told you I almost got married."

"You didn't tell her it was to me." Tessa had her hands on her hips.

"Why would that matter?" Michael asked.

Tessa groaned. Ava put a hand on her head like it had started to ache.

He had to be kidding. This was the perfect reminder that he wasn't the man for her. She pushed back her chair and stepped away.

"You might have mentioned that you used to sleep with the woman you assigned to be my in-club mentor."

"Honestly, at the end there wasn't much of that. There wasn't much of it in the beginning either," Tessa admitted. "Sometimes I have no idea why we even moved in together."

"Your apartment flooded, and you didn't want to move back in with your mom," Michael replied. "Vanessa, I'm sorry. I didn't mention it because it didn't matter."

"Michael," his mother admonished.

"I didn't mean it that way." Michael groaned. "Vanessa, let's talk about this in the car. Tessa, why are you here? Where's Kyle?"

Vanessa turned to Tessa. "Do you have a car here?"

Tessa nodded before looking back to Michael. "He's trying to work out something at his bank. I didn't have an assignment today so I told him I would cover for him."

"Good." It was late, and she didn't want to talk to Michael. He would simply give her more excuses. "You can drive me to work. Michael, I won't need a ride home. Your ex can give me one."

Michael stepped in front of her. "I honestly didn't think about telling you her name. I didn't think it mattered. I did talk to you about the fact that I'd been engaged. I'm sorry I didn't sit you down and explain the whole situation, but I wanted to focus on us."

"There is no us." The words were stubborn, but she was kind of feeling that way. She needed to think about this, about what the hell she was doing with a man she couldn't trust. "I would like for Tessa to take me to work. She's proven she's good at watching me, so I don't think we'll have any problems."

"Come on, please." Michael stared down at her, a stark look on his face. "Let's go get some coffee and talk about this. I wasn't trying to hide something from you. Or maybe I was. Maybe I didn't want you to think about the fact that I almost made a huge mistake. Not because Tessa isn't wonderful, but because she isn't you. I should have been patient. I should have waited until I met the right woman. Until I met you."

He was so earnest, but she needed time. And space. She wasn't sure she could believe him, and even if she did, wouldn't it all fall apart? "I need to go to work. I would like for Tessa to drive me. I would like some time to process what I just learned. I'm asking you for that time."

Michael let out a long breath and then backed away. "All right. Please come home tonight."

She frowned up at him. "Where else would I go?"

"You can yell at me all you like." He reached out and smoothed back her hair. "As long as you come home."

She hated how this man could make her feel. But wasn't that the point? He could make her feel safe and loved and he could irritate the fuck out of her. Because somehow he'd found a way to make himself a place in her stupid, never-endingly open heart. "You should have told me."

"I'll have a list of everyone I've ever slept with by tonight. It's not as long as you think it is," Michael promised. He swept in and kissed her.

Asshole. "I don't need that."

"No one needs that, Michael." His mother looked horrified. "Please tell me you don't actually keep a list of your conquests."

"No, there's not a list, Momma." Michael's hands had come up. "It's just that I remember the women I shared a bed with. And they are obviously not conquests. Could you stop making me sound like a seventeenth century duke working his way through the women of the *ton*?"

Tessa's jaw had dropped, and she leaned over and whispered to Vanessa. "I don't know which is more horrifying. The fact that Michael is talking to his mom about the women he's slept with or the fact that Michael knows what the *ton* is. Do you think he's been reading historical romance?"

"Well, I'm sure at least the duke would have mentioned to the love of his life that he'd been engaged to a woman she knew," his mother argued. The petite woman got into his space.

"I didn't think about it." Michael backed off. "I wasn't trying to hurt her. Did you hear my whole 'I should have waited for her' speech?"

He was an adorable asshole. Especially when he was being taken down by his mom.

"And JT's done way worse." Michael threw his brother under the bus. Or at least he tried to. "What about all the times JT said he was me so he didn't have to deal with a woman he'd previously slept with?"

Vanessa kind of wanted to watch this play out because Ava started in on what felt like a long speech on how JT had left his playboy past behind him. Michael argued that unlike JT he'd never actually had a playboy past.

"They'll be at it for a long time." Tessa finished her coffee. "We should sneak out or they'll start asking us to pick sides."

"I would pick Ava's side." Vanessa knew she should still have anger thrumming through her but it was at a simmer because watching Michael have to deal with his mom was fun.

This was what family felt like. They could argue and fight and it was okay because they would get through it all. There wasn't a question of whether Ava would turn her back on her son. She wouldn't. Michael could throw JT under a bus all day, but they were still brothers.

She and Nicki hadn't been taught this. They hadn't been taught how to love like this. When they'd disappointed their mother in any way, she simply shut them out. She would never have spiritedly argued, pointing out what a douchebag one of them had been, all the while obviously adoring them.

She hadn't been taught how to fight and forgive and love through it all.

George had been easy to love. All he'd wanted from her was companionship and comfort and someone to talk to about his daughter.

She hadn't been his great love. That had been his wife who'd died years and years before. She'd been a way station, a nice place to rest while he was waiting to be reunited with his soul's mate.

"Could we not do this around Vanessa?" Michael was clearly exasperated. "Could we hide the crazy until she can't run away?"

"Well, she should know what she's getting into," Ava replied.

Ava had called her the love of Michael's life.

Vanessa brushed away tears. He was almost certainly the love of hers. She needed to think, needed to figure out if she could learn to love the way he did.

"We should definitely go." If she stayed she worried she might tell him to take her to Vegas and marry her before she could change her mind.

She started for the door, Tessa following after. "Hey, are you okay? I know he's in the wrong here, but…"

She shook her head. "It's fine. I need to get to work."

Maybe at work she could think about something other than Michael.

Maybe…

* * * *

Where else would I go?

He held on to those words as he walked into the elevator that would lead him up to the McKay-Taggart offices. Vanessa had said the words with an unsounded "duh" to them. Like it was a foregone conclusion that the condo was now her home, and he should think about that because she could be the one kicking him out.

She'd sounded like a woman who was deeply annoyed with her man. Not one who was about to walk out.

Every night he felt like he made a tiny bit of progress. She let him hold her, let him carry her to their bed, and this morning she'd flat-out let him make love to her. She wouldn't shower with him, but they would get there.

Except he'd taken two steps back because he hadn't told her about Tessa.

How would that conversation have gone? Probably about the way this morning had gone except maybe his mom wouldn't have been there to call him out. Vanessa had been able to slip away while he'd been trying to explain to his mom that he wasn't trying to embarrass his whole line.

Only his mother still referred to her family line.

The door started to close when a big hand came out from the other side, slapping the sensors and forcing them to come back open.

Deke hopped on, a frown on his face and his cell phone in hand. "You didn't tell your girlfriend about Tessa?"

Michael felt his jaw drop. They'd had the fight less than an hour ago. "How the hell do you know that?"

Deke's shoulders shrugged as he pressed the button to close the doors again. "Grapevine. I managed to get on the text loop many of the ladies use when they need someone to pick up the kids or they need to talk about how dumb their men are. It's entirely entertaining."

The carpool loop was legendary. It was also supposed to be all female. Not that the men didn't drive the kiddos around, but they weren't on that loop. The "grapevine" as they called it was used to plan and organize the McKay-Taggart world. Everything from potluck menus to carpool schedules were devised and carried out over that text loop. "I'm sorry. What the actual hell, man? How did you end up on there?"

"Oh, Big Tag sent me undercover. It's part of my job." Deke slid his phone into his pocket. "I was to infiltrate and report back. My oldest sister's potato salad recipe got them to notice me. But then Seth broke his arm and Charlotte's Navigator was in the shop, and he couldn't get into Big Tag's truck, but my SUV was perfect and comfortable, so I drove him to school when she couldn't. Two weeks later, Luke had that crazy accident during his football practice and then I was driving two of them. So Charlotte added me to a text that got me in the loop. I started replying with helpful hints my sisters fed me. Then I threw all the guys under the bus and I was in."

"And you report back to Big Tag?"

"Oh, yeah, but only the good gossip like what I got this morning about you. Charlotte caught on very quickly and turned me with a combination of fear and her chocolate chip cookies. I'm way more scared of the ladies," Deke admitted. "So I'm a double, but I'm pretty sure Big Tag knows that, too. I'm a pawn in their game of love."

His workplace was weird. He knew they were all in the information game, but still, this shit had only gone down an hour before. "So who the hell told? Tessa's not in that loop."

It wasn't that the women of MT weren't nice to his ex, but she wasn't in need of help with childcare, and he couldn't imagine tough-chick Tess trading key lime pie recipes with the girls. In that Deke really did belong more.

"Oh, no. Tessa told David, who told Kyle, who texted MaeBe, who went straight to Charlotte, who texted the group," Deke said like it was a totally normal thing to do. "MaeBe tells Charlotte everything because when she finally gets married and has kids, she wants on that loop. She thinks loyalty will get her there. Then Charlotte posted the whole thing as a poll on our Facebook page."

That was news to him. "There's a Facebook page?"

"It's more of a group. Charlotte found it was more versatile than texts," Deke explained. "You should know you're not polling well."

There was a quiet ding, and the doors opened. Michael thought seriously about quitting and walking away now. He could move to a deserted island and live off the land. He wouldn't have to face anyone again.

Oooo, he could kidnap Vanessa. She'd mentioned at one point that she might think about forgiving him if he was the last man alive. He wouldn't technically be the last man alive, but he could be the only one she could talk to. Maybe forcing her into complete isolation with only him as a companion would make her rethink her stubborn stance.

Or he could take his medicine and be the man she needed.

Damn it. "I think I need a sparring session. See you downstairs at 10?"

Beating the crap out of Deke would make him feel better. And he might let Deke get in a shot or two. If he came home looking pathetic and damaged, Vanessa's tender heart wouldn't let her ignore him.

Although his mom would point out he'd probably started the fight and go into all the ways he and JT used to get in trouble.

He was calling his dad because he needed to get his mom out of here stat.

"Dude, I'm not sparring with you when your life is this fucked up," Deke announced as he slid his security card to open the door.

Yasmin gave them a cheery smile from the reception desk.

"Morning, Michael. Morning, Deke. Michael, MaeBe asked me to tell you she's got some info for you," she said before touching her earpiece. "McKay-Taggart Security Services. How may I help you? Wow, that is a lot of gunfire. Hold on." She pushed another button, her voice staying cool as a cucumber. "Big Tag, I've got Tennessee Smith on the line, and he is under heavy fire. Uh huh. I know you told him not to get involved, but I think he did. Sure thing. I'll put him through now."

So Ten's latest endeavor was going gangbusters. "Thanks. I'll go find her."

Yasmin gasped and then hung up. "That was a loud explosion, but Mr. Smith was still talking. He's very cool under pressure. It seems like he started a small war. I don't think Big Tag gave him a per diem for arming rebel forces."

You never knew with Tag.

"I'll go and get right on that." Deke stepped away.

Michael was about to go find MaeBe when he stopped. Yasmin was level-headed. She was a divorced mom with a daughter. Since every woman in his life seemed pissed at him, perhaps he should get an outsider's view. "Hey, can I ask your opinion?"

Her brown eyes came up to find his. "About per diems? Big Tag is actually quite generous with them. He even gives a daily allowance for condoms. Even for the female employees. He's a little too generous, if you ask me. Some of the guys take advantage. Like there's no way they're going through that many condoms. I've seen some of them. They do not have a whole box of game, if you know what I mean."

The expense reports at MT could get kind of weird. "Not about that. All right. This is a hypothetical. You're dating a man."

Yasmin's mouth went flat. "He's wrong."

"I didn't finish."

Yasmin nodded. "All right, but the answer's going to be the same. And I assume we're talking about a friend who is you, so you're wrong. But go ahead. I can be fair."

Oh, she so couldn't be fair.

He was about to tell her to forget it when a deep voice spoke.

"He wants to know if he was right to not tell his girlfriend that he was engaged to a woman he had spy on her." Kyle had slipped in behind him. "According to what I've managed to uncover, Vanessa knew he was engaged, but she didn't know it was Tessa. Who seems to have slipped up and spilled the secret when she took over for me today because someone stole my identity and I need to talk to a lawyer. Also, I'm probably going to have to have my mom cosign for my car. So I feel very adult and ready to face the world."

Yasmin's eyes had widened in obvious awe. "You figured all of that out this morning?"

Kyle nodded. "I'm a good operative."

He was an ass. "He found it out from his brother, who found it out from Tessa, who can't keep her mouth shut. He's not good at finding out intel. He's good at reading texts."

Kyle shrugged. "You say potato and all that. You should have straight up told her. I knew this would all go wrong, but hey, no one listens to me. Including the guy at the bank."

Yep, he should have taken the day off. "I've got to go find MaeBe. You're an asshole, Hawthorne."

He strode toward the bank of cubicles where the tech team was located. Thankfully it was on the opposite side of the building from Big Tag's office. Although he could hear the man yelling something about starting rebellions in foreign countries and how insurance didn't cover that.

Those were management problems. He had worries of his own.

"Are you trying to put MaeBe back out in the field?" Kyle was right on his ass. "Because you saw how that went last time."

"No, she's got information for me." Michael managed to avoid turning and confronting the kid.

"Okay, because she got hurt last time, and I'm not merely talking about the knife wound she took. She's not like us, man."

That did get Michael to stop. "What do you mean she's not like us? She works here, too. You have to let her do her job."

"She isn't an operative," Kyle insisted. "She can hack all day, but putting her in that role will kill a part of her soul. I'm asking you not to do it. She wants to please the people around her, and she'll hurt herself to do it."

Michael sighed, his irritation gone in the face of Kyle's open longing. "Man, why don't you tell her you love her?"

Kyle's face went blank. "Because I can't. Because I won't."

He had no idea what had happened to Kyle, but he knew a tortured soul when he saw one. "Saying those words doesn't make them true. You're in love with her. You can't stay away from her. All you're doing right now is delaying the inevitable."

"No. I'm saving her right now. My life… I'm not in a place where I'm good for her. I can't even get a freaking car loan without something exploding. The last year of my life has been this weird slow burn of a shit show that I can't get a handle on. It's one thing after the other, and she doesn't need that." Kyle sighed. "I thought I would get a job and a car and then I would look for a place of my own. When I can be a real functional adult, I can have a girlfriend."

"And if she finds someone in the meantime?"

Kyle shrugged. "I think she knows how I feel, and I think she's giving me some time. She's not dating right now. I hope I'm ready before she's done with me. But that's my problem, not yours. However, I need to know you'll watch out for MaeBe. She's getting along with Vanessa again, and that friendship is important to her."

All of MaeBe's friends were important to her. "Vanessa's definitely softened. I think all her anger is directed at me now."

Kyle patted his shoulder. "As it should be. If it helps, she thinks Vanessa's going to come around."

"She does?" He would take any good news he could get.

"Dude, you lied about something that was fairly reasonable and you have a shit ton of money to lavish on her," Kyle replied.

"The money might be part of the problem." Vanessa didn't trust that his family would stand by her. She had all kinds of evidence that they wouldn't. Her relationships before had gone wrong, and the one good relationship she'd enjoyed had been doomed from the start.

"Nah, she might shy away in the beginning, but what she really wants seems to be people who care about her enough to let themselves need her. She wants to be part of a family, and not a distant one, if you know what I mean. Her sister didn't even tell her she had a brain tumor. My brother lets me know when he stubbed his toe. Like that family shit can fuck a person up."

Her sister hadn't told her she was dying.

He and JT had been so close at one point it had been suffocating. They'd found a balance, but he had no idea how he would survive if he found out his brother kept a secret from him. Some part of him would die.

He hadn't even thought about that. God, how must that have made her feel? She'd barely talked about it, and he hadn't asked. He'd let her stew in it for a week without offering her comfort. He'd been so wrapped up in his own guilt and misery that he hadn't considered how alone she was in her mourning. How she'd thought she was doing something—one last thing—good for her sister, and that rug had been viciously pulled out from under her.

He wasn't the only one who'd hurt her, but he'd neglected to confront the situation because he'd selfishly thought only of himself.

"Hey, Michael. I was looking for you. I've had some movement on the George Jr. front, but I'm not sure what to make of it." MaeBe had a thermos in her hand. She smiled Kyle's way. "'Morning."

The fucker actually blushed. "'Morning. You doing okay?"

MaeBe nodded. "Yeah. How about you?"

They should just fuck already, whether or not Hawthorne was an actual functional adult. He should start using up his condom per diem and put the rest of them out of their misery.

"Okay. I had some business stuff to get out of the way," Kyle replied, seeming to get his cool back.

"He got turned down for a car loan." Michael wasn't so nice that he would let Kyle totally get away with it.

Kyle frowned his way. "Thanks, man."

"You're welcome." He turned to MaeBe. "Before you start to soothe his wounded ego, what do you have for me?"

MaeBe looked to Kyle like she wasn't sure what to do.

"Let's go to your desk." Kyle put a hand on her back as she started to walk. "And it's a little hiccup with an old credit card of mine. Nothing I can't fix. What did our least favorite billionaire do now?"

"Well, you know I've been poking my nose around, and I've heard a couple of rumors." MaeBe made it to her desk. She had a double cubicle with three different monitors and so much computer equipment, Michael couldn't name it all. She also had shelves of pop culture memorabilia. Michael was sure the blonde figurine with a stake was Buffy, but he had no idea why Rose Apothecary was such a big deal to the woman.

"By poking around I assume you mean you've been hacking," Michael said.

"And looking around our beautiful interwebs," MaeBe replied with a smile. She sank down to her chair and started typing. "I found a couple of boards where former employees of George Jr. commiserate on what an ass he is. I infiltrated."

"Of course you did, you sneaky little catfish." Kyle stood behind her chair, watching the biggest of her monitors. "Do they think you're an employee, too?"

"A former assistant," MaeBe replied. "Though I told them I worked for his second wife. Everyone here is involved in the corporation, so I was hoping they wouldn't know much about the domestic side."

Kyle might be right about MaeBe when it came to working in the real world, but damn she was a master when it came to this one. "How long have you been on this?"

"About six weeks," MaeBe explained. "When Julian asked Big Tag to look into the Vanessa situation, he thought it would be good to check out all the angles. He wanted me to get some insider info. So I was in place when it was time to pivot and get the downlow on Junior himself. Everyone hates him, by the way."

"That is not surprising." Big Tag had spectacular instincts when it came to these things. "Are these active employees? Or former?"

"It's a mix of both," MaeBe replied. "The group started so they could network, but it morphed into more of a support group. From what I can tell, it's not easy working for Junior. So, his current assistant is on here. She's trying to find a new job. He passed her over for a promotion again, and she's figured out that he's never going to let her move into that marketing job she wants. So she was talking last night about him moving money around. Large sums."

"How large is large?" Michael asked.

"Two hundred and fifty *K*," MaeBe replied. "I know that's not much to a billionaire, but she says it's very odd for him to do it personally. So odd that he wasn't sure how to do it himself and he had to ask her for passcodes."

Okay. He was intrigued. "Do we know what account he moved it from?"

"A personal account, but not one he shares with wife number three." MaeBe brought up a screenshot of a banking record. "And he didn't exactly move it. He made a purchase. Bitcoin. She had to help him do that, too. He then shifted the bitcoin to another account. He told her he was paying his lawyers."

"Lawyers don't take cryptocurrency." Kyle frowned. "Does she have the account number?"

"I couldn't easily ask." MaeBe turned her face up from the screen. "I'm looking into it though. The assistant thinks it's hookers. Apparently Junior likes hookers."

"I doubt a hooker would make him go to so much trouble, and she would have to be a spectacular one to charge a quarter of a million." Michael didn't like it. He didn't like that number at all.

"It's some kind of shakedown," Kyle said with a shake of his head. "Cryptocurrency is the chosen payment form of the mafia these days. He's in charge of a multinational corporation. Does he have ties to any of the heavy mob countries?"

MaeBe nodded. "The company works all over the world. He's got ties to both Russia and Ukraine. There's a big office in Tokyo, too."

"Don't discount the Italians." He'd made a study of the Benedict Group. "The company owns some hotels in Italy. So we're thinking he's paying mafia contacts?"

"Or he's had a ransomware shakedown," MaeBe mused. "But I suspect the assistant would know something about that. And he would likely use corporate funds."

"Unless it's personal servers they're shutting down." It wasn't likely though. Ransomware attacks were more and more common these days, and they'd gotten far more sophisticated. The attacker would target certain systems, take control over them, and hold the very important system hostage until demands were met. The government had been battling them for years.

MaeBe knew a lot about those kinds of attacks.

"I'm looking into it, but I doubt it. I've heard absolutely nothing about a coming attack. He's in town today, by the way," MaeBe mentioned.

That was news. The last Michael had heard, Junior was holed up in Houston. "Junior flew in?"

MaeBe shook her head. "No. He drove up here. The assistant thought it was weird because he didn't mention he was going anywhere, and he didn't use a driver. She only knows about it because she overheard him talking on the phone. Said it sounded supersecret. That's why she thinks it's hookers."

Why would he drive? It was five hours on the road but roughly thirty minutes in the air. "Is there something wrong with the corporate jet?"

"No. He's supposed to use it tonight. He's due in New York for meetings tomorrow. That's the weird thing. He's got a flight scheduled for midnight and a hotel room booked," MaeBe replied. "So I have no idea why he's up here."

Michael didn't like it. He looked Kyle's way.

Kyle nodded. "I'll help MaeBe figure out where he is."

"The Benedict family has a suite at the Fairmont." MaeBe picked up her cell. "I'll make some calls."

Kyle looked to Michael. "We'll figure out where he is and what he's up to."

"Thank you. I'll be in my office. I need to make a call. Let me know if you find anything."

He didn't like the idea that Junior was in Dallas. He definitely didn't like the idea of the man sending a quarter of a million out in crypto. Something was about to happen. It was an instinct he'd honed over the years. Things were starting to converge, and Junior was getting nervous. It was precisely why he'd tried the dumbass blackmail setup on Vanessa.

The thing is it might have worked if Michael hadn't been around. If they hadn't been investigating Vanessa, no one would have turned on the cameras and gotten proof that someone had messed with her computer. Otherwise, her reputation might have doomed her.

A reputation she hadn't earned and didn't deserve.

He glanced down at his cell, and his mother had left him a text.

Darling, I'm taking Vanessa some lunch and then heading back to the ranch. Be patient with her. We'll win her over.

He loved his mother so much. She might be his secret weapon. Not money or good sex or the fact that he adored Vanessa. His mother being kind to her, offering her real maternal affection, might be the thing that got Vanessa to forgive him.

He walked to his office, his brain humming with thoughts.

Did he really want a relationship that was predicated on Vanessa's need for a loving mother?

Yes. No question about it. He would take her any way he could get her, and he would make it work. He would love her so long and so well she would forget how they started. He would make her such a part of the Malone family that the neglect she suffered would be a distant memory.

He dialed her number and got sent to voice mail. He started to hang up, but decided he needed to say something to her. Right now.

"Hey, sweetheart. I know this is weird because we're in a fight, but I need you to know that I love you. No matter what. If you can't love me back, I still love and support you. My family does, too." He had to take a breath to steady himself because emotions flooded through him. "And your sister was wrong to not tell you. I think she would have eventually. I think she thought she had more time. But you deserved the chance to say good-bye. You deserved the chance to try to take care of her, and I know you would have. You would have stayed with her until the end. The way I'll always be there for you. I know I screwed up, but I want to share this life with you. I want you there by my side through everything. I won't lie to you again. I won't omit a thing. I'll share it all if you can find a way to forgive me. I love you. Maybe we can talk tonight. Have a good day, baby."

He hung up and realized he hadn't shut his door.

Charlotte Taggart stood in his doorway. There was a fine sheen of tears in her blue eyes. "That was beautiful, Michael. I'm so glad you found her."

At least it was Charlotte. Ian would have given him hell. "Now the problem is keeping her."

Charlotte sniffled and straightened her shoulders. "Oh, it's worse. I came to bring you to the conference room. One of the big talk shows is running an interview about Vanessa, and it's not pretty."

Fuck. It was one more thing converging on a day that felt like it was the beginning of a whole bunch of dominoes falling. He followed Charlotte toward the conference room, a sinking feeling in his gut.

Chapter Eighteen

"Are you sure she shouldn't join us? It feels weird to have her standing there."

Ava smiled and waved over to where Tessa stood inside the private dining room Julian Lodge used when he entertained clients. It was on the floor above the club, and Vanessa couldn't stop thinking about what happened right below where they sat. Michael had offered to take her in a few days, to let her play and talk to her friends and be the person she got to be when she was in The Club.

She really had made friends here. She'd spent much of the last week trying to convince herself that everyone she'd met here had used her. But it wasn't true. Dani had been a true friend to her. The women of The Club didn't treat her like she was something to avoid. They laughed with her in the locker room and offered to help her with her corset.

Even Tessa had kind of become a friend.

"She wouldn't. Tessa's working, darling, and when she's working she's very focused. She'll watch the door and do her patrols," Ava said with an elegant wave of her hand.

Tessa nodded, but her face stayed blank. She'd started to think of it as Tessa's working face.

"What does she think is going to happen?" Vanessa took a sip of the iced tea the server had offered to go along with the chicken parm Ava had arranged to be delivered from Top. Michael's mother had walked in and declared it was lunch time and she had to make up for the terrible breakfast scene her son had made this morning.

"Oh, I think Tessa is ready for anything." Ava wore a Chanel jacket over her silk blouse. "But we're perfectly safe here. It's why I didn't invite you out. I thought you might need a break from reporters."

She did, although Michael and the whole team had done a good job of getting the press off her back. She hadn't been mobbed in the last few days. "The publicist warned me there's some kind of interview coming out. I suspect my old bestie is at work again."

The salads were swept away, and the perfectly heated entrée set in front of them. The smell alone told her this would be delicious. And she didn't give a crap about carbs anymore.

"This is that Ashton person, correct?" Ava frowned as she picked up her knife and fork.

"Yes." At least she was almost certain it would be. "She always crawls out from under a rock anytime there's a chance to talk about me."

"Why does she hate you?"

Vanessa sighed. "I feel bad saying this because it's not true in most cases. You know when two women are friends and they break up and they both blame the other because they're jealous?"

"Ah, but it's often true, love." Ava sat back. "Human beings can be jealous creatures, but women are taught not to help each other. We're taught to compete against each other. I think it's changing a bit, but the instinct is instilled in us."

"Well, Ashton thought she could get into the business through me. I suppose I always knew that," Vanessa explained. "I needed an assistant. I advertised for one and interviewed about ten before I found her. She told me she wanted to be a screenwriter. I didn't know that she was lying and had been in LA for a year auditioning with no luck. The thing is I would have sympathized, but she hid it. She did a good job in the beginning. She traveled with me. It can be lonely on the road. You know how they talk about a film crew is a family?"

Ava nodded. "Yes, I've heard that said."

"It's true, but it's a family that changes every couple of months when you get a new job." It was the part Vanessa loved and hated. She loved getting to know everyone and hated the fact that none of the relationships lasted. "Ashton was the one constant. She became my closest friend, the only family I had at the time. I didn't realize how she was manipulating things behind the scenes."

"Manipulating things?" Ava prompted.

"She would talk to people about how difficult I was. She would tell industry people all these outrageous stories about how mean I could be. It was all to gain sympathy, to try to show that she was more worthy than I was. It worked. She got some small parts. I didn't know how she'd gotten them at the time, so I was supportive. She didn't have a ton of chemistry on the screen. It wasn't that she was a bad actress. She didn't have the sparkle that's necessary," she explained. "Then the rumors started, and I met Lara. Ashton tried to manipulate her and Lara laid it all out for me. I fired Ashton, and she's never forgiven me."

"It sounds like you didn't need forgiveness."

"Well, she'd done her job for long enough. She spread rumors for years. It hurt my career." Vanessa sighed. "Lara and I spent time together. We made three movies together. She was…she was a light in the world, but she had her darkness, too."

"I'm so sorry you lost her." Ava sat back. "I've watched those movies. They were your best work."

"Why would you watch them?" She hadn't talked much about her career with Ava. They'd spent quite a lot of time together in the last few weeks, but Ava hadn't asked many questions about her time in Hollywood. It had been refreshing, but now she was surprised.

"Because I want to support you. Because my son loves you, and I've come to adore you, darling. I wanted to know more about you. Those films you made with her, they were personal to you."

Lara had made films about women. About their worries and struggles. About how women fit into a world that hadn't been made for them. She'd told her own stories. "They were always about her, but she was so good at what she did that it was easy to see myself in every role. I felt like a real actress for the first time, not just the star of a film."

"You were very good in them." Ava's lips had turned up in an almost sad smile. As though she knew how hard it was to think about what could have been.

"I wish she'd lived. That was what George and I talked about a lot in the beginning. What she could have done if she'd lived, the people she could have touched with her unique talents."

"I don't understand how a woman like that…" Ava stopped as though realizing she was about to say something wrong.

But she wasn't. Staying silent about these problems exacerbated them. It made the problem something to hide, and this was a problem that flourished in the darkness, that lived in the shadows and fed on shame. "She struggled to fit in all of her life. Wealth doesn't necessarily equal happiness. Her mother and father loved her, but they didn't always understand her. She spent much of her life with undiagnosed clinical depression. Her mom didn't want her to see someone because of how it might look to the family."

"But I knew her mother," Ava began.

"Her mother didn't understand," Vanessa pointed out. "No one talked about mental health in her world, and even if they had, she'd been raised to believe it was a weakness and something to hide. It's hard to break out of a lifetime of teaching, and a lack of courage doesn't mean someone is terrible. George felt that guilt. It was only after her mother passed that Lara sought some help, but she would get on her meds and feel good and then get off them because she thought they held back her creative process. She didn't talk about the issues behind her drug use in public because it was shameful to her and her family. But talking is exactly how to address the problem. Talk and support. She was about to go into rehab. That's the ironic part. She was supposed to go in when we finished filming, but I think she wanted one last night."

"I'm so sorry, darling."

Vanessa took a long breath. It did feel good to talk, to process through emotions that still swirled inside from time to time. If there was one great thing that had come from this, it was spending time with her therapist. Michael had forced it on her, but it was a good process. Emotions weren't a thing a person confronted and then discarded. They lingered and had to be brought out time and time again, examined with new facets found and explored. There was often no "getting over" a trauma. There was hard work to do to ease the pain and work around it or work with it, because sometimes trauma could bring about strength and empathy that hadn't existed before. "She was part of my family. The one I chose. Nicki and I weren't close. Our mom…well, she made us compete. If one of us got better grades, she would use it against the other."

Ava reached out, putting a hand over hers. "That wasn't right of her. You can't do that when you have children. You have to love and appreciate them for who they are separately. I should know. I sometimes worry I treated Michael like he was another JT. JT was easier. He was a clone of his father. Michael was someone different. I think I pushed him away sometimes."

Vanessa turned her hand over so she could hold Ava's. "He adores you. And he knows who he is now. He loves his job. He needed the military, and he needed to be away from the world he grew up in for a while. But never doubt how much he loves his family."

Ava sniffled and gave her a squeeze before she sat back and dabbed at her eyes with her napkin. "Thank you, dear. I needed to hear that. And you need to understand that not all women in your life will be like this Ashton. Or your sister. I know she was a good woman, but she hurt you, too."

Vanessa's heart ached. "She didn't understand me. Very few people do. She understood that I cared about George, but she didn't understand why I had to marry him. Sometimes I think that was the mistake I made. If I'd told him no, simply lived with him those last few years, maybe the press would have been easier on me."

Ava's head shook. "I assure you that they wouldn't have."

There were some things she needed to ask. "Does it bother you that I was married to him? That I had a relationship with a man who could have been my grandfather?"

Ava's eyes went soft. "I was concerned with it at first. Mostly because of busybodies who stick their noses into things they shouldn't. I was reminded recently that I don't want to be one of those people. Things can look different from the outside. The truth of the matter is only you and George can ever know what happened between the two of you. I'll ask the only important question, and you can tell me as much or as little as you like. Did you care about him?"

"I loved him very much." She could feel tears in her eyes because she'd never talked about him with anyone but Nicki, who'd been a bit brusque about the whole thing. "He was a great man, the first man who was truly good to me. He was lonely, and I was lonely. If we'd been the same age, no one would have questioned it. It would have been seen as a proper transaction. I would have been a trophy wife in the public's mind. I've been thinking about that a lot lately. What my life might have been like if he'd been younger."

"And what have you concluded?"

"That it wouldn't have worked," Vanessa admitted. "That sometimes we have relationships we need, and they don't have to be some happily ever after. I could love George because he was older, because he needed me. I wasn't ready then to be in a partnership of equals. I needed a father figure, and I know that sounds…"

"It sounds like a woman who is being honest with herself," Ava said. "I will say the age difference bothered me at first, but then my son pointed out that I was being small-minded. Who is to say what emotions are worthy? Does love mean less because it doesn't fit some perfect narrative? Is a personal relationship supposed to check off boxes the public expects them to?"

"Apparently. I know I was expected to."

"We are all expected to. Especially women. We're born, and by the time we're teenagers, we're put in boxes, and it takes a lot to get out of that box. I have to say the truth is my box was comfortable. I went from being protected by my parents' status to being protected by my husband's. I didn't have to worry about what people thought of me." Ava frowned. "So I did nothing to truly push against those boundaries. Why would I? The world was made for me. But Sophy changed that. I love my nephew like a son and Sophy like a granddaughter. What if she doesn't want to marry a wealthy man and live a fairy tale? What if she wants a life where she's judged on her merit? She sings quite beautifully. What if she chooses that life? What box will they put her in? How will I feel knowing I did nothing to change that?"

Vanessa could feel tears falling on her cheeks because no one had ever put it so simply. She'd been put in a box when she'd started her career. Scream queen. Bombshell. Pretty but probably dumb, and when she tried to bust out of that confinement, she'd been punished. She knew other actresses who had done much worse than she had, but the media had placed them in a different box. They could talk about feminism and they were considered activists. When Vanessa did, she was pushy. "I tried and I failed."

Ava suddenly had a couple of tissues in her hand. "Oh, darling girl, you are far too young to have failed. You had a setback. A spectacularly painful one from what I can tell, but only a setback if you choose. You didn't let them keep you in the box, and you paid the price. Nothing changes if no one is ever willing to pay that price. We merely push the charge off on our children and grandchildren. So I would like to thank you for pushing back."

They were both crying now.

Ava dried her eyes and sat back. "Are you done with my son? Is there anything he can do to make up for what he did? I have to ask because I'm his mother, and I truly believe he will be alone for the rest of his life if he can't be with you. Is there any way to forgive him?"

She'd been taught that when a person hurt you, you shut them out. That's what her mother did. She punished every infraction and let her daughters know that her love was something they earned.

She didn't want to live that way. She loved Michael. She could accept that he was a dumbass who'd screwed up. That wasn't the hard part. The hard part wasn't forgiving. "I'm afraid he'll wake up and not want me anymore."

Ava shifted from the chair across from Vanessa to the chair next to hers, opening her arms. "Oh, my darling, we're all afraid of that in the beginning. Love is a giant leap of faith because it only makes sense to the heart. Do you love him?"

She had to nod.

"Then take your time and decide if he's worth the risk. You don't have to say yes now. You don't even have to stay with him. If you need space, come out to the ranch with me. Or take a place here, but talk to him, try to work this out if you think it could be something good for you."

"Shouldn't you tell me to forgive him?"

Ava's hand came up to cup her cheek, rubbing away her tears. "No. I have to think about you, too. Your mother isn't here to advise you. I don't think she ever was. It's not a good idea for me to listen to all your complaints about my son. And there will be many. There always are in a marriage. You need someone to talk to, someone who will listen so you can get it all out. You can't keep these things inside. But if you have questions, need advice, I'm here for you. My advice is this—don't let past heartaches rob you of future joy. Life seems long but it's not. It goes by so quickly. Build joy where you can."

"I do love him." It was good to admit it.

"Then trust that things will be all right if you put in the work," Ava replied. "Hold on to him and your family even when the storm seems at its worst."

The storm had already taken her life and ripped it apart. But she could put it back together. She could choose to take this chance with Michael. She didn't have to make the decision now. Everyone was giving her time, but wasn't she making the choice by not walking away? Did she need another three weeks or three months to think over whether or not to forgive him? That wasn't the question. Forgiveness would come, and she knew it deep down. It was the choice to trust him again that was hard.

Because everyone she'd trusted had somehow turned on her.

Could she try one last time? If Michael betrayed her again, she would likely close herself off. She wouldn't lie down and fade, but she would close her heart off because she'd found her mate and wouldn't take another.

Wasn't that worth the risk?

"I'll talk to him tonight. I promise. I do love him. I want this to work."

Ava gave her a glorious smile. "And I will support you both."

Because that was what families were supposed to do.

Sometimes a person was born into her family. Sometimes she had to search the world to find it. Sometimes blood bound people together, and for others it was forged in love and commitment, the bonds chosen freely, the choice made every single day.

She could choose to be part of the Malones. To stand by them and allow them to stand by her. She could have faith that Michael wouldn't wake up and decide the love he felt for her wasn't worth the trouble. She could value herself enough to know that it was. That she was worth trouble and pain because she could bring him joy.

It wasn't sacrifice she'd been offering them. It was the denial of her own worth. She'd fought for it once and lost.

She wouldn't stop fighting.

"Hey, Vanessa, there's something you should probably see." Tessa had a worried look on her face. "I just got a text from the office. According to Charlotte, there's an interview playing on one of the big daytime talk shows."

Her phone was likely blowing up. The publicist had warned her. This was the moment when she would usually panic.

She felt nothing but calm. "Is it Ashton?"

Tessa nodded.

It was odd how she'd gone from resenting Ashton to feeling sorry for her. One of the things they'd bonded over was a shared family experience. Ashton's father had ignored her utterly, and everything she'd done had been in a vain attempt to get his attention. Now she realized Ashton had focused all that negative energy on her. She'd fired Ashton over all the manipulations, and here they were years later with Ashton still trying to get her attention.

"Do you want to watch it?" Tessa asked. "I can ask the servers to turn on the televisions."

Vanessa looked to her mother-in-law. Well, the woman who would one day be her mother-in-law. "Are you concerned?"

Ava waved her off. "I'm far more concerned about our lunch getting cold. Let the lawyers and publicists handle all of this. We should talk about nicer things."

"I agree." She was sure Michael was watching it somewhere. He would tell her what she needed to know, and they would figure out how to handle it together. She glanced up at Tessa. "But I think I'll be going home early. I finished up everything I needed to do. I want to be ready when Michael comes home."

Tessa's eyes widened. "Ready to leave?"

She had that desperate *Please don't make me be the one to tell my ex that his current is leaving him* look. If there was an acknowledged look to go with that situation, that is. Vanessa merely smiled. "I guess he'll have to wonder."

She got back to her lunch and was ready to enjoy the rest of her day.

Because tonight would change everything.

Two hours later Vanessa stood in the lobby of the building she'd come to think of as home. Tessa was with the manager of the building, a frown on her face. "What do you mean there's been a problem on the penthouse floor?"

There were several workers in uniforms, toolkits at their sides, waiting in the lobby. It looked like two different crews from their uniforms.

The manager was an older, distinguished-looking man. "It's been a crazy day. Everything has gone wrong. Our plumbing system here on the first floor went insane. There was some kind of commotion up on the penthouse floor. One of the two units had an alarm go off. We think it's malfunctioning, but we can't be sure."

"Oh, it's all kinds of malfunctioning." Chelsea Weston sat on a bench, her daughter by her side. Sophy had a tablet out, obviously playing some sort of game. Chelsea had a laptop open in front of her. She'd dragged a table over to form a desk. "Some asshole tripped the entire floor and I panicked, and now I can't get back up until some Agency dudes check it out because I have classified shit up there."

Tessa's jaw dropped. "I thought you weren't supposed to admit you still did that."

Chelsea shrugged. "Maybe if I admit it enough they'll fire me. It's only part time. Only when the really bad stuff happens. Sorry I said *shit*, baby."

Sophy's lips curled but she didn't look up from her game. "I didn't notice, Mom. And you help keep us all safe. You know if they fired you, you would sit up all night wondering what's going on and driving the rest of us crazy. It's best you stay close. Dad's proud."

"Well, Dad's going to be annoyed," Chelsea said with a sigh. "Because he's coming home in a couple of hours, and we'll probably still be down here. He's going to give me so much hell about not being able to deal with the security system."

"Can I go up and check it?" Tessa asked.

The manager perked up. "You're on the list. I can let you go upstairs. I'm still waiting on the work orders for these gentlemen, but my system is down. I'm trying to get the homeowners to verbally approve them. Thank god one of them is a plumber because the men's toilet is overflowing, and my super had a car accident this morning."

It sounded like the manager was having a day.

Chelsea looked at Tessa over her laptop. "That would be great. We can't stay up there. The alarms won't turn off. It's something wrong with the physical system. I tried to fix it online, but it's the actual unit that's got the issue. You've installed them?"

Tessa nodded. "I had some of the installers teach me the system, and I'm handy with a wrench when I need to be." She looked over at Vanessa. "Stay here with Chelsea. It shouldn't take long. I think this is one of the older units. I can get it fixed quickly."

"The system cut off the elevators," the manager said. "Well, the private elevators to the penthouse floor. You can take the regular elevators up to eight, but you'll have to walk from there."

Tessa turned distinctly disgruntled. "Yeah, I remember. Damn paranoid people." She held up her phone. "Give me a heads-up when the suits get here. I'd like to not get shot."

"Oh, they don't wear suits," Chelsea said with a frown. "Today's Agency asshole is surprisingly casual."

"Mom," Sophy groaned.

"Sorry." Chelsea looked Vanessa's way as the doors to the elevator opened and Tessa hopped inside. "We tried to use a curse jar but we were going to go broke."

It looked like she wouldn't have as much time as she'd wanted. She'd intended to prepare the small playroom Michael kept for a superhot scene with her Dom. At the end she'd intended to tell him that she wasn't going anywhere and that they had some talking to do.

She'd listened to his voicemail after lunch. Ava had left to go back to the ranch with promises of visiting very soon and then Vanessa had sat down and turned on her phone. Michael had said all the right things, and now she knew he meant them.

He wasn't going to change his mind. They couldn't know the future, but he wanted one with her. He cared about her, and she was worthy of that care.

They could build trust from here. Starting tonight.

Well, starting after the security system got fixed.

"Baby girl, are you piggybacking off my signal?" Chelsea's lips turned down in a frown.

Sophy kept her eyes on her game. "I'm one level from beating Devi."

"And I am working on national security issues," Chelsea argued.

"How did you get my password?"

It sounded like the Westons were having a family dilemma. "I'm going to the bathroom. I'll be right back."

If she stayed down here much longer, Michael would likely walk into the lobby, and she wanted to look halfway decent. She strode over to the elevators and took a right. The bathrooms were hidden away behind them. She noticed the plumber on one knee in front of an open tool kit. Even kneeling she could see he was a tall, lanky man.

Unlike her broad, gorgeous guy. She slipped inside the women's room and moved to the mirror. She didn't look half bad. If Tessa couldn't get the security system under control, maybe she could convince Michael to go to The Club for the night. They could check into the hotel portion of the building where each room was sumptuous and designed for play.

She should text him. She hadn't replied because she'd been so emotional. And there was a devil inside her who wanted him to sweat a little.

She pulled her phone out because there wasn't time for punishment. Ava was right. Life went by in a blur, and she wanted every moment she spent with Michael to be as sweet as they could possibly make it.

"Please hand me the phone, Miss Hale."

She looked up, and the plumber was standing in the sitting area.

And he had a gun in his hand.

Vanessa gasped and took a step back, fumbling with the phone. There was a button on the side and if she pushed it three times, it sent out the emergency signal. It would go to all her emergency contacts. There was only one.

It would go to Michael.

"Touch that button and I'll have my friend in the lobby kill Chelsea and Sophy Weston." The man had a deep voice. "He's out there with the others, and no one will suspect a thing until he draws out his gun and shoots them both in the head." He touched his ear. "Stand by. The target might need persuading. Take the adult out first. Then we'll go for the kid."

Little Sophy. Ava loved her so much. Chelsea was part of the family, had been for years.

She couldn't take the risk.

She let the cell drop to the tiles below. "What do you want?"

"I don't want anything but cash, honey." The man moved in, picking up the cell and pocketing it.

Vanessa kicked out and started for the door, but the man had an arm around her waist in a heartbeat.

"Can't damage you. You have to look good for your final act." The words were whispered in her ear before he placed a cloth over her mouth and nose.

Chloroform. The astringent smell assaulted her.

"I'm bringing her out the back. Get ready for transport."

They were the final words she heard before everything went black.

Chapter Nineteen

Pulling into the parking lot at your building. I'll take her upstairs and wait for you to get home. She's in a good mood. You might be a lucky bastard.

Tessa's text should have sent a surge of hope, but the last few hours had done nothing but enrage him.

"I'm ready to start again," MaeBe said quietly.

Kyle clicked the button that started the stream, and the interview proceeded.

Michael felt his fists clench as he watched the woman on the screen's eyes go soft, her lips trembling as she stared at the camera.

"I love Vanessa. She's like a sister to me, but I'm so worried that she's going to try to hurt herself." Ashton Banks had the concerned friend act down. "It's what she does when she gets put in a corner. She turns to drugs and alcohol, and one day she's going to go too far."

"What does she get out of this?" MaeBe had real tears in her eyes. There was a combination of pain and rage on the hacker's face.

"Attention." Kyle sat beside MaeBe in the darkened conference room.

In the hours since the interview had aired, Michael had watched it all the way through three times, looking for anything he could use to take this woman down.

"I think it's something more," Michael murmured, his eyes on the woman who seemed so determined to keep Vanessa in the spotlight through her lies. "What do we know about the timing of these interviews she's done? She goes quiet for periods of time, right?"

"That could be dictated by whether the tabloids are interested or not, I would think." Kyle sat back. "Wouldn't she interview more when there's more interest in Vanessa? So I would think she would have more people asking for her input when something happens with the trial."

"Or something scandalous happens like her stepson trying to set her up," MaeBe pointed out.

"But there's been very little press about Junior." It bothered him. He'd thought about it all week long. The press had quieted, but he doubted that would have happened if Junior's plan had gone through.

"The major news outlets all covered the story." MaeBe had been tasked with watching the media when it came to Vanessa. "But it was very upfront coverage. Most of the major newspapers and entertainment outlets were fairly uniform. They put the facts out. The tabloids are a little different. There are some stories that question whether or not the Malone family put pressure on the police to hide Vanessa's actions."

"I want a deep dive into everything the Benedict Group is invested in, and Junior personally." Something about the timing bugged him.

On the screen Ashton was continuing to tell the sympathetic-looking reporter how worried she was for Vanessa's life, telling her stories about other times Vanessa had tried to hurt herself to get attention.

Bullshit. He'd talked to Vanessa's therapist half an hour ago. She'd gone over the interview Ashton had given, too, and found none of it credible.

Vanessa is a strong woman. She's determined to make something of her life. I do not believe she would hurt herself. Especially when things are looking up for her.

The therapist's opinion had bolstered his own. Not for one second did he believe what Ashton was saying. If Vanessa had ever had a problem with drugs, she would have told him, would have owned it. She didn't flinch in the face of any weakness. She dealt with it.

He so admired her for that.

"You think he has sway with some of these tabloids?" Kyle asked.

"I think the timing is interesting." His brain was working overtime. "All of this happens just as he figures out my family won't be swayed. He tried to force a rift between me and my mother over Vanessa. I've read Ashton's other interviews. She's never mentioned a drug problem before."

"No," MaeBe agreed. "This interview is so weird. I've watched and read them all. Ashton usually paints herself as the victim of Vanessa's cruelty and lies. Now she's making Vanessa seem fragile. Almost sympathetic."

"Yeah, like the part where she talks about how hurt Vanessa is by bad press and how it sends her into a downward spiral," Kyle commented. "What was that about? All she's had is bad press, and she seems fine to me."

He wouldn't trust Kyle to psychologically evaluate a person, but he was right in this case. Despite the fact that she had a tender heart, she was tough. Yes, she cried, but that was a measure of her strength, too. She hadn't hardened her heart against the world, hadn't cut herself off from forming relationships even though her foundational ones had been dysfunctional.

Vanessa hadn't stopped fighting for what she believed in. She'd hit the ground and was working on getting back up.

"She's strong as hell, and I assure you there's no way she's thinking about hurting herself. She might punch me." He would take it. He would take any punishment she needed to mete out as long as he was with her at the end of this. "But she won't hurt herself."

MaeBe was going through her files. "I got a report from our forensic accountant. The company is huge, but they do have a majority share in a news group that includes several tabloids." MaeBe groaned. "Including the ones that are so harsh on Vanessa. He's using these papers to build a narrative. I would bet he's paying Ashton, too."

"Then what's the narrative now?" Kyle asked.

The conference room door opened, and Deke strode in. "Hey, I know Vanessa isn't staying at her sister's place anymore, but something weird is happening, and I'm going over to check it out."

"Weird?" Michael didn't like the sound of that. It was a lot of movement around her at one time. First the surprise interview, and now something at her old place. Probably coincidence, but he had a nasty feeling in his gut that something was about to happen, some line of dominoes being set up to fall.

"The power went out for the whole community," Deke said. "I've been monitoring the community message boards, and the power went out about ten minutes ago. I checked Vanessa's cameras. They're off."

"And the gate wasn't fixed," Kyle stood. "So it's probably the press trying to get in."

Michael joined him, pushing back his chair and getting to his feet. "No. They know she's staying with me. We talked about it in our interview last week. There's no need for them to go to her old place. I'm calling Tessa. I want to make sure she lets no one into our condo."

He dialed her number, and Tessa came over the line.

"Hey, Michael," Tessa said, sounding slightly out of breath. "You owe me a beer after having to climb all these stairs."

"Why would you climb stairs?" He didn't like the thought of the elevator being out. Vanessa had worn heels today. They were little kitten heels, but they were still heels. "Did you talk to the manager?"

"There's something wrong with your security system, and apparently it's screwed with the private elevators," Tessa said over the line. "Don't worry about it. I can get it back online in no time."

His heart rate ticked up. He hadn't gotten a message that the system had a problem. If there was a security issue with the system, the guys who monitor it should have let him know. "Let me talk to Vanessa."

"She's downstairs," Tessa replied. "But it's okay. I left her in the lobby with Chelsea, and the manager's got the whole place in lockdown. He won't even let workmen up in the building."

Oh, his every sense was flaring now. He looked at Deke. "My security system is down."

Deke's shoulders went back, his whole body going on alert because he would understand the issue. Tessa might know the system, but she didn't understand the controls he had put in place. "I'll go check."

Deke jogged out of the conference room.

MaeBe pulled her cell phone out and dialed a number.

"Tess, I need you to get back to the lobby," Michael ordered. "I know Chelsea is trained, but she's been out of the field for a decade, and her daughter has to be her priority. Something's going on. Something's happening, and I think it's about Vanessa."

"I'm on it. I'll call you as soon as I'm on the ground and have her in sight." The line went dead.

"I can't get Vanessa to pick up, but it's ringing," MaeBe said. "It's not going straight to voicemail, so it's still on. What's happening?"

"I don't know, but I want her found now." His gut was in a knot. Something was happening, and he wasn't putting all the pieces together. They were all laid out for him, but he hadn't snapped them into place yet.

MaeBe turned to her laptop and started hitting keys.

Kyle moved in behind her, his hands on her shoulders. "You do what I think you did, nosy little hacker?"

MaeBe didn't look up. "Of course I did. I do it to everyone I like. Let me get a connection."

"What did she do?" Michael asked.

Kyle's head tilted, eyes turning Michael's way. "MaeBe likes to track people via their cell phones. You know how you can turn that function off if you like? Well, MaeBe can turn it back on without you knowing it. Even if Vanessa looked on her phone, she would have no idea that MaeBe's still got access. She could have been a supervillain."

"I only use my powers for good." MaeBe frowned at the screen. "I think she's moving. Like in a car. Her phone is heading north on I75. Is she coming here?"

Michael moved in so he could see the screen. Sure enough, MaeBe had pulled up a map of Dallas, and there was a small icon moving down the major freeway that ran close to the MT building and led north. This wasn't the app a person could use to check up on their wayward teens or make sure grandma was where they'd left her. This was all MaeBe.

She really would have made a good supervillain.

"So we know at least her phone is on the move." Though he would bet a lot of his wealth that Vanessa was in close proximity. "Where are they going? Can you pull up the traffic cams?"

"Of course, but as long as they're on the freeway I won't get much," MaeBe admitted. "I need her to exit or get on a toll road."

Michael heard a dinging sound that let him know he was getting a text. He pulled out his phone. It was from Vanessa.

I'm sorry. I can't do this anymore.

That was it. A chill went down his spine as things started to fall into place.

Junior had paid someone a quarter of a million dollars and tried to hide his trip into town.

Ashton went on television and declared that Vanessa was fragile and known for hurting herself.

His security system went south long enough to separate Vanessa from her guard. She should have been safe in the building, but the management system used a janitorial service, and the turnover was high. It wouldn't be hard to slip someone in.

They would need a place to carry out their plan.

The gates at Vanessa's community were open, and suddenly all the security cameras were down. No one would notice a car pulling in. They would all be trying to get their power back on.

Ashton had claimed Vanessa had tried to kill herself before.

"Fuck, they're setting her up." He knew where they were going. "That car will get off at the next exit. It's going to Vanessa's house."

"Why would they take her there?" Kyle asked.

MaeBe looked up. "They exited."

He was right. "Call Derek and explain the situation. I'm going now. I can probably get there before the cops send someone out."

"I don't understand the situation." MaeBe stood.

Michael started for the door. "Junior couldn't make his blackmail plot work, so he's falling back on an old standard. He's going to fake her suicide, and he's doing it this afternoon. I got a text from her saying good-bye, and I assure you she wasn't planning on saying good-bye to me."

She wouldn't have left him. He knew that deep in his soul. She would have stayed and fought like hell with him. She would have yelled and talked it through, and maybe forced him into couples therapy, but she knew they were endgame.

She loved him. She wouldn't leave him.

Deke jogged back in the room. "Someone has to have fucked with it physically because according to the guys in security, nothing's wrong. I'm surprised Chelsea didn't catch it."

But Chelsea was consumed with work and her kid. Years of being happily married had softened Chelsea's instincts. She'd likely heard the alarm and thought it best to get her daughter somewhere safe.

"I know where they're taking her. We have to go." He had to get to her.

"I want to come with you." MaeBe held her cell in hand.

"No." Kyle stood in her way. "They need you here. I need you here. Call the cops and then interface with me. Get those cameras in her place back on. They've got backup batteries. Get it up again and tell the guys in security to capture it all."

MaeBe nodded and then she was on her phone. "Yes, I need…"

That was all Michael heard because he was running out the door, Deke and Kyle behind him.

He had to get to her before they could play out this scene they'd planned.

Because it couldn't be Vanessa's last. It just couldn't.

* * * *

Vanessa watched as they turned into her sister's driveway, her heart pounding. The driver put the car in park and went to manually open the garage door. He moved quickly, looking around to see if anyone was watching.

"Don't move," her kidnapper said. "I'll shoot you right here if I need to and then I'll go after your neighbors. The power's off so the cameras are, too."

"No wonder you wanted my daddy's money. I wouldn't let my cats stay here," Junior said with utter disdain.

Junior had been the fun surprise hoisted on her when her kidnapper had taken her out the back of the building and shoved her in the waiting car. She'd woken up to the sound of Junior talking about what fun he was going to have.

Her kidnapper had been in the back seat with her, a gun against her side. There had been a driver and Junior in the front seat.

That was when she'd known they were going to kill her.

She'd already tried to open the door. She'd attempted to roll out of the car when they'd pulled off the freeway, but they'd been careful. The child locks were on. She'd been willing to risk the pain of the fall or the bullet he might put in her, but she hadn't had a chance.

Now she had to worry that he really would shoot whoever happened to be walking by if she tried to scream. The neighborhood was full of kids. She couldn't risk them.

She had to pray Tessa wouldn't take too long or that Chelsea would wonder where she'd gotten off to. Someone would call Michael, and she kind of prayed he'd done underhanded spy stuff to keep watch on her. Like maybe he was tracking her phone. They'd been very interested in her phone. Her kidnapper—who was probably also going to be her assassin—had forced her to open it. She had no idea what he'd done, but it had sounded like he'd sent a text or an email.

The driver hopped back in and moved the car inside.

"This place is a dump." Junior seemed intent on letting her know how far she'd fallen.

The driver shut off the car and made for the door again.

The garage door started to go down behind her, wiping out the late afternoon sunlight and sending her into the gloom.

"We need to move quickly," the man with the gun said. "I sent the text to her boyfriend. He hasn't texted back. Hopefully he's in a meeting or somewhere he can't check his phone. We have to get this done before he comes looking for her."

Junior wore slacks and a collared shirt, his head covered in a ball cap and sunglasses over his eyes. He took them off now, and in the dim light from the single bulb overhead she could see the way he sneered. "She left early. He'll be at work for another hour or so. There's no need to hurry. I'd like a talk with my dear stepmother."

She still had no idea what this was about. Every time she'd tried to ask, the man with the gun had pressed it harder against her. Junior was wrong, of course. Tessa would figure out something was up very quickly, and she would call Michael. He wouldn't scratch his head and wonder where she'd gone to.

Unless she'd convinced him she didn't love him and never would. He might think she'd walked away from him. And then there had been whatever her kidnapper had sent.

"You sent a note to Michael, didn't you?"

The man stayed beside her as the driver moved around, opening the door and getting a hand on her arm.

"Of course. The note is important," her kidnapper explained simply, as though his job was normal. "What I love about these modern times is that I don't have to match your handwriting. I can open your phone and send your lover a sad good-bye without too much trouble."

So Michael might think she'd left. She was hauled out of the car. It was a shame she'd cleaned up the garage. The only thing in here was her own crappy car, the one she'd been forced to buy after Junior had kicked her out of her home and left her with nothing. It was a sedan she had to maneuver around. After she'd moved in, she'd cleaned out the whole place to make room for her car so she wouldn't have to leave it in the driveway. Her tidiness worked against her now. There was room for both cars, and there weren't any handy weapons she could use, and she couldn't get the garage door open fast enough that she could get away. She would have to bide her time. "What exactly do you think you're going to get out of this?"

"Satisfaction, bitch." Junior walked ahead of her and tried the door. It opened easily because someone hadn't locked it.

She knew she had. She locked every door and checked them all before she went to bed or left for the day. So it had to have been one of Michael's men who forgot to lock it. Deke had been out here. She would be having a long talk with him about home security.

If she survived. She didn't think she was here for a long talking to.

Please don't let Michael accept whatever that damn text had said. Please let him get angry about me leaving. Let him find me.

Junior strode into her kitchen and turned when he reached the big island in the middle. "I get to watch you get what you've always deserved. I get to play a part. Do you know how much I've dreamed about this? Bill, I want half an hour with her."

A chill went down her spine as "Bill" dragged her into the

kitchen. "We talked about this." He turned to his driver. "Go and wait in the car. We'll need to move out fast when this is done."

Vanessa didn't like the sound of that. "What are you going to do?"

"We're going to take care of you the way I should have in the beginning," Junior said as the door closed behind the driver.

Vanessa's brain whirled, trying to figure a way out of this. She couldn't simply wait and hope Michael decided to hunt her down. The front door was her best bet. The back fence was pretty high, and she probably wouldn't make it over before someone could shoot her. But the front door was another situation. It had a deadbolt. She would have to get that open and then get the lock open on the screen door. If she could make it to the front yard, someone would see her. There were tons of cameras in the neighborhood. Everyone was freaked about porch theft. All she had to do was make it to her neighbor's porch and at least there would be a record of her murder.

"You're going to remember what I told you," Bill said. "We talked about this. I thought it was stupid as fuck for you to come here."

"I'm the one who paid you. You work for me, and I want to watch," Junior snarled back.

He wanted to watch what?

He wanted to watch her die.

"You've only paid me half, and if you screw this up, you're going to be the one I deal with, not her," Bill vowed. "If this is going to work, she's got to be pristine. You damage her and the cops will have questions."

They were going to do it. Junior was going to have her killed.

"Everyone will know it was you." What was he thinking? "You recently tried to frame me. Do you honestly believe the police won't ask questions if I turn up dead? It won't matter if you don't pull the trigger yourself. Only one person in the world wants me dead, and that's you."

"I think I can handle it. You know a good lawyer can get a man out of anything," Junior said.

"It certainly seems to have gotten you out of paying me what your father wanted me to have." She still wasn't sure what was going on. If Bill was going to shoot her, why hadn't he yet? Why bring her back here? Why not kill her and put her in a dumpster somewhere?

"Move toward the bedroom," Bill ordered, the gun trained on her.

She needed more time. Bill was a professional. He would do his job as quickly as he could, but Junior would want to make it last. Junior had an odd obsession with her, and she needed to play to it.

What was in the bedroom that she might be able to use? There was an alarm clock, but it wouldn't do much damage. She might be able to pick up one of the lamps and knock a skull around.

Or two.

Her heart was pounding in her chest as she followed Junior back to the bedroom she'd used before she'd moved in with Michael.

She wanted to see him. Even if it was the last time. She wanted to see him and tell him that she wished they'd had more time together, wished she hadn't spent the last week holding part of herself back from him. She wished she'd shoved away all the anger and simply let herself love him.

"I don't care what my father wanted. My father was an idiot. Nothing but a sentimental old man," Junior was saying. "And he betrayed his family."

"By wanting something to honor his daughter?" It was what she'd never understood. "All he wanted was to help people like Lara."

"People like my sister don't deserve help. They're fucking addicts. Let them all die." Junior slammed the door open. "Do you have any idea how hard I worked? And all my dad could think about was my pathetic sister."

Yes, she knew how Junior felt. There was zero question that Junior had no empathy for his sister. Lara had been everything Junior was not. Kind. Artistic. Thoughtful and caring.

She'd only had one real flaw.

Vanessa moved into the bedroom and realized her time was running out. She couldn't simply let them shoot her.

She had to move now.

Someone had been in here. She hadn't been back to this house since the day she'd moved in with Michael, but she knew she hadn't left things like this. She'd neatly made the bed that morning she'd left, but it was turned down now. Other things had been moved around. There were candles around the bed.

She maneuvered her way to the bedside table. The lamp was

heavy. It would do the job. She was far more worried about Bill. Junior was a coward.

He was also a hothead, and maybe that was the way she should go. Everyone had been so calm up to this point. It might be time for some chaos.

"She wasn't pathetic. She's not the one who can't keep a wife," Vanessa pointed out. "How long before this one leaves you? They never stay long because the truth of the matter is that women want more than a paycheck, and that's all you are, Junior."

She shifted her gaze around the room, seeking anything she could use against these men.

"My wife isn't going anywhere because I'll ruin her if she does," Junior replied. His tone seemed calm, but he couldn't disguise the way his skin had flooded with heat. He'd gone red, his jaw tight. "I'm not an idiot this time. I have plenty of shit on her, and I'll make her life hell. You taught me exactly how to treat a woman."

Bill put the small bag he was carrying on the dresser.

He'd shut the door so she couldn't run through. She watched Bill carefully, waiting for any moment when he would be distracted. Somehow he managed to get the zipper open with one hand, even as his eyes stayed on her. Bill had his back to the bathroom. The doors were closed, but she knew that part of the house well. The big bathroom led to the walk-in closet. There was a window in there. It was small, but she could probably wriggle through if she had enough time to get the sucker open.

How long had it been since anyone had opened that window? She would have to push through the screen.

It wasn't a viable option, and the French doors that led to the closet didn't lock.

She had to get to the front door. It was the only way she was getting out of here.

"You taught me that women are only after one thing," Junior continued. "Money. And they have to be controlled like a dog. You gotta have a leash. I signed a prenup with my latest wife. Bitch still hasn't given me a kid. I need to divorce her and find a fertile one."

"Three wives and not one kid," she taunted. "I think the problem is in your dick, Junior."

His hand came out and she braced for impact, but Bill intervened.

"Don't you fucking dare." The gun was pointed at Junior's head. "I told you this doesn't work if she's damaged. The cops will ask questions if the side of her face has your fucking handprint on it."

She gasped as Junior turned to Bill.

"We can say it was her boyfriend," Junior said. "Beat her up a little and make it look like that Malone asshole did it. I would love to see him in jail."

She stood in front of the bedside table. She could reach the lamp from here and pray it moved easily. She would only have one shot. Bill just had to come a little closer.

"We don't have time for that," Bill insisted. "I told you how this would go, how this has to go to make it look right. She's correct. If the police think for a second that she was murdered, they'll look at you. They look at you, they might find me, and I'm not going to risk that."

"They'll know I've been murdered." Vanessa wasn't sure what he was talking about. "The bullet hole will tell them."

She gripped the lamp, her heart thundering in her chest.

"Oh, honey, do you think you're about to be murdered?" A nasty smirk hit Junior's face. "You're going to kill yourself. You're going to be the new Marilyn Monroe. I've been setting it up forever. Your friend gave the performance of a lifetime earlier today. She told the whole world how fragile you are, how you turn to drugs when times get tough."

"I don't use drugs, asshole." Beyond the occasional glass of wine, she didn't touch anything that could remotely be considered a drug.

Not that the rumors weren't out there. Ashton had hinted at it before. She'd spread rumors among their friends and coworkers. She'd told a couple of directors that Vanessa couldn't be trusted because she used. After Lara had died, there had even been some rumors that Vanessa had supplied her with the drugs.

George had shut those down quickly, but she still ached with the thought of anyone believing she'd had a hand in that magnificent woman's death.

Vanessa hadn't watched the interview today. She'd ignored it. Maybe she should have paid more attention.

"Everyone thinks you do," Bill said, lowering the gun. He was obviously satisfied that Junior wasn't going to smack her and screw up his plan. "No one is going to question that a woman like you would meet a tragic end."

"Michael will." There were so many things wrong with this plan, but it occurred to her that Junior couldn't see it because he'd never truly seen her, never looked past her shiny exterior to see the woman underneath. He'd slapped a label on her and expected her to behave according to plan. His plan. "Michael won't believe for a second that I took a bunch of drugs and overdosed. Is that the text you sent?"

Bill pulled out a couple of vials and bottles. "You're depressed. You've been through a lot lately, and today you had to listen to your friend betray you once again."

"I didn't watch it," she replied.

Junior frowned. "No one will believe that."

"I have witnesses." There was so much they weren't thinking of. "I hope you didn't pay this guy too much because this isn't going to work. Tessa's been with me all day. I was with Michael's mother when the interview came out. They both know I didn't watch it. And Tessa's going to figure out very quickly that I didn't leave on my own. She knows I wouldn't. She'll also figure out that you're the one who screwed with the security system."

God, she prayed Tessa would know and call Michael.

"No one will be able to trace that back to me." Bill had been wearing gloves the whole time. He was a careful killer. "It'll look like a power outage. I know what I'm doing."

"I assure you McKay-Taggart will figure it out," she promised. "You should think about this, Bill. My boyfriend works for an investigative firm. I don't know what Junior's told you, but they won't buy that I killed myself. Michael knows what this means to me and how hard I want to work against it. They won't stop until they figure it out, and when they connect this to Junior, he's going to hand you up on a silver platter."

"No one is going to figure out anything because no one cares about you," Junior said with a frown. "You're a piece of trash, and everyone will shake their heads and say they always knew you would end this way."

"You told me the boyfriend wouldn't be a problem." Bill had stopped, staring at Junior.

"He won't."

"He works for an investigative firm? I know the name Taggart," Bill said. "I don't know why I know it, but I do."

Junior turned to his assassin. "I don't care. I can bury that motherfucker and his company. I'll handle it."

"Like you handled me?" She needed to push Junior a little further. He could go over the edge. Chaos would be her friend.

"I handled you fine," he shot back. "The way I handled my delusional father. I found the right doctor and now you don't get a dime."

"Your father wasn't senile." She'd always known Junior had paid the doctor. If George had lived, they would have been able to prove it.

"Of course he wasn't," Junior conceded. "But he proved he wasn't worthy of everything he had because he was stupid enough to fall under your spell. Bill, do what I paid you to do or we'll have a problem."

Bill had gone still. "I don't know. I believe her. This is going to be more trouble than it's worth."

"More trouble than a half a million," Junior argued.

Something moved behind Bill, the door to the big bathroom flying open and a whirl of motion coming out. There was a loud scream and then something hard smacked against Bill's head.

Bill went straight to the floor.

Ruby stood there, the heavy toilet tank lid in her hand and a wild look on her face. "I'm sorry. I still had the key and I needed…"

They didn't have time to talk it out. Vanessa started for the door. "Come with me."

She jogged out of the door, Ruby behind her.

"You ruin everything." Junior was screaming as she got Ruby in front of her.

She wasn't about to let Ruby get caught.

"Go to the front," Vanessa ordered. "We have to get outside."

They would run and hide somewhere, hide until Michael could find them.

"I hid when I heard the men," Ruby said as she ran. "I just needed to be alone for a while."

"Move or we'll be alone for a long time." Though she did seem to have gotten Bill out of the picture. That hadn't been a little tap. It had been rough, and he'd hit the floor hard.

There was a loud boom as they made it to the living room, and Vanessa felt fire along her arm.

Ruby turned down the foyer.

"I won't let you get away, bitch," Junior shouted.

Vanessa stumbled, her knees hitting the hardwood floors, pain flaring through her, but she could hear sirens in the distance.

She'd fallen right in front of the foyer. She could see the door, see how Ruby was rushing to get it open.

But something was wrong with her arm. She tried to use it to push herself up but pain bloomed.

Ruby threw open the door, and the late afternoon sunshine blasted through. She heard Ruby cry out.

"Go. Run." Vanessa tried to force herself up, ignoring the pain in her arm. She managed to turn over and get to her knees.

Junior was right there, and he kicked her chest, forcing her on her back.

He looked like a monster standing over her, wielding that gun. "I don't care who finds me. I'll tell them what you did to my family, and no one will convict me."

He pointed the gun at her, and she knew she was about to die and all she wanted was Michael. The moments with him flashed through her, every one precious. Even the hard ones because they'd been a part of their story.

She loved him. She would love him always.

A shadow moved across the door, and then there was a loud crack. Junior frowned, and his arm fell to his side before he slumped down and hit the floor.

"And I won't let you hurt mine."

Michael. He was standing in the hall, a gun in his hand and an implacable look on his face that fell the minute he looked down at her. Her big, strong guy paled and rushed toward her. "Baby." He fell to his knees. "He shot you."

Ah, that's where all the blood was coming from. And the pain. It didn't matter because he was here. She reached up for him. "How did you find me?"

He took her good hand in his. "A combination of sneaky things I might have done to keep track of the person I love most in the world."

He glanced back. “Kyle, tell the cops we’ve got one dead.”

“And there’s a guy in the garage, and I think Ruby might have killed a guy in the bedroom.” She had to tell him everything because she was getting a little woozy.

She watched as a big guy moved toward the garage. Deke. She was pretty sure it was Deke.

It didn’t matter because Michael gingerly picked her up and started moving out of the house and into the sun. She felt it warm on her face, and she cuddled close to him.

She was safe.

Chapter Twenty

"All right, so let me get this straight. Junior planned on staging Vanessa's drug overdose," Kyle began, a frown on his face. "That's the stupidest thing I ever heard."

Michael sat on his couch, Vanessa wrapped in his arms. It was getting late, but no one seemed ready to leave. They'd all gone to the hospital, and then the whole group had moved over to his condo.

"Yes. It was a very foolish thing to do." His mother had rushed out the minute she'd heard Vanessa was in trouble. It was obvious she was his mother's newest darling, and Vanessa would discover that his mom knew how to take care of a person. She passed Vanessa a mug of what Michael was sure was some sort of healing tea. "No one would believe that our Vanessa would ever do such a thing. Ruby, dearest, I've got some hot chocolate for you."

His mom had also taken a shine to Ruby.

"Thanks, Mrs. Malone." The teen sniffled. "I'm glad I didn't actually kill that guy with a toilet bowl lid."

The assassin had survived his encounter with the hacker girl, but it seemed to have wiped out his short-term memory. He couldn't remember anything that had happened today. But he did seem to be talking about other things.

"He doesn't know who John Smith is," Michael said flatly. "Neither does the driver. I don't like it. It feels too coincidental that Vanessa is almost attacked a few weeks ago and then we find out Junior hired an assassin to fake her overdose."

"It also could have been viewed as suicide." Vanessa sounded entirely too peppy for a woman who'd almost been murdered this afternoon.

"It's all very Marilyn Monroe." MaeBe sat beside Ruby.

"It's all very fucked up, and I did that." Tessa had a grim look on her face, the same expression she'd had for hours. "I can't believe I fell for it."

David put an arm around his fiancée. "Baby, it's not your fault."

Vanessa held up her good arm. "It's my bladder's. If I hadn't gone to the bathroom…well, they probably would have found another way. You told me to stay with Chelsea. You know I now get why women die in horror films. It's not about hunting down a scary noise. It's about needing to pee."

His girl was a little loopy from the pain killers they'd given her when they'd dug the bullet out of her arm.

His heart threatened to seize every time he thought about how close it had been.

"I would have done the same thing." Kyle sent his almost sister-in-law a sympathetic look. "I would have left her with Chelsea and gone to check on the security system."

Tessa had apologized over and over again. Michael didn't blame her. She was forgetting one very important part of the assignment. "You were supposed to protect her from the press. She should have been safe in the lobby of the building. We had no idea Junior would take things this far."

Damn, but he was glad the man was dead.

"I still should have been more careful," Tessa insisted.

Vanessa shook her head. "No. You did your job, and I'm glad it went down this way. It would have happened at some point. What if he'd tried to take me when I was out with Ava? Or the kids? What if I'd been totally alone and no one had missed me for hours? No. If there is one thing I've learned from all of this it's that Shakespeare was right. All's well that ends well. If it hadn't happened this way, it could have gone more wrong. I will take this outcome over all others because the people I love are alive and healthy."

She'd whispered the words to him before she'd gone into surgery. *I love you.* He'd felt them in his soul.

"Well, I would have preferred you didn't get shot." He would have nightmares about that moment for the rest of his life. He would dream about the look on Ruby's face as she'd opened the door, the way she'd pointed back and told him Junior had a gun.

He would never forget shooting that fucker who'd been about to end the life of the woman he loved.

"I don't know. It'll be a cool scar story." Vanessa grinned at him. "How'd you get that one? Well, my deranged, older-than-me stepson hired a killer to stage my death, but my hacker friend is good with toilet lids and then my boyfriend saved me."

She was a little high. Thank god she hadn't been when she'd told him she loved him.

Or had she? Had she already had some pain meds by then?

"Well, I'm still sorry it happened on my watch." Tessa leaned against her fiancé, but her eyes were on Michael, beseeching him to forgive her.

"Vanessa's right. It all turned out for the best." He meant that on several levels. He needed Tessa to know that everything they'd been through had been okay because it had led to this place. Tessa had found her professor, and Michael had his leading lady. They were good.

Tessa nodded his way. "I'm happy she's okay, too. And that Ruby's smart as hell." She looked to the teen. "You know we might still be at the police station if you hadn't recorded everything those men said."

Vanessa held her good arm in the air. "Ruby rocks."

Ruby grinned. "Well, I was hanging out in the bedroom because it's where the best Wi-Fi is. I was actually about to leave because the power went out. I had my hand on the door when I realized that asshole was bringing Vanessa in, and she was in trouble. That was when I texted MaeBe."

"We were already on our way," MaeBe admitted. "But it was good to know what we were up against and that we were going to the right place. Though I do remember telling you to hide."

Ruby shook her head. "They were going to kill Vanessa. I

couldn't hide. I turned on the recorder on my phone and taped everything they said, but I couldn't hide."

"Of course, you couldn't." His mom handed Ruby her hot chocolate. "You were brave. You were a hero, darling."

Ruby accepted it with a smile. "Vanessa was calm the whole time. And she gave me a chance to get away. I don't know what would have happened if you hadn't shown up when you did."

Michael knew. Junior would have let his rage lead him. He would have killed Vanessa.

"Next time pick up the gun," Kyle advised.

"There will be no next time," Michael replied. "I'm not letting her out of my sight ever again."

"Hey, you never know. It's always good advice. If a killer drops his gun, pick it up," Kyle said. He looked MaeBe's way. "We should get this one home. She's got school tomorrow, and I'm sure she doesn't want to miss it."

Ruby frowned. "Yes, I do."

"After all the news reports?" MaeBe asked. "They're all saying you're a hero who took out an assassin. You're going to be a star at your school."

Ruby's lips turned up in a savage grin. "Yeah, all the bullies should beware."

Ten minutes later, he was escorting his guests out. He hugged Tessa and promised her everything was all right before she left with David. Kyle was escorting MaeBe and Ruby home.

The big guy shook Michael's hand as the ladies headed for the elevator. "It could be a coincidence, you know."

Michael knew exactly what Kyle was talking about. It had bugged him since the moment he'd found out the hired guns didn't know a thing about the John Smith who'd attacked Vanessa that day at the café. "Or Junior could have hired someone else. No one but the reporters we called knew where she was that day."

"And that part of Dallas is pretty safe," Kyle agreed. "I don't know. I'll look into it. I've got this feeling that we're missing something."

He held a hand out. "I appreciate it. And why don't you skip the bank and let me loan you the money for the car?"

Kyle shook his hand. "Absolutely not. I'm good. Honestly,

something's weird about that, too. A month ago I got approved for a credit card with far higher standards than that car loan. Weird things are happening around me. All of them annoying. Bad karma or something."

"You think someone's fucking with you?"

Kyle shrugged. "I don't know who would want to. The only person who ever hated me that much is dead."

"You sure about that?"

"I killed her." Kyle said the words in a flat tone. "She was part of my past. The worst part, and killing her was necessary. It was in the line of duty. Killing her saved a lot of people. And the shit that's been happening to me, well, it's all little crap. Like I said it's annoying, but it adds up, you know." He sighed. "I shouldn't have told you that."

Michael knew he wasn't talking about the annoying stuff. "I won't say anything. Your past is yours to deal with any way you need to."

Kyle's lips turned up in a ghost of a smile. "Everyone is giving me time, but I don't know I'll ever be ready to share that whole story. It's not a good one."

"You survived." He'd had this lesson reinforced. "That's all that matters to the people you love."

"Kyle, the elevator's here," MaeBe called out.

That smile of Kyle's became a radiant thing. "I'm coming." He shook Michael's hand again. "Take care of your girl."

"And you take care of yours." No matter what Kyle said, MaeBe was the center of his life.

Kyle nodded and strode down the hall.

Michael closed the door.

"Darling, I think Vanessa needs to go to bed." His mother had set herself up in the guest room. She was staying on until she was sure Vanessa was all right. "Take her and I'll clean up out here."

He stared down at his mother, the woman who'd taken such good care of him all these years. "Thank you, Mom."

"Of course. You know I adore her."

"I meant for everything. And I mean everything. I love you very much, and I don't say it enough."

His mom went teary and hugged him. "And I love you. I always knew, Michael. Even when you were far away, I knew you loved me.

You simply needed time to find yourself. Your father knew, too. And your brother."

It felt good to hug her without worry between them. "Liar. JT did not, but thank you for giving me the space to figure out who I am."

There was a sigh from his left. "You're an asshole liar."

He turned and Vanessa was standing there, looking at him with an oddly soft expression on her face.

"Vanessa, we should get you to bed." They would talk again in the morning.

She moved into his space, putting her arms around him and his mother. "But you're my asshole liar, and you're not going to investigate me again, are you?"

"Never," he promised.

She smiled. "Good, then after a reasonable amount of time I will likely accept a proposal from you."

"Don't forget some groveling, darling." His mother gave Vanessa a squeeze and stepped back. "He should do some serious groveling. And I'll start working on the wedding. You can never start too early."

She walked away.

Michael stared down at her. "I will give you all the groveling you need. And I won't ever lie to you again."

She frowned. "Not about anything important. Now if I ask you if my butt looks big…"

"Your butt is always perfect." He smoothed back her hair. "I hope you still feel this way tomorrow when you're off the drugs. Know I won't hold you to anything."

She went on her toes and kissed him. "I'd already decided to stay with you. I love you. That won't change. I forgive you and you forgive me because that's what people in love do."

He kissed her back. "I promise I will never betray you again. I love you so much."

"Then take me to bed. I'm tired. In the morning we'll have to face the press again." She let him pick her up, her arms going around his neck.

"I'll be right beside you."

He carried her to their bed. He would be beside her for the rest of his life.

* * * *

Julia Ennis sat in the parking lot and watched the front of Michael Malone's building and considered how pathetic her fall had been.

At one point in time she'd been the CIA's It Girl, the one everyone wanted to know and have on their side. She wouldn't have been stuck in a car watching and waiting for the man she loved to show up. She would have been in a comfy office surrounded by technology most people didn't even dream of because they didn't know it existed. She would have control of all the cameras. She wouldn't have to use something as sad as her own eyes to verify the target was on the move.

There was a soft knock and then the passenger door opened, and her partner in this endeavor slid in beside her.

Partner? He was really more of a professional lackey looking to make his way in the world. In their world.

Of course she used to have a foot in both worlds until she'd let her stupid heart rule her head.

"I brought you some coffee." He slipped the cup into the holder beside her. "I didn't know how long we were going to be here…watching."

"I told you this is a personal job. You don't have to hang out," she murmured. "You can head back to LA. I'm worried about one of his employees. She's got connections I don't like."

Her new job took her across the world, but all roads seemed to lead her back here. She'd heard that McKay-Taggart no longer did work with the Agency, but the firm seemed to have their fingers in every pie. Even when the connection wasn't direct.

Maybe it was fate. Maybe destiny was bringing them back together again.

Maybe she was going to kill MaeBe Vaughn. She watched as the doors opened and her rival strode out, laughing at something the hacker kid said.

What the fuck did Kyle see in her? She wasn't his type at all. Kyle liked his women elegant and beautiful. Mae Beatrice Vaughn was neither.

"Hey, she looks pretty good," her partner said, nodding toward MaeBe. "I did that up right. Missed all the vital organs and still managed to get away with it. I heard they think I was going for the actress chick. Did I overplay that? From what I knew about her, I thought going after the other chick would be the only way to get MaeBe in the alley."

John was annoying. John also wasn't his real name, but even she wasn't sure what it was. He had a Colorado driver's license, but that could change in a heartbeat. The ID she was carrying proclaimed she was Anna Sinclair. His name didn't matter. He was an employee like her now. She wasn't sure how he'd gotten here, but he'd likely fucked up somewhere along the way, and now he had no connections to the world beyond the group she worked with.

He was also halfway good in bed. Oh, not like Kyle had been. Kyle had been transcendent, but then that was the way it was between soul mates.

Too bad hers had decided to kill her.

"You did a good job," she murmured, her eyes on that door because he wouldn't be far behind MaeBe. He never was. "I don't think they even understand that Vanessa Hale wasn't the target."

"I could've killed her and gotten her out of the way," John offered. "I know you don't like her."

She actively hated the woman, but that wasn't the point. "A good predator never simply deals the killing blow. A good predator likes to play with her food. The terror makes the meat taste better."

There he was. She wished he wasn't so gorgeous. Six foot three, with eyes as green as a forest and a body she couldn't forget. He jogged down the steps, his head swiveling as though looking for threats. He stopped when he got to the ground, and for a moment she thought he would look her way.

For a moment she prayed he would because it would mean he still felt the connection between them, the one not even his betrayal could sever.

You were going to kill hundreds of people, Julia. How could you?

She'd thought he'd understood the nature of her job. She was a goddess, and she'd tried to make him a god. The little people didn't matter. They were chess pieces, and a few of them had to be sacrificed for the good of the game.

His bourgeoisie morality had been their downfall.

"Sometimes you scare me," John said quietly. "Is that him?"

John had been helping her on their corporate rounds, ensuring the tycoons of the world kept their places and everyone made cash. The world needed to keep a certain balance, and she ensured that the right people got ahead. And the wrong people died or found themselves in bad situations where they needed to sell their shares in an all-important new invention to the right ones. Or at least that's the way her last assignment had gone.

Fucking with Kyle was merely a hobby. Her favorite hobby.

"Yes." All John knew was she'd had a relationship with Kyle that had gone wrong, and she wanted some revenge.

He didn't know that she had a very comfy cage ready for Kyle. She could change his mind. All she needed was a little time.

But first she was going to show him how awful the world could be without her around to make things nice for him.

"Remind me not to piss you off," John said. "You've made that dude's life hard the last year."

It was the little things. That's what she'd learned. Oh, she could announce herself and start their war, or she could play some fun games with him. Games he didn't even realize they were playing.

She'd watched him for a while and realized that fucking with his family could be so much fun. After all, he'd chosen them over her. He'd chosen all the fairytale crap they'd crammed into his head about fairness and the sanctity of life over her real-world views.

Over her love for him.

So she'd studied them all and started small. Calling in the health inspector on his stepfather's restaurant. Catfishing his little sister and outing the fact that she had two boyfriends to everyone at her high school. Paying someone to fuck with little brother's sports equipment so oops, he broke a leg.

All in all, it had been a hard year for the Taggarts.

Now the poor man couldn't even buy his own car.

And she'd been merciful with that bitch of his. She wanted to see how far he would go to protect her.

He wasn't sleeping with MaeBe. That was why she was still alive, why Julia had ordered John to miss her vital organs.

"I wouldn't play with you." She kept her eyes on Kyle. He'd joined MaeBe and the other one, walking toward MaeBe's car.

Wouldn't it be sad if someone stole it?

"That's good to know," John said. "I like you, too, Jules."

She couldn't leave the poor boy with a misconception. "I would kill you quickly."

"Okay." John huffed.

He would still put out. She could insult the man and two hours later, he was in her bed. And she would close her eyes and think about Kyle.

The new job she was on had one of those odd connections to Kyle's company, one that might force them back together.

And then it would be time to show Kyle exactly how she felt.

Epilogue

Six weeks later

Vanessa Jones laughed at something her future brother-in-law said and took a sip of champagne. Oh, JT wasn't exactly her formal future inlaw, but she'd caught sight of a small Tiffany blue box in Michael's boxer drawer, and she'd overheard him talking about how he would "do it" during their trip to Paris next week.

She was absolutely going to say yes.

Nina joined them, taking her husband's hand. "It was a beautiful ceremony, wasn't it?"

David and Tessa were officially husband and wife, and the entire McKay-Taggart world was out to celebrate. She felt a little sorry for the academics David had brought in. They looked slightly afraid of the motley group of ex-soldiers. Except that one woman who kept trying to get them to talk about former missions. For history's sake, she'd told them.

"It was lovely." Michael handed her another glass. "And not at all weird like JT said it would be."

JT pointed his brother's way. "Hey, it was only comfy for you because you found your girl. If you were doing this solo, it would be weird."

He didn't have to worry about that. That man was hers, and he wouldn't be solo again.

Michael started to argue, but JT's cell rang, and he went slightly pale.

"It's the babysitter." He put the phone to his ear. "Hey, how's it…okay, you have to coax him down easy. Whatever you do, don't panic. He can sense it."

Nina glanced back as her husband walked away. "Poor girl." She turned to Vanessa. "She doesn't have your touch, dear. No one handles Jasper the way you do."

She adored her almost nephews and Sophy. Getting to be the kids' aunt was almost the best thing in her life. She squeezed Michael's hand. Almost. "You have to give him something fun to do. I can't wait to see how his kindergarten teacher handles him."

Michael shuddered. "Whoever that is deserves hazard pay."

"I'm already prepared to bribe the woman to not quit on the second day," Nina replied with a smile. "So is it true? I caught a bit of the news on the way out here. Are you actually working with Junior's widow?"

It had been the craziest turn of events. "She inherited everything. Since they didn't have kids, there wasn't even a fight. Everything went to Camilla. I thought she'd take up Junior's suit to keep me out, but she called and told me she's dropping the whole thing and offered me everything George wanted me to have. I explained what I wanted to do with the money, and she offered me more if I let her help me. Turns out she lost a brother to addiction."

"I think she's grateful," Michael added. "I know that sounds terrible, but she knew she was on her way out. Junior wasn't exactly kind. Camilla married him to help her family financially. She signed a prenup that would have left her with nothing. Now she's set for life, and she seems to want to use the money for good. She's going to give Vanessa enough to fully fund the Lara Benedict Foundation for a long time."

It was exciting. She was finally going to get to work. Finally going to be able to fulfill her promise, but beyond that she was looking forward to making meaningful change in the world.

So the world was better for Jasper and Ryder and Sophy. So it was better for the kids she and Michael would raise.

"That's incredible news." Nina leaned in as the music changed to a slow song. "I also heard that you have a couple of offers on the table. Are you getting back in the movie business?"

She wasn't sure about that. After all the fallout, some directors had come calling. "I don't know. I think I'm happier behind the scenes. I'm thinking about producing."

She would find talented women directors who hadn't gotten a shot and give it to them. She would use her resources to give them a voice. Even the "difficult" ones. She'd found that being difficult was sometimes a necessity.

"I think that sounds wonderful," Nina said.

JT rejoined them, sliding his cell in his pocket. "She'll be okay. I think. Come on, baby. Let's dance. We might have to leave and save the world from our son at any moment. I want to enjoy the time we have."

She took her husband's hand and started for the dance floor.

Michael offered her his. "Want to dance with me?"

"Always." She took it and joined her family.

* * * *

Deke Murphy popped the top of his second beer and looked across the table. "Is insurance going to pay for that?"

It was almost midnight, but after David and Tessa's wedding some of his friends had wanted to keep the party going, and his place had been closest. Which was important to a couple of his buddies because transportation had become a problem.

Hutch finished up his turn and nodded Kyle's way.

MaeBe frowned. "I mean, they will eventually. I just can't believe someone stole my car. I paid that sucker off six months ago, and they're not offering me anywhere near what it was worth to me."

If he didn't know better, he would start asking which supernatural being Kyle and MaeBe had pissed off because they were having an incredible run of bad luck.

"I'll talk to the adjusters," Kyle promised, putting a hand over hers.

"And I just moved into a new building," Boomer offered. "I can walk to work so if you need to use my truck for a while, it's all yours."

That was Boomer. He was the single most generous dude Deke had ever met. Except when it came to his lunch. Boomer liked to eat. Did he have enough snacks?

"I can pick her up." Kyle pulled a card from the stack. "I finally got my car."

"But you live all the way across town," MaeBe argued. "I can take the train. I just miss my car."

Hutch's wife, Noelle, stared at Kyle. "Are you trying to block me?"

Kyle's brows came up. "Uh, I'm not trying, but if it happens, well, that's part of the game, right?"

Noelle turned MaeBe's way. "I blame you for teaching him how to play."

MaeBe grinned. "He thought it was silly at first, but now he's really good."

Deke was pretty sure Kyle had started coming to game night because he couldn't stay away from MaeBe. Her game nights were legendary around the MT offices. The younger generation met up almost every Thursday to play boardgames. It was often the highlight of Deke's week.

Since it wasn't like he had a lot to look forward to. He loved his friends, but they were all pairing off, and he never would.

"Hey, Deke, I have a friend," Noelle began.

Deke frowned. "Absolutely not. No setups. I'm done dating for a while."

Boomer polished off the chips Deke had set out. "That's smart, man. You told Charlotte you didn't want to go out with her new friend, so she better not find out you've been letting Noelle set you up."

He would never hear the end of it. He would be kicked out of the grapevine, and he enjoyed being a part of that.

Damn, that was probably his last bag of chips. The food at the wedding had been good but not plentiful enough to fill Boomer's gut. "I think I'll order some pizza."

Boomer got cranky if he didn't eat.

"That sounds good," MaeBe said. "I'll go in with you."

He shook his head. "Nah, I've got it."

It wasn't like he had anything or anyone to spend money on. He'd saved a lot over the years. He didn't need much more than his two-bedroom condo. He'd bought it with the thought of having visitors, but he always went home to see his family. They'd never been to Dallas. His sisters rarely left the Northern California rural town he'd grown up in.

He excused himself to call in the pizza order, walking into his neatly kept kitchen. It was neatly kept because he almost always ate out. He took extra shifts or met his friends for dinner because eating alone was sad and made him think about big family dinners with all the chaos and energy they brought.

He'd found a family here, and he genuinely loved them. He wouldn't leave Dallas. He belonged here.

But damn he missed his hometown.

You don't miss that town. You miss her. You'll miss her until the day you die, you idiot.

Deke shook that thought off because he wasn't going to spend his night mooning over his high school girlfriend. He'd broken that relationship off because Madeline Hill was not meant to live her life in a small town waiting for her dumbass boyfriend to come home from the military. She'd been stubborn, ready to turn down a full-ride scholarship to Yale to stay behind and help out with his family.

So he'd made sure she didn't. He'd broken her heart, and he'd been right to do it. She'd gone to Yale, and now she worked for one of the country's top inventors. She lived the high life in LA, and someday he would find out she'd married a man on her level and started her family.

God, he still missed her.

He ordered five pizzas. Two for Boomer and three for the rest of them and hoped he would have leftovers because he was pretty sure the milk in his fridge was bad, and all he had for breakfast was cereal.

He could hear Noelle and Kyle arguing about whether or not he really needed to call yet another auction for a railroad.

Kyle probably thought he had enough points to win and wanted to end the game.

Kyle kind of bulldozed his way through games.

Like Maddie used to bulldoze her way through problems.

Why was she so on his mind tonight?

Because he'd been to another wedding. Because he was pretty sure the reason none of his relationships worked was because he'd never gotten over her.

Because she was the one, dumbass.

There was a knock on his door.

"That was quick," Hutch said. "Do you live next to the pizza place?"

He didn't. It would be at least another half hour before the pizza showed up. He moved to the front hall. "Nah. It might be Jamal. He said he would head over if he had time."

But it wasn't a six-and-a-half foot tall bodyguard standing in front of his door when he opened it.

He damn near felt the breath knock out of him. Maddie Hill was standing there, clutching a backpack and looking even more delicious than she had in high school.

"Hey, Deke."

He stared at her. "Hey."

Yeah, that was good.

She bit her bottom lip and looked up and down the hall. "Can I come in? I'm afraid I've got a problem and you're the only one who can help me."

"I am?" Also good. He was not on his game tonight. "I mean what kind of problem?"

"The national security kind," she said quietly. "I'm in over my head. Please, Deke."

He opened the door, and the love of his life walked in.

Maybe he was about to get a second chance.

He wasn't going to waste it.

Deke, Maddie, and the whole McKay-Taggart team will return in *The Man from Sanctum*.

Author's Note

I'm often asked by generous readers how they can help get the word out about a book they enjoyed. There are so many ways to help an author you like. Leave a review. If your e-reader allows you to lend a book to a friend, please share it. Go to Goodreads and connect with others. Recommend the books you love because stories are meant to be shared. Thank you so much for reading this book and for supporting all the authors you love!

The Man from Sanctum

Masters and Mercenaries: Reloaded, Book 3
By Lexi Blake
Coming March 8, 2022

A painful past

Deke Murphy and Maddie Hall should never have worked as a couple in high school. She was the class valedictorian and he the jock who took nothing seriously…except her. Together they formed an amazing team, and young love blossomed into something that strengthened them both. Until tragedy struck and Deke made a sacrifice that split them up forever.

An unexpected reunion

Seventeen years later, Maddie is living her dream working for a brilliant tech guru in the beauty of Southern California. She's made a life for herself and it's first class all the way. She rarely thinks of the jock who dumped her all those years ago. But when Maddie realizes her boss might be part of an international conspiracy, she can't deny Deke might be her best bet to solve the mystery. Her one-time sweetheart works for one of the world's premiere security and investigative firms. She'll hire him and prove to herself their relationship could never have worked.

A dangerous future

As Maddie and Deke begin to uncover her boss's secrets, they can't deny the chemistry that has reignited. But before they can explore the connection growing between them, they must survive the deadly forces hunting them down.

About Lexi Blake

New York Times bestselling author Lexi Blake lives in North Texas with her husband and three kids. Since starting her publishing journey in 2010, she's sold over three million copies of her books. She began writing at a young age, concentrating on plays and journalism. It wasn't until she started writing romance that she found success. She likes to find humor in the strangest places and believes in happy endings.

Connect with Lexi online:

Facebook: Lexi Blake
Twitter: authorlexiblake
Website: www.LexiBlake.net
Instagram: www.instagram.com/lexiblakeauthor